KINGDOM
KEEPERS
DISNEY IN SHADOW

BOOK THREE

Also by Ridley Pearson

Kingdom Keepers—Disney After Dark
Kingdom Keepers II—Disney at Dawn
Kingdom Keepers III—Disney in Shadow
Kingdom Keepers IV—Power Play
Kingdom Keepers V—Shell Game

Steel Trapp—The Challenge
Steel Trapp—The Academy

Writing with Dave Barry

Peter and the Starcatchers
Peter and the Shadow Thieves
Peter and the Secret of Rundoon
Peter and the Sword of Mercy
The Bridge to Never Land

Escape from the Carnivale
Cave of the Dark Wind
Blood Tide

Science Fair

BOOK THREE

DISNEY • HYPERION BOOKS

New York

If you purchased this book without a cover, you should be aware that this book is stolen property. It was reported as "unsold and destroyed" to the publisher, and neither the author nor the publisher has received any payment for this "stripped" book.

Printed in the United States of America
First Disney • Hyperion paperback edition, 2011.
10 9 8 7 6 5 4 3 2
V475-2873-0-12132

ISBN 978-1-4231-3856-3 (pbk.)

visit www.disneyhyperionbooks.com
www.thekingdomkeepers.com
www.ridleypearson.com

The Kingdom Keepers series is dedicated to Storey and Paige, for helping me see the world through their eyes. . . .

KINGDOM
KEEPERS
DISNEY IN SHADOW

BOOK THREE

1

FINN WHITMAN RAN HARD, then all the harder still, Donnie Maybeck by his side and keeping up. By day, Tom Sawyer Island in the Magic Kingdom was an intriguing tangle of trees and bushes interrupted by meandering pathways. By night, it was something altogether different.

Especially with four insanely angry, sword-carrying pirates bearing down on you, followed closely by an alien with a genetic malfunction that posed like Elvis Presley and looked slightly like a cross between a koala bear and a cuddly dog.

The guys in the torn T-shirts and calf-length pants had leaped from the shadows surrounding Pirates of the Caribbean—the park having been closed for nearly three hours—immediately in pursuit. Stitch, on the other hand, had appeared out of nowhere.

Finn made the mistake of glancing back at them.

"Don't look back!" Maybeck called out sharply. "Your face, your skin is like a flashlight. You'll give us away! Believe me, Whitman, this is when it pays to be yours truly."

Maybeck thought of himself as God's answer to everything, and wasn't afraid to share that opinion. If given half a chance, he would make the point that his great-grandparents had been slaves, and his grandparents sharecroppers on Florida sugarcane plantations; he was fiercely proud of his African American heritage and of the fact that his family were some of the original Floridians, instead of being descendants of snowbird retirees, like Finn and so many of his friends—and their fellow DHIs.

DHI stood for Disney Host Interactive, or Daylight Holographic Image, depending on who you asked. There were five DHIs, including Finn and Maybeck—holograms of teenage hosts that, by day, acted as guides to guests at the Magic Kingdom. (The other three, Philby, Willa, and Charlene, were by now supposed to be awaiting the two boys in the Indian Village across the water from Tom Sawyer Island.)

There was a glitch in the software that projected the holograms in the park: when any of the five teens who'd originally modeled for the DHIs went to sleep at night, they would wake up, not as themselves, but as their holograms, *inside* the Magic Kingdom. As it turned out this was no glitch—an old guy, a Disney Imagineer named Wayne, had intentionally made this "crossover" possible by rewriting the projection computer code. He'd done this because he'd needed the help of the DHIs to solve a riddle left behind by Walt Disney years before.

But tonight was different: the kids had gone to sleep; they'd crossed over, becoming their DHIs inside the Magic Kingdom at night—something they were used to by now. They had left a special fob with a button, like a garage door opener, inside a teepee, to ensure that they could all simultaneously cross back over, retreating into their sleeping bodies in their homes. That was all pretty much the same as usual; what made it different was why they were here in the first place.

Wayne was missing.

He'd been missing for nearly three weeks, ever since one very long day inside Disney's Animal Kingdom where the teens had battled the wicked fairy Maleficent and the gargoyle beast Chernabog.

It was unacceptable to leave Wayne missing. He was the last Imagineer alive who'd known Walt Disney personally, who'd known Walt's plans and intentions for the parks and characters. Wayne had created their ability to cross over. He was their mentor and their leader in trying to fight Maleficent and her ambitious plans.

Wayne had explained it all to Finn, what seemed like a long time ago now.

"You know the movie *Toy Story*?" Wayne had asked.

"Of course."

"Andy's toys come alive when he leaves the room."

"I know," Finn had said.

"Well, that wasn't exactly a new idea around here. Walt designed it so that when the last of the humans—the guests, the cast members, the cleaners, maintenance personnel, even the security guys—leave the Magic Kingdom, the characters get to have it all to themselves."

"Yeah, right."

"I'm serious," Wayne had said. "We began to suspect this as odd things started happening, like finding equipment moved or an Audio-Animatronics in a different position than it had been left in the night before. Strange, unexplainable events. But Walt had wanted it this way, and we left it alone. That is . . . until the trouble began. Even now, security rarely patrols the parks at night, and when they do, the good characters are left alone to enjoy their freedom as Walt wanted."

The good characters, Finn thought.

He would later discover that Wayne was telling the truth, but when he'd first heard the story, he'd thought the guy was nuts. He hadn't believed a word. Having been raised to be polite, he kept quiet and didn't challenge the old man.

"I had a pet monkey when I was a child," Wayne said. "My mother gave it to me for my thirteenth birthday."

"Fascinating."

"A terrific pet, a monkey. A real friend. Except the more freedom I gave him, the more freedom he wanted. The more freedom he *took*. I eventually had to give him back to the store that had sold him to us because he would no longer get back into his cage at night. He couldn't give up his newly found freedom.

"Well, the same thing has happened to the characters," he continued. "Turns out some of them like having the park all to themselves. Mostly the villains, as it so happens. They enjoy bossing around the likeable characters, sabotaging the more popular rides, and generally making trouble. We think a group of them—we're not exactly sure who all of them are—have decided to drive the good characters out, to take over the park and make it a dark, evil place. The plan seems to be a simple one—if they can scare away the good guys, only the villains will be left. Eventually only people attracted by evil will come. That's why we call them the Overtakers. Their mission is to change the park forever."

Wayne had studied Finn's face to see how much, if any of this, Finn believed. He couldn't read him.

"We had it wrong for the longest time," Wayne

said. “We thought it was about them turning it into a ‘dark park’—a place where, instead of being magical and happy, it would be villainous and dark. We’re no longer certain that’s the case. We now think instead they want the parks—maybe all the Disney properties—for themselves. The more playgrounds, the better.”

Finn remembered the day clearly, remembered how he’d felt about the idea of losing Disney World, Animal Kingdom, Epcot, Hollywood Studios. As DHIs—nonhuman holograms—he and the four others could infiltrate the park at night, making efforts to spy on and bring down the Overtakers. This had been Wayne’s grand scheme, his big plan in making the kids DHIs in the first place. Their most recent effort had been in the Animal Kingdom. They’d managed to save a friend from the Overtakers. But only Wayne saw the bigger picture. Only Wayne fully understood any of it.

They had to find him.

This was their fifth night searching the Magic Kingdom; their last now that they’d been spotted by the pirates and Stitch, now that all the Overtakers under Maleficent would be looking to . . . eliminate them. Or at least to trap their DHIs, a situation that left their sleeping bodies back in their parents’ homes unable to wake up. They called the condition the Syndrome—short for Sleeping Beauty Syndrome. Maybeck had experienced it once. So had Willa and Philby, briefly, in the Animal Kingdom. The Syndrome was nothing to mess with.

"Note to self," Finn said, intending it for Maybeck, "we are glowing bodies of light running through the dark jungle. You really think *my face* is going to give us away?"

Of the five DHIs, Finn had the most control over his crossed-over state as a hologram. The four others existed in a kind of suspended state when crossed over: half DHI, half human kid, susceptible to getting hurt by accident or at the hands of others.

Finn had learned with Wayne's guidance to separate himself from fear, from all sensation—touch, sound, taste, smell, sight—and in doing so to make himself pure light, a stream of energy, a hologram just like his DHI that Disney used as the park guide. He couldn't maintain this pure state for long—a minute or two at most. But he liked to rub his skill in Maybeck's face.

Finn ran right *through* three palm trees, not bothering to get out of their way. Maybeck weaved and bobbed, avoiding collision.

"Show-off!" Maybeck said.

"Elitist!" Finn fired back. His body passed transparently through a huge rock that Maybeck had to scramble over.

"Know-it-all!" Maybeck said.

"Eye candy!" Finn said. Maybeck was popular with the girls at school.

They both heard the footfalls at once: the pirates had closed the distance and were only a matter of yards behind them now.

"We should continue this later," Maybeck said.

"Agreed."

"Right now we need something resembling a plan."

"I have one," Finn said. "Do you?"

They continued running, Finn out of breath, Maybeck not winded at all.

"That would be *no*," Maybeck said.

"All right then."

"All right then, *what?*"

"We'll go with my plan," Finn said proudly.

"Only if you have a plan in the next five seconds," Maybeck countered.

At that instant, Finn felt a burning sensation on his arm. He didn't really have much of a plan, and Maybeck's reliance on him had taken him out of his pure holographic state. He wasn't glowing as brightly. He was part human again.

He kept running.

"Dude," Maybeck said. "Your arm is like, gushing blood."

Finn looked down. He'd been caught by the tip of a pirate's sword. It was a nasty cut, but he wouldn't have called it "gushing."

Whoosh! Whoosh! Finn heard the sword slicing the air just behind him.

"Slowpoke!" Maybeck chided. Maybeck ducked to his right and went down onto his hands and knees, tumbling over. He tripped up three of the pirates, sending them flying. He jumped to his feet and caught back up to Finn.

"You do make yourself handy," Finn said.

"What are friends for?" Maybeck asked.

"Here's the plan. . . ." Finn said at last. "How are you at swimming underwater?"

2

AT FIRST, FINN ASSUMED THE alligator was a Disney prop. But then a flicker of doubt crossed his mind: Tom Sawyer and Huck Finn were Mark Twain Mississippi River characters. Alligators and the Mississippi River didn't fit.

Swiss Family Robinson, maybe. Or the Jungle Cruise. The doubt—the fear—made him less DHI and more human, less pure light and more flesh and blood. Swimming underwater, glowing slightly, his eyes wide open, with Maybeck swimming to his left, Finn came to a major realization: the alligator was for real. It was swimming right at them, its mouth wide open.

He didn't know much about alligators, but this one looked hungry. And big.

Finn reached over, grabbed Maybeck by the hand, and pulled him lower. The alligator misjudged and swam above them. It turned with a flick of its massive tail and came at them again.

At that same instant, the pirates or Stitch must have stepped into the river water that surrounded Tom Sawyer Island. A splashing sound was familiar to any alligator—it often signaled an animal's arrival at the water's edge for a drink. To an alligator that sound meant a chance at a meal, and for this particular alligator the instinct proved too strong to resist. Only a foot or two from being able to bite off Maybeck's feet, the beast reversed course with another fierce lash of its tail and headed for shore.

As Finn and Maybeck scrambled up the muddy bank on the far side, winded and spitting out river water, there came a cry of terror from across the way: one of the pirates had nearly lost his leg to the alligator. He and the others and Stitch were in full retreat, running as fast as they could in the opposite direction.

"You're late," Philby said. Philby was maybe the biggest techno-geek Finn had ever met, but he looked more like a soccer player than a nerd. Finn supposed that all the DHI models had been chosen for their "average" looks, their "all-American" qualities; all but Charlene, who was anything but average. She stood just behind Philby in front of one of the teepees, and looked more like a teenage movie star. She had blond hair and a cheerleader's body, but she didn't fit the stereotype of what all that implied. She was smart and athletic, cautious and curious.

"We were worried about you," she said. She pointed across the river. "Looks like for good reason."

"Yeah," Finn said, "you might say we were delayed."

"You might say the pirates were *waiting* for us," Maybeck said. "Waiting to grab us. To trap us in the Syndrome. They chased us onto the island and Whitman figured a way off, but it was close."

"Waiting," Philby said, "as if they knew you were coming?"

"That's the way I read it," Finn admitted. "Someone had spotted us in the park and alerted the pirates. Maybeck's right: it was a close call."

"Come on!" Charlene said. "Before they come back."

The way the DHIs crossed over into the park was to go to sleep in their beds at home. Once asleep, they "woke up" inside the Magic Kingdom; but that meant that whatever they wore to sleep was what they were wearing when they appeared as DHIs in the park. Knowing this, Finn always dressed in normal clothes before going to bed. He pulled the covers up so his mother didn't see what he was wearing as she said goodnight. Charlene, on the other hand, had a mother who insisted on rubbing her back and talking to her each night before bed, so Charlene always arrived in the park wearing a nightgown, as she wore tonight. The boys had a hard time keeping their eyes off her.

Willa, on the other hand, who looked Native American or Asian with her hooded, inquisitive eyes and dark braided hair, wore cargo pants and a T-shirt that read: BITE ME. On the back it had the picture of a shark—some kind of promotion for a seafood restaurant.

Once inside the nearest of the six teepees, the Kingdom Keepers were in an electronic shadow, an area where the DHI projection system could not reach. They became invisible once they moved a few feet from the teepee's door. Only impressions in the sand showed where any of them were sitting. Though their DHI projections sometimes did not project in certain locations, they remained in the park, just as when light is showered onto a shadow, the shadow disappears but the object that was casting the shadow remains. In projection shadow the DHIs could still touch, feel, talk, smell, and hear; they left footprints. Invisible to the eye, they were not beyond detection, and therefore had to be careful. Now inside the teepee, their four voices rang out from the darkness. To anyone looking inside, it would have appeared that no one was there. The only thing that seemed out of place was a small black plastic fob that looked like a garage door opener, hanging from a nail in a pole by the teepee's open door.

Philby remained as a lookout somewhere outside the teepee. This, because they'd had unwanted visitors before.

"So? What now?" Willa asked. "I mean we've looked for Wayne everywhere and I just don't think he's here in MK."

"If he is here," Charlene said, "we're not going to find him. I agree with Willa."

"We can't give up," Finn said.

"That was a trap tonight, Whitman," Maybeck said. "You and I . . . we walked into it. We can't be hanging around MK anymore. They're onto us."

"I'd like to disagree with you," Finn said, "but I can't. I say we move on to the Animal Kingdom."

"But our DHIs aren't set up there, right?" Charlene said. There had been a time when Charlene had understood little of the technology that allowed them to cross over and become DHIs by night inside the park. But now she spoke as the expert they all had become.

"Correct," Finn said. "If we look for him inside AK, then it has to be during the day, and we have to go as ourselves."

"We'd be mobbed," Maybeck said. He made a valid point, Finn thought. The DHIs had become so popular that even at the mall and at movie theaters the five kids were approached and often overwhelmed by fans. Inside one of the parks it would be insane. There were also contractual rules limiting their visits to the Disney parks in order to protect the "brand" of the Disney Hosts. The kids often ignored these rules, going in disguise, but. . . .

"My parents would kill me if I got caught," Willa said. "Now that they've added us into Epcot and the Hollywood Studios, the cruise line and the ice show, my parents are freaking. It's apparently a lot of money Disney is paying into the college account. I blow that and I'm dead."

"Yeah, same here," Maybeck said. "My aunt has lectured me about a million times on not messing with that college fund."

"So we don't look for Wayne?" Finn said. "That's not happening."

"If it means we have to go into AK, Epcot, or the Studios as ourselves, I'm out," Charlene said. "Or, if we go in, we've got to tell the company, and everything the contract says to do. I'm in the same situation as Maybeck and Willa. My parents are counting on this college money."

"I can't believe you guys would bail on Wayne," Finn said. He found it a little strange to be talking to a dark, empty teepee, but it wasn't the first time.

"Psst!" It was Philby just outside the door of the teepee. His DHI glowed in the darkness. "We've got company." He stepped inside and, as he crossed into the projection shadow, a black line sliced through his image and slowly ate him. His DHI disappeared.

"Ouch!"

Philby had sat down on Finn's crossed legs. Finn moved over, and Philby's butt made an impression in the sand beside him. "Not a peep," he whispered. "It's all of them!"

A moment later, the crunch of dry palm fronds and jungle leaves could be heard as the pirates entered the Indian Village.

"They probably skedaddled," said a man in a low and ominous voice. It sounded as if he had gravel in his throat.

"Footprints!" called another man's voice.

A shudder passed through each of the Kingdom Keepers. They had gotten careless. A year earlier they would have taken the extra precaution of dragging a branch behind them to erase their footprints. When Finn was pure light, a true DHI, he didn't leave any footprints, but that wasn't often and it wasn't for long. The other DHIs were always part human, and therefore left tracks. Finn and the others understood perfectly well where those footprints led: directly to the teepee they now occupied. They'd trapped themselves. Their only defense was their invisibility, and their invisibility lasted only as long as they were deep within the teepee and in the projection shadow.

The voices drew closer—the pirates were following the footprints closer and closer.

"It's here," a low voice growled, immediately outside the teepee.

A face appeared, partly in silhouette, with a scraggly beard, dark brown moles like warts, and winding scars. The man stepped inside.

Finn spotted the black plastic fob hanging from the pole by the door of the teepee. The remote control device could send them all back to the safety of their beds. Their homes. But it was out of reach now. The pirate blocked the way.

In the past, Wayne had typically kept the fob himself. But without Wayne around, they had to hide the fob safely in the park so they could use it to leave. They'd been using the teepee as a hiding place, but now that would have to change.

Finn's hand nervously clutched into a fist. In doing so, he gripped a handful of sand. He reached out, his hand searching, and he bumped into Charlene's arm. He let some of the sand cascade onto her skin, hoping she would get the message.

Over the next few seconds he heard the soft trickle of sand spilling. She had understood! The sound moved from DHI to DHI in a semicircle inside the teepee.

The pirate heard it too, but couldn't figure it out.

Finn scooped up two big fistfuls of sand. His heart pounded in his chest.

The pirate looked searchingly into the teepee.

"Ain't no one here," he said.

"But them tracks go in and don't come back out," said the man with the gravel voice. "Don't make no sense."

"Them kids is cagey," offered a third voice. "Wouldn't trust them with my teeth."

"You ain't got no teeth," said the man in the doorway. "Come take a look yourself."

A second face appeared in the doorway. This man had long, greasy hair, a gold hoop earring in his right ear, and a left eyelid partly sewn shut. He smelled like bacon fat and fish guts.

He also stepped inside. "Them tracks don't make no sense." He looked up into the peak of the teepee, searching for the kids. "And them tracks don't lie. They're here somewhere."

He looked *right at Finn.*

"Maybe they done dug themselves down into the sand like a flounder."

"You mean a stone crab," said the first man.

"I mean a flounder, you landlubber. Or a ray. What's it matter what kind of fish, you ninny? Point is, they could be hiding 'neath the sand and we wouldn't know it, now would we?"

The two were standing inside the teepee now, one

so close to where Philby had sat down that he had to be just about touching his DHI. The pirates used their feet to disturb the sand, digging down.

"How would they be breathing?" the gravel-voiced pirate asked.

"How should I know?" answered the one-eyed stink bomb.

"Now!" Finn shouted. He stood and threw both handfuls of sand directly into the faces of the two pirates.

The men screamed. Covering his face, clawing at his eyes, one fell to his knees as Philby tripped him.

Finn snagged the remote control fob on the way out the door as the other Kingdom Keepers charged for the doorway. Two more pirates appeared.

Startled by the kids appearing out of thin air, the two men went wide-eyed with surprise. Willa and Charlene filled those eyes with flying sand. The two pirates hollered and staggered back.

The Kingdom Keepers rushed out of the teepee as a group. Finn, the fob in hand, ran smack into what felt like a giant sponge, bounced back, and fell to the sand.

Stitch stood over him.

"You don't belong here," Stitch said. He showed his teeth. It looked as if he could bite Finn's head off—and maybe had that in mind.

Maybeck, who had run past Stitch, now daringly crept up behind the blue alien and knelt down on all fours.

Finn got up.

"Neither do you," Finn said. "Shouldn't you be back in space? And you want to know something? I *liked* you until just now. My sister thinks you're cute."

This caused Stitch a moment of thought.

Finn took the opportunity to step forward and shove the creature over Maybeck's back. Stitch went down hard.

Maybeck jumped up. He and Finn took off, turning left down an access trail, back toward the park.

The pirates were up now, angry as hornets, and running hard to catch them.

"Ready?" Finn called out. "Keep close together. Everyone hold hands."

No one argued. They closed ranks and all held hands.

Finn had never tried to use the remote control device on the run before. They'd always been standing together as a group. He had no idea if it would work. He hoped that by holding hands. . . .

"One . . ." he counted.

The pirates were only a few feet behind them. He heard the ring of steel as swords were drawn.

"Two . . ."

Whoosh! A sword blade passed frighteningly close to his head.

"Three!"

He pushed the button. All the holograms disappeared at once. The black fob fell into the bushes at the base of a palm tree—a location Finn would etch vividly in his memory.

3

FINN OPENED HIS EYES. It was the same as always: he could barely see. His bedroom was cloaked in a midnight darkness, the only light coming from the colorful LEDs on his computer and his DS. He could make out the poster of Matt Damon overhead, taped to the ceiling alongside a glow-in-the-dark mobile of the solar system. He reached out and touched his face, pulled on his ear—he was human. He'd crossed back over again. He could never really be sure if the experience was anything more than a vivid dream. If the other Kingdom Keepers had not had the *exact same* dream as his he might have questioned all of it. But there was no doubting the phenomenon anymore. As unreal as it was, it was for real.

As if to confirm this, he felt his left arm stinging and, reaching over, felt it sticky with blood. He raked back the bedding, worried about staining the sheet—worried his mother would see the blood—and sure enough there was a smear on the sheet. The pirate's sword had caught him. The cut wasn't deep, but it was five inches long and still bleeding a little. He jumped up. He'd worn his regular clothes to bed—a pair of cargo shorts and a Rays T-shirt—and he was dressed the same way still, including his Keens. His clothes were wet and, turning on a light and looking back, he saw that the bed was too.

Dang! Finn thought, considering the damage control necessary to put things right. He cleaned and closed the wound with two Band-Aids. He'd have to wash the top sheet, dry both sheets, maybe the mattress pad too, and remake the bed before getting any sleep. The dryer was in a laundry room by the kitchen. It would wake his mother. He frantically rubbed a wet face towel on the top sheet, combatting the bloodstain. He tried some soap and more water and got most of it out. He stripped the bed, made sure his bedroom door was closed tightly, then closed his bathroom door to make an effective sound barrier. He hung the sheets over the shower curtain rod and used his blow-dryer on them.

His clothes were a bigger problem. How would he explain to his mother that his clothes had gotten soaked while he'd been asleep? A year ago he might have invented some fairly believable story, but now both his parents watched him like hawks. The Kingdom Keepers had acquired legendary notoriety. There had been newspaper stories about "rumors" circulating around Orlando and on Internet chat sites that five kids had somehow "saved" the park. A book had been written. Their adventure inside Animal Kingdom had been witnessed by hundreds of park visitors, adding credence to the rumors. While most adults would not, could not, fully believe any of the stories, kids had no problem doing so. Finn's parents fell somewhere in between doubt and fear. They doubted Finn could leave his room at night and enter the Magic Kingdom as his DHI; but they secretly feared it was true. More importantly they believed—falsely—that he sneaked out at night and violated his contract with Disney by visiting the parks.

They'd installed an alarm system, claiming the neighborhood had had some trouble; in fact it wasn't to warn them if burglars tried to get into their house, but if their son tried to get out. He didn't know the security code—the house was, in fact, an effective electronic jail. But if, without explanation, he dumped a pile of wet clothes into the laundry, questions would be asked that he couldn't answer. He had sworn not to lie to his parents, a promise he'd made himself years before. He had no desire to break that promise, so he had to find creative ways to sneak around the truth without outright lying. He settled on an idea. His effort on the sheet had failed miserably: it looked as if he'd smeared ketchup on it.

The thought of ketchup steered him toward the

kitchen and a possible solution. He loved potato chips with ketchup and his mother had long ago denied him permission to eat the combination in his room, because he always made a mess of it. So he made up a plate of it—ate some, since he was constantly starving—and put the plate on his bedside table. He then smeared some ketchup on his clothes and the sheets and bundled them up and put them into the washer. He set his alarm clock for ten minutes before his parents would wake up, and climbed into bed between a blanket and the mattress.

He slept soundly, woke with the alarm, and quickly started the washing machine.

Five minutes later his mother, wearing a knee-length pajama top, knocked on his bedroom door and entered. His mother didn't look good in the morning. In fact, she looked kind of scary—her hair tangled, her face plain and pale, her eyes unable to open all the way. She scratched at her collarbone, rubbed her eyes with her knuckles, and yawned.

"What are you doing?"

"Laundry. Sorry."

"*You* are doing laundry?" she asked. "So what's going on?"

He made a point of pretending to try to hide the plate of chips and ketchup beneath a sheet of Kleenex tissue. It was such a lame attempt, he wondered if he'd overdone it—but she was not fully awake. She raised her voice.

"Ah, Finn . . . I thought we talked about that! You're not allowed to bring food into your room."

"I know. I'm sorry. I was famished."

"You eat like a horse. You ate a gigantic dinner!"

"Sorry."

"You know the rules."

"I kind of . . . I dropped a couple of chips, but . . . I put everything in the wash."

"That's a first."

"I really am sorry."

"No more. Okay? We've talked about this."

She turned and headed back down the hall.

Finn celebrated his small success. It wasn't easy trying to save Disney World from the Overtakers.

Harder still being the son of disbelievers.

He rode his bike to school. It was a serious stunt bike and he was proud to be seen riding it. He locked it with two locks along with a bunch of other bikes, but in his mind none were as slick as his Hawk Tracer BMX. He rounded the corner from behind the gym where the bikes were parked and headed for the entrance.

He wasn't sure exactly how it happened, but he caught sight of a woman on the sidewalk out in front of the school. She was walking slowly, carrying a purse over her right shoulder, and a Disneyland 50th Anniversary Celebration tote over her left. Finn knew that particular khaki-colored tote bag—and it was a big deal, a serious collector's item. He could see a couple dozen pins attached to the tote's fabric handles and didn't need to get any closer to know that these, too, would be collectible pins—the ones that sold for hundreds of dollars on eBay. He knew women like her. He could spot the Disney freaks a mile away.

What raised his hackles was that she was looking at him. There was a huge distance between them—fifty yards or more—and yet Finn knew what he knew: she was focused only on him. Him, and him alone. It wasn't something that made any sense; nor was it something he could explain; he just knew it. That was all.

What made matters more complicated was that this was not the first time he'd seen her. Yesterday, after school, he'd seen a woman—maybe this same woman—out there. She hadn't been carrying the tote. Was that some kind of signal for him? he wondered. Was he supposed to go out there and talk to her because she had a collector's-item tote? Did that make *any* sense?

Just the idea sent shivers through him. Disney freaks came in all shapes and sizes—and all ages. He'd learned that the hard way. He didn't want some grown-up stalker following him around. Maybeck had reported a woman window-shopping too long outside his aunt's pottery shop. He'd seen her out there a couple of times.

Was this the same woman? Finn wondered. Was she an adult Kingdom Keepers stalker? How random was that? Were they all going to need bodyguards before long? What had started out as something cool focused only on the Disney parks had now grown considerably with the DHI program's expansion. Was it going to wreck his life and leave him hiding from adult freak shows, like this woman stalking him here at school?

He hurried up the stairs, stopping just outside the front doors. He looked back toward the street. The woman had moved on, showing absolutely no interest in him or the school.

So was he making this up? he wondered.

Or was she some kind of professional?

4

FINN WASN'T SURE WHAT IT WAS. All his male friends hated girls. They made fun of girls behind their backs, went to great lengths to embarrass them in person, and yet never stopped talking and complaining about them when they weren't around. Making things more complicated for Finn was that he didn't mind girls so much. One in particular he didn't mind at all.

He'd met Amanda in a weird sort of way and had eventually been involved in saving her sister—in fact, a girl who wasn't really her sister, a girl once called Jez, now it was Jess or Jessica, depending on what week it was and what color hair dye she was using; girls liked to change their names, their looks, and their friends as often as possible. Amanda, sometimes called Mandy, wasn't like the other girls—though Finn had said that to his friends once and had been laughed at until he'd turned red. So now he kept thoughts like that to himself, a process that, as far as he could tell, only caused him to think about her all the more.

For a long time, Amanda and Jess had lived in an

abandoned church on the outskirts of Orlando. No one knew for exactly how long (except them), but Finn knew *why*. Both girls were orphans, both had been in foster care in a home for kids with "special needs"—only in their case it was more like "special powers." Jess had dreams that turned out a lot like the future; Amanda could move things with the power of thought. Neither girl understood her gift, but each had learned to accept it. Since the crazy events inside Animal Kingdom on a particular Saturday, the girls had been swallowed up by Family Services. Living in the church was history. They were in foster care now.

"Rumor is that they're going to move us back with the Fairlies," Amanda told Finn. She called the gifted residents of their former foster home Fairlies because she considered them to be fairly human.

Finn and Amanda were sitting across from each other at the far end of the cafeteria normally reserved for Losers, over by where kids returned their dirty plates. But it was a place they could talk without fear of being overheard and recently they'd spent a lot of lunches there together.

"No way!" Finn said. He took a bite of cold pizza the texture of extruded plastic. He spoke with his mouth full and watched Amanda wince as he did.

"They can do whatever they want," she said. She

indicated her lip to signal to him that he had some cheese stuck on his.

He wiped it off—and then ate it. She winced again.

"We have no parents, no relatives to object," she continued. "Never mind that we both like school here. Never mind that we have new friends." She let that hang there a second. "We are at the mercy of a social worker from—you get the idea. From no place you want to be from. He's decided that the paperwork is a whole lot easier if we go back to Maryland. Foster care isn't about how to find the right home for a kid," she said cynically, "but how to get rid of kids with the least amount of paperwork."

"There is no way they're sending you back."

"You want to bet? And don't even mention the word *fair* because Jess and I have this thing about *fair*: it's the worst of all four-letter words, along with *hope* and *trust*."

"*Trust* is five letters."

"Yeah, but it's just *rust* with a *t* added on to disguise it."

"Aren't we in a sunny mood?"

"Excuse me if I don't want to leave here, if I don't want to be moved against my will, if I don't want to be treated like I'm always in the way and that I'm an expense someone has to justify. People get *paid* for taking kids in foster care. Did you know that? Jess and

I are somebody's paycheck. Nothing more."

"But not with the Fairlies," he said. "You didn't feel like that there."

"No, it's more like a family there. That's true. But it's so far away from here. You know?" She looked at him levelly in a way that he knew he was supposed to understand, but he was back at the idea of people being paid to take kids into foster care, so he missed her meaning. "Don't you care what happens to us?"

"Totally."

"Because you don't sound like it."

"I totally care," he said.

"How'd last night go?" she asked. When Amanda changed the topic you didn't try to revisit the earlier subject matter.

Finn went with the flow. He debated trying to explain their search for Wayne and the sudden and surprising pursuit by pirates. Instead, he rolled up his sleeve, revealing the poorly bandaged cut.

"Yikes!" she said.

"A sword," Finn said.

"First comes love, then comes marriage. . . ." said Greg "Lousy" Luowski, returning a plate that had been licked clean.

"Then come morons," said Finn.

Luowski, roughly the size of a soda machine and

probably just about as smart, stepped toward Finn in what was intended to be a menacing gesture. But his running shoe hit some spilled tomato sauce and he slipped and nearly fell and ended up looking like the idiot he was. His threat destroyed, his crush on Amanda obvious, his face about the same color as the sauce, he retreated to plan another insult.

"He likes you," Finn said.

"I don't lose any sleep over it," Amanda said. She reached out and touched Finn's wounded arm at the wrist. He checked to see if the emergency defibrillator was still mounted to the cafeteria wall. It was.

"It got a little dicey," he said, wondering how far he could play it.

"But you'll survive," she said, withdrawing her hand.

"No sign of . . . our friend." He checked the immediate area to make sure no one could possibly be listening. Luowski, at a table with four other like specimens, seemed to be monitoring them closely.

"Don't let the EMHs bother you," she said.

"EMH?"

"Early Modern Human," she answered. "We're studying them in science. Cavemen."

"I like it," he said.

"You don't want to mess with Greg," she warned. "You heard about Sammy?"

Sammy Cravitz had had his nose broken by Greg in a fistfight that Greg had started. The whole school had heard about it, except the teachers, apparently. Only the thing was, the teachers probably *had* heard about it, but they were as scared of Greg Luowski as everyone else.

Finn had one thing going for him that no one else had: he'd learned how to briefly become his DHI *while still awake*. It still took concentration and practice, but he could suspend himself for a few seconds—sometimes for as long as a minute or two—becoming nothing but light. If a guy like Luowski took a swing at a hologram, he wouldn't connect. He might even lose his balance and create an opening for a return punch. Finn was almost eager to test his theory. He liked Sammy Cravitz; and besides, Luowski had it coming.

"We have a favor to ask," Finn said.

"We?"

He lowered his voice. "The Keepers."

"Which is?"

"We're not allowed to go into any of the parks without permission."

"I know that."

"We've looked all over MK for our friend, but we got nothing. The abandoned truck was found near Epcot, so we want to check out Epcot next. Most of the others are afraid to go without getting permission, and they don't want to ask their parents for permission, because they already know the answer. I'm willing to go, but apparently I'm alone."

"You? You're like only the most famous of all of the hosts."

"Am not."

"Are too. You'd be recognized in a nanosecond."

"It's too big a job for one person."

"Count us in," she said.

"I haven't even asked yet."

"How dumb do you think I am?" she said. "You want to ask me and Jess to do it for you, but you're worried about Jess because of what happened last time, and yet you're worried about *our friend* even more, and so you don't know exactly how to ask without seeming selfish, when in fact it's not selfish of you at all, because it's all about *our friend*, not about you." She pushed her plate to the side. "Are we done here?"

"Jeez," he said.

"And the answer is yes. And the second answer is no: you can't come along. You're a liability—look it up if you don't know what it means."

"I know what it means."

"But how are we supposed to find him?" she asked.

"I don't know. Philby has this theory that if we get close to him—"

"The temperature will drop," she said. "Yeah, I heard that one. Like it did last time. Because of her."

"Her *and* him," he said. *Maleficent and Chernabog*, he was thinking. "They both need the cold. Yes. But who knows? Either that, or the Overtakers will react to our snooping around."

"I thought you said the Overtakers chased you in the park last night."

"They did."

"So why doesn't that count?"

"I can't tell you that we're right about any of this," he said. "But there was no sign of her. No cold. Nothing felt right. It felt much more like we'd stepped into a snake hole than a beehive."

"You're really weird. You know?"

He didn't comment.

"Good weird," she said. "But weird." She picked up her tray and stood from the table. "Check your e-mail," she said. Neither she nor Jess had cell phones like the rest of them. "I'll let you know what we find out, if anything."

Good weird, Finn was replaying in his head. He hardly heard the rest of it.

And there was Greg Luowski staring him down from across the cafeteria. Big, tough Greg.

Once again Finn debated the unthinkable. This time Amanda wasn't there to warn him off.

* * *

Finn was able to check his e-mail during last period study hall.

wer goin 2day aftr skool. c u 2nite

Knowing their plans made things easier for Finn. He grabbed a baseball cap from his locker and donned a pair of shades on his way out of school. He biked to a bus stop, locked up, and rode the twenty minutes out to the Disney Transportation Center, where he hopped a bus to Epcot. He couldn't use his Magical Memories Pass to enter the park (a rare VIP pass issued to his family because of his status as a DHI) because it would alert the computer system that he'd entered the park, and he was forbidden from doing so without applying for permission beforehand. But Wayne had given Finn and the other Kingdom Keepers fake employee passes during their search for Jess in Animal Kingdom, and he'd used the pass twice since, and it still worked.

Finn used it now, entering Epcot through a special turnstile for employees and guests and then hiding himself among Leave a Legacy's rows of stone monoliths, which were covered with one-inch-high metal plates bearing photographs of faces of former park guests. Leave a Legacy had always given Finn the creeps—instead of feeling futuristic, it felt more like the cemetery where the ashes of Finn's grandparents had been buried.

He knew that Amanda had P.E. last period on Tuesdays, which meant she would shower and change afterward. He felt confident he had a head start on her and Jess. So he waited it out, pacing among the marble markers and keeping a sharp eye on the gate entrance to the park. Five minutes passed. Ten minutes. It was dizzying trying to study the faces of the hundreds of people who entered Epcot each minute. He didn't spot either of the girls, but he did jump back as he recognized the face of an adult.

The woman.

He peered around one of the marble slabs and checked again. He'd only seen her from a distance at school, and yet . . . he couldn't be absolutely certain, and yet . . . he was seeing her in profile now . . . and yet. . . .

Something tugged at him, told him to look over at the gate.

Amanda and Jess were just coming through one of the turnstiles.

Had the mystery woman's entrance been designed to coincide with the arrival of the girls? Had she been following them, only to slip into the park ahead of them?

Finn located the woman again in the crowd. She was with the crowd, walking to the left of Spaceship Earth, the giant golf ball for which Epcot was known. In the few seconds he watched her, she didn't look back once.

"Hey!" Finn called out as Amanda and Jess approached.

They took no notice of him, continuing along, talking to each other.

He tucked his chin low to keep his face from being recognized, and hurried to catch up.

Coming up from behind, he startled them both.

"*Psst!* Amanda!"

She spun around and puckered her face dismissively, not recognizing him. Then her expression changed.

"What are you doing here?" she said, aghast. "I thought the whole purpose of our—"

"I didn't want you guys doing this by yourselves," he said. "Hey, Jess."

"Hey there, Finn."

Jess was exotic looking. He found it difficult to separate what he knew about her from her looks, but the fact was her ability to dream the future seemed to agree with her intense beauty, as if she were a fairy or a witch or some kind of unknown being or alien. Her natural hair color was not natural at all, a shocking white, like a grandmother's. It had gone that color after Finn had rescued her from the clutches of a spell cast by Maleficent. She hid the white hair by dyeing it, becoming sometimes a brunette, sometimes a redhead. For the past month she had been a strawberry blonde, an appealing look that made her seem more outdoorsy and playful than he knew her to be.

"Aren't you taking a risk by coming here?" Jess said. Her voice revealed no emotion, no judgment. She sounded half asleep, as calm as the waters of the lake they now approached. "Amanda explained your . . . situation."

"You two are doing Wayne and all of us a great favor," Finn said. "I couldn't let you go alone."

"So it isn't that you wanted to hang out with Amanda?" Jess said.

"Jessica!" Amanda snapped, blushing.

"I wanted to hang out with *both* of you," Finn answered without missing a beat. He could see he had caught Jess off guard. He suppressed a grin.

"And protect us, I suppose?" Amanda said.

"It's not like that," he said.

"No, it's not," Amanda said, "because if anyone

recognizes you—and they are bound to because that disguise is . . . *pitiful*—then you mess us up a lot more than if we were just on our own."

"So you want me to leave?" he said.

"No," Jess answered, stealing the moment from Amanda. "She wants to pretend she isn't thrilled that you took a very big chance by coming here to protect us, and she wants to make it seem like it's no big deal when we all know that it is a big deal. I, for one, want to thank you. I like it that there are three of us. I feel better that you're here, and so does Amanda, though she'll never admit it."

"I don't have to admit what isn't true," Amanda said.

"There's a lot of park to cover," Jess said. "Three people are better than two."

"It may be more complicated than that," Finn said. He took each girl by the arm and led them behind a stand selling all kinds of merchandise. They quickly picked up on the fact that he was using the stand as a screen, and that made them both curious to try to look around it and see who or what they were hiding from.

"It's a woman," he said. "I'm pretty sure I saw her in front of school this morning."

"Seriously?" Amanda asked.

"And Maybeck said some woman was lurking

around Crazy Glaze. Window-shopping, but less interested in the pottery than the people inside."

"And she's *here*?" Jess said.

Finn nodded. "I saw her enter just before you two. If she is following you, she's good at it, because she never looked back toward the gates, never gave any indication . . . and I don't see how she could have followed me, but I'm not ruling that out either."

"So what do we do about it?" Jess asked.

Amanda lifted onto her toes to see over the stand, but Finn pulled her back down.

"I think I take the woman, while you two search for a temperature drop."

"We don't have phones," Amanda reminded him. "So what good does your following the woman do?"

"If I keep my distance, I can see if she eventually tries to follow you two. If she does then we know she's trouble—probably an Overtaker—and maybe by me following her she leads us to Wayne."

"You're dreaming," Amanda said.

"That's genius!" Jess said.

"And if she's following *you*," Amanda said, "which makes sense if she was watching you from in front of the school, then by following her you could be led right into a trap. Then, instead of looking for Wayne, we'd be looking for you and Wayne. That's helpful."

Amanda was typically gentle and good-natured. Yet it seemed that the closer they grew as friends, the more sarcastic she became. Or maybe it was the foster-home situation and the threat of her and Jess being sent back to Maryland that was making her this way. Whatever it was, he didn't like her like this and wanted to say so, but Jess interrupted.

"I say we call for a vote," Jess proposed. "All in favor of Finn following the woman?"

Jess and Finn sheepishly raised their hands.

"Whatever," Amanda said. "But listen up, Alex Rider: if anything happens, you'd better leave us some clues. This park is gigantic and we're leaving here together—the three of us—you got that?"

She sounded concerned—deeply concerned.

Finn bit back a smile. "Sounds good to me."

"And me," Jess said, chiming in.

Finn spotted a bright green balloon for sale on the cart. It was the only green balloon.

"Keep a lookout," Finn said, "for that green balloon. I'm going to carry it low unless there's trouble. If you see a green balloon following you, it's probably me, and it means something's wrong—like maybe the woman is following you, or I've been spotted, or something like that. If that happens, you split up. No matter what, we all meet back here in two hours so I can get home by dinner, and you guys can get to your place before curfew. Sooner than that if there's trouble. Agreed?"

"I suppose," Amanda said.

"You're good at this," Jess said.

"I've had a little practice," Finn said.

He bought the balloon, and hurried off to catch up with the mystery woman.

5

"YOU WERE A LITTLE HARD ON HIM, don't you think?" Jess asked as she and Amanda headed toward The Land. Not only was Soarin' their favorite attraction in Epcot, but The Land offered a controlled environment—a cooler environment—and because of that, it seemed a good place to start in their search for signs of Maleficent or Chernabog.

"I was only messing with him," Amanda said, answering her. "He shouldn't be here. That's the whole point of our being here, right? So what's with that?"

"He's worried about us."

"Yeah, right. And who's the one always getting in trouble?"

"We've had our share," Jess said.

Neither of them could forget the nightmare of Jess's being captured by the Overtakers, her escape that had led to her being trapped, and the resulting ordeal inside Animal Kingdom. Finn had been the one to find her, and Jess nearly reminded Amanda of that, but knew she didn't need to.

"He's handy to have around at times like this," Jess said.

"I suppose. But it's risky for him—for all of them. I think it's stupid of him to come."

"You're *worried* about him! Do you have a crush on him?" Jess said.

"As if! You're the one he can't keep his eyes off of. Him and every other boy."

"That is *so* not true!"

"We both know it is," Amanda said. "Hey, I'm good with it, so don't fight it." She lowered her voice. "Why do you keep checking your watch? We've got plenty of time before we have to be back."

"It isn't that," Jess said. "My watch shows the temperature. Elevation. A bunch of stuff. It's like for rock climbers or something."

Amanda moved closer trying to see the watch face. "And?" she asked.

"No change so far. Eighty-two degrees."

"As in, boiling."

"Yeah, but my watch may pick up on a change before we do. You realize we're lucky it's so hot out?"

"Because?"

"Because it'll be more obvious if the temperature drops all of a sudden, like Finn says it will. And because any kind of sudden chill will need some kind of explanation. It's not as if anything's getting colder out here, you know?"

It was true. Everything around them was concrete or stone, storing or reflecting the intense afternoon heat. Any drop in temperature could only be explained by something man-made or *unnatural.*

The Land was housed in an inelegant glass-and-concrete structure with a huge sign bearing its name. As the girls approached it, they walked slowly, trying to sense a change in temperature. Jess monitored her watch carefully.

"Nothing but hot," Jess said.

"Personally, I think this is hopeless," Amanda said. "I mean I know Finn and those guys have felt a chill before, but you've got to be kidding me."

"Any other ideas?"

"No. That's the thing, I guess. Finn is super-close to Wayne. His being missing is eating him up. We've got to do something, but I'm not sure there's any point to—" Amanda turned because Jess had stopped walking. "Sis?" she said, using a favorite nickname.

Jessica stood there staring into space. She looked as if she was studying the sign on the building, but Amanda knew something was wrong. She hurried back to her.

"Sis?"

"I don't want to lose it," Jess said.

Amanda was about to say something when she thought better of it. Her "sister" was a rare and unusual creature herself; her gift of "sight" made her different in the same way that Amanda's own gifts separated her from others. In this way neither of them felt that she belonged, which only solidified their friendship and their bond. Amanda knew better than to speak. She knew it intuitively without needing to be told. She took Jess gently by the arm and steered her toward a concrete bench. At the same time, her concern for their safety told her to search for any security cameras in the area; in the Magic Kingdom, Finn had believed some of the security people worked in concert with the Overtakers.

Again, she was about to speak; again, she controlled herself.

"Pencil," Jess said. She sounded sleepy. "Something to write on."

Amanda dug through her purse. No pen, no paper, but she found some mascara. She slipped Jess's purse off her shoulder and rifled through it as well. She came up with a Winn-Dixie receipt. She put the mascara brush into Jess's right hand and the receipt onto her leg and steered Jess's hand to the receipt.

"Okay." She spoke softly.

Jess had that faraway look going. But her hand

began to move, and the mascara brush smeared black onto the receipt. It was no good: her effort was illegible. Amanda frantically dug through Jess's purse. In a zippered pocket she found a stumpy wooden pencil. She replaced the mascara with the pencil. Jess's hand began to scribble again.

She shaded and crosshatched, making the receipt darker. Then she pressed hard and wrote several letters, making them fat and black.

MKPFP IFP

Amanda looked up. Later, she wouldn't be sure exactly why she did this. Had something instinctive told her to do so, or had it been only coincidence? These kinds of questions pestered her lately, the reasons behind events, the power of intuition and thought and what role fate played in her life and the lives of others. She didn't mention any of this to anyone—not even Jess. It was "heavy," deep stuff—and she was afraid she'd be teased for thinking about such things—but she lay awake at night considering the connection of her life to the lives of others, what her life might have been like had she not been orphaned, what it would mean for her and Jess to be sent back to the Fairlies, whether Finn liked her as more than a friend, where she was going to be in another three years when she turned eighteen and the foster-care system released her.

She spotted a green balloon coming toward her. Carried high above the heads of the guests pouring in to The Land, it bounced with the movement of the person carrying it.

Finn? If so, they had no time to hang out on a bench.

"We've got to get going," she said to Jess, whose hand suddenly went rigid as she stopped writing. She blinked.

"Jess!" Amanda continued. "The balloon. Finn. The woman. We can't stay here."

Jess looked over at Amanda, then took in her surroundings. "Whoa," she gasped. She looked down at the receipt as if seeing it for the first time. "What's going—?"

"Now!" Amanda said, grabbing the pencil and receipt and stuffing them into her purse.

The green balloon wasn't traveling at the speed of the other guests, but much faster. She knew it was Finn. She knew it meant trouble was coming toward them as quickly as the balloon.

She pulled Jess to her feet. "You okay?"

"Yes. Fine."

They started toward The Land.

"It was like . . . one of my dreams," Jess explained.

"You know? Like when you get in the zone. In a daydream? Like that."

"You were totally gone," Amanda said. "Like sleepwalking."

"Exactly! That's exactly it. That's never happened to me before. Nothing like that. I mean, when I'm asleep, sure. In my dreams. But never like that. Never awake."

Amanda glanced back. Her eyes fell briefly on a woman coming toward them, a woman more put together than ninety percent of the other park guests. She had her hair up in a fancy way, and wore a nice necklace, a pressed white shirt. Amanda knew immediately it was *the woman*, though she spent no time considering how that might be possible.

"It's her," she told Jess. "Follow me."

She picked up the pace, leading Jess into the enormous, circular pavilion. There was an escalator and stairs ahead. A balcony running around the perimeter looked down into the lower plaza. Miniature hot-air balloons were suspended from the peak of the tent with colorful streamers cascading down on all sides.

She avoided the pileup at the escalator and took the stairs, careful not to run and draw further attention to them.

Below them was a sea of tables, most with colorful umbrellas overhead. The umbrellas did not exactly hide whoever was sitting beneath them. So she plotted a course away from the stairs.

"This way!" she whispered as they reached the plaza. She glanced quickly up. There was the green balloon, now only a few feet behind the woman. Finn was taking a huge risk getting so close to the woman.

Amanda cut quickly to the right and dodged a few tables, now in a location screened from the stairs. For the time being, they'd ditched the woman. She wanted to keep it that way.

"How are we supposed to hide in this place?" she asked Jess. But there was no answer: Jess seemed dazed, like she'd just woken up.

Amanda considered the girls' room, but they'd only trap themselves.

"Can't see the forest for the trees," Jess said. She was pointing at the waiting line for Living with the Land.

Amanda tried to make sense of what Jess had just said. *Trees?* There were fruit trees inside Living with the Land, but if they tried to jump out of the boat they'd be busted.

"It's a basketball team, right?" Jess interrupted, sounding much more awake. "Or volleyball, maybe. Come on!"

Jess reversed their roles, taking Amanda by the hand and steering her toward the line.

"I don't think this is such a good idea," Amanda said. She spotted a group of tall girls all wearing a team uniform. *The forest for the trees*, she realized. "We don't want to get stuck on a ride."

But Jess ignored her.

"Excuse me," Jess said, maneuvering the two of them between the team and the far wall, as if keenly interested in the wall's photographic mural. The athletes continued talking among themselves, not the least bit interested in the two girls.

Jess had effectively put a human screen between herself and Amanda and the mystery woman. There was no way the woman would see them unless she, too, joined the line and pushed forward; but that would be nearly impossible: several families had filed in behind the team. The woman would have to cut the line to have any chance of seeing the girls, and that would only draw attention to her.

The hardest thing for Amanda was not looking. She kept an eye for the green balloon but made no effort to see through the tall girls, for fear of her being seen.

"Good call," she said to Jess.

"Finn had better be careful," Jess said.

"Yeah, I know."

The line surged forward. The sisters stayed with the

team, keeping up against the wall and out of sight of the vast hall.

"Oh, no," Amanda said. The green balloon appeared and stopped about five yards behind them.

Finn was in their line. He had not lowered the balloon, which meant only one thing.

"No more looking," Jess instructed. "We keep our backs to her. We'll be on the ride—in the boat—in less than a minute. What's she going to do then?"

"No idea," Amanda answered, "but I don't think I want to find out."

"We've just got to hope—" Jess cut herself off. It was too late: the volleyball team filled up the back of a boat. This forced the two girls into the front of the next set of boats. Behind them, other park visitors took their seats.

Amanda stole one look in that direction. The balloon, still aloft, had moved farther back in line. Finn had stopped, allowing those in line to pass him.

In that fleeting glimpse, Amanda spotted the woman as well. She was boarding the ride on the same set of boats as Amanda and Jess, only a few behind.

"She's right behind us. Like three rows. What do we do now?" Amanda whispered into Jess's left ear.

Jess stared ahead.

"You got us into this," Amanda complained.

"First we calm down," Jess said without any trace

of tension in her voice. "I'm coming up with a plan."

"Now? Now you're coming up with one?"

"I am," said Jess. "If you'll allow me to think, that is."

The guide was saying, "Please remain seated. Please keep your legs and hands inside the boat at all times. . . ."

"That's it!" Jess said.

Amanda looked quickly around, expecting to see something.

"Where?" she said. "What?"

"Do exactly as I say," Jess instructed.

"Oh yeah, that's worked real well so far," Amanda snapped sarcastically.

"There's no room for hesitation," Jess explained. "As in *none*. We either do this together, or it's your turn to come up with a plan."

"Okay. I get it."

A recorded female voice took over from the guide. The narrator warned of a storm, then identified the rain forest, and the desert. There was a brief explanation of the diversity and importance of each to the earth's ecosystems.

"The American prairie once appeared as desolate as the desert," the voice continued.

"Get ready," Jess hissed.

"*Psst!* Girls?"

Jess and Amanda froze. It was a woman's voice

coming from directly behind them. They didn't have to guess which woman it was.

"*Psst!* You, two! I need to talk to you. It's about—"

"If you'd please keep your voice down," said the guide, cutting her off.

The boats had moved into a dark tunnel where movie screens showed working farms, ladybugs, and beetles.

"Now!" Jess said. She stepped off the boat and onto a walkway, ducking down into the dark to hide. Amanda was right behind her.

An alarm sounded. The boats stopped immediately. Several guests were talking at once.

"They got off! . . . I saw that! . . . You can't do that!"

They had tripped some kind of emergency stop.

"Come on! Let's go!" Jess said.

Together the girls headed for the light ahead and reached the greenhouse where banana and other fruit trees rose from a beachlike floor of sand.

Two men in coveralls appeared.

"You can't leave the boat!" one of them hollered.

"My sister can't hold it in another minute," Jess said. "Mexican food, you know?"

A twitter of laughter carried to them from down the tunnel. The guests on the ride had heard her.

"Oh . . . thanks," Amanda said through clenched teeth. "*This* was your plan?"

"You can't leave the boat!" the greenhouse worker repeated.

"Mister, if you don't get my sister to the girls' room, *you're* going to need a boat. Or at least some rain boots."

The alarm stopped. The boat started moving again.

"Your tickets will be pulled for this," the worker said. "You're through for the night—probably for the year."

Through for the night, Amanda heard. They'd barely just gotten started. Then again, Jess's plan had worked: the woman was stuck back on the boat. They'd gotten away from her.

Probably for the year.

Could Disney do that? She supposed they could probably do a lot of things that didn't seem possible.

"There's a lavatory down there," the worker said, pointing, having ushered them away out of view of the ride.

Jess elbowed Amanda.

"Huh?" Amanda said.

"The girls' room," Jess said emphatically.

"Oh, yeah," Amanda said, "right." It wasn't a stretch to try to look embarrassed. She headed toward the sign.

Behind her, two workers in lab coats appeared and moved directly for Jess.

Amanda hoped they weren't Overtakers, hoped like mad that Jess hadn't gotten them out of one trap only to lead them into another.

6

Mrs. Nash, arms crossed, looked down on Jess and Amanda with fire in her eyes. She was a woman who, to judge by her appearance, ate well, and had no love of cosmetics, nor of hairdressers or fashion magazines. She was currently stretching out a green T-shirt to the point that the writing on it was too distorted to be legible. Her arms bore white patches of dried skin scratched to scarlet, flaming islands that came down her arms like the Alaskan archipelago.

"What exactly were you thinking?" she wheezed. Mrs. Nash had trouble breathing.

"Amanda had to use the facilities," Jess said.

"I thought we had an understanding that the Disney parks were off limits," Mrs. Nash said. "After everything that happened to you, Jessica, I'm surprised you'd get anywhere near that place."

"I love Disney World," Jess said. "Especially Epcot. And it had been forever, and we just wanted to go there."

"Did you plan on missing dinner and curfew as well? Did you realize you might lose your passes?

You know how much one of those costs?"

For Mrs. Nash everything came down to dollars.

There was a stomping upstairs that won her attention and distracted her. Seven other foster girls lived in the house along with Jess and Amanda, in a total of three bedrooms, with two baths. Making a ruckus was strictly forbidden and the rule against it even more strictly enforced. Mrs. Nash had been born strict.

"We had no intention of missing dinner," Jess said. "The meals here are so . . . wonderful."

"There's no need for sarcasm, young lady."

There was great need for sarcasm where the meals in this home were concerned, but Jess held her tongue. "Yes, Mrs. Nash."

"Why wouldn't you wait for the weekend?" she asked, still concerned with the money involved.

"We acted spontaneously," said Amanda, answering her. "We realize now that was a mistake."

"You're both grounded for two weeks. Do you understand me? Directly from school to this front door. 'Do not pass Go. Do not collect two hundred dollars.' Are we clear?"

"Yes, Mrs. Nash," both girls said, nearly in unison.

"Your behavior reflects poorly on this house and my ability to care for you girls. I hope you'll consider that the next time you think about doing something as foolish as what you've done. And next time," she said directly to Amanda, "you think about going on a ride, you might think about using the girls' room first. You're a young woman, for heaven's sake, not a four-year-old."

"Yes, Mrs. Nash."

"Up to your room," she said. "You will do your homework and miss dinner. I'll keep plates for you in the fridge. You can warm them up after you show me your homework."

"Yes, Mrs. Nash." Again, nearly in unison.

Mrs. Nash eyed the girls suspiciously, wondering if they weren't mocking her by saying her name in concert. But Mrs. Nash wasn't intelligent enough to understand fully what people were thinking or trying to do; it was everything she could do to understand what people were actually doing. She understood punishment. If something confused her—which was often—she punished the offender. It was a simple formula for her that had worked nicely for nearly twelve years of looking after wayward girls: punish first, figure it out later.

"Well? What are you waiting for?"

The girls took off upstairs. Suzie Gorman and Patricia Nibs had been spying on them from the stairwell. The girls took off as Amanda and Jess approached. Upon their arrival at Nash House, Amanda and Jess had been hazed and harassed by the other girls. But then, one day, after Amanda had peed into a toilet with plastic wrap over the bowl, all the furniture in one of the rooms had instantly rearranged itself—*with no one in the room*. From that moment forward, the tricks had stopped and Amanda and Jess were kept at a respectful distance, never included in anything to do with the other girls, but never tortured or threatened either. It was a workable, serviceable arrangement.

In their room now, open to the hallway—there were no doors on any of the bedrooms, only half-hinges left where the doors had been removed—the girls sat down on Amanda's lower bunk and pulled out their notebooks. There were no desks or bookshelves in the room. All available space was given to the three beds—a bunk bed and a twin-size roller bed—and a single, four-drawer dresser that the girls shared for their few clothes.

Amanda started in on her math assignment. But she looked over at Jess and saw that instead of her homework Jess had her diary open in her lap and the wrinkled, mascara-stained receipt unfolded next to it.

"What's up?" Amanda said.

"It's just. . . . It was like a dream. You know? One of *my* dreams."

"Outside The Land?"

"Yes. But I didn't get it all. Nowhere near all of

it. And I thought. . . ." She sketched into the diary a clearer image of what she'd begun on the receipt. It looked to Amanda like a piece of a wall, but with horses drawn on it. And then, the same letters as before:

MKPFP IFP

It was almost like a torn piece of a photograph; part of the picture was there, part missing. The horses looked as if they'd been stabbed from the top with what appeared to be lances.

"Do you remember it?" Amanda asked.

"Not all of it, no. But what I do remember is pretty clear. Like the rest of them."

"And you think it's important?"

"It has never happened to me like that: during the day, in the middle of everything. It's always at night when I'm dreaming. It's always when I wake up and I can't get it out of my head. But today, in the park. . . . it just hit me all of a sudden. Like you'd put a bag over my head or something. Like I'd walked into a movie theater. Yeah, more like that. Only now I can't remember exactly what I saw. All I know is that it scared me, whatever it was. I didn't like it. I didn't want to see it. Most of the time, you know, it doesn't feel like that. I don't really care one way or the other—it's just sort of there, like that glow in your eyes after a camera's flash. Like that."

"So you think it means something?"

"It must," Jess said, nodding. "I mean it seems like they all mean something. And this one . . . this one was different."

An hour later they'd made it through their homework, microwaved their dinners, and hurried to get in line for the bathroom so they could take showers before bedtime. Another hour later they were both in their beds reading prior to lights-out at ten o'clock.

Amanda leaned out of her upper bunk to speak to Jess. "I wish we could have talked to him," she said.

"Shh!" hissed Jeannie Pucket from the rollaway. Jeannie made a point of being obnoxious whenever possible. She was Mrs. Nash's favorite and, as a result, got all sorts of privileges the others girls did not. Amanda suspected she was also a spy for Mrs. Nash, so she didn't mention Finn by name.

"He figured it out," Jess said. "He's smart that way."

"But still."

"I'll see him tomorrow at school. You'll see. I'm sure he's worried about us, but he won't be mad."

Mrs. Nash didn't allow the girls to take phone calls. Finn had no way to reach them, even if he wanted to.

"Be quiet," Jeannie said. "It's disrespectful. I'm trying to read."

Amanda groaned and lay back in her bed. Not long after that, the lights were turned off and Mrs. Nash patrolled outside the rooms, prepared to punish anyone who spoke after curfew. Amanda fell into a troubled but deep sleep, drawn down by what had been an exhausting afternoon.

Sometime in the middle of the night, the bunk shook and Amanda felt herself torn from a strange dream that involved Finn in a boat in the middle of white water. She sat up to see an indistinct shadow cast onto the wall, only to realize that the glow casting the shadow was coming from a portable reading light in Jess's lower bunk. Amanda hung her head over the edge.

Jess was sketching in her diary again.

"What are you doing?" Amanda said in a thin whisper to avoid waking the spy.

"Go back to sleep."

"It's the middle of the night."

"I had a dream."

"That's the idea," Amanda said. "That usually happens when we sleep. I was just in one myself."

"One of *my* dreams," Jess said. "The same dream I had at the park today."

"The same one?" Amanda tried to view Jess's dream

diary upside down, but finally slithered off the top bunk and pushed Jess over and climbed into bed with her.

"Is that who I think it is?" Amanda said.

"I think it is," Jess said.

"And what's that behind him?"

"I don't know, but it was *exactly* the same as I saw this afternoon, only this time I got the whole thing."

The image she'd sketched was striking. Amanda felt tempted to point out how much of what she had drawn borrowed from this very room, for it appeared to be an older man sitting on the edge of a bunk bed with a string of gibberish written on the wall behind him.

"So you dreamt this twice, exactly the same?" This fit a pattern for Jess, and they both knew it: her dreams that repeated eventually came true in the future; this had happened too many times for them to believe it had anything to do with coincidence. It was a gift—Jess's gift—nothing less.

"And that's who I think it is," Amanda continued.

"Wayne," Jess said. "Has to be."

"He knows about your . . . ability. About your dreams," Amanda said. "You suppose he's trying to communicate with you?"

"Who knows?"

Jess was still drawing. She was adding a horse to the background behind Wayne.

"We've got to show this to Finn," Amanda said.

Jess continued to shade the sketch by adding dark circles under Wayne's eyes. He looked haggard and much older than Amanda remembered.

"He's in trouble," Jess whispered.

"I think we all are," said Amanda.

IF FINN HAD RIDDEN HIS BIKE straight home, none of it ever would have happened. So in a way, Amanda was to blame, because she was the reason he walked his bike rather than riding.

He'd just been climbing onto his bike when she'd come running up to him, red-faced and out of breath.

"Oh, good. I thought I'd missed you."

"I'm right here."

"I have something I have to show you."

"Ah . . . okay." He climbed off the bike.

She reached into her backpack, slipped her hand inside, and then happened to look over her shoulder.

"Oh, no," she said.

Lousy Luowski was coming toward them, flanked by Mike Horton and Eric Kreuter. Smarter than Luowski by a long shot, both Mike and Eric wished they were as tough. They worked hard to act and look the part. Finn thought of them as pilot fish, the fish that swim with sharks and feed off the scraps that spill out of the scavengers' mouths while they feed.

Amanda was holding a small book—no, Finn realized—a journal or *diary* in her hand.

"You and me . . . we're going to fight," Lousy said.

"You're kidding, right?" Finn said.

"Do I look like I'm kidding?"

"That's original," said Finn.

When Lousy Luowski stood next to you, it was like putting your face into a laundry bin in the gym locker room. He had a string of zits stretching away from his nose, several with hairs, like tiny antennas, sticking out of them.

Finn worked hard not to show his fear. His only advantage at the moment was that the bicycle remained between him and Luowski—a small advantage at that.

"Hey, Greg, can't I talk to a friend if I want to?" said Amanda.

"Him and me, we've got some business to settle," said Luowski.

"Spoken like a true diplomat," said Finn.

Amanda shot Finn a look, chastising him for provoking Luowski.

"Why don't we take it off school grounds?" Luowski said.

"Because," Finn answered, "if we take it off school grounds then you will feel free to beat me to a pulp, and something tells me I wouldn't like that."

"You got that right."

"So I think I'll stay put," Finn said.

"You can run, but you can't—"

"Don't even *go* there," said Finn. "Mike," he said to Horton, "you've got to get this guy a better speech-writer."

Mike Horton bit back a smile, then lost it completely as Luowski looked his way.

"You gotta go home sometime," said Luowski.

It was true. And it would be easy for Luowski to wait for him in any number of places along his route. He might be able to lock up the bike and call his mom to come pick him up, but he'd never live that down. He saw his dilemma for what it was, even if Amanda didn't: a confrontation with Luowski now seemed inevitable.

"So," Luowski said, "whadda we got here?" He snatched the diary from Amanda's hand and waved it over his head tauntingly.

Finn lurched forward, but Luowski fended him off with a straight arm. It was like hitting a steel post.

"That's private property," Finn said. He'd seen Jess's diary before and understood its significance as a portal into the future. If Amanda had brought him the diary, then it had to contain something significant.

"As if I care," Luowski said.

"You'd better care," Finn said. He'd made promises to people—Wayne, chief among them—as well as to himself, never to cross over outside the parks, never to reveal his abilities to people who wouldn't understand. Wayne believed that to do so would jeopardize the future of the DHI program inside the parks, and therefore the existence of the Kingdom Keepers. But at the same time Finn's friendship with Amanda and Jess demanded that he act. Luowski had no right to steal Jess's diary, no right to enter its pages without her approval—a permission she would never give. Finn felt bound to do something more than just stand there watching this moron misbehave.

Rather than anger, Finn sought the inner quiet that freed him. He divorced himself from the moment, no longer fully present. His vision blurred. His skin tingled. He felt a lightness in his being. Freedom. He began to cross over.

It wouldn't last long. He had to take advantage of the moment—become part human, part DHI.

He charged Luowski, ducking under the boy's surprised reaction, a hastily lifted arm.

Finn snatched the diary from Luowski's grasp and threw it at Amanda, knowing that as he transitioned fully, his DHI might no longer be able to hold on to anything material.

"Go!" Finn shouted, wondering if he was the only one to hear the electronic buzz in his voice.

The diary flew in slow motion, its pages fluttering like a bird's wings. Amanda caught it and stuffed it into her purse. She turned and ran.

Luowski pulled back his right arm, loading it with purpose. He planted his feet and delivered the swing from low to high—a punch designed to deliver the most impact while, at the same time, snapping his opponent's head back. It was a roundhouse punch, meant to clock Finn unconscious.

A second before, Finn felt his entire body tingle like a limb that's fallen asleep. He'd done this enough times to understand that now he'd fully crossed over. So he stood there, chin out, awaiting the full brunt of Luowski's fist.

The blow failed to land. Luowski's knuckles went right through the space that should have been Finn's face. Luowski fell forward and, off balance, onto the ground. As Finn ducked back, the fear of the moment overcame his ability to cross over and he transitioned. Mike Horton would swear he'd never seen someone move so fast, convinced that Finn must have somehow ducked the punch. Eric Kreuter would claim that Luowski hit Finn squarely in the jaw, but that nothing happened. For this, Luowski later punched Kreuter in the jaw, knocking him down and asking him if he still thought nothing had happened.

Finn mounted the BMX and was speeding away before Luowski had regained his balance.

"Get onto the seat!" he called to Amanda, who had turned to witness everything.

He slowed. She swung a leg over and slid onto the seat, reaching out to Finn's waist as he stood, driving the pedals faster and faster. The bike wobbled and then sped away, Luowski cursing and shouting that he would do things to Finn that, technically speaking, were impossible.

"You're insane," Amanda said, her legs dangling on either side, her hands gripping him all the harder.

But the way she said it he could tell she didn't mean it. She meant it as a good thing. A good insane.

Finn pedaled all the harder.

8

FINN STUDIED THE PAGE in Jess's diary while the buzz of conversation swirled around him and Amanda. The Frozen Marble enjoyed a rush of middle school students each afternoon, loading up on chocolate, doing homework, teasing, conversing, and generally annoying one another. Their table was near the back, but Finn kept one eye on the front door in case Luowski happened inside.

Finn had put a shout-out—a text—to the other Kingdom Keepers to join them if possible. They attended schools spread throughout Orlando, so Finn doubted that Philby would make it—he had the farthest to travel—though he thought Charlene and Maybeck might show up. To his surprise Philby was the first to arrive. He wore a ball cap pulled down tightly to hide his face, as did Finn. The celebrity thing had gone from exciting to annoying; neither of the boys wanted to endure a half hour of signing autographs or answering stupid questions.

"Hey," Philby said, pulling over a chair and sitting down.

"Hey, yourself," said Amanda.

Finn picked up a spark between the two and wondered if he was imagining things.

"You made it here quickly," Finn said, suddenly questioning Philby's motivation.

"Caught the right bus. What's up?"

Finn slid Jess's diary over to Philby. At the same moment Jess entered the shop. Finn was going to ask Amanda how Jess could possibly know they were there, but he wasn't sure he wanted the answer—the "sisters" had an eerie connection and seemed to possess powers that had yet to be fully explained. But as it turned out, he was being overly dramatic.

"We can't stay long," Jess said. Thanks to Mrs. Nash, she and Amanda attended different schools. They met here each afternoon before heading home. She sat down and pulled her backpack into her lap. "Mrs. Nash grounded us, in case you didn't hear."

Amanda said, "We've got to stay at least a few minutes. Finn wants to talk to everyone."

"About?" Jess looked over at Finn. She had an intensity about her that other girls didn't have, a way of looking *through* you as if reading your thoughts. He was partly afraid of her, partly intrigued. Always curious. Her looks changed with her moods—today she was bright and cheerful, but that wasn't always the case.

Her skin shimmered, catching the light in an unusual way and making it appear translucent.

"You," Finn answered. "This," he said, indicating the diary. "Your encounter with security."

Mention of that caused Philby's head to snap to attention. Philby's expertise was in all things technical—he was a computer nerd, electronics wizard, and all-around techno-geek. He also loved anything to do with security because security represented his chief nemesis.

As Amanda was about to explain their escapade in Epcot, Maybeck, Charlene, and Willa all arrived together. Maybeck ordered a double scoop of vanilla mixed with peaches and almond crunch. That forced everyone else to order something. A few minutes later, the group sat in a circle around the two café tables wolfing down their orders.

Amanda spoke between mouthfuls, detailing the events of their ordeal, Jess's spacing out and the first sketch she'd made. Jess then explained her "nightmare" and the sketch that they all studied individually.

"It's Wayne," Amanda said.

"Has to be," Philby agreed.

"What do we *do* about it?" asked the ever practical Maybeck.

"We help him," said Charlene. All eyes fell on her. "What?" she inquired.

Willa said, "I mean I get that you're a rally girl—the cheerleading and all that. Right? But since when are you so eager to dive into action?"

"I've changed," Charlene said.

"I'd say so," said Willa.

"The stilts. Everything we did at Animal Kingdom. I can do stuff that you guys can't. Gymnastics, for instance."

"No one's questioning your contributions," Willa said.

"But *I* was," she said. "Look. I know that Disney hired me because of the way I look. Okay? Miss Middle School USA. I get it. I fit whatever they were looking for in a DHI the same way Maybeck does, and *all* of us really. But once this whole other thing got going, I had no idea what I was doing with all of you. You're smart," she said, looking at Finn, "or creative"—Maybeck—"or able to figure stuff out"—Philby—"or daring"—Willa—"and where was I supposed to fit into that? But AK changed all that. I'm a jock. I can fold myself in half, or do the limbo, or walk on stilts, or climb a climbing wall. Maybe I can't climb as good as Philby, but I can still climb. I think I needed that. I needed to figure it out, whatever *it* is. And for me *it* is athletics. So now I'm . . . different, I guess. I'm kinda charged up about doing whatever it is we're doing, and right now

I think what we're doing is trying to rescue Wayne. Right? I'm all over that."

For a moment no one said anything. It was as if someone had paused the DVD player. No movement. They all stared at Charlene.

"Alrighty then," Willa said, breaking the ice. "So how do we find Wayne?"

"I don't mean to be hard on anyone," said the ever-skeptical Maybeck, "but this drawing . . . He could be anywhere."

"Check out his jacket," said Finn.

Maybeck took the diary out of Charlene's hands without asking. He leaned in close to the page. "You're kidding me, right?"

"It's a shield," Willa said, leaning over Maybeck's arm to look.

"It's an EC shield," Finn said. "An Epcot Center windbreaker. Old guys get cold. My grandpop shakes like a leaf when it dips below eighty."

"Give me a break!" exclaimed Maybeck. "That logo is tiny! You can't see a thing. It could be anything."

Finn passed Maybeck his phone. "I went on eBay," he said. "Check out the black stripes on the arms." The image on the phone—an Epcot windbreaker for sale—matched what Jess had sketched exactly.

Maybeck said under his breath, "You're dreaming."

But he no longer sounded so sure of himself.

"The point is," Finn said, "we won't know until we find him. Okay? And what about those horses? They could be a carousel."

"A carousel in a room?" Maybeck snapped cynically.

"We have to start somewhere," Finn said. "Jess got . . . I don't know . . . a *signal* . . . when she was at Epcot. Then she got more last night in a dream."

"It's some gibberish on a wall, some horses, and an old guy in a chair," Maybeck complained.

"It's a place to start," said Charlene. "We have to start somewhere. Right? We wasted enough time in the Magic Kingdom these past couple weeks. What's wrong with trying Epcot?"

"But our tickets—our passes—were pulled," Amanda reminded them. "Every girl in Mrs. Nash's house was given a year's pass for free. But they took ours. And it's not like we can afford to buy tickets."

"Which is why I'm going to suggest something radical," Finn said. "I've thought about this a lot, so before you go shooting it down"—this was aimed directly at Maybeck—"at least think about it a minute. Okay? Give it a chance."

"That's some setup," said Philby.

"I'm not saying it's going to be easy," Finn said. "And I know that we can make all sorts of arguments against it, but I also know that when you look at it from every side, as I have, it makes total sense. It may seem random, but it's not. I promise."

He had everyone's undivided attention, especially as he lowered his voice so that it wouldn't carry.

"The point is, Jess will tell you that she hasn't completed the sketch. Amanda said she saw her go into kind of a trance when they were in Epcot. I think that's because she can feel Wayne there. She dreamed about him later, but the inspiration for that dream came from what had happened at Epcot. Now they've both been told they can't go back in any of the parks. Security will be watching for them: they're on the list. They certainly can't get in with us, at night—because we aren't exactly ourselves then, are we? As it is, we're going to need to get our DHIs from MK over to Epcot. And even if we figured out a way to get Jess and Amanda inside the center with us, since they're human, they could be caught. If we're chased, we can zap the remote—cross back over and be in our beds at home—like we did the other night. They can't do that."

"Are you thinking what I think you're thinking?" Philby asked.

"Do you see any other choice?" Finn asked him right back.

"Will someone clue me in?" said Charlene.

"Yeah, me too," said Willa.

Maybeck sat up and stared across the table at Finn intently. If anyone was going to make a fuss, it was going to be Maybeck. He nodded slowly. "Okay, I get it. I see where you're coming from."

"Well, I don't!" Charlene announced.

All eyes found Finn as a moment of expectation overcame them all. The buzz of the conversation in the room swirled around them. Spoons clinked against dishes. As the door came open, sounds of traffic out on the street could be heard.

Finn leaned forward, as did everyone else. For a moment they were in a tight huddle.

Finn said, "I think it's time we turn Amanda and Jess into DHIs."

9

THE MAGIC KINGDOM closed at nine o'clock that night; Finn went to bed at nine-fifteen. So did Philby, Maybeck, Willa, and Charlene. Had their parents and guardians communicated, perhaps the plans of their children might have been revealed, perhaps someone would have stopped them. Instead, Finn said good night to his parents, who were currently caught up in an episode of *Survivor*, closed his bedroom door and, fully clothed, climbed between the sheets.

He'd long since learned that he couldn't will himself asleep. If he tried to make it happen, he only prolonged his wakefulness. Philby had given him a book on self-hypnosis that included a series of relaxation techniques; Charlene had given every Kingdom Keeper *A New History of the Roman Empire*, a book so dense, so turgid, that no human being could read it for more than ten minutes without dozing off. Maybeck had recommended some songs to be downloaded to their iPods; he found them soothing and a gateway to sleep. Finn used a combination of all three: he listened to music while reading about the Romans and flexing his ankles and doing deep breathing exercises. He fell into a deep sleep ten minutes later.

* * *

The air smelled bitter, the result of the fireworks at the park's closing. Finn found himself sitting on a low concrete retaining wall next to a life-size bronze statue of Mickey Mouse holding hands with Walt Disney. Beyond Walt and Mickey, Cinderella's Castle was washed in a rich blue light, its spires stabbing the night sky. No matter how many times he visited, the magic here remained. For all the cynicism of his jealous friends at school who teased him about his now permanent connection to this place, he loved the Magic Kingdom and understood it would always be a part of him.

"Fancy meeting you here." Maybeck was sitting on the concrete walkway, his back against the metal fence. His eyes hid behind a pair of sunglasses. His dark clothing would help him blend in with the night and included a pair of black Converse basketball shoes. He looked cool, and that annoyed Finn. Maybeck couldn't help himself—he was the kind of guy who didn't ever try for cool, but always had it. Maybe it was the artist in him. Maybe it was that he didn't have parents and he'd had to forge an identity for himself out of what his aunt offered. Maybe some kids understood stuff others didn't and Maybeck was one of the ones who did. He had this *thing* about him, part attitude, part confidence, part selfish knuckleheadedness. Whatever it was, Finn would have given up a lot to understand it. To grasp it. There were times he disliked it, was revolted by it. There were other times, like now, when he coveted it.

"Have you seen the others?"

"That would be no," Maybeck answered. He opened his hand and showed Finn that he'd retrieved the fob from the bushes where Finn had tossed it. Maybeck passed it to Finn, who pocketed it.

The Kingdom Keepers each had to hit a patch of deep sleep in order to cross over. They seldom all arrived at once, but instead appeared over ten to twenty minutes. Finn now carried the device that could alone return them to their beds. At some point he would hide it so that any of them could use it, in case he were captured. He couldn't allow the remote to be captured along with him.

"Are you okay with this?" Finn asked. Maybeck had been an outspoken opponent of the idea in the ice cream parlor.

"It's not that I don't see your point. I do. I think, all things being equal, it would be good to have the sisters with us. Maybe we can't find Wayne without Jess, like you said. Maybe that's true. But . . . and it's a big but . . . I think it's too big a hassle to make it happen. Right? First we've got to record them somehow, then Philby has to upload the data. That's a lot, in my opinion."

"Jess only got part of the picture."

"We don't know that. I mean . . . I know what you're saying, it's like half drawn, but we don't exactly know what's real and what isn't. We never have. Right? I'm supposed to believe this is real. You kidding me? A couple holograms talking to each other. Who knows, Whitman? Maybe you know what you're doing. But maybe you don't. In which case this is a big waste of time."

He sounded so matter-of-fact, so convinced. Finn found it depressing. He looked around, hoping someone else—anyone—had arrived. The place was empty.

"We voted," Finn reminded. He didn't want Maybeck thinking he'd forced this on them.

"Yeah, yeah. And I was the minority. Imagine that."

"You're mad about it."

"Not true. Chill. I'm along for the ride, dude. Baa baa black sheep, that's me. I'm going along with you."

"Why do you do that?"

"Do what?"

"You know."

"Point out that we're different?" Maybeck asked.

"Make a deal out of it."

"It's me, Whitman. It's like Philby and his brain,

or Charlene being hot. I'm not saying that makes me special, but I'm different from the rest of you and I'm not going to dance around it as if it isn't there. I'm African American. So what? Right? There's good parts of that and bad parts of that, but I'm not going to pretend I'm white and I'm not going to not talk about it just to make you comfortable."

"I'll tell you something: I don't think of you as African American. I don't even see that part of you anymore. Maybe I'm supposed to, maybe it's disrespectful not to, but I just see you as . . . Maybeck. Listen, there are kids at school . . . you know who I'm talking about. They try to be . . . cool. They make a big deal about listening to rap, wear the lowriders, talk ghetto talk. I hate that kind of stuff. They want to act like they're something special. But then there's you calling yourself a black sheep and making these little jabs and reminders like I owe you something for who you are, what you are—and I don't get that. I just end up not knowing which is the real you."

Maybeck eyed him. "So how cool am I?" he asked.

"Shut up," Finn said, smiling.

"Ultracool, smokin' cool, plain old cool?"

"Uncool," Finn said. "Did you mishear me?"

"I heard you okay, Whitman."

Philby arrived. He was lying down on the grass

behind Maybeck. He spoke as if they were already in midconversation. "It's a cryptogram." He held a piece of paper in his hand. He waved it as he sat up. The edges of his image were sparking.

Finn was having the same problem: a strange static coming off him.

"What is?" Finn asked.

"The letters behind Wayne's head are a cryptogram."

"Is that supposed to be some sort of hypnosis?" asked Maybeck.

"A code," Philby said.

"A letter code," said Finn.

"Exactly."

"An engram?" said Maybeck.

"Anagram?" Philby said, correcting him. "No. A cryptogram substitutes letters of the alphabet for one another. It's like spy stuff. Tricky-to-solve stuff used by the CIA and people like that."

"How tricky?" asked Finn.

"Seriously harsh," said Philby. "And because it's Wayne, I'm thinking it'll be tough toenails. But if it's for real, if it really is Wayne, and he somehow knew Jess would dream it—and I know you believe that, Finn, but I'm not so sure I do—then he'd make it solvable. At least I think he would. He'd know I'm on it. And he'd know I'd Google it and find sites that could help decipher it."

Since Philby had been working with Wayne when Wayne had been captured, he blamed himself for it. He'd dragged around for the first couple of weeks after the event, only snapping out of it when Finn had suggested they start trying to find him by crossing over into the Magic Kingdom.

Philby had supported Finn's call for the sisters to become DHIs because it promised to keep him busy. He acted impatient, picking at the grass behind Maybeck, sitting with the low metal fence between them. He was the first to spot Charlene and Willa. "All here," he announced.

"How are we going to do this?" Maybeck asked.

The others gathered around, all five kids standing in front of the statue.

"You mean leave the park?" Willa asked.

"We've never done that before," Maybeck reminded her. "Not as DHIs. We don't even know if it'll work."

"There are DHI projectors in Hollywood Studios now," Philby said. "They project *us* there as guides. It makes sense that we should be able to see ourselves, see each other, once we're there. When we're away from the projectors, I don't know, it's like when we're inside the teepee, I think. We're there, but we're in shadow so we can't be seen."

"We're invisible," Maybeck said. "How cool is *that*?"

"Totally," Philby said, agreeing. "But being invisible is not going all-clear the way Finn can. We're still physically there . . . here . . . whatever. That's why we can pick up sand and throw it. And if we can touch stuff, then stuff can touch us. . . ."

"As in the Overtakers," said Charlene.

"That's my point," Philby continued. "We're still at risk. And we'll be in Epcot, whether in projection shadow or not. Who knows if the Return—the remote button—is going to work anywhere but here? This is where Wayne brought us. This is where we were when he sent us back. Maybe the fob will work inside Hollywood Studios or Animal Kingdom or Epcot, but who knows until we try? We'll bring it with us and try to Return from the Studios. And if we get separated, if we can't all get back here to cross back over together . . ."

"Then whoever was stuck here would be stranded," Willa said. "The Syndrome."

The DHIs glowed slightly. More static sparked off Philby. It went away as he set the paper down. Finn set down the history book and his static stopped as well. Finn tucked Philby's sheet into the book and showed the others that he was leaving the remote there as well. He hid them beneath a bush within reach of the path. He double-checked that everyone knew the location.

"Let's face it," Finn said, "there's a lot more that

we don't understand than what we do. This stuff . . . We're not going to figure out any of this stuff until we try." He looked around at the others. "The buses and the monorail run until midnight. We can get from here to the Transportation Center, and from there to Hollywood Studios."

"We need to get back as well," Charlene reminded. "So we've got to be back here by midnight."

"I would suggest we don't touch anyone. We don't bump into anyone. We don't speak," said Philby. "Chances are we won't be able to tell who's where or what's going on once we're outside the range of the projectors. So if we get split up by accident, we meet by the Kodak shop just inside the Hollywood gates. No one leaves there until we're all there together."

"Agreed," said Finn.

The others nodded.

"I'm a little scared," Willa said. "I'm not so sure I like this."

"We're all a little scared," Finn said.

"Speak for yourself," said Maybeck.

10

AMANDA SAT UP IN HER BUNK, Mrs. Nash's voice ringing in her ears.

"Did you just hear that?" she asked Jess.

"Yeah," Jess said, swinging her legs off her lower bunk. Her voice signaled her mutual surprise. Mrs. Nash *never* called for them. She scolded them. She bossed them around. But she never barked their names up the stairs—shouting at Nash House was strictly forbidden and universally punished.

Jess slid off her bunk. Both girls hit the floor at the same time. Jeannie, who had been given DS privileges, looked up from the device.

"What's up?" she asked.

"Who knows?" Amanda said, unable to keep the terror out of her voice. She didn't know how to respond to Mrs. Nash calling them this way. The girls looked at each other; Jess shrugged; they both finger combed their hair (Mrs. Nash was a stickler about appearances) and hurried out of the room.

"Girls?" Mrs. Nash was calling from the bottom of the stairs. She sounded so . . . sweet.

"Maybe she's had a stroke," Jess said, cracking up Amanda.

Standing to the side of the stairs and sneaking a peek down, the girls saw a tall woman standing inside the front door. She was a woman of thirty, properly attired, hair perfectly coifed. She was too well dressed, too pretty, to be from Social Services.

"Oh, no," Amanda gasped. She grabbed for the banister to steady herself.

"Amanda?" Jess said. "What is it?"

"It's *her*. I mean she was way far away, so I suppose I can't be sure, but I *am* sure. It's the woman who was watching the school. The woman Finn said was following around the Kingdom Keepers. She'd been at Maybeck's before."

"You're sure?"

"Pretty sure. And what's Mrs. Nash doing accepting a visitor this late? Curfew's in twenty minutes."

"We can't just hide up here," Jess said.

"Girls?" Some of the sweetness was gone.

Jess took Amanda's hand and the two descended the stairs together.

"You have a visitor," Mrs. Nash said. "This is Ms. Alcott, from the Timmerand School in Charlottesville, Virginia." She introduced both girls by first name only, and led the three into the small public room. She was just about to sit down when Ms. Alcott spoke for the first time.

"If I could visit with the girls in private . . ."

Mrs. Nash looked as if she'd been slapped in the face. "Of course," she said.

"The four of us can have a discussion just as soon as I've met the girls and had a chance to visit."

"That's fine," Mrs. Nash said, clearly upset by the rebuke. She pulled the pocket doors separating the parlor from the hallway shut on her way out.

The woman calling herself Ms. Alcott looked over both girls carefully.

"You look terrified, child," she said to Amanda. "Is it me scaring you? I promise you there's nothing to fear." She lowered her voice. "I'm not from Timmerand, though I am on their board of trustees, and I did go there, years ago. I find the telling of small lies is most convenient, though I do not advocate the practice as it's an extremely delicate matter, an art form of sorts. Bending the truth is like pulling back a spring—more often than not it snaps back and hits you. Stings like the dickens when it does."

"Why have you been following my friend?" Amanda asked, careful not to give Finn's name, but also wanting this woman to know that she, Amanda, was aware of her recent actions.

"For the same reason I've come here," Ms. Alcott

answered. "Because I need your help. And you need mine."

"I don't understand."

Jess looked on, saying nothing. Amanda expected her to join in, and was disappointed when Jess did not.

"Wayne," she said, surprising both girls.

"What about him?" Amanda asked.

"Your friends are his only hope."

Amanda said nothing. She had no way of knowing if this woman was an Overtaker posing as a friend, or an honest friend of Wayne's desperate to find him.

"The Kingdom Keepers," Ms. Alcott said. "Finn Whitman, Terry May—"

"We call him Donnie, by the way, not Terry, but we know who our friends are," Amanda said.

"You have something of Wayne's," Jess said quietly. Her sudden participation surprised Amanda.

Ms. Alcott took a deep breath and sat back in her chair. "How could you possibly know that?"

"What is it?" Jess said.

"It's something I need to get to Finn or one of the others. I've tried several times to make contact, but it hasn't worked out."

"You've been *stalking* them," Amanda said.

"I'm an adult. You all are not. That makes things . . . difficult sometimes. Furthermore, I had to make sure the Overtakers were not following either of us—me or them—and I could never be absolutely sure."

"Are there Overtakers outside the parks?" Amanda said.

"Wayne has always believed so. But he tends toward the paranoid when it comes to his enemies. I have no proof either way. But he warned me, and I've always taken his warnings seriously."

"You've known him a long time," Amanda said.

"You might say that," she said. "I'm his daughter. Wanda. Get it? Like Mickey's wand?"

"Aha," Amanda said.

"What is it?" Jess repeated. "This thing you've brought?"

"My father has a very active imagination. It's why he's been such a successful Imagineer. That includes . . . well, I don't know how to put this exactly, but he can 'see' things. Or he thinks he can. He claims it's an extension of his imagination. Most of the time it's little things: he'll mention someone's name and within a matter of minutes that person calls him—I've seen that happen a lot with him. Or he'll know, five minutes before it happens, that all the lights are going to go out, that there's going to be a power failure. It's not that he talks about these things. But he'll go get a flashlight out of the garage, and right then all the lights go out. That sort of thing. As a child I always considered these things coincidences. As I grew older I saw them more for what they were: prescient moments. *Prescient,* meaning—"

"We know all about prescience," Amanda said. "'Knowing beforehand.'"

"It's a gift."

"Or a curse," said Jess, winning a sympathetic look from Amanda.

"Yes, I suppose," said Wanda. "Though for my father, a definite gift. He would do things like pull over to the side of the road without explanation. A minute later a car would come zooming down the wrong lane head-on at all the traffic. That kind of thing. Quirky things."

"You still haven't told us what he gave you," Jess said.

"I didn't say he gave it to me," Wanda said, correcting her. "I merely told you I had something of his."

Amanda said, "Jess has a similar gift to your father's."

"I'd like to see it," Jess said, sounding somewhat trancelike.

"Please," said Amanda.

"Of course. I have no problem with that." Wanda reached into her purse. "He made this the day before all that craziness at the Animal Kingdom, the day before he disappeared. He'd kept everything about your friends private until then. I hadn't heard anything about it. But we spoke that day—he called me, not the other way around, which was the far more common occurrence. He told me in detail about the Overtakers, about Finn and Maybeck and the others. You two included. He'd not done that before and I knew just his talking about it meant it was significant. I'm now of the belief that he might have foreseen his being captured, that he called me because of this. He was laying the groundwork for your friends to save him, or at least to save the parks if it came to that."

She withdrew the item from her purse, opening her palm to reveal a small, white cube made of typing paper. There were symbols written and drawn on the cube's six surfaces.

Jess picked it up and studied it, spinning it and taking in the various images. She closed her eyes, opened them and looked over at Amanda. She shook her head slightly: she hadn't immediately flashed on anything to do with the box.

"We can get it to Finn," Jess said, not wanting to surrender it.

"Oh, yes! Could you, please? As soon as possible!"

"Tomorrow," Amanda said. "I'll see him tomorrow."

"I can help your friends," she offered. "I want to help."

"We can show the box to Philby," Jess said. "He's smart. He might know what it means."

"I looked up each symbol on the Internet," Wanda said. "They were all easy enough to find. But none of it added up. And who can tell what order they're supposed to be in? Without the order, the message—if there even is a message—keeps changing. But he didn't intend it for me, did he? I don't think so. I think it was for your friends. I think that's what he was trying to tell me in the phone call, without actually saying it. He was always convinced the Overtakers were listening, watching. I think some of that rubbed off onto me, which is what made actually contacting Finn or Maybeck so difficult for me. But then it occurred to me to talk to you. They'll believe you more than me, anyway."

"We'll make sure they get it," Amanda said.

"I want to help," the woman said. "There are any number of ways I can help your friends. Access to the parks. Research materials. I'm very close to my father. I know much more than I probably should—about the parks, the Overtakers, Maleficent, even Chernabog. I'm not claiming to be as useful as my father—there's only one Wayne. But he called me for a reason that day, and I think the reason was for me to be involved in his rescue. I'm not saying I can take his place, but I want to help."

"We'll tell them what you've told us," Amanda said.

"I want to leave you with my phone number," she said, scribbling out a number and offering it first toward Jess, but then passing it to Amanda as Jess's concentration remained fixed on the paper cube she held. "Day or night, doesn't matter. Please call."

"Okay."

"I have access to all of my father's things. His notebooks, keys, computer. There are any number of ways I can help."

"We have to come up with something believable for Mrs. Nash," Amanda said.

Mention of the woman's name snapped Jess out of her trance. "Yes, there is that."

"I can take care of it," the woman said. "We're recruiting you as boarding students. I'll have the school mail some brochures and applications as a kind of follow-up. I'll call you. I can make it convincing, I promise. I can be very convincing."

"And so can your small lies," said Amanda, who still didn't know if she could trust this woman. She might not have anything to do with Wayne whatsoever.

If not, then what had been her purpose in coming to the Nash House, and what damage had they done by talking to her?

"I realize it may be asking a lot to expect you to trust

me. My father has spent the past ten years training me in all things Disney. It's a matter of pride for him. He loves the parks . . . well . . . like he loves his own children. And that's me. With or without you, I'm going to do whatever it takes to find him, to rescue him." Her voice choked and she looked down, breaking eye contact with Amanda. "My father has spent basically his whole life making the parks magical places—including creating the DHIs, I might add. The Overtakers will do whatever is necessary to corrupt the parks, to drive guests away, to ruin the experience for everyone. Whether or not they have ambitions beyond the parks, who knows? But I'm not going to allow everything my father has worked for to be taken away. At least, not without a fight. Maybe you don't trust me—I can't speak to that. But I can tell you it isn't easy for me to put my faith in a bunch of kids. That may sound harsh, but that's just being honest. That's not a little lie, or a big lie, but the truth. But I don't know where else to turn, and my father believes in your friends. He believes very deeply in them. He thinks they can accomplish what he has not been able to. I've never doubted my father, and I'm not going to start now. That's about it. That's about all I can tell you."

"What's it like?" Jess asked, her voice soft and comforting.

"Excuse me?" Wanda asked.

"Having a father?" Jess said. "We've . . . neither of us . . ." Her voice trailed off.

"It's amazing. It's the best there is."

Amanda swallowed deeply. She had a decision to make that wasn't easy. "I know where you can find them—our friends," she said. "I think they could probably use your help."

Wanda pursed her lips. Her eyes welled with tears. "Thank you! Thank you for trusting me! You won't be sorry," she said. "I promise."

11

THE TRIP FROM THE MAGIC KINGDOM to Hollywood Studios was a strange mixture of an eerie sense of nothingness combined with a heart-stopping awareness of imminent danger. Things Finn had taken for granted, like having a bus driver hold the door open, were not available to the invisible. Only he, Charlene, and Philby made it on board the first bus; Willa and Maybeck were left behind as the driver, seeing no one, shut the bus door, closing them out. For the fifteen-minute ride to the Transportation Center Finn hadn't been sure which of them had made it on with him. Once at the center, he tried talking, only to discover that he had no voice. Sound, it turned out, was part of the projection process. Until he reached Hollywood Studios, he was not only invisible but wholly alone in a way he'd never experienced before. It was a condition, a state, he found unsettling and frightful: no one heard him; no one felt his presence.

"It was as if I didn't exist," he told Charlene once they were both through the turnstiles. Entering the Studios had been tricky. He'd had no idea when, or even if, the projectors would pick up and start displaying his DHI. To complicate matters, he spotted two night watchmen. They might allow characters their freedom, as Wayne had told him, but they wouldn't appreciate kids running around.

He'd timed his entry until a guard passed. He made a run for it: straight up the street toward the Kodak shop. One second he was invisible, the next a glowing blur of colorful light. He could see his arms and legs. As it turned out, Charlene was right behind him. The two sprinted up the empty street together, their attention on the back of the guard who'd just passed.

"You!" came a man's voice.

A different guard; one neither of them had seen.

He and Charlene skidded to a stop.

"Do as I do," Finn said under his breath.

Suddenly Philby appeared from the turnstiles. Thankfully the guard's attention had been on Finn and Charlene at the time, meaning that he missed a boy appearing out of thin air.

"Hello, there, park visitor! My name is Finn," Finn said in an extraordinarily happy voice. "Can I help show you Disney's Hollywood Studios?" He struck a pose—one hand out, the other on his hip.

Charlene caught on. Like Finn, she had little difficulty recalling the lines she had once said repeatedly during the DHI recording sessions.

"Hello, there, park visitor. I'm Charlene, a Disney Host Interactive. I'm sorry, but I'm not able to read your identification pin. Please recite the guest number on your Disney Pass and I'd be happy to show you around."

The guard reached out. His hand swiped right through Finn, accompanied by an electronic buzzing.

"Dang," the guard said. He ran his hand through Finn again. He reached for his radio. "Hey, Tim . . . it's Tanner. Can you check—?"

"We . . . are experiencing a DHI server malfunction," said Philby coming up from behind the guard. "Please . . . stand by."

"Tanner?" It was a man's voice over the handheld radio.

"Yeah, I'm here. Ahhh. . . . For some reason those host things didn't shut down properly. You'd better ask tech services to look into it. I've got three of them out here talking to me."

"Talking to you?" the radio voice said.

"Offering to show me around the Studios."

"Okay. I'm on it," the man's voice replied over the radio.

Finn searched his memory and said, "I'm sorry you won't be joining me today. Maybe another time. Advance reservations can be made through the dining hotline. Do you have any more questions?"

"Umm . . . That would be *no*," the guard said.

"Have a star-filled day at Disney Hollywood Studios." Finn walked mechanically toward the camera shop. He'd studied his real DHI enough to know that while the 3-D projections were phenomenally lifelike, movement was not perfect. When walking slowly, the DHIs tended to have stiff knees. When running fast, they blurred.

A few minutes later, all five DHIs collected outside the Kodak shop. The guard had moved on from Finn, eyeing Maybeck and Willa as they arrived late. Finn didn't feel like pushing his luck. "Split up in groups and meet over at Soundstage B in ten minutes. If you're stopped by a guard, stick to the scripts we recorded for our DHIs."

"Is that how you got around him?" Maybeck asked. "Willa and I saw you talking to him—"

"Later," Finn said. "We can catch up later." He and Charlene took off up the street, mapping out a route in his head to the soundstages.

"You were amazing back there," Charlene said, running at his side.

"It's amazing that he didn't question the way we're dressed, that we're out of costume. He must not know the DHIs very well. He's probably a night-duty guy."

"Do you think they're watching us now?" she asked.

"Could be," Finn answered. "Philby would know about the security cameras, but we've got to assume they're watching us."

"Then what'll we do?"

"It may make some kind of weird sense to them to see us all meet up outside the same soundstage where we were created. That may give us an excuse to get inside."

"Isn't that a little risky?" she asked.

"You saw what happened with his hand," Finn said. "It went right through me."

"Yeah. So?" she said. "That's you. Most of the time our DHIs are kind of half and half. You know that. They can catch *me*. The rest of us. Besides, what if they shut down the projectors like that guy said. . . ."

"The servers are always running," Finn reminded her. "Philby said so and so did Wayne. They'll close our programs and assume we're shut down. If they see us after that they'll file a maintenance ticket and forget about it."

"If you say so."

"Look, this is our chance to scout the soundstage. To see if we can figure a way inside and if Philby can figure out a way to shoot what we need to turn Amanda and Jess into DHIs. It was a hassle getting over here. You want to leave? We can leave. But—"

"I'm not up for leaving," she said, "but I also don't like the idea of their checking us out, knowing where we are. The Overtakers have guys in security. We all know that. Getting lucky once doesn't mean it's going to happen every time."

"The cameras aren't everywhere," Finn said, as Soundstage B came into view. It was a large, sand-colored building, like a giant box. "The attractions, mostly. Philby will know exactly where. I get what you're saying: it's better if we don't advertise. But at the moment they're thinking we're part of a computer glitch. We can use that to our advantage."

"Behind us," Charlene said, having glanced over her shoulder.

Finn looked back. Whoever, whatever it was, was tall, clearly an adult, and moved like a woman. She seemed in a hurry to reach them.

"What do we do?" Charlene asked.

His temptation was to run first, answer questions later. But they'd had success fooling the guard. To run was to look guilty of something.

"I think," he said, "we just do like before. We play our DHIs."

"You sure?"

The woman was closing the gap between them.

"Ah," Finn said. "You know the woman I told you

about? The one at the school? The one Maybeck saw?"

"Yes."

"I'm pretty sure it's her."

"So what do we do?" Charlene asked.

"Walk faster," Finn said.

He stole another look back: the woman was still gaining on them.

"Should we run?" Charlene asked.

"Where to? We can't lead her to the soundstage, that's for sure."

"Then what?"

Finn stopped and turned around.

"Earth to Finn," Charlene said nervously. "We're supposed to be running away, not waiting for her to catch up."

"I know. But we're DHIs, not kids at school. What's the worst she can do to us? Scold us? Shout at us?"

"How about bust us? What if she's like park Security or something? What if it's her job to verify violations and pull passes? What if she was at the school to keep an eye on you? I cannot get caught. My parents would kill me for being here."

"Disney would never allow her to stalk me at school. She can't be park Security. It's got to be something else."

"Like an Overtaker?"

"You take off," he instructed her. "Go around the other end of the soundstage. Find the others and hide. I'll stall her."

"This is no time to get all heroic there, pal." Charlene sounded concerned. "Why don't we just both take off?"

"Because I'm done with her following me," Finn said. "Go on!"

Charlene hesitated at first, but then took off at a run.

Finn waited. The mystery woman caught up. They were standing face-to-face, about five yards apart.

"You're Finn," she said. He could tell she was marveling at the realism of the DHI. Everyone did the same thing the first time they saw him or the others. He could feel her wanting to reach out and try to touch him.

"What do you want?" he asked.

"Amanda told me I would probably find you here."

"That's a lie."

"It's not. Do you want to call her?" she reached out and offered him a phone.

He stepped forward and waved his arm through her.

She gasped.

"I've heard the technology described so many times. But . . . in person . . . it's really quite amazing."

"What do you want?" he repeated.

"It's not about what I want, Finn," she answered. "It's about what Wayne wants."

He wondered if somehow this was Maleficent in disguise—if he'd walked into a trap, if she'd figured out how to transform herself into things other than animals. He thought he should have listened to Charlene; he should have taken off with her. He wondered if it was too late.

"What do you know about Wayne?"

"That he's missing," she said. "That you and your friends are the key to finding him."

"You think?"

"I'm his daughter. I'm Wanda. Wanda Alcott."

"Wayne's daughter?"

"You don't have to sound so skeptical. Don't I look at all familiar? Even vaguely familiar?"

"I saw you outside the school, if that's what you mean."

"No, it's not. I meant, don't I look even a little like my father? People say we do."

"No. Not to me."

"He said you were the natural leader, the smartest one of the group."

Finn swallowed dryly. He remembered Wayne saying that about him—not that he believed it.

"Not the smartest. Not by a long shot," Finn said. "That would be Phil— That would be one of my friends."

"Philby," she said. "He's kind of your wired guy, isn't he?"

He felt a chill. How did she know so much?

Charlene was gone. Out of sight. He'd bought her the time she'd needed to get away.

"Don't do it," Wanda Alcott said, reading his thoughts. "I can help you."

"I don't think so."

"You're concerned I'm . . . her. Maleficent? No. Hardly. I'm as afraid of her as you are." She answered his stunned expression. "Oh, yes. I know all about her. All about you. My father told me everything."

"How am I supposed to believe you're Wayne's daughter?"

She smiled a small smile. "You're going to have to decide if you trust me or not."

"Not."

"I thought the resemblance might help."

"Nope, don't see it."

"The first time . . . the very first time, you ended up on a bench next to Goofy. My dad was there. He drove you around in a golf cart."

Finn felt as if somehow all the oxygen had been sucked from the air. He thought he might faint.

"I can help you, Finn. You can help me, find him. Please." She reached into her purse. "I showed this to Jessica earlier tonight. We agreed that you and Philby should see it."

"I don't believe you," he said, but it was a lie. He did believe her—he just didn't want to.

Her hand came out of the purse and opened.

Resting in her palm was a small white paper box.

12

WANDA ALCOTT PRODUCED a sizable set of keys from her purse and unlocked the door to the soundstage.

If she was Wayne's daughter, it wasn't immediately noticeable. She had auburn hair, a pleasant face, and vivid green eyes. She was wearing loose brown pants, a scoop-neck top, and a black sweater. Her earrings were silver cursive letter *D*s, the first letter of the trademark Disney logo. Finn had never seen a pair like them. Though her physical presence was anything but that of an eighty-year-old man, she had the same self-assurance as her father. This, among other things, convinced Finn she might be telling the truth about being Wayne's daughter.

It was the keys that actually sold him: who else but a friend or relative of Wayne's could possess a ring of so many keys, one of which opened the door to Soundstage B?

And even though his brain processed these qualities about her, making every effort to convince him of her legitimacy, he wasn't about to go through the door. He advised the other Kingdom Keepers to stay put.

"One of us will go first," he said. "We don't all go at once."

"But this is why we came here," Philby protested. "Besides, it's far safer inside. Security could come along at any time."

"Speaking of time," Willa added, "we've lost a bunch. The Transportation Center shuts down in just over an hour. Whatever we're supposed to be doing here, we'd better get to it."

"It could be a trap," Finn reminded her.

"She does look like him," said Maybeck, the artist. "Her chin and eyes are the same."

Wanda's face warmed. "I'll tell you what," she said, working the door's key off the ring and then returning the ring to her purse. "Finn, if you'll give the paper box to Philby, my work is done here." She offered him the key to the soundstage. "Jessica isn't the only one who has vivid dreams. My father has had some powerful and unusual dreams for decades. Dreams that led him to unusual discoveries. He constructed this box the day before he went missing. He drew the images. He'd told me about Jessica's ability to see the future on the same day he gave me the box. Because of this, I know it means something. I showed it to her earlier this evening, and she said to show it to Philby. If I've accomplished that, then you can have the key and I can go if you like."

"No," said Charlene. "I think you should stay."

"I agree," said Willa.

Finn groaned.

"What if it was *your* father?" said Willa. "If we can help her, then we should."

"We're already trying to help," Finn pointed out. "That's why we're here."

"Wayne is counting on you, on all of you—" Wanda said. "On all of *us* to save the parks. His concern is always for the parks first, and his own safety second. The Overtakers want the parks to themselves. He has taken so many risks over the years."

"We need to get inside," Philby said anxiously. "It's not safe out here. There are no security cameras inside. What they shoot inside is classified, like the DHI work. It would be a lot safer."

"He's right," Wanda Alcott said. "Security doesn't have keys to Soundstage B, the work done here being classified. Once inside, you'll be safe."

Finn tensed. He and the other DHIs were the product of the "classified" work she referred to.

"Give me five minutes," he said. "If I don't come back out, take off."

"I'm coming with you," said Maybeck.

When Maybeck made up his mind, there was no use arguing.

"Okay," Finn said. "Let's go."

Finn opened the door and the two went inside. There was a second door, meant to block light and sound when cameras were rolling. Maybeck pushed this second door shut behind them and together they entered the windowless, cavernous building. Maybeck found some light switches. It was an area the size of a big airplane hangar. The ceiling had to be fifty feet high. Hundreds of theatrical lights hung suspended from a steel superstructure. A massive green screen lined the entire length of one wall. In front of that green screen was where Finn and the others, wearing motion sensors, had elaborately acted out all kinds of movements in order for the computers to program the holograms. Seeing the space took him back to the auditions and the weeks of work here that had led up to his becoming a Disney Host Interactive. He'd never known then—none of them had—that Wayne had been secretly planning to cross them over and solicit their help in defeating the Overtakers. It seemed like he was a different Finn now than the kid who had first auditioned here.

"Not so different than when we were here," Maybeck said.

"Kind of . . . weird, you know?" Finn said. "Like we never left."

"Yeah."

They searched the interior, including the two bathrooms, a small office, changing rooms, and a control room filled with electronics.

Maybeck climbed a ladder well up into the catwalks and rigging above the soundstage. His voice echoed as he called out. "There's no one here. We're good."

They admitted the others.

"We can make this work," said Philby, exiting from the control room. "The cameras, video, sound editing—it's all here. All we need is—"

"Don't say it," Finn said, interrupting.

An awkward silence hung in the air.

"It's about the girls, isn't it?" Wanda said. "They've been grounded, so there's no way to get them out to help you here. But if they were like the five of you . . . well, that would change things."

Finn didn't like it at all that she could know this.

Charlene shot Finn a look that cautioned him not to try to stop her from talking. "It's that, yes," said Charlene, "and also that they've been put onto park Security's watch list. There's no way to get them out of the foster home or into the parks."

"But if they were DHIs. . . ." said Willa. "If they could cross over along with us. . . ."

Finn bit back his tongue, furious that they were sharing so much with a complete stranger.

"I understand," Wanda Alcott said. "But please, whatever you do, don't forget the box." She addressed this to Philby. "It must be important."

"I promise to take a look at it," Philby said.

"How did you get into the park?" Finn asked suspiciously. "How did you get past Security? Tonight? Just now? Why didn't they stop you?"

"Finn!" Charlene chided. "She's offering to help us."

"It's all right," Wanda Alcott said. "I'd expect no less after everything my father has told me about all of you. You haven't exactly had it easy. If you weren't careful you wouldn't have made it this far."

"I'm not accusing you of anything," Finn corrected. "You've misunderstood me. I'm just curious for my own reasons."

"Because you need a way to get Amanda and Jessica into the soundstage undetected," she said.

Finn withheld comment, but the surprise on his face gave him away.

"But when can you possibly do this?" Wanda Alcott asked. "The girls are grounded."

"The woman who runs the foster home—" Willa began.

"Mrs. Nash. Yes, I met her," Wanda Alcott said.

"—attends Mass every Friday night and every Sunday morning for two hours—nearly three including driving back and forth."

"But the other girls . . . all they'd do is have to report them and—"

"They won't report them," Maybeck said, "because the other girls won't be there. They've received complimentary sessions at my aunt's pottery shop—to 'a program on Friday evenings and Sunday mornings provided to deserving institutions in the Orlando area.' I'll be at the shop, keeping them busy and monitoring them."

"I'm impressed," Wanda Alcott said.

"We've learned to work as a team," Finn said. "Maybeck talked his aunt into doing this. She doesn't know the full story, only that she's helping homeless girls."

"She has a big heart," Maybeck said.

"But none of it means anything," Finn said, "if we can't get onto the property without being seen. Same goes for Jess and Amanda."

"If I remember right, my father gave you all employee ID cards."

"Yeah," Philby said. "But it's a long way from either employee entrance to this soundstage. We can wear hats and glasses, but it's still a pretty big risk."

"You won't need the hats and glasses," Wanda Alcott said. "I can get you onto the property. The girls, too."

"But how?" Finn asked.

"You'll need to use your employee passes to get backstage. Name a time, and I'll meet you at the costume shop," she said.

Finn hoped for more of an explanation. He didn't get much.

"Make sure one of you has Maybeck's employee pass with you. If he's going to be at Crazy Glaze, he doesn't need it."

"We can do that," Finn said, but his voice revealed his skepticism.

"My father had more than a few tricks up his sleeve," she said. "It all comes down to trust, Finn. Leave it to me."

13

FINN FELT THE PRESSURE of time running low as, on Friday evening, he, Jess, Amanda, Willa, Charlene, and Philby entered through an employee gate on the back side of Disney's Hollywood Studios. Amanda used Maybeck's employee card to enter; Jess used Wayne's, provided to her by Wanda Alcott.

The time pressure arose from Mrs. Nash's schedule. She spent two hours at Mass. It took her a half hour to reach the church in Friday traffic, and she remained at least thirty minutes after the service, praying for the welfare of her girls. That totaled a minimum of three hours she would be away from Nash House—the same three hours the girls of Nash House would be at Crazy Glaze.

But it had taken Jess and Amanda thirty minutes to reach the Studios. With another thirty set aside for their return, that left the Kingdom Keepers only two hours to accomplish what they'd come to do.

Wanda Alcott's plan to get them inside the Studios required some humiliation. The kids were shown into costume storage and made to dress up in *High School Musical* outfits, either as basketball players or cheerleaders.

"Do we really have to?" Finn said, adjusting a headband.

"Cast members are used to seeing *High School Musical* kids here because of the street show. They won't think anything of it. The only thing we have to be careful of is—"

"Being in the same place at the same time as our DHIs," said Philby, interrupting, "because our faces are the same, and we might be recognized."

"Exactly."

They divided into the two groups: the DHI/film characters and the *HSM* gang, and entered onto the streets of the Studios. Wanda Alcott went ahead of them, both as a scout looking for the real DHIs, and to unlock the door to Soundstage B ahead of the kids' arrival.

Nearing Soundstage B, only fifty yards away, Finn was approached by a round, red-faced kid who had a bully's mischievousness in his beady eyes. This was something Wanda Alcott had not considered: DHI fans. Finn had encountered enough of these kinds of kids at school to know what was coming.

He whispered under his breath so that Jess and Charlene could hear. "Don't let him try to touch me! He'll either try to push me or punch me. He's expecting his hand to go right through."

"How do we stop him?" Charlene asked. She looked several years younger with her hair in braids and wearing a blue-and-white gingham jumper and red slippers.

"I don't know," Finn answered. "Step between us."

As expected, the boy delighted in seeing what he believed to be a hologram that would serve as a punching bag. He stepped up to Finn, raised his fists and said, "Whatcha got, pal?" He took a swipe, his bunched knuckles coming straight for Finn's chin.

Finn leaned back, the blow just missing.

The boy staggered, off-balance.

"That wasn't a very nice thing to do," Jess said, moving between them.

The boy's brow furrowed and he stopped, stone still, utterly taken aback.

"Who are you?" the boy asked. He stepped toward Jess. She stepped back, still blocking Finn.

The boy took a step toward her. She stood her ground.

"This DHI is our guide," she said. "You'll have to get your own."

"Jimmy?" called an adult from down the street.

The boy's mother, Finn guessed.

"I'll just borrow him for a minute," the boy said in a mean voice.

Finn stepped back. But the boy was athletic. He'd anticipated Finn's move and actually moved closer to him. He swatted out, grabbing for him. He'd expected Finn to be nothing but light. His face twisted into surprise as he caught Finn's basketball shorts.

"What the . . . ?" he mumbled.

Finn broke the contact and pushed the boy to the asphalt.

The boy just sat there, dumbfounded. "You're no DHI," he said.

"Go!" Finn told thc girls. They obeyed, heading away.

"Jimmy?" his mother called out, concern now filling her voice.

Finn, worried the boy might tell on him, said, "I'm a generation-three DHI, Jimmy." He reached out his hand. "More human than ever."

Finn helped the boy up. Jimmy stood slowly, awe-struck at touching Finn.

"But how . . ." the boy said meekly. "I thought . . ." He couldn't finish a sentence. "This is . . . *way cool!*" He reached out while wearing a mask of incredulity, once again trying to touch Finn.

But Finn moved away from the effort.

"James Francis McConnor!" the boy's mother shouted. "You come here this minute!"

"I must catch up to my guests," Finn said. He turned and hurried off.

Reaching Soundstage B out of breath, Finn glanced around trying to make sure no one was watching. There were too many people milling about for him to know. At last it came down to a decision.

He turned the doorknob and opened the door.

Inside, he found everyone waiting.

14

PHILBY RAN THE CONTROLS. Jess and Amanda changed into skintight green leotards and tights that included booties, gloves, and full hoods that covered their heads and faces like ski masks. Patches of green plastic mesh had been sewn into the hoods to provide a way to see out, and to breathe.

Charlene attached the thirty-five wired sensors to each of the girls. The sensors would measure every kind of joint and muscle movement. Then the girls took turns on the green stage in front of the green background as Philby directed them to squat, stand, walk, lie down, run, crawl, dance, and jump. He thought up dozens of combinations of movements as Finn and Willa ran video cameras that captured and recorded, from multiple angles, every move the girls made. The girls made some mistakes and had to repeat their movements, many of them several times.

Philby worked a pair of computers, one recording the video, the other recording the digital output from each of the thirty-five sensors. The computers measured and recorded the similarities and differences between the way each of the girls moved compared to a database of how dozens of other people moved, including all the Kingdom Keepers, each of whom had been part of the database nearly from its inception.

Philby completed the recording with just fifteen minutes to go until Jess and Amanda absolutely had to be headed back to the Nash House. He had a good deal of work yet to accomplish, work that had to be done in Soundstage B, with its phenomenally powerful computers.

"No way I can get this done in time. And we still have all the voice work to do," he said from his seat in the control room.

"Red alert!" came the voice of Wanda Alcott, issuing a warning that meant someone—Security?—was heading toward the soundstage.

The kids had practiced their roles for such an event: Willa stood poised, ready to kill the overhead lights; Philby put both computers into sleep mode; Finn and Charlene shut down the stand-alone lights and all the cameras; Jess and Amanda disconnected the main cables from their suits, the umbilical cords that fed the computers. Everyone was intent on hiding.

All the kids scattered, having elected hiding places earlier.

Jess—in the green suits it was hard to tell the

girls apart—had difficulty unclipping the large plug at the end of the master cable. Amanda made it off the all-green stage, but Jess was still struggling with the oversize connector. There was no way she could leave the stage so long as that huge cable was attached to her suit.

Finn, who'd hidden behind a wall of plywood panels on casters, watched helplessly, desperately wanting to run out and help her.

Jess lay flat down onto the stage. The green of her suit and the cable blended perfectly with the green of the backdrop and flooring—she all but disappeared.

The lights went dark, and Finn heard Willa scamper to find a place to hide.

Only seconds passed before the door swung open and the lights came on again.

"I don't see what all the fuss is about," one of the two night watchmen said. "Do you see anything?"

"The report was someone *hearing* something," the other man said. "We might as well look around."

Leaving the door open behind them, the two walked to the center of the soundstage. Only then did Finn, peering out, see that a light on one of the cameras was still glowing. His eyes darted between the camera and Jess, who remained flattened on the green deck, only a matter of yards from where the two men stood.

One of the guards lit up a cigarette.

"You can't smoke in here," his partner said.

"Correction: I can't smoke *out there*. No one's going to see me smoking in here, unless, I suppose, you're going to turn me in?"

"No."

"Then what's the problem?"

"No problem."

"Okay, then."

The smoker remained where he was. The other guard grew restless and headed for the control room. Philby was somewhere in there.

"You know what they use this place for?" the smoker called out. "Those hologram kids."

"DHIs," the other called back.

"The kids, yeah. You gotta admit, they look freaking real."

"I know."

"They give me the weebies, to tell the truth. I mean, if you want guides, why not just hire real kids?"

"It's Disney World, you moron. Don't knock it: it's a paycheck." He entered the control room. Finn lost sight of him, concentrating instead on the smoker, who stood less than twenty feet from Jess, his back to her.

She seized the opportunity, crawling on her

stomach across the green stage, the cable dragging behind her like a green snake.

The man took another drag off the cigarette and slowly turned in Jess's direction as he exhaled. If he looked down, he'd be looking right at her.

Finn willed her not to move, not to so much as *breathe.*

The ash from the man's cigarette broke loose and fell slowly to the floor. His head dropped, his eyes following it.

Finn couldn't take it. He spotted a group of push pins stuck into the plywood. He withdrew one and threw it across the room. It clattered and rolled.

The smoker turned away from Jess with a start. Finn backed up, deeper into shadow.

"Hey!" the smoker called out.

The other man reappeared from within the control room. "What?"

"Something . . . I don't know . . . over there."

"Where?"

"I don't know. I'm just saying I heard something."

"So?"

"So what?"

"So check it out, you doofus. And put out that cigarette before you burn the place down."

Finn stepped forward and sneaked another look.

The smoker smudged out the burning cigarette against the sole of his shoe. As he did, Jess once again crawled toward the edge of the green stage behind him. She reached the length of her cable and stopped, face down.

The smoker headed in the direction of the sound of Finn's pin. He searched the area near the door they all had come through. His partner joined him.

"Well," said the smoker, "I heard something too, but it wasn't much. How do you want to deal with it?"

"It's a nonevent. I'll call it in." He snagged a radio from his belt as the two men made for the door. His voice could be heard faintly reporting in as they shut the door.

Five minutes passed. "*All clear*," Finn announced in a forced whisper.

"We were probably talking too loudly," Philby said, once they'd gathered in the control room. "We can do this. We just can't be so loud about it."

"We can't do it tonight," Finn corrected. "Look at the time."

To everyone's surprise, they'd lost nearly a half hour.

"We're going to be late," said Amanda. "That won't be pretty."

"We can't be late," Jess said. "There's no telling what Mrs. Nash might do. That woman is . . . Well, let's just say she's not normal."

"We made a lot of progress on the imaging," Philby said. "But there's more to do, and don't forget the voice recording. We've got to have Sunday if we're going to pull this off."

"Then we can't be late," said Jess.

"But we already are," said Amanda. "Unless anyone happens to have a helicopter handy?"

"Maybeck," Finn said.

They all looked at him.

"We've got to get Maybeck to delay the other girls. If they're late, and if Jess and Amanda arrive at the same time—"

"Then Mrs. Nash won't know," said Willa excitedly.

"But the girls will," Charlene said. "What about the other girls?"

"Jeannie's the only one who might put up a stink," said Jess. "The others couldn't care less."

"But Jeannie," Amanda said, "will definitely tell on us."

"Then you'll have to bribe her," said Charlene, as if she knew all about such things.

"How?" said Jess.

"There must be something. Money?"

"No, not Jeannie. All she does is read books from the library. She couldn't care less about money."

"Music?" Philby asked. "Movies?"

Amanda said, "I know!" She looked over at Jess. "Her poster."

Jess looked at Finn, then at Amanda. "That could work," Jess said.

"What?" Finn asked. "Whatever it is, we've got to do it. We can't have her wrecking this."

The two girls giggled. Amanda said, "Are you sure?"

"What?" Finn asked, feeling he was being left out of some joke.

"Jeannie's poster is of you, Finn. Your Magic Kingdom DHI poster."

"Me?"

"What if we could promise her she could meet you?" Amanda asked.

"That hardly qualifies as a bribe," Philby said. "More like a penalty."

"Thanks a lot," Finn said.

"Well?" Jess asked.

"If it means your getting back safely tonight, then absolutely," said Finn.

He glanced over at Amanda. Something felt wrong about agreeing to do this. But he just had.

15

JEANNIE PUCKET REFUSED TO LIE about Jess and Amanda's whereabouts, but her compromise position was to agree not to tell on them. If Mrs. Nash didn't ask, she agreed to keep her mouth shut, so long as she got to meet the boy who her favorite DHI had been modeled after.

Mrs. Nash didn't ask. Having returned home to an empty house, she had been on the phone trying to find all her girls as they climbed the front steps. Amanda and Jess were among the group, having timed their arrival perfectly. Not so much as an eyebrow was raised.

Sunday's foray into Hollywood Studios went much the same as the first session: the Kingdom Keepers met Jess and Amanda backstage, courtesy of Wanda Alcott; everyone donned costumes and, using employee ID cards, gained access.

Philby completed the task of translating as many of the girls' movements and spoken phrases as possible into computer code. He assembled the code and then dumped it onto a hundred-gigabyte portable hard drive, about the size of a paperback book. The creation of the

DHIs was hindered by the pressure of time—while each of the kids had spent over a month in the soundstage modeling for their DHIs, Jess and Amanda had spent a grand total of four hours. It meant that, without a doubt, there would be gaps in their motion and speech, like a DVD or CD skipping. They were certain to "go digital" at times. What that would mean for the two human girls asleep in Mrs. Nash's house, or the appearance and performance of their DHIs inside the parks, no one knew.

Philby had a number of new concerns and he shared them with Finn as the two, in the guise of their DHIs, sneaked from in front of Cinderella's Castle toward a Cast Member Only entrance to the Utilidor, the underground tunnel system that connected attractions below the Magic Kingdom.

There was no way, yet, for Philby to select who crossed over and who didn't. The only control they had over their transitioning was the black fob that also returned them. Finn had discovered that pulling out the fob's small battery prevented their crossing over. Without the small watch battery in place, the kids got a good night's sleep; with the battery installed, they crossed over—all of them. There was no way yet to send just one or two of them. It was something Philby hoped to remedy, perhaps even that same night, but as it was, they'd left the DHIs of Willa, Maybeck, and Charlene in Walt's apartment at the top of Cinderella's Castle, awaiting their return. Maybeck had the all-important fob. They would hide it in the apartment as they crossed back.

If the two boys weren't back by midnight, Maybeck was to use the fob to cross all three back over, stranding Philby and Finn and delivering their human selves into the Syndrome. The DHI servers shut down at midnight—that was part of the fix that Imagineers had believed would solve the Kingdom Keepers "problem" once and for all. This midnight curfew was another of Philby's intended targets when he and Finn reached the computer server farm thirty feet beneath the surface. If he could defeat the curfew installed in the software, they could stay in the parks longer as DHIs.

"It's complicated," Philby said.

"That's an understatement," said Finn.

The two boys moved quickly between bushes, keeping low and working their way toward the ice cream shop on Main Street. The park came alive at night with all the Disney characters. It was difficult if not impossible to identify Overtakers, unless a particular character was seen doing something suspicious. He and Philby stuck out. They needed to make it underground as quickly as possible.

They paused, well hidden, allowing a golf cart to make it down Main Street and turn into Tomorrowland.

"At this point, servers project DHIs into the four different parks," Philby explained. "Magic Kingdom, Animal Kingdom, Epcot, and Hollywood Studios. Our crossed-over DHIs always land in the Magic Kingdom. That's okay, but time consuming if we want to be in Epcot looking for Wayne. What I have to do is figure out why the Magic Kingdom is the default landing and change it, at least for the time being, to Epcot. That's something Wayne set up, so hopefully I can distinguish the instruction within the existing code, the problem being that if it was easy to find, then the guys who scrubbed the code to 'fix' the KK problem should have found it in the first place."

"Unless they *did* find it and Wayne reentered it recently," Finn suggested.

"That would explain why we suddenly started crossing over again. Good point."

"And no one's been told to clean the code since, because we haven't been spotted."

"Another reason not to be spotted now," Philby said.

"How long to install the girls?" Finn said.

"Around twenty minutes. Once they're installed here, they should self-propagate and install onto the other servers. They're all linked by fiber optics. They share resources, which makes the refresh faster, and keeps the feed hot if one of the servers fails. I'll use those twenty minutes to try to change the landing default to Epcot."

"And you're going to show me how to read the Epcot maintenance stuff?" Finn reminded.

"Piece of cake. I can get that started the minute the download begins."

Philby hoped that Epcot maintenance reports might reveal something of the Epcot infrastructure, might show or suggest to the boys where to find the various utility rooms, places where Wayne could be locked up. Philby had once been led by Wayne into a powerful graphic representation of the Magic Kingdom's schematics. If such a thing still existed—and there was no reason to think it didn't—it would likely be accessible from the Utilidor's computer room.

Finn didn't trust Philby's optimism. When it came to computers, Philby seemed to think all things were possible, whereas his own experience had often proved much different. Half the time Finn couldn't get his printer's scanner to work, much less crack the code of Disney's maintenance server.

"Let's go!" he said, the golf cart having passed and disappeared.

They ran for the boardwalk that fronted the ice cream shop, turned left, and found the sign that read CAST MEMBERS ONLY. They hesitated, alert for the sound of anyone coming.

Finn used hand signals to motion for Philby to follow him. They slipped through the short turn in the fence that led them backstage, where they saw permanent office trailers and employee parking, empty at this hour. To their right was a small set of stairs leading to an elevator. The door beside the elevator led to a set of descending stairs where a sign was posted high on the wall: WELCOME TO THE UTILIDOR—WATCH FOR VEHICLES, AND HAVE A MAGICAL DAY!

Finn felt Philby place his hand on Finn's right shoulder. If they failed at this, in the morning their parents would find their sons lying in their beds, impossible to awaken. It would scare their families to death.

No matter what, they could not allow that to happen.

16

FROM THE MOMENT FINN'S DHI entered the Utilidor tunnels he had a bad feeling. It didn't come from anything obvious. There were still a few Cast Members milling around. Most of them were the women whose costumes required wigs, makeup, and extra attention. The wigs had to come off and be put away in the wig shop, the makeup removed, the costumes hung up and put away. But there were also other workers driving the golf carts laden with bottled water, soda, sweatshirts, boxes of 3-D glasses, popcorn, costumes, books, pins, lanyards, cotton candy, DVDs, and all the hundreds of items for sale in the park's various gift shops. It all moved through the Utilidor—some of it well past the hour of the gates' closing.

Finn and Philby, shimmering slightly under the fluorescent lights, were greeted with nods and smiles. The DHIs were genuinely well liked by Cast Members, and though it should have occurred to some of them that they never saw the DHIs in the Utilidor, instead the two were met with a joyful surprise and they actually felt compelled to wave to several of those who were most eager to greet them.

Philby, who managed to keep far too many facts in his head, led Finn to the right at the first intersection, and to the left at the next. He then waved Finn across the hall and they busied themselves at a bulletin board, standing with their backs to an unmarked door. Finn recognized the door from an earlier visit to the computer room.

"Our problem now," Philby said, "is that the door will be locked."

"Which is why I came along," Finn said. "You tell me when, and I'll do it."

"And if there're people inside? How are you going to explain that?"

"If there are still people inside, which I doubt since there's no light coming out from under the door, and they see me, it won't be me doing the explaining. Right? They're the ones controlling the computers, *including* the DHI server. It isn't shut down, or we wouldn't be here right now, but we don't know what the software does, how it deals with us once the park is closed. We probably aren't supposed to be here. Not at this hour. So I imagine my showing up will surprise them *just a little bit*," he said sarcastically. "All we can do is try it, and see what they do. If they head for a keyboard, I'll know we're in trouble."

"If they shut down the server," Philby said in a cautionary voice, "the Return button won't work. It won't just be you and me—all of us will be trapped in the Syndrome. All of us will be lying in our beds at home like we're half dead."

"We're either doing this, or we're not," Finn said. "It's a little late to be debating the merits of the plan. Forget us. Forget the Syndrome. Think of Wayne. Think of Jess's dream, or premonition, or whatever it is that Jess has. Wayne's in trouble and he needs us. End of story."

Philby looked over at Finn and nodded. "You're right."

"I know I'm right."

"Okay. So do it."

"I'm going to do it now."

"So why aren't you moving?" Philby asked.

"Because now you'vc scared me. I mean, what happens if there are people in there?"

"I thought we just got past that."

"I thought so too," Finn said, turning around and crossing the wide tunnel to the door on the opposite side.

He paused there in front of the unmarked door. A pair of voices came and went at the far end of the tunnel they were in. He knew he mustn't be seen going into this room, and so he waited to make sure the voices weren't coming toward them. But there was more to it than that. He also stopped there to clear his head. He forced his fear into a tiny box at the back of his mind and he closed the top of that box and he locked it. He washed all concern and all sensations from his body, taking a deep cleansing breath and feeling his connection to his senses expelled with his exhalation. Even thought left him, so that he existed in an ether, a fragile place where he wasn't even Finn any longer. He wasn't even sure he *was*—that he existed at all. He was a bundle of jumping atoms, light generated by a series of computer-controlled projectors. If he could become pure light, without thought and without form or shape, no physical barrier could stop him.

He imagined the train coming down the tunnel and he stepped forward and passed right through the door into the humming room on the other side. The light from his own projection created a glow in the otherwise dim room. He looked left: no one at the desk there; right: row after row of shelving lined up in stacks like a library. The shelves were not filled with books but with computer servers, network hubs and switching, terabyte hard drives, routers, and thousands of flashing, colorful LEDs. It was all neat and organized with labels attached to each shelf below a device.

Old McDaniel's Farm read a computer printout, hanging like a sign on the endcap of the one of the stacks. A server farm. A computer nerd's paradise.

Slowly, Finn allowed his thoughts to flow again. His senses came back online and he not only processed cognitively but he felt his fingers and toes tingle.

He turned and reached for the doorknob. His hand went right through the door. He withdrew it and closed his eyes, trying to speed himself back to a less pure condition, where his body would be more than light.

He hadn't told any of the others, but this transition had become increasingly difficult for him. He could easily—perhaps too easily—transport himself into the state of pure DHI—*all clear* he called it—a state in which he possessed no material quality, in which he was capable of walking through walls or on top of water. But the way back to his human self was sometimes harder. It occasionally took him more time to transition back to being part DHI–part human. He wasn't sure when that scale had tipped, but it had; he didn't know what it meant, but knew it meant something. He tried the handle again, and this time it turned. But he looked down at his own hand as if it belonged to somebody else.

And maybe it did.

Philby came through quickly.

"Jeesh! What took you so long?"

Finn shut and locked the door behind them.

"Heaven!" said Philby, spreading his arms as he faced the stacks of servers. Finn's primary job was to get them in and out of the locked room, a job half accomplished. His other job—checking the maintenance records—would have to wait.

Philby searched the aisles, row after row of servers, inspecting the labels taped beneath each black brick. Unlike Finn, he didn't seem the least bit intimidated by the maze of wires and display of blinking lights. He located a vertical column of six machines and a keyboard and screen that accessed them. Within minutes he'd removed the portable hard drive and was downloading the data from the Soundstage B shoot.

He typed frantically, at a speed Finn had trouble believing.

"Done a little bit of this, have you?"

"For me," Philby said, never slowing, "this is like a violinist playing a Stratosphere—"

"Stradivarius," Finn corrected him.

"Whatever. Just like that. I dream of messing with this stuff. For most companies, it would be a major deal to have one of these SGIs. I'm looking at six right here. Four more, a couple rows behind us. They've got everything in here: Solaris, Red Hat, Linux. All the top-of-the-line Macs. For all I care, you can just leave me here."

"Don't get too carried away, okay? You're freakin'."

"The girls are downloading," he said. "It's going to take me a while to try to find that Easter egg of Wayne's—the remote."

"And the curfew limits," Finn reminded. "How about you lift those first?"

"I've got to do this in the order I've got to do it. But yes, I'll lift the midnight curfew if possible."

"I knew you'd say something like that."

"Maintenance!" he said, as if remembering to keep Finn busy. A flurry of typing. "Hang on a minute."

He led Finn to a computer terminal in the next row. On the screen was a familiar layout.

"Is that VMK?" Finn gasped. Disney's online Virtual Magic Kingdom had been shut down over a year earlier. Finn had missed going on the site.

"VMN, actually—Virtual Maintenance Network—but it's just like it," Philby said. "That's why it'll be easy for you."

He worked a boy avatar up a ladder, through a door, and into a tunnel. At the other end, a door came closed behind the avatar.

"Okay, you're in," Philby said.

Finn's avatar faced a large screen listing all kinds

of locations within Epcot: attractions, foreign countries, buildings, restaurants, even a graphic labeled PYROTECHNICS.

"Start with the obvious things like electrical and phone," Philby said. "You're looking for junction boxes, places all the wires or pipes come together. Those might be actual rooms in the real Epcot—utility rooms where they might have put Wayne. There will be a code at the bottom of each of those kinds of places. Write down the code. I can probably figure out pretty closely where it is inside the park."

He took off, back to his own aisle. They talked through the gaps in the stack that separated them.

"How are you doing?" Philby asked.

"Getting the hang of it." Finn moved his avatar through the puzzle of colorful tubes, ladders, and pipes. "What *is this* exactly?"

"The maintenance guys created a virtual world that would let them fix a lot of stuff remotely. Wayne knew about it."

"Wayne knows everything," Finn said. Talking about Wayne made Finn miss him all the more. He found an intersection of purple and blue tubes. There was a pulsing code beneath the box where they met, just as Philby had said there might be. He wrote it down. He moved his avatar in front of the graphic—a door—and then forward. The door opened and the screen changed to put Finn inside a small room where the various colored tubes terminated in boxes on the walls.

The code below one of these boxes was flashing red and blue.

"Is it okay if I try to open a box?" he called out.

"Go for it," Philby replied.

But Finn hesitated even so: Philby was not bashful when it came to computers.

Finn used the mouse to move over to the box, and then right-clicked, bringing up a menu. OPEN, REMOVE, OFF, and REPORT were the only highlighted menu choices; the rest were grayed out. REPORT was pulsing. Finn clicked on it.

A pop-up window zoomed open and lines of code scrolled, pausing briefly as they filled the window. Each paused but seconds before they began scrolling rapidly up. Finn clicked on one of the lines to stop the scrolling. Most of the words had been condensed, so that power was written as PWR, and temperature as TMP. He studied the strings of code and numbers, then tried to make sense of the time code that ran on the left.

"I've got something here," he said.

"Write it down," Philby said. "I've hit a line of code that could be Wayne's Easter egg. It requires a password to edit the code, which could be why the guys repairing the code didn't remove it."

"No, I mean I've really got something here," Finn said. He wrote down two of the lines verbatim. "I think . . . If I'm right . . ." He backed the avatar out of this wall box, then out of the room in order to take a wider view of the overall screen. Several of the codes beneath various boxes were pulsing. But not all, by any means.

"I'm busy here," Philby said.

Finn drilled down into a similar box—entering a room that also showed a pulsing code and then a junction box with a flashing label. By the time he opened the pop-up window, he'd convinced himself.

"Temperature drops," he said.

"What's that?"

Finn took notes furiously. The pop-up window appeared to be an error log, the scrolling lines a nearly minute-by-minute cataloguing of significant variations in temperature swings, all recorded in centigrade. *Temperature drops*, he noted. In each case the temperature had fallen dramatically before it slowly climbed again.

He backed out of the error log and found his way to the wider view that showed the tubes and wires. There were six codes pulsing. He wrote them down and circled them repeatedly so he wouldn't forget them.

At the bottom of the screen Finn saw an identifying marker change. Beside CURRENTLY ONLINE: 1 flashed and then changed to 2.

"Philby . . . I've got a visitor."

Philby didn't hesitate this time. He hurried to Finn's side and ran a finger along beneath the Cast Member Monitor line.

"Dang," he said. "We need to find an exit."

"An exit? Can't I just close the session?"

"It doesn't exactly work like that. Once you're in this world, you're in it."

"Sounds familiar," Finn quipped.

"The main problem being," Philby said, taking a look at the door leading to the Utilidor, "as long as your avatar's online they may be able to determine which station you're using."

"What! So get me offline!"

"I just told you: it doesn't work like that," Philby replied anxiously. "It's a virtual world. And . . . maybe . . ." He sprinted around the stack and into the next aisle and began tugging on cords and trying to sort through the massive bundles of multicolored wires. Finn was alongside him now. Philby grabbed and pulled Finn's finger so that it pointed to a particular blue wire. Philby then followed that same wire as it twisted and traveled along the stack to another set of boxes. He pinched a plastic clip, and pulled the wire from a box.

Together, they raced around to the other side. Finn couldn't remember seeing Philby so flustered. He'd been mumbling to himself for the past thirty seconds.

"Tracers . . . user logs . . . spiders . . . not good, not good. . . ."

They reached the terminal Finn had been using. His avatar was gone.

"You did it!" he said, pounding Philby on the back.

"No . . . no . . . no. . . ." Philby muttered. "Not really. Not so fast. Not quickly enough."

He sprinted to the next aisle and typed even faster than before. But he kept looking at the room's main door as if expecting someone.

"What the heck is going on?" Finn said.

"You know that wire I disconnected?"

"Yeah?"

"You've got to reconnect it."

"What?"

"We can't leave that kind of thing behind. It'll give us away. Don't you get it?"

"Apparently not," Finn said.

"These are computers."

Finn waved for him to give him more, like they were playing a game of charades.

"They're self-monitoring. They keep logs of everything

they do. Every computer does, these especially so because they're like ten times more serious than anything you've seen. Our being on here—it's all there. That's not a worry as long as no one goes looking for it."

"But now . . . my avatar . . . someone's going to come looking."

"It's possible. That's all I'm saying."

"Do they know I was in this room?"

"By now? It's possible," Philby repeated.

"So what are we doing here?"

"Plug that wire back in," Phiby said. "I'm wrapping up."

"But—"

"The wire!" Philby yelled.

Finn took off, slipped and fell, got to his feet and found the wire. Philby had reached the door by the time Finn caught up.

"Go!" Finn said. "Don't wait for me. I'll meet you in the apartment. We left the remote at the Studios, remember? We'll have to go back there to return."

"But—"

"Don't wait for me!" It was Finn's turn to yell.

Philby nodded.

They unlocked and cracked open the door. Philby peered out. "It's clear," he said.

Finn pushed his DHI out the door.

He locked the door from the inside, and attempted to calm himself, to clear his mind. His fingers tingled. He stepped forward.

He crashed into the door. He was not yet pure DHI, not yet able to pass through the door. The more he thought about someone coming for him, the more difficult it was to make himself clear enough. He debated just leaving the door unlocked, but it was sure to give them away, certain to make them audit the computers and discover the intrusions. He had to do this.

He closed his eyes and focused on a song, humming to himself. Out of nowhere Amanda's face appeared in his imagination. That combination: Amanda in his eyes and the song "With You" in his ears and. . . .

He walked through the door and into the hall.

Looked both ways.

No one coming.

He walked out, in no particular hurry, his feet and fingers beginning to tingle again. The song stayed in his head, the image of her in his mind.

He felt safe. He felt good.

He felt totally confused.

17

"HOW DID YOU SLEEP, sweetheart?" Finn's mother asked him the next morning.

In the midst of cooking pancakes and bacon, she had her hair pinned up with what looked like a chopstick, her sleeves rolled up past her elbows, and her right hand on the wrong end of a spatula, scraping some burned stuff off the blade with a determined red fingernail.

"Okay, I guess," Finn replied. His knees ached, his head felt fat, and he was beyond thirsty. He swilled down a glass of orange juice and went to the fridge to pour himself another.

"Anything fun going on at school today?"

"No."

"There must be something."

"No. It's boring. Same as always."

"But you like school."

"Sometimes."

"Then let's make today one of those times!" she said brightly.

He could have bitten her. She came out with lines

like this that didn't even sound like her. She was probably reading another book like *Parenting Your Teenage Monster* or *Be-Teen the Terror*. She tended to quote whatever advice she was getting, whether from a friend, a book, or a podcast.

"You lose any more weight, Mom, and you're going to disappear."

"I'm just keeping fit. Fit is it!"

She flipped the pancake.

"Not too long on that side, okay?" The up-facing side was the color of coffee grounds. She was an okay cook most of the time, though she could trash the entire kitchen just making peanut butter-and-jelly sandwiches. There was currently not an open square inch on the countertop, unless you counted the half acre of spilled pancake flour, or the used teabag with Lake Earl Grey surrounding it.

"Disney sent us a letter about the DHIs being installed on the cruise ships. They're still working on that."

"That would be pretty good," Finn said.

"That would be *very* good," she corrected. "For your college fund especially."

"You know Wayne?" Finn said.

"Yes?"

"He's missing." The words came out of Finn's

mouth and he wondered exactly where he'd thought he was going with this.

"Missing?"

"Never mind." He wished there were a rewind button for real life, like Adam Sandler's in *Click.* He could have put it to good use.

"Missing, how?" she said.

"As in no one can find him."

"There's no reason to be fresh, young man."

She delivered the pancakes. He considered asking her for a jackhammer but worried she might send him to school with no breakfast at all.

"That's none of your concern," she said quickly, her mind jumping to the obvious next step.

"I know."

"Finn?"

"I know, *Mother*. I get it."

"Tell me you won't get involved in something like that."

"Something like what?"

"Don't avoid the question."

"Don't jump to conclusions," he said, trying to move her away from the promise. He wouldn't lie to his parents. He would, and could, stretch the truth to the cosmic edge of reality, but not tell an outright lie.

"Should I call someone?" she asked. "About Wayne I mean?"

"I don't know. Who would you call?"

"I'm asking you."

"No clue."

"But you're worried about him."

"I like the old dude," he said. "I figure he's just taken a vacation or something. Maybe he's on one of the cruise ships trying to set us up, like you said. Maybe that's all it is. If he was on one of those ships we'd never know about it."

"Well then, I helped solve it!" she said in a cheery but creepy voice. She was watching way too much *Desperate Housewives*; she was beginning to sound like those women.

"Whatever," he said.

"You haven't brought Amanda by in a long time."

He'd brought her by exactly once, and one time she'd come on her own.

"So?"

"So, you're welcome to do so anytime you want. We could have her over for dinner?"

To eat hardtack? "No, thanks."

"Or for a movie or something."

"Yeah, right."

The pancakes tasted pretty good given that he had to break an outside shell to eat them.

"How are they?" his mother asked, hovering.

"Ummm," he said through a full mouth, avoiding the second outright lie of the morning.

"I don't want you worried about Wayne."

"I shouldn't have said anything," he said.

"Older people. Well, sometimes they need a visit away from home, or fresh air, or even a day or two in the hospital. But I'm sure he's fine."

"That's not exactly reassuring. What do you mean: the hospital?"

"I shouldn't have said that. I didn't mean that the way it sounded. I'm sure he's with friends somewhere."

"Enemies is more like it," he told his pancakes, quietly enough that she couldn't hear.

"Your cell phone buzzed."

"What? When?"

"While you were sleeping. Just now. A text I think. A short buzz."

He'd left it charging the night before amid the sea of wires and wall warts at the end of the kitchen counter. He extracted it and unlocked the keypad.

"Hey, where's the rat?" Finn said.

"You will not call your sister derogatory names. Not in this house, young man."

"Student council," he said, answering his own question. "Dad dropped her?"

"Uh-huh."

jess crosd ovr lst nite. finishd her dream . . . cll me–pby

"Anything important?"

"Huh?" Finn stuffed the phone into his pocket. "No. Nothing. Just stuff. Boy stuff. You know?"

"Boy stuff as in boy-and-girl stuff?"

It was all his mother could think about. He was supposed to be the one thinking about girls, but he could have sworn that she spent ten times more time than he did thinking about all that stuff. He barely thought about girls at all—except Jess and Amanda, and they didn't count. Not exactly, anyway.

"Just stuff."

"No more of that Kingdom Keepers nonsense. We're clear on that, young man. Yes?"

"You've made yourself very clear on that," he said, dodging yet another straight answer. Three in one morning. That was close to a record. He didn't want to push it. She was the one who always told him to quit while he was ahead.

"I think I'll ride my bike, if it's okay. Maybe I'll walk Amanda home today, if you wouldn't mind?"

As expected, she practically exploded. "Mind? Why would I mind? What a lovely idea, Finn. You could ask her for dinner if you wanted."

How could he bring a girl home for dinner with his mother analyzing every word spoken, every gesture? She treated him like a lab rat.

"Maybe so," he said, not wanting to hurt her feelings.

He'd just bought himself at least two hours after school, but he walked calmly to his bike, not wanting to appear too anxious.

He successfully flew beneath his mother's radar. He pedaled as fast as his bike would carry him. Jess had crossed over, confirming that Philby had successfully installed her—and presumably Amanda too—onto the DHI server. Their mission at the Studios had been a success. She'd apparently finished her dream of Wayne while crossed over.

He couldn't wait to see whatever she'd sketched.

He one-handed the bike and called Philby, reaching him on the second ring.

18

SCHOOL COULD SEEM ENDLESS. Days could stretch out for an eternity, as if someone had put weights on all the hands of every clock, slowing them down. This must be how prisoners look at clocks, Finn thought, the days stretching out impossibly long, compounding their incarceration. He felt like a prisoner himself, knowing what lay ahead when the bell rang and the doors opened.

Amanda was waiting for him at the bottom of the steps.

"Jess crossed over last night."

"I heard. And you?"

"No, I don't think so."

"Oh, you'd know, believe me. But that's strange. Was it into Epcot?"

"Yes."

"Then Philby got it right."

"I suppose."

He walked his bike, Amanda alongside him.

"I could sit on the bar, you know," she said. "It would be faster."

Finn's throat tightened. If she sat on the bike's top

bar it was going to be cozy—real cozy.

"What about your bag?" he asked, looking for an excuse to prevent this from happening.

"I can put it with yours. Unless you don't want me to. . . ."

Trapped. "No, that's okay. Sure. I guess." He held the bike for her, steadying it.

She slipped onto the bar, held the handlebars and waited for Finn to mount the saddle. Amanda was tall, and it suddenly felt as if she were sitting in his lap. Her left shoulder was touching his chest, and her long, dark hair tickled his chin.

"I've got a better idea," he said, their faces nearly touching, his voice sounding like air leaking from a balloon. "Why don't you take the saddle?"

"I'm good here," she said.

"No . . . I think it would be safer with you on the seat. I can stand on the pedals."

A moment later, rearranged on the bike, they were heading down the sidewalk, shouting at students to get out of their way. Amanda tried to steady herself by gripping the saddle, but gave up after a block and placed her hands on Finn's hips. He stopped pedaling, allowing the bike to glide, then drew a deep breath and continued riding. Five minutes stretched to ten. She talked to pass the time.

"When she was crossed over, she walked around the park. It was nighttime, of course, and there wasn't anyone around for the most part. She saw some movement across the lake, and she hid out of sight. She said it was kind of creepy, being there all alone."

"I'll bet it was. The Magic Kingdom's the same way."

"She felt drawn to certain attractions. But that's how she is: all sorts of stuff happens to her and a lot of it can't be explained."

"How did she cross back?"

"I have no idea."

"What time was it?"

"She woke up in bed, just before midnight."

"That was us," Finn said. "That was when Philby and I and the others crossed back. We met up in the apartment. But it doesn't make sense that she crossed over. We always have to be together for that to happen."

"But she was in one of her dreams right then. Maybe that had something to do with it. One minute she was walking past France, the next she was in her bunk. But she had the picture in her head. A perfect picture of Wayne—the same dream she had before, only this time it was all there. At least she thinks it's everything."

Finn glided to a stop in front of The Frozen Marble

ice cream shop. Philby was waiting at a table inside with a strawberry concoction in front of him. It occurred to Finn that he'd never seen any of the DHIs' houses except Maybeck's, not counting the church Amanda and Jess had squatted in for a few months. He had no idea how or even where some of his closest friends lived.

"Hey," Philby said.

"Hey," said Finn.

"Hey," said Amanda.

She went to the counter and ordered a mocha mini with graham crackers, M&M's, and chocolate syrup, and returned with two spoons, handing one to Finn. He regarded the spoon carefully. Sharing an ice cream was something he'd never done with a girl. It felt to him like some kind of contract, some kind of commitment, and he was leery of entering into it too quickly.

"Don't worry, my spoon won't touch your side," she said in an openly mocking tone.

Philby arched his eyebrows and kept his mouth occupied with his strawberry whatever.

"I didn't say anything," Finn said.

"Eat," she said.

He stabbed into the ice cream recklessly, took a spoonful, and hummed as the combination hit his taste buds.

"Whoa!" he said.

"Yeah," said Amanda. "I thought you'd like it."

"Double whoa," he said, winning a chocolate smile from her.

"It's a cryptogram," Philby said. He pushed a photocopy from the page in Jess's diary in front of Finn. It showed an old guy that looked surprisingly like Wayne sitting in a chair. On the wall behind him was the image of a horse, a pole, and in the distance, a mountain and some trees. Across it all was written a string of letters and numbers.

MKPFP IFP TDIEPR VKPFP RMIFR
CQW'M JFQV HT 2736/2730

"What the . . . ?" Finn said.

"It's a kind of code," Philby explained.

"He is always doing this," Finn complained. "Why is nothing ever simple with him?"

"He's secretive," Philby answered. "It's like the Stonecutter's Quill, only different."

"Different, how?"

"That was an anagram. This, clearly, is not."

"None of this is exactly clear to me," Finn admitted.

"He expects us to break it."

"But how?" Amanda said.

"Are we sure this is right?" Finn said, puzzling over the combination.

"Jess's dreams are accurate. You know that, Finn. Remember the Animal Kingdom?"

"I know, but that was animals. This is . . . I don't know what it is! Gibberish?"

"Not exactly gibberish," Philby said. "Though it won't be simple to figure out. He's left us a few clues."

"More than this?" Finn asked.

"Within this," Philby answered.

"Clues within clues?"

"Exactly."

"He's either way too smart, or way too crazy," Finn said.

"A little of both," Philby said.

"What clues?" Amanda asked. "I love puzzles."

"These numbers at the end are a clue. But the apostrophe's the biggie."

"Huge," Finn said, mocking him. He didn't like the way Amanda and Philby were suddenly so buddy-buddy.

"Break the numbers apart and you get—"

"Two-seven-three-six—"

"Twenty-seven and thirty-six," Philby said, correcting her.

"And that's significant because?" she said.

"How many letters are there in the alphabet?"

Philby wanted her to think it out for herself.

"Twenty-six. But oh . . . my . . . gosh . . ." Amanda said ecstatically.

"That's big news?" Finn asked. "I know that much."

"But if you add in the ten numerals," Philby said. "One through zero."

"Not zero through one?" she inquired.

"No, I don't think so. You'll see why. . . ."

These two were speaking a foreign language. "Back up!" Finn said.

"By including the number thirty-six," Philby explained, "he's telling us that he extended ten characters—or numbers—past the end of the alphabet. So twenty-seven is—"

"The numeral one," she answered.

"And thirty-six—"

"Is zero!" Amanda said excitedly. "One followed by a zero—is ten."

"Yes. All together it's a date, I think. Ten-fourteen. October fourteenth."

"Whoa!" Finn said, seeing the solution. "But that's . . . what . . . two days from now?"

"Exactly," Philby said, agreeing. "And since that date makes at least some sense in terms of the code, it shows us he was using a system—"

"Where each letter and each numeral represents a

number," Amanda said. "Or in the case of the alphabet, a different letter."

"Yes," said Philby. "That's it: a cryptogram."

"So another clue is the letter *M*," she said.

Finn was lost. "We know this because?"

"Because it follows the apostrophe," Philby said.

"So *M* either represents an *S* or a *T* or a *D*," Amanda said, "because those are the only three letters that ever follow an apostrophe by themselves, except for *M*, and I don't think *M* is likely to be *M*. Also, it's probably not *D*, since I bet this message is in the present tense—apostrophe *D* would be short for *had*, the past."

"She's fast," Philby told Finn, who mugged, trying to appear that he was following them.

"And where does this get us, exactly?" Finn said.

"Cryptograms are about patterns. Words follow patterns. Vowels are in certain places in most words. Wayne wouldn't make it ridiculously difficult, just hard enough that the Overtakers couldn't understand it when they found it."

"He'd have had to actually write on the wall," Amanda explained to Finn. "Otherwise Jess would not have seen it. Her dreams, her visions, are like snapshots of the future. She wrote down each of these letters. She saw this clearly."

"But all we have are a couple of numbers and an

S or a *T*," Finn said. "I don't see how that helps us. Wayne needs us *now*."

"The most common letters are vowels," Philby said. "I'm pretty sure I can decode this. The *P*'s repeat. The *I*'s. Therefore they're probably vowels. It's going to come together easier than you think. It's like Scrabble in a foreign language."

"When?"

"Finn!" Amanda said, complaining. "He just got it today. It's not *that* easy."

"But I thought we were going after the temperature records. I thought that was the way we decided we might find Malef—" He caught himself. "You know."

"Then you want the Engineer Base." A woman's voice turned the heads of all three kids.

Wanda stood there looking down at them.

"Where'd you come from?" Finn said, his suspicion obvious.

"You will need to learn to pay more attention to who's behind you, who's watching you. I followed you and Amanda from school."

"You're freaking me out," Finn said.

"You were so busy with getting her onto the bike, you never looked at what was going on around you."

It was true: at the time, Finn hadn't been thinking about anything else.

"But the Overtakers don't go outside the parks," Philby said.

"They did at least once," Finn corrected. "*She* did. I saw her drop Jess off at the car wash that time."

"An air-conditioned car," Amanda said.

"You don't know that was her," Philby said.

"Sure I do. Sure as I'm sitting here."

"I would err on the side of precaution," Wanda said, "if I were you."

"What's the Engineer Base?" Philby said.

"Where you'll get your answers. Data from the Studios, Epcot, and the Animal Kingdom are fed into a central office that's housed in the back lot of the Studios. The Imagineers refer to it simply as the Base."

"What about the Magic Kingdom?"

"No. Their equipment is older, and with the Utilidor, that park is basically self-contained and self-sufficient when it comes to engineering. But Epcot, yes. If you get into the Base you'll have all the temperature data you want."

"It's too risky," Finn said. "We just barely got out of there the last time."

"Yes, but the last time you were you," Wanda said, "and the Studios still had people inside."

"Yeah? So?"

"What if this time you went back as your DHIs, at night, after it closed?"

"Same answer: too risky. And complicated. Philby programmed us to cross over into Epcot."

Finn looked at Philby, whose face was all in a knot.

"Didn't you?" Finn asked.

"Not exactly. I opened a backdoor on the software so I can control it."

"Control it how?" Amanda asked.

"The projectors," he answered. "I can control the DHI projectors from any laptop, any computer. I can decide which park a DHI lands in after crossing over."

"Wait a second! I didn't hear about this!" Finn said.

"It wasn't like we had a lot of time to talk," Philby said, reminding him. "I'm pretty sure I can control who crosses over into what park. I turn the projectors off in the parks we don't want to go, and leave them on in the one where we do. It's pretty basic."

"We can cross over into the Studios?" Finn said curiously.

"We should be able to cross over into anywhere there are projectors: the two kingdoms, the Studios, and Epcot. And it gets better than that," Philby said.

"Meaning?" Amanda asked.

"I think I should be able to toggle our DHIs on and off."

"Same question," Amanda said.

"It means I can decide who crosses over and who doesn't."

"Cannot," said Finn.

"Didn't know I could until I was in there debugging, but yeah, I think I can. And there's only one way to find out."

"Why do I not like the sound of that?" said Finn.

"We just have to make sure that whoever's on the list to go—one of them has to be able to get to the remote, or there's no return. And I realize that Jess crossed back over from Epcot when we hit the return in the Studios, but I don't think we should count on that always working. It would be better to all return together, like we usually do. We don't want to get someone stuck—as in the Syndrome."

"That doesn't exactly sound reassuring," Amanda said.

"And Wanda . . . we're going to have to trust Wanda to move the remote for us," Finn said. "It's currently in MK. It'll have to be in the Studios if Philby and I are going to get out without having to go all the way over to MK."

"I can do that for you," Wanda said. She pulled up

a chair to the table, grabbed a napkin and a pen, and started to draw. "Let me show you where to go once you're inside," she said.

Finn looked over at her, wondering if he could trust this woman with the fob. There was only the one fob, as far as he knew. If they ever lost it, there would be no crossing back—their DHIs would be stuck, their human selves would be caught in the Syndrome. It required an enormous leap of faith—just the kind of thing Wayne would use to test Finn. "The Base," Wanda said, "is going to have everything you want."

19

FINN OPENED HIS EYES to find himself lying beneath what looked like a giant mouth. He flinched, flailing his arms, still half asleep.

"You're all right," he heard Philby say.

It wasn't a mouth about to eat him, Finn realized, but the bottom of Mickey's giant sorcerer's hat in the Hollywood Studios plaza.

Philby sat off to the side, cross-legged.

"You're late," he said.

"You ever have it where all you want to do is sleep, but it just isn't happening?" Finn sat up.

"All the time."

"That was me tonight."

"We should get out of here," Philby said. "You're glowing like a night-light."

"As if you aren't."

"Not exactly subtle. Someone could see us."

"Did you bring the napkin?"

Philby fished it out of his pocket for Finn to see. "Remember, she warned us that it's not different from MK over here: the characters come alive, and some of them are bound to be Overtakers."

"So, we stay out of sight," Finn said. He'd had an encounter once with pirates from Pirates of the Caribbean that had cost him a laser burn. He still had the scar to show for it.

"Out of sight and no confrontations," Philby agreed. "We don't want them to know what we're up to."

"Duh," Finn said. The sound of an explosion rocked them both. "What was that?"

Philby checked his watch. "How incredibly stupid," he said.

"What?"

"Fantasmic! Sometimes they do a couple of shows."

"But it's almost ten o'clock!"

"And they don't start until it's dark. What can I tell you?"

"You can tell me that we did not mess this up!" Finn said. "You want to think about who's in Fantasmic!?"

"Ursula, Cruella De Vil, Scar, Jafar—" Philby was being his usual encyclopedic self.

"Chernabog, Maleficent!" Finn said. "Let's not forget where that ice cream truck was found. Fantasmic! is like an Overtaker convention. What were we thinking?"

"You were the one," Philby reminded, "who got freakin' about Epcot."

"Jess had that dream there," Finn explained. "It

wasn't me. Don't lay that on me. I never said Maleficent was there. But if Wayne's locked up there, Maleficent can't be far away." He added, "What are we doing arguing about this, anyway?"

"The point is," Philby said, "Maleficent and Chernabog could hide a lot easier in Fantasmic! than anyplace else, and they'd be protected here, too. Not only that, but who knows what they might be planning? Mickey defends *all magic* in Fantasmic!"

"So?"

"So they absolutely could be here in the Studios. The real ones, I mean."

"Okay, they could be here. But it's Wayne we're worried about. If we're going to take on those two, we've got to have Wayne on our side."

"If that's possible," Philby said. "Yeah, I agree."

"So let's take advantage of everyone being out at Fantasmic! Right? I think we're going around in circles."

"I'm just saying: if we find Wayne . . ." Philby said.

"*When* we find Wayne," Finn corrected him. "Look, we've got to trust Jess's dream and that means Wayne is somewhere in Epcot. If they've captured him, then Maleficent's involved."

"Up to her elbows."

"So if we track temperature changes in Epcot—"

"Maybe it leads us to Wayne. I get all that."

"It *will* lead us to Wayne," Finn said. "And once we find Wayne we'll help him trap Greeny whether that's here or wherever."

"Greeny . . . I like that."

"Thanks. So you're the one with the map," Finn said.

Philby got his bearings. "This way," he said.

* * *

ENGINEERING BASE read the lettering on a door in an orange building that looked like a giant shoe box. It was situated behind Lights, Motors, Action! past a sign that read: CAST MEMBERS ONLY. Finn did not hesitate; he walked his DHI through the door's glass, turned around and unlocked it for Philby. After relocking the door they climbed some stairs, as sketched out on Wanda's napkin.

"Five minutes," Philby reminded, marking the time on his watch.

Wanda had warned them that the door coming open might trip a silent alarm to Security. It was only a warning; she didn't know if it would actually happen.

"If they receive an alarm like that," she'd said, "you'll have at least five minutes, but I wouldn't take much more than that."

They arrived in a room that looked like a miniature NASA control center. There were office cubicles around the small room's perimeter separated by gray sound baffles and, in the room's center, an island of computer terminals. Philby circled the island until arriving at a terminal marked HEATING, COOLING.

"You're good," Finn said, awed by the ease with which Philby navigated a variety of screens, drilling deeper and deeper toward the information they sought: PARKS, EPCOT, MAINTENANCE. The screen showed Epcot as a graphic. It took Philby four tries and nearly another minute to start the screen flashing.

"What's this?" Finn asked.

"Anything flashing has recorded temperature swings that exceed acceptable limits—in this case, ten degrees."

Philby used the touch screen to navigate into each of the flashing pavilions. He called out times and dates for Finn to write down.

"Can't we just print it out?" Finn said.

"I don't see how, no. I don't think so."

Finn grabbed a pen and paper and began taking down the dictated data. But Philby could talk faster than Finn could write and he quickly fell behind.

Now that he had the hang of it, Philby was flying through screen after screen of maintenance reports.

"You see what's happening?" Philby said.

"No," Finn said sharply. "I can't keep up, and even if I could, it's not like I have time to think about what I'm writing down. So, no. Emphatically, no."

"The times," Philby said. "The times!"

Finn had written down dozens of times. Philby was still spouting off even more times and numbers.

"I'm sorry," Finn said.

"We need more than five minutes," Philby announced. "This is the—"

Voices.

He checked his watch.

"Not possible!" Philby whispered frantically.

"What?" Finn whispered back.

"Seven minutes! We've been here *seven minutes*!"

"Not possible," Finn said.

"I just said that!" Philby complained.

They both heard the door come open downstairs. The voices grew louder and more easily understood. Security patrols traveled in twos. Judging by the voices this was a man-and-woman team. They thumped their way up the stairs.

Finn pulled Philby into one of the office cubicles and sat him down on a chair next to him. He hung his arms at his side and indicated for Philby to do the same. He hung his head, so that he looked half-asleep. Philby mirrored Finn's position.

"Door was locked," the woman said. "It's not like we've got anything to worry about. Could be a faulty wire. Coulda been somebody shook the door or something. I've seen that throw off a false alarm before."

"Check it out!" the man said.

Out of the corner of his eye, Finn saw the man approach.

"What's this?"

"Well, I'll be," the woman said, now standing directly in front of Finn. "These are those things. You know: those new things they installed. What-cha-ma-call-its."

"Halo . . ." the man said, fishing for the word. "Hollow?"

"Holograms!" the woman shouted, as if she'd won a game show competition.

"What are they doing here?" the man said.

"Whaddaya mean whadda they doing here?" she barked. "It's engineering, you moron. I've always wanted to try this." She waved her hand through Finn. It passed smoothly, with only a brief static buzz as her hand swiped through Finn's upper body. "Whoa, is that amazing."

She lifted her arm, about to do the same thing to Philby. But if she tried to wave her hand through

Philby, it would likely not pass through. In all likelihood she'd knock Philby right off the chair.

Finn lifted his head and moved it robotically. "Welcome to Disney's Hollywood Studios," he said.

The guard jumped back, startled. "Jeez!" she snapped.

"Welcome to Disney's Hollywood Studios!" Finn repeated, continuing to move his head in the same, jerky motions.

"Look what you done!" the male guard said. "Don't mess with those things. Who knows what kind of trouble you might make?"

The female guard eyed Finn curiously. "I'd say this fella has a chip loose."

The male guard chuckled.

"You don't suppose it coulda been them tripped the alarm," she said.

"These two? You're joking, right? You just waved your hand through that one."

"Yeah," she said, "you're right." But her tone of voice indicated otherwise.

"More than likely, Mr. Potato Head again. He loves to mess around."

"Or Tigger," she countered. "I've seen him snooping around lately, out of bounds, back in here where it's Cast Members only. I caught him following Ursula the other night. It was like he was spying on her. And when I accused him, he got all in a knot, like I had it all wrong."

"Knowing you, you probably did."

"Thanks for the vote of confidence there, big guy."

The two roamed the room for a minute, checking under desks and doing a thorough job of securing the office.

The man spoke into his radio asking whoever was on the other end to "activate the motion sensors in Base." Only a few seconds passed before a voice came back confirming that the sensors were now active, and telling the guard he had thirty seconds in which to leave the building.

As they were heading down the stairs their conversation faded.

"You didn't tell the boss about Tigger," the man said, his concern obvious.

"We agreed not to say nothing to no one about what goes on here. I, for one, would like to keep my job."

"Keeping the job is a good thing," the man said.

Then the front door shut and Finn couldn't hear anything more of them.

"Okay," Finn said.

"You saved my butt," Philby said.

"Keep your head down and *do not move*," Finn said, his eye on a small wedge-shaped device way up high in one corner of the room. "They activated the motion sensors."

"Dang!"

"You know what this means? It means you've got to go *all clear*. Tonight. Right now."

"I've never been able to. You know that," Philby complained. "You're the only one—"

"I'm not the only one. I can't be the only one."

"You're it, dude. None of the rest of us can completely get ourselves out of our DHIs *or* cross over in the middle of the day. And don't think we haven't tried."

"That's not true: Maybeck pulled it off that time he was trapped in Space Mountain. You've got to try harder."

"No point. It's not going to happen."

Finn had never been comfortable having more abilities than his friends. Nor had he appreciated Wayne telling him that he was, and would be, the team's leader.

"So what do we do now?" Philby asked, his head hanging down. "The moment I move, that alarm is going to trip, and that's going to bring those two back, and fast."

"Not if we can get you to the staircase. You can do

this," Finn repeated. "I talked Maybeck through it. I can do the same thing for you."

"I don't think so."

"That's because you're afraid you can't do it. But you *can*. What I want you do—*without moving!*—is picture a blank wall. There's nothing on it. There are no images in your head, no thought. Are you with me?"

"Okay, I guess."

"No thought. No fear. Now there's a light coming toward you—like the light on the front of *The Polar Express*, you know? One bulb, really bright, out of the darkness. That's all there is—the darkness and that one light. The closer the light comes, the less darkness. The light takes over everything. There's no room for fear, or thought, for anything. Can you see that happening?"

"I can! My arms are . . . tingling."

"No, they aren't," Finn said, trying to coach him, "because you don't have arms. You don't have legs. The light gets close enough and you *become* the light. You *become* the hologram. That's all we are right now—light. Projected light. You don't have to think about that, you just have to . . . I don't know . . . *know* it."

Finn stood from his chair, his eye on the sensor in the corner. It didn't flash; it didn't sense him.

There was no easy test to know if Philby had succeeded. Finn couldn't drop a book through him without the movement of the book setting off the motion alarm.

Then he remembered back to one of the first times he'd been able to all-clear his DHI, and his surprising discovery.

"You know," he said, "when we're *all clear*, when we fully cross over, then even though we can shape ourselves to fit onto a chair, the chair doesn't actually hold you up."

Instantly, Philby fell *through* the chair and onto the floor, so that the seat of the chair was mostly inside his chest.

"No way!" he said, realizing what had happened.

"Don't do that!" Finn cautioned. "Don't question it, or challenge it, or even *think* about it. Just stand up and keep thinking about the train and that light. You've got to focus on that light. And get yourself over to the stairs—halfway down the stairs where the sensor can't see you. I'll handle the temperature log."

Philby stood up. The motion sensor didn't respond.

"I'll memorize what I can," Finn said. "I can't use a pen to write anything down without tripping the sensor. I'll call some numbers out to you. Then we'll get out of here."

Philby made it partway down the stairs. "What if my hands are tingling?"

"Picture the train."

"Okay, but they're still tingling."

Finn stood at the computer monitor; he called out some of the data and memorized what he could. Then he got down the stairs. Philby looked worried, and Finn knew he'd lost his all-clear.

"I'm going to wait here and lock the door behind you," Finn said. "But I'm guessing when we open the door they're going to know about it somewhere and come after us."

"There's that construction shop Wanda told us about. It's right next door. We should be able to hide somewhere in there for a while. We can take our time getting back to the remote."

"'Kay, then that's the plan."

Philby unlocked the door and stepped outside. Finn pictured getting caught, and he could feel his DHI shape shifting; his fingers tingled. He turned the lock. Then he cleared his thought and stepped through the glass door and outside.

"You want to know what's weird about that?" Philby said as the two DHIs ran toward the construction warehouse.

"Everything?" Finn answered.

"It's how hard it was to keep from having a negative thought. And that was, what?—one minute? Two, at the most."

"Tell me about it," Finn said. "My personal best is five minutes, thirty-three seconds."

"How messed up is that?"

"Messed up," Finn said. "But you've got to admit, it's majorly random to be *all clear*, even if it's only for two minutes."

"I fell through a chair," Philby said proudly.

"You fell through a chair," Finn said.

They ducked into shadow, their DHIs glowing, as a golf cart zoomed down an opposing lane—the same two Security guards.

"Close," Finn whispered.

"They'll never figure it out," said Philby, a smile overtaking his face. "I fell through a chair," he mumbled.

20

ANOTHER TWO SCHOOL days passed uneventfully. Text messaging among the Kingdom Keepers established that no one had crossed over, confirming that Philby had full control over the DHI system. Through the backdoor he'd left in the software, he could determine who crossed over, and into which park or kingdom. They would still need the remote to return.

The two days felt like an eternity to Finn, his concern over Wayne's whereabouts and condition deepening with each passing hour. But something bigger was taking place in him as well—not only his confused feelings about his so-called friendship with Amanda, but his bigger understanding of what the Overtakers might be up to. He felt in his gut that he needed to see the goal of the Overtakers in order to know how to stop them, and so far that goal had eluded him. Wayne's abduction obviously played a part, just as Jess's abduction in the Animal Kingdom had. They feared Jess and her ability to dream the future because for them it was like playing a chess match where the opponent knew their next move. The question was: did they fear Wayne, and his considerable understanding of everything Disney, or did they *need* him for something they had planned? To Finn, these were two very different possibilities, each presenting its own challenges. Until they found Wayne they wouldn't know the answer, but he was beginning to realize that he had to face the possibility that they might not find Wayne. If that proved to be the case, then he had to *become* Wayne: he had to get out in front of the Overtakers and whatever they had planned, because falling behind was not an option. There would be no catching up if the Overtakers took control. Their powers were too substantial; their reach, too pervasive. If Wayne was testing him, then he was failing. It was time to do something. The trouble was, he didn't know what he was supposed to do.

"Your friends are waiting," his mother said, as Finn came through the front door to his home.

Finn glanced into the living room.

"Hey," Philby said.

"Hey," said Willa.

"Hey there," answered Finn.

"We're here for the *project*," said Philby, aware that Finn's mother did not approve of Finn's association with his fellow Kingdom Keepers.

"The inter-school math competition," said Willa.

His mother, standing a few feet behind Finn, seemed to relax a little.

"You didn't say anything, dear," his mother said.

"I wanted to surprise you," said Finn, surprised himself.

"We've been given a *code*—" Philby said proudly, addressing Mrs. Whitman.

"—that we have to break," said Willa.

"At least that's what we hope," Finn told his mother. "If the other teams break the code first—" He left it hanging there because he wasn't sure how to finish it.

"Then we lose," Philby completed.

"How . . . interesting," said Mrs. Whitman.

"Would you like to see it?" Philby offered. "Other kids' parents are going to help. That's a no-brainer."

As his mother stepped forward, Finn used her as a shield and shook his head violently at Philby, who had just taken things way too far. What Philby didn't understand—had no way of knowing—was that Finn's mother had, until five years earlier, worked at NASA on the Space Shuttle program. After the birth of his sister, she'd tried mostly working from home, but had finally given up her job amid a budget cut.

The thing was: his mother was a rocket scientist. The real thing. She could do advanced calculus *in her head*.

"Well, I could take a look, I suppose," she said.

Finn squinted and hung his head and knew it was

too late: there was no way they would be getting rid of her now.

Philby got one chance to look Finn's way as Mrs. Whitman sat down onto the couch beside him. His expression said, *Who knew?* But Finn's heart sank because *he knew*.

Philby unfolded the piece of paper and placed it in front of her.

MKPFP IFP TDIEPR VKPFP RMIFR CQW'M JFQV HT 2736/2730

1	2	3	4	5	6	7	8	9	10	11	12	13	14	15	16	17	18	19	20	21	22	23	24	25	26
A	B	C	D	E	F	G	H	I	J	K	L	M	N	O	P	Q	R	S	T	U	V	W	X	Y	Z
					A					T				A	A						N				
					E					S				E	E										
					I									I	I										
					O									O	O										
					U									U	U										

mkpfp = vkpfp words ending in a i o u? p = e?
e e e e if p= e then f = r
ere ere if f= r, then k = h
here here

Mrs. Whitman studied the page for less than a minute as the three looked on.

"Your assumptions are clever," she said.

"With cryptograms," Philby said, "we were told the whole thing is repetition. So the two words that are the closest are the VKPFP—"

"—and the MKPFP," said Willa, who wanted in on this.

Finn looked on, a bit bewildered.

"The apostrophe," said Philby, "tells us *M* is an *S* or a *T*. A possessive or a contraction. And that means that *W*—"

"Could be an *N*," said Mrs. Whitman, "if it's part of a contraction. Very good. Let's play with that for a moment." She focused on the page and reached over, accepting a pencil from Philby as if she'd asked for it, which she had not.

"So *P* has to be *E*," she said, erasing and adding to Philby's chart.

"Because?" Philby asked.

"Because probability favors *R*, in TDIEPR, as the plural, *S*. And if *R* is *S*, then—"

"*P* is a vowel, and it's an *E*!" Willa nearly shouted. "And if *R* is *S*, then *W* can't be *S*. It has to be *T*, making the apostrophe a contraction, just as you said, Mrs. Whitman. I get it."

Mrs. Whitman showed the others her work.

The chart was beginning to take shape. Finn could even understand the substitution of letters.

Not wanting to be left out, he said, "So *M* and *V* have to be consonants in words like *there* and *where* . . . and . . . What other five-letter words end in *here*?"

"There aren't any," his mother said with complete authority. "There are a couple six-letter words, like *adhere*, but no five-letter words. So, you're right, Finn. *M* and *V* are either *T* or *W*."

"And we already know that *M* is *T*," Philby proclaimed, pointing to the chart.

"So *V* is *W*," stated Willa.

"*V* is *W*," said Mrs. Whitman, adding this to the chart. "I love this kind of puzzle!"

Indeed, Finn's mom was leaning over the table, writing and erasing. She turned and presented the page to the others.

MKPFP IFP TDIEPR VKPFP RMIFR CQW'M
JFQV HT 2736/2730
THERE —E ——ES WHERE ST—S —' T

"Whoa!" Finn gasped. "We have all that already?"

"Finn," his mother said, "Google four-letter contractions. That's the next piece of the puzzle. I'm going to get us all cookies."

Finn felt as if he'd entered a parallel universe where an alternate life-form had taken over his mother. There was a good deal of evidence to support his theory: first, his mother was asking him to get *on* the computer, not *off* it; second, she was offering cookies *before* dinner.

He knew his mother to have a nearly uncontrollable addiction to chocolate, an addiction that especially revealed itself when she was nervous or anxious. That in turn told him something about her current condition.

"I'm on it," he said.

By the time he returned, there was a plate of chocolate chip cookies on the coffee table, along with three glasses of milk and a glass of water.

Another piece of evidence: his mother spoke with her mouth full of food. *Unthinkable.*

"So . . . what'd you find?"

"There are four: *isn't*, *won't*, *don't*, and *can't*," Finn reported.

"Two with *O*s, one with an *I*, and one with an *A*," his mother said, licking chocolate off her front teeth.

She adjusted the chart accordingly.

She had shaded the letters that they felt certain about.

"You missed a couple *F*s," Philby said, pointing to her chart and, more importantly, to her line of deciphering:

MKPFP IFP TDIEPR VKPFP RMIFR CQW'M
JFQV HT 2736/2730
THERE —E ——ES WHERE ST—S —'T

He changed it to:

MKPFP IFP TDIEPR VKPFP RMIFR CQW'M JFQV HT 2736/2730
THERE -RE —ES WHERE ST-RS —'T -R-W

"So I did! Good catch!"

"*I* is *A*," Finn announced loudly, wanting to be more than the errand boy.

His mother nodded and scribbled in the letter.

MKPFP IFP TDIEPR VKPFP RMIFR CQW'M JFQV HT 2736/2730
THERE ARE —A-ES WHERE STARS —'T -R-W

"We're getting there now," whispered Willa, as if by speaking too loudly she might jinx it.

His mother read, substituting words. "'There are . . . traces . . . spaces. . . .'"

"Places," Willa said.

"Places," Mrs. Whitman said, nodding. "Yes, I think you're right: 'There are places where stars. . . .'"

"*Isn't*, *won't*, *can't* or *don't*," Finn said, supplying the only four-letter contractions that seemed plausible.

"We can eliminate *isn't* because 'stars' is plural," Mrs. Whitman said. "We can eliminate *can't* because we've identified the letters *A* and *W* and there's no *A* or *W* in the word. So it's got to be *don't.*"

"*P*!" Willa announced. "The *T* of the code—the last letter—is the same as the first letter of *places.*"

Finn mumbled to himself. "He made it so we could figure it out."

"Your teacher?" his mother said. She never missed anything. He could be *thinking* something up in his room and his mother could somehow *overhear* it.

"Our teacher," Philby answered for him, seeing that Finn was tongue-tied.

"Up," said Willa. "The last word is *up*. There are places where stars . . . don't . . . grow up."

"We did it!" Willa proclaimed.

"*You* did it, Mrs. Whitman," Philby corrected.

"We did it as a team," Mrs. Whitman said in a tone of voice that Finn recognized as preachy. "I really had nothing to do it with. I was more of a coach than a participant." His mother was always trying to turn everything into a life message. If a bug died on the porch light it was a life message. If a mirage appeared on the highway, instead of just being cool it had to be a life message too.

"Mo-om!" Finn said in his best whine.

"Okay," she said, anticipating his objection before it was enunciated.

"The Milky Way," Willa said. "Stars just don't grow up—they burn out and die."

"But of course they grow up," Philby said. "They can't die unless they are created. Stars are constantly being created and burning up."

"It's the natural order of the universe," said Mrs. Whitman.

"You worked for NASA, mom," Finn said, giving her a chance to redeem herself. "What's with stars not growing up?"

"It would appear to be some kind of riddle," she answered. "What teacher assigned this? Science or math?"

Willa answered, "Math," at the same exact instant Finn answered, "Science."

His mother gave Finn the evil eye; she knew something was up.

"Finn?"

Philby stepped in. "They're both right in a way," he said, sounding typically Philby-convincing. "Because it's an inter-school competition, several teachers from each school were involved in creating the code and, I suppose, whatever riddle is involved."

Philby was presently the color of a ripe raspberry. Finn hoped his mother didn't know him well enough to notice—but his mother didn't miss much.

"Well, that makes sense," said Mrs. Whitman.

"What kind of riddle?" Finn asked.

"Philby is right," she said. "Stars are constantly being created, and stars are constantly burning out after millions of years of burning. What makes it more complicated—much more complicated—is that we are seeing the stars, thousands, hundreds of thousands, of years *after* whatever happened. It takes light all that time to reach earth. So by the time we identify a star it may actually no longer be there."

"An illusion," Willa said.

"Yes!" Mrs. Whitman said. "In a manner of speaking. But not exactly an illusion, since it did exist in the first place, perhaps for millions of years."

"'There are places where stars don't grow up,'" Willa repeated.

"On a Christmas tree," Mrs. Whitman said. "Or in a stained-glass window."

"A church!" Finn said.

"Do you suppose it's some sort of scavenger hunt?" Mrs. Whitman asked.

Finn glanced at the others. "I . . . ah . . . I think we can take it from here, Mom."

Mrs. Whitman bit down properly on her cookie and chewed with her lips pressed closed tightly. She looked at each of them, one by one. She took a sip of water, looking right over the brim of the cup at Finn.

"A starfish that has been preserved," she said. "A museum comes to mind."

"A church or a museum," Finn said. "That's really good, Mom. I think we'll take it from here."

"Doesn't one of the car makers use a star as its hood ornament?"

"Really," Finn said, *"we're good."*

"Thank you for the cookies and milk," Willa said, trying to help Finn.

"They were delicious," said Philby. "And your code breaking was awesome."

"I hope it doesn't disqualify you that I helped," Mrs. Whitman said.

Both Finn and Philby screwed up their faces in confusion.

"The competition!" she said.

Both boys nodded. They were becoming trapped by their own story.

Mrs. Whitman returned the empty cookie plate to the tray and accepted the empty glasses as well. She left the room.

"Whoa," Finn said.

"Museums?" Willa said in a whisper. "Churches? Christmas? What's he trying to tell us?"

"One Man's Dream is like a museum," Philby said. "It's not impossible to think of Cinderella's Castle as a cathedral."

"At Christmas all the parks go wild with decorations," Willa added. "There must be a million stars."

"Fireworks!" Philby said. "That's one place that stars never grow up. They go up, and they come down."

"The numbers at the end!" Willa said. "We forgot the numbers at the end."

"No we didn't," Philby said. "I solved that first: ten-fourteen. It's either a time, or a date."

"And if a date, it's tomorrow," Finn said.

"So what stars just don't grow up tomorrow, and only tomorrow?"

"We should check a Disney calendar," Willa said

"I'm on it." Finn took off to Google a Disney calendar. He bounded up the stairs.

He was at his computer—having no luck at all with the calendar—when his mother cleared her throat from his open door.

"Hey," he said, paying her a passing glance over his shoulder.

"Hey there yourself."

"You did awesome," he said.

"Did you solve it yet?" she asked.

"I'm Googling some stuff."

She didn't say anything. She just stood there, leaning against the doorframe.

"What's up, Mom?"

"I was hoping you'd tell me."

He didn't dare turn around. If she got a good look at him she'd know something was going on. He couldn't hide stuff from her even when he wanted to. He'd learned to avoid some of her more penetrating questions, but outright lies were beyond him; he didn't even want to lie.

"You know," she said, "when you can't look at me, it tells me a lot."

"Who said I can't look at you?" he asked, not looking at her. "I'm just busy, that's all."

"While you're at it, why don't you Google, Orlando School Code Contest, or Orlando School Challenge, or . . . *any other combination you can think of.* Or I could save you the trouble. The last one listed was in 1996."

Finn panicked. His lungs stung, as did his eyes. His fingers felt cold and his throat dry. All this in a matter of seconds. *Her*, he thought. Only his mother could have such an effect on him.

"It's the Kingdom Keepers, isn't it?"

"Mom . . ."

"Is that your answer? 'Mom?' That's . . . pretty lame, Finn."

Lame? Since when did she talk like he did?

"It's complicated," he said.

"You are so grounded."

"Mom. . . . We're just figuring stuff out."

"You're just putting your college education at risk," she said. "That's all. Do you know what your father would do?"

"Please don't tell him! *You* helped solve it, after all."

"Under false pretenses."

"No. Not exactly."

"Exactly and completely."

"You're part of it now. Think what Dad would think of that."

"You're threatening me? Do you really think you're in any kind of position to threaten me? You're about to turn grounded into grounded forever. As in infinity. Have you studied infinity?"

"The code," he said, spinning around. "The code is nothing, Mom. A friend *dreamed* it. I swear that's the truth. *A dream.* But she remembered it exactly, and we decided to try to solve it for her."

"That is even lamer," she said.

"But it's the truth. I promise! Amanda's friend, Jess. She dreamed the whole thing. We thought it might actually mean something and so we tried to decode it."

"And it does mean something," his mother said.

He stared at her, knowing her as he did, knowing that her arms and ankles being crossed suggested a confidence she rarely displayed. This was the Ph.D. mom, the math mom, the rocket scientist.

"You solved it," he said, aghast. "You solved the riddle."

"And wouldn't you like to know the answer," she said, not denying it.

"You gotta tell me," he pleaded.

"I 'gotta' do nothing of the sort," she said. "I gotta ground you."

"So ground me. A couple days, a week? I can take it."

"Two weeks. And we say nothing about this to your father," she said.

"As if I'd object to that," Finn said.

"When I tell you the solution, you're going to do whatever it is you're all doing—*here*. Here, tomorrow night, where I can be a part of it. Where I can keep an eye on you. You'll have your friends over, and if I find out you're lying to me about any of this, then not only is the deal off, but I'm calling all their parents, and I'm putting an end to this—to whatever it is you aren't telling me about."

"It was a dream, Mom. I swear." Was she going to make him beg for the solution? The official Walt Disney World Resort calendar had nothing of interest for the following night. It left him with the fireworks displays at the various parks, and not much more.

"Television," his mother said.

"Excuse me?" Finn said, as politely as possible.

"On television, stars don't grow up. They stay the same age."

Finn's jaw dropped. She could have put a golf ball into his open mouth.

"Genius," he said.

21

"DUMBO?" Maybeck groaned in complaint.

"It's so sad," Charlene said. All the kids looked over at her in disgust, including Amanda and Jess, both too embarrassed to admit they'd never seen the movie.

"What?" Charlene said defensively. "Those ears?"

"Give me a break," Maybeck said. "*Bridge to Terabithia* is sad. *Dumbo* is just . . . stupid."

"Is not!" said Willa.

"Is so," said Philby, supporting Maybeck and quickly drawing a line between the boys and the girls.

Gathered in Finn's basement family room around a behemoth of a rear-projection television, they talked through the ads while Finn had it on mute.

"I think Wayne meant *Wizards of Waverly Place*," said Philby.

"*Cory in the House*," said Maybeck. "Has to be."

"We're missing the bigger point," Finn said.

"Which is?" asked Amanda.

"Cartoons," Finn said. "There's a place where stars don't grow old: cartoons. Even child actors grow up at some point. Not Dumbo. Not any of the other cartoon characters. That's why this show is important to us."

"And because any of those other shows could be on any night," said Willa. "This is the fourteenth. This is the night he wanted us to watch, and this is the only night *Dumbo's* going to be on. The only night it has been on the Disney Channel in . . . what?" She addressed Philby, the fount of all knowledge.

"Two years," Philby said. "It's tonight's special movie."

"It's gotta be it," agreed Finn.

"But it's torture," Maybeck said.

"It's not either. It's a good movie," Charlene insisted. "And it has a good message."

"Which is: 'You're never too young for plastic surgery,'" said Maybeck. They all laughed, even Charlene.

The ads stopped and the movie continued. Over the next hour, Mrs. Whitman delivered popcorn, soda, cupcakes, milk, and hot chocolate. Finn and Philby took notes about the characters in the movie as well as tracking the plot. Willa wrote down the settings of the various scenes. Maybeck snorted and made derisive comments, some of which would have gotten him thrown out of class at school. Amanda and Jess watched enraptured, with Jess displaying a serious appetite for kettle corn and Amanda for lemon cupcakes with cream-cheese frosting.

By the end, Maybeck said, "I don't get it."

Finn muted the television. "Wayne never makes it easy, you know that."

"Admit it, Whitman," Maybeck said. "You don't have a clue why we just watched that movie."

"We watched the movie," Finn answered, "because Wayne told us to watch the movie."

"That's only if you interpret the coded message a certain way."

"And how do you interpret it?" Philby asked.

"How should I know?" Maybeck said.

"Meaning you don't have a better idea," Philby said.

"All I'm saying is, none of us knows why we just watched that movie."

Silence settled between them. Finn studied his notes and Willa leafed through hers. They looked at each other and Willa shook her head. "I'm not sure."

"Any ideas, people?" Finn proposed. "Remember, the Stonecutter's Quill was no cakewalk. He never makes it easy."

"No one could accuse him of that," Charlene said. "Elephants? Ears? Mother–daughter? Determination?"

"Try, try again," contributed Philby.

"Stupid, stupid, stupid," said Maybeck. "It's a geek elephant with ear-wings. An overweight Will Smith."

He won another laugh from everyone.

"The circus," said Jess.

They all looked at her. She hadn't spoken a word in nearly two hours.

"It's true," Willa chimed in. "We're talking specifics like elephants and ears, but the theme, the overall setting is the circus."

"The horses are from a carousel," said Amanda. "In Jess's diary. The picture she drew. The horses aren't being stabbed. They're on a carousel."

"I pointed that out before," Maybeck reminded, "and nobody thought to consider it."

"A chair in front of a carousel," Finn said.

"The Dumbo ride in Magic Kingdom!" Charlene said.

"Just one problem with that idea." As the resident expert Philby won the group's attention. "Dumbo the Flying Elephant is not a carousel and there are no horses on the ride."

"Other than that," Maybeck said, "it's pretty much a perfect match."

"So, it's Cinderella's Golden Carrousel," Charlene proposed.

"I hate to be a stinker," Willa said, "but one of the horses in Jess's drawing has straight legs."

The boys eyed Willa suspiciously. Was this a girl–boy trap they were being led into? A joke or prank?

Charlene quelled that notion. "She's right! And on Cinderella's Golden Carrousel all the horses have bent knees."

"You can't possibly know that," said Philby, believing himself the expert in everything.

"How many times have you ridden it?" Charlene inquired. "Trust me: bent legs."

"And there's the jacket, people," Maybeck said. "Let's not forget the jacket."

"The Epcot jacket Wayne is wearing," Finn said, nodding.

"Carousel horses in Epcot?" Willa questioned. "I don't think so."

"When in doubt . . . ?" Philby said to Finn.

"Google it!" Finn answered. He returned less than five minutes later carrying a printout.

"So, I tried a bunch of things. Epcot carousel—got all these hits for Carousel of Progress. It's in MK and is rarely opened. Circus, Epcot was a waste. But circus tent, Epcot, was it. Fun Facts of Epcot came up with the words circus tent highlighted. It's a blog," he said, showing them the printout, "from 1997. I searched it for circus tent, and got this part that talks about a field trip to Wonders of Life. There was a hallway with a circus tent at the end of it. And in the very next paragraph, there's a lounge mentioned that has a Mary Poppins theme with . . . get this . . . carousel horses painted on the walls."

"Mary Poppins!" an excited Charlene shouted too loudly. "I knew I recognized those horses. That's it!" At Charlene's beckoning, Jess handed her the photocopy from her diary and placed it for all to see. The kids gathered around. "These carousel horses are from Mary Poppins. Absolutely. I can't believe," she said to Jess, "you got it as perfect as you did."

"I've never even heard of Wonders of Life," Maybeck complained.

"Neither had I, so I Wiki'd it," said Finn. "It was closed in 2004. And get this: it's used sometimes for receptions and—"

"Field trips," Philby said.

"That's where they're holding him," Maybeck said, sitting up and paying more attention.

"I thought you didn't believe any of this," Willa sniped.

"I was locked up by those bad boys," Maybeck reminded everyone.

"So was I," said Willa. "The Animal Kingdom Lodge, remember?"

"So you know, and I know, how bad it is. I was waiting for you geniuses to figure it out. But now that you have and it's time for action. . . ."

"Maybeck to the rescue," Charlene said.

"Don't knock it until you've tried it," Maybeck said.

"Tonight?" Finn asked. He slowly looked around the room, from face to face. He realized how these six people had become his closest friends. He didn't see that much of Dillard, a neighborhood pal, anymore. These six and their mission to stop the Overtakers consumed him. He could use his being a Kingdom Keeper as a convenient excuse with his other friends. The role required him to record vocal tracks and occasionally model a new move or two for the hologram Imagineers. But more than any excuses, he wanted to be with the Kingdom Keepers; he wanted to find Wayne and take on Maleficent and Chernabog and get them locked up again. To voice that aloud would get him an appointment with a psychiatrist, but these six others understood; they had been there.

"Tonight," Maybeck said. "Tomorrow is Saturday. We can sleep it off."

"What time?" Amanda asked. "We're kind of new at this."

"It's late already," Finn said. "If we all try to get to bed by quarter of eleven, we should cross over about a half hour later."

"We left the fob at the Studios," Philby reminded him.

"I'll pick up the fob," Finn said. "Fantasmic! Friday will mean there are buses running late."

"Won't you be spotted?" Jess asked.

"My projection will die somewhere outside the Studios. I can get on a bus without being seen. If I happen to pop on and off a couple of times, it'll only convince the other guests that I'm my DHI. That's all that matters."

"So," Philby said, "eleven-fifteen, the bathrooms on the way to Test Track."

Each of them nodded.

"We wait for everyone," he said. "I'll use the back-door in the software to send us all. I'll turn the Studios on for you, Finn." Finn nodded. "Once Finn is there with the fob, we'll wait until eleven-thirty and then head for the Wonders pavilion. If you're late, you can catch up to us there."

"The lounge," Finn said, "is on the second floor."

"What if the Overtakers are using Wonders as a kind of base?" Charlene asked.

"We're not going to just barge in there, if that's what you're asking," Philby answered.

"We should go to bed wearing dark clothing and running shoes," Finn advised.

"I'll bring some rope," Charlene said.

"Bring your phones with you," Philby told them.

An anonymous benefactor—Wayne?—had sent all five Kingdom Keepers free phones as a reward for their efforts in the Animal Kingdom. The phones, which could connect to the Internet as well as send texts, had a direct-connect feature—like an intercom—just between the five of them. "And flashlights," Finn said. "And, Jess, make sure you have paper and pencil, in case you have one of your . . . you know. . . ."

"Trances?" Jess said.

"Whatever it is you have," Finn said.

"Anyone up for s'mores?" Mrs. Whitman shouted down into the basement.

"Quick!" Finn said, "get out of here before you don't fit through the doors!"

22

"ARE YOU KIDDING ME?" Everything had gone smoothly for Finn. He'd made it into the Studios, had retrieved the fob, and had been about to board the last bus back to the Transportation Ticket Center, when he realized he'd be stranded there. He'd gone invisible shortly after leaving the Studios' gate and had been standing near the bus loading area wondering what to do when he'd overheard a conversation behind him.

"Catch a ride back to Epcot with you?" Printed in large yellow letters across a windbreaker Finn read: ORDNANCE CREW CHIEF.

"Sure, climb in! Don't know what we'd have done without you, Pete," the driver of the pickup said. Pete climbed in. A Mickey Mouse bobblehead nodded at the two men from the dashboard. "Would have been a disaster without those pyro effects."

"Without problems," said Pete, "I wouldn't have a job. Happy to help out. I just wish we weren't doing the run-through of Fantasmic! at five again tomorrow."

"Every morning this week."

"Don't remind me. I can hear my alarm ringing already."

As Pete pulled himself up into the cab, the invisible Finn stepped onto the bumper and pulled himself into the truck bed.

The problem came as the pickup truck was passing through Security backstage at Epcot, for, as it turned out, the Epcot DHI projectors could reach all the way out to the checkpoint. Finn's DHI began flashing and flickering on and off in the truck bed, only seconds before the pickup pulled to a stop at the Security blockade. There was no tarp to hide under. No empty cardboard box. So he rolled to the side of the truck bed nearest the guard station and hid as best he could. Hiding his projected image was one thing—his effort accomplished that. But there was nothing to stop his pulsing glow from illuminating the back of the truck. He feared either the guard, or Pete, from the passenger seat, would pick up on his blinking glow and discover him. He was like a neon sign going on and off. He tried to think of how to talk his way out of this if spotted, but couldn't come up with any decent excuses.

The driver announced himself and must have passed the guard some identification for him and his passenger. Would the guard check the back of the truck?

He didn't. The truck pulled forward. Thirty yards

past the checkpoint Finn's DHI stopped flickering. He was fully projected now, and he had to get out of the moving truck before being spotted. He calmed himself, repeating the procedure he'd outlined for Philby, not forcing, but *allowing* his DHI to realize all-clear. Then he rolled over the side of the moving pickup truck and dropped. If he'd been human, he would have broken bones and suffered a road rash that would have stayed with him through Christmas. Instead, he fell to the pavement and bounced. No matter how prepared he'd been, he couldn't keep fear entirely out of his system. He felt the contact with the asphalt; his elbows and knees hurt as he rolled and sat up, now on the edge of the access road. His palms were scraped, though not badly, and it occurred to him he'd have these wounds when he awakened later that morning, that he'd need an excuse for them to use on his mom. But he was in surprisingly good shape for a kid who had just jumped from a moving vehicle.

He stood up, took his bearings by locating Epcot's famous golf ball, and headed off to join the others.

His surprise, upon arriving at the rendezvous, was Philby.

He was standing there, wearing only his underpants.

"No, I'm not kidding you," Philby said. "It was a situation beyond my control."

"As in?" asked Charlene, who couldn't keep the smirk off her face.

"As in, I happened to fall asleep before I expected. I was getting dressed—putting some dark clothes on—when I heard my mom coming to check on me. She'd probably heard my dresser drawers or something—"

"Your drawers?" Maybeck said, winning a volley of laughter.

"And I had to get into bed fast, and next thing I know I'm waking up here."

"Here," said Jess, who'd worn a sweater. Philby thanked her as he tied it around his waist.

"I can all-clear into one of the gift shops and borrow you a pair of pants. We just have to put them back before we leave."

That's exactly what he did on their way to the Wonders of Life pavilion. Finn walked through the front door of the Future World gift shop, found some clothes for Philby, and shoved them through a mail slot. Philby ended up in sweatpants and a Test Track T-shirt.

"Okay, that's the entrance," Willa said as they approached a line of potted evergreen trees. The trees had been cleverly placed to both block the entry ramp and screen the closed pavilion from view.

"Over here," Finn said, moving them into the planting to hide. He lowered his voice. "We'd better split up." He'd long since accepted that the other Keepers looked to him to have a plan. "That way if there's trouble, maybe one group can help the other. Or, at the very least, not all of us get caught at the same time."

"That doesn't sound great," Charlene said, the climbing rope carried over her left shoulder.

"Do you feel like climbing?" Finn asked.

She peered out at the round pavilion. "I should be able to get up those *X*s to that lip in the middle of the glass. It looks like I can get clear around the building."

"There's a sunroom terrace, over there," Philby said, pointing. "If you could lower the rope—"

"Yeah!" said Maybeck.

"You'll need to tie off both ends," Charlene told Maybeck. "I'll double it, like we do for climbing, so we can pull it down from the bottom after we leave."

"No sweat."

"Philby, Willa, and Maybeck will climb and meet you on the balcony," Finn said. "Philby, you or Maybeck could all-clear and go through the door and get it open.

"Amanda, Jess, and I will hang near the front doors. Once you guys are in, if there's no one watching the front door, one of you will come let us in. You guys will take the second floor, we'll take the ground level."

Charlene held up her mobile phone. She wore a

black baseball cap to help hide her blond hair. "I'll call if I spot trouble."

"Might be too risky," Finn said. "Too noisy. Let's stick with the flashlights. Three flashes is *clear*. One means we hang here and wait for you to come back."

"Okay," Charlene said, the strength in her voice belying her pretense of bravery. "But you'll need a view of the sunroom."

"I'm with you," Maybeck said. "I can give you a leg up, then I'll get around to the side and wait for your signal. I'll pass it on."

"That works," Finn said.

"Are you sure you're okay with this?" Jess asked Charlene somewhat timidly.

"She's fine," Maybeck said, resenting Jess's voicing her concern.

"Help me tie this on," Charlene said.

Amanda and Jess knotted the coil of rope into a figure eight that fit snugly on Charlene's shoulder. She double-checked the flashlight, cupping it to avoid giving their position away.

"One last thing," Finn said. "If it goes bad in there, we rendezvous in two stages. First, here, if it seems safe. Then, where we crossed over, over near Test Track. If some of us miss the first crossover, I'll leave the fob on the water fountain by the bathrooms. We'll need a better hiding place for it after the final crossover, so keep that in mind."

"We're good," an impatient Maybeck said. "Let's do this thing."

He and Charlene slipped out of the bushes and, ducking low, ran quickly toward the looming pavilion.

23

FINN KEPT AMANDA and Jess close, crouched and sneaking through the trees and shrubs, with Philby and Willa lagging slightly behind. The group gathered where they'd have a view of Maybeck, who had scurried off into the overgrowth after boosting Charlene up into the superstructure. Maybeck had taken a position where he could see around to the back of the pavilion.

The five watched in amazement as Charlene scrambled up the crossbeams like a monkey. She threw a knee over the rim that stuck off the curved surface like a shelf, and then rose to her feet, leaning against the wall and inching her way to her left. After a few minutes, she disappeared around the curve of the building.

"We wait for Maybeck's signal."

"Finn!" hissed Jess. She was pointing toward the pavilion. "On the ground."

"I don't know what you're pointing at."

Amanda shuddered. "Is that a—"

"Snake?" gasped Willa.

"Not just a snake," Philby answered. "A python. A giant python."

"That's Gigabyte," Finn said, finally seeing the thing. "It's from Honey, I Shrunk the Audience."

The python was over fifteen feet long and a foot in diameter, with a diamond-shaped, oversized head the size of a large pumpkin. He was patrolling through the grass and the landscaping along the base of the pavilion. "What's he doing here?" Willa whispered. "We aren't anywhere near Honey, I Shrunk the Audience."

"He's with *them*," Finn answered.

"And if he's guarding Wonders," Philby said, "then it's pretty obvious who's inside."

"Seriously?" Willa sounded terrified.

"An Overtaker for sure," said Philby. "Interesting that the characters come alive here the same as in MK and AK. If we thought it was limited to just—"

"Spare us the Nutty Professor routine," Willa said, uncharacteristically harshly. "If the Overtakers are inside, then Charlene's in trouble, big-time."

"We should have set up a system to do this in reverse," Finn said, withdrawing his flashlight and preparing to signal Maybeck.

Philby slapped his hand over the front of Finn's light, stopping him.

"Wait a second!" he hissed. "Think this through. If you signal Maybeck, and he signals back, guess who'll see it?" He stared off into the general direction of where they'd last seen Gigabyte.

"Note to self," Willa said. "Where's the snake now?"

"I was watching him," Jess said. "But I lost him by that column."

"What if he's headed here?" Willa said, speaking what they were all thinking. "Don't snakes have amazing noses?"

"They do have an olfactory ability," Philby said. "They don't have noses. But yes, they can smell things a long, long ways away."

"Like nervous girls?" Willa said.

"We have to warn Charlene," Finn said.

"Not with the flashlight," Philby cautioned. "That'll backfire."

Willa quickly tried to reach Charlene by phone. She shook her head. "Must have turned it off when we nixed it."

Finn felt responsible for that decision. He toed a rock free of the dirt at their feet and picked it up. "What if we could distract the snake? Turn him around so he doesn't see our flashlights?"

"I think it may be too late for that," Amanda said. She was looking off toward Maybeck, and when Finn looked in that direction he saw what she had seen: a small white light flashing three times, pausing, and flashing the same signal again. Maybeck was relaying Charlene's signal.

"She thinks everything's okay," Finn gasped.

"And maybe it is," Philby said. "Maybe it isn't the Overtakers inside, but Wayne. Maybe the snake is on his own, patrolling Wonders *for* the Overtakers, sure, but not *with* them."

"That would be a lucky break," Finn said.

"Only one way to test it," Philby pointed out.

Finn nodded. He extended the flashlight through the wall of leaves and pushed its button once, signaling: *danger.*

24

THE AREA OF THE BUSHES where they'd seen Maybeck's flashlight remained dark. But from the grass there appeared a silver gray flash of a different sort: snakeskin. As Philby had predicted, Gigabyte had seen the signal and had taken off in Maybeck's direction to determine its source.

"This is our shot," Finn said. "Maybeck just bought us the front door. We can't wait for Charlene."

"Are you *nuts*?" Willa said.

"We go now!" Finn said. He reached out, took Amanda by the hand, and led her out of the shrubbery, somehow knowing that the others would follow—that Jess would stay with Amanda, and Philby would join him; Willa wasn't going to remain in the bushes alone.

Their DHIs sprinted across the lawn, jumped a rail, and hurried up the ramp leading to the pavilion's front door. All of them were panting, and Philby bent over to catch his breath.

"Give me two seconds," Finn said, closing his eyes and attempting to settle himself into all-clear. But it required a profound depth of concentration, mixed with a surrender and the subsequent removal of any fear. Standing in the dark, in front of an enormous abandoned pavilion with a fifteen-foot python somewhere out there, he found it difficult to picture the pinprick of light in the sea of darkness inside his eyelids.

"How do we know it isn't coming this way?" Willa asked.

"Shh!" Philby understood the challenges of all-clear.

"How do we know there isn't something, someone, much worse inside?"

Amanda tapped Willa on the shoulder and pointed to Jess who, standing alongside Finn, had her eyes squeezed shut.

"I know that look: she's picking up on something," Amanda whispered so softly that not even Philby could hear her.

In the gloomy darkness, Jess's right hand reached for her back pocket and pulled out a small spiral notebook, her eyes still pinched shut. Her left hand found a mechanical pencil in her front pocket and, as she slowly came out of her trance, began to sketch.

Finn passed through the glass of the pavilion's front door and turned to face them. He could be seen taking a deep breath. He tried to push the door's panic bar, to open it, but his hand slid right through the glass barrier, and he pulled it back inside. He shook his arms.

"It's coming back," Willa announced, pulling Philby and the others down to a crouch.

Philby peered out to see the silver python slithering toward them at a high speed. "Stay down," he said.

Finn tried a second time, and his glowing arms went right out the door. The third time was the trick: the door opened.

The others slipped inside and Philby quietly pulled the door closed. Willa backed her way through the door, never taking her eyes off Gigabyte.

"Look!" she said pointing. "Where's he going?"

The python reached the path and headed off, his body maintaining a giant *S*-shape yet still propelling himself forward, moving toward the center of the park *away* from the pavilion.

"Reinforcements. If we could follow him—"

"He might lead us to the Overtakers," Philby concluded for Finn.

"And maybe Wayne."

"You can't be serious!" Willa complained.

"It's too late," Philby said. "He's too fast. The only way we'd be able to follow him is at an all-out run, and he'd spot us."

Jess gasped and they all looked at her and her pencil that had stopped in the midst of making the sketch.

"What is it?" Amanda asked.

"It's me. . . ." Jess answered. "They're coming for me."

For a moment Finn couldn't think. His mind, free of all thought only seconds before, was bombarded with reality—the hardest part of going all-clear. It was like being jostled awake from the deepest sleep ever. Like waking up in the middle of a class only to realize the teacher has just called your name. He shook his head. His hands were doing the tingling thing, and his feet felt as if he were walking on a bed of a thousand needles.

"Where?" he managed to say.

"The image stopped," Jess said, shrugging her shoulders. "The minute I realized it was me, the image stopped."

"We've got to get her back," Willa said. "Cross her back over."

"We need her," Finn said, without thinking. He looked at her, knowing the kind of pressure they were putting onto her, but not seeing any choice. They had come a long way to reach this moment. "It's up to you." They were where they were because of Jess's original dream, because of her powers as a seer. He believed they needed her to search the pavilion, to confirm that they had the right place. "No one will hold it against you if you go. It's probably the smart thing to do."

"They will come from my left side. Two of them. A

man with a red beard and a green tunic, and a boy much like him wearing blue. I know that sounds ridiculous, but. . . ."

"Trust me," Finn said. "Everything we do is ridiculous. No one would believe half of what we've seen."

"Vikings," Philby whispered. "Norway. There's a father-and-son display. It's just about as she has described."

"What about . . . cavemen?" Jess asked. "I know that also sounds stupid but—"

"Nothing is stupid," Finn said. "You know that! Not here. Philby? Cavemen?"

"Spaceship Earth. Another father-and-son team. In the scene, the two are looking at pictographs on cave walls. The guests see them from behind, never see their faces."

"They're part of this too," Jess declared.

"Overtakers," Willa and Finn said in unison.

"How do we protect her?" Amanda said anxiously.

"We know what to expect now," Finn said. "Or *who* to expect."

"Keep them away from me, and I'm safe," Jess said.

"We don't know that what she just saw will happen tonight," Professor Philby pointed out, raising his index finger perfunctorily. "The future is longer than just the next few minutes."

"But what she saw *could* also happen tonight," a troubled Amanda said.

"If we stopped talking and started looking for Wayne," Finn said, "tonight would be over a lot sooner."

Maybeck appeared at the top of the stairs and stopped abruptly. "I thought . . ." he whispered, seeing them already inside.

"Change of plans," Finn hissed back.

Maybeck made a series of hand signals that apparently Finn was supposed to understand. He didn't.

"He and Charlene will stay upstairs," Philby translated. "No sign of the Overtakers. Should we split up Jess and Amanda?"

"You got all that," Finn asked, bewildered, "from him pumping his fists a couple times?"

"No. That last part was me. What about Jess upstairs, Amanda with us? If anyone comes after Jess, maybe we can act as decoys, buying Charlene time to get Jess out of here."

"Works for me," Finn said. "Jess?"

"Sure. Why not?" She gave a fleeting glance in the direction of Amanda and hurried up the stairs. Finn, Willa, Philby, and Amanda crept forward and moved past groupings of gray machines with bold white numbers on their fronts. Philby explained, a little heavy-handedly, that Wonders had been known for its interactive stations long before *interactive* was even a word. There were all sorts of games and demonstrations surrounding them that involved participation, but their plugs were pulled and they were stacked randomly together—it looked more like a technology graveyard than a Disney attraction.

A doorway opened into a vast space beneath a dome.

"This reminds me of The Land," Willa said. "Only different."

A gray glow from the path lighting outside leaked through the skylights, playing on the contents like moonlight. At the center of the circular space was a theater; there were structures made to look like tents, and seats and tables; the whole pavilion was deserted in a way that suggested that the guests had fled in a hurry.

"Creepy," Willa said.

"Times ten," Amanda said.

There was a sign for BODY WARS on the opposite wall in front of a queue with stanchions and chain.

"It was originally all about stuff to do with health," Philby said. "Body Wars, Cranium Command, The Making of Me. Some of it was really gross."

"A lot of places to hide a person," Finn said.

"And totally empty," Philby said. "It's pretty weird to see an entire pavilion totally empty."

"You think?" Willa snapped sarcastically.

A whistle caught their attention. Finn looked behind them to the second floor—an enclosed sunroom that ran fully around the building. Maybeck was waving for them to come up.

Philby gestured in hand signals. Maybeck gestured back.

"Did I miss a class or something?" Finn asked.

"He wants us all up there," Philby said. "There's something to see."

"That's not so smart," Finn said immediately. "We're more effective in two groups. As a single group we're vulnerable."

Philby nodded. He flashed Maybeck some hand signals, and Maybeck turned from the railing and disappeared.

"Okay, Maybeck's coming down," Philby said. "You and Amanda will go up to Charlene and Jess."

Finn remained skeptical that Philby could have gotten that from Maybeck's few quick gestures, but a moment later Maybeck appeared.

"You're not going to believe it," Maybeck said.

"Keep an eye out," Finn said. "All phones on vibrate. Call me if there's trouble." He and Amanda took off.

Finn and Amanda hurried back to the main doors

and were halfway up the stairs when Finn tripped. He fell flat into the stone stairs and struggled to stand back up, desperate not to look too much like an uncoordinated dork. But Amanda crawled up his back and lay down on top of him, holding him down, squeezing the breath out of him, before sliding off to his side, her left arm still around him. "Outside!" she whispered.

The exterior wall was glass. Finn edged his eye over the edge of the staircase and spotted what Amanda had seen: the giant gray python, squirming toward the pavilion, with four shapes following close behind. Two adults, two children, judging by their size.

"Vikings and cave . . . people," Finn said. He rolled over and quickly texted all the others.

MAYDAY!

Finn was lying face-to-face with Amanda, so close that he could smell a flowery sweetness. Her hand had seemed to burn his back where she'd touched him.

Philby, Maybeck, and Willa appeared, moving toward the front door.

"Pssst!" Finn caught Philby's attention and tried his best to hand-signal him to crouch and hurry to join them. He then took Amanda's hand and, bending low, the two raced for the top of the stairs.

They ran down a hall and into a room where a real-life fabric circus tent had been erected inside the reception area. Beyond the circus tent, Charlene was waving them ahead.

As Finn reached Charlene and Jess, the other three were fast on his heels. Finn stepped into what turned out to be a conference room with a long oval table surrounded by a dozen or more comfortable chairs. But it wasn't the chairs or the table that caught his eye. It was the walls. They'd been painted with carousel horses from *Mary Poppins*, so he felt as if he were at the very center of a carousel, looking out.

"Oh my gosh," he said. "This is it."

He immediately identified the panel and chair that Jess had sketched in her diary. The resemblance was uncanny. She'd captured it perfectly.

"But no code on the wall," Jess pointed out. "Or if it's there, we can't see it."

"Maybe it's invisible ink or it needs a special light or something in order to be seen," Philby said.

"And no Wayne," Charlene said.

"We're out-a here, people," Maybeck said as he arrived. "Those four aren't sightseeing."

Finn said, "We'll go down Charlene's rope, as soon as we're certain those four are inside."

"What four?" Charlene asked.

"We'll explain later," Finn said.

"We have visitors," said Amanda. "Two sets of fathers and sons."

"And don't forget the snake," said Willa.

"I'll stand watch," Maybeck offered. "The moment they enter the building, we go over the side."

"What about the snake?" Willa asked in a dry rasp.

"I can deal with the snake," Finn said. If he could maintain himself fully crossed over in all-clear, the snake would have nothing to attack.

If, he thought.

"Follow me!" Charlene said, leading them through a jumbled room where there were cloud figures on the wall.

Jess stopped as if she'd hit a wall of glass.

Finn grabbed her.

She said, "I know this place. I've seen those shapes." She pointed to a hot-air balloon and a spaceship—small plaster reliefs hanging on the wall about fifteen feet above the floor.

"We've got to go," Finn said, pulling her after him. They entered a spacious patio enclosed in walls of glass that met overhead like a greenhouse. One of the windows was open and Finn spotted Charlene's rope looped over a pipe and doubled, dropping down to the ground.

"Philby first. Then Jess, then Amanda."

No one argued with him. When Maybeck appeared, frantic and excited, Philby hooked the rope in his feet and lowered himself. Jess went next. They went quickly, in an orderly fashion, and Finn thought back to Wayne telling him that some people were born to lead and that he was one of those people. He hadn't believed it at the time, but he was slowly coming around.

"I'm last," Charlene told him, when only the two of them remained. "I'll take the rope out so they won't even know we were here."

"How can you do that?" Finn asked.

"Same as in climbing. I'll loop the rope over a bar up top. We'll climb on a double rope and then pulling it out is a matter of just tugging one end of it."

"But no funny business," Finn said.

"None," she said.

A moment later they were all in the shrubs at the base of the pavilion. Willa helped Charlene coil the rope.

Then, from their left, a thick shape emerged, worming across the grass—*Gigabyte*. Finn tried his own sign language. He held up six fingers and then motioned toward the thick vegetation twenty yards across the open grass. Philby nodded to signal that he had understood. Maybeck pointed back at Finn and shrugged as if to say, *What about you?*

Finn thumbed his own chest and then pointed at the fat gray python, its tongue slurping into the air, searching for a scent. Finn banged his fists together.

At that instant, Gigabyte turned toward the Kingdom Keepers.

"Now!" Finn said.

25

FROM THE MOMENT FINN took off running, he was afraid. He hated snakes. Any kind of snake gave him the weebies. A python as thick around as a basketball and nearly twenty feet long was the stuff of his worst nightmares—he'd never even had a dream that bad. Somewhere inside him he understood how stupid he'd been to offer to play the decoy. Somewhere in him he understood how fast a snake that big could travel across level ground and how if there were any small piece of him not fully crossed-over when the snake caught up to him—for Gigabyte would catch up to him no matter how fast he ran—that he would be caught, crushed, and consumed. But he ran straight at the snake, as fast as his legs would carry him.

At first, Gigabyte didn't see him, concentrating on the group of six others. The snake moved over the grass in an almost lazy motion, as if filled with such confidence that catching the kids was never in question, that instead it was only a matter of when, and how many, and what to do with them once they were caught. Such confidence terrified Finn; it was the confidence of a predator, a killer.

Despite his proximity to the disgustingly large reptile, the beast didn't turn in his direction. "Hey!" Finn shouted, trying to win his attention.

The huge head pivoted toward Finn, one yellow eye taking him in, but the giant tube of his body kept sliding ahead, aimed now at a precise point directly ahead of Charlene, who had just overtaken Philby in the footrace to reach the jungle's edge.

It took Finn a second to realize what was happening: the snake wasn't interested in having one kid for dinner when the opportunity for six remained only a few yards in front of him.

"Scatter!" Finn shouted. With that, he briefly closed his eyes and summoned the locomotive's light in the darkness—the pinprick of purity that would allow him to fully cross over to all-clear. Shutting his eyes also had the advantage of eliminating the snake from his view, and thereby removing it from his thoughts and from an imagination that could easily picture him as an appetizer ahead of the main meal Gigabyte would make of the others. Not only did Finn think he was about to die, he thought he was also about to fail in his campaign to save his friends.

Finn opened his eyes to find himself within a few yards of the thing. Gigabyte, responding to the distraction, suddenly straightened out from the winding *S* that had been propelling him forward and bent into a giant *C*, with Finn at the center.

Out of the corner of his eye Finn saw the snake's tail recoil and come at him with blinding speed—like the tip of a cracked whip. Gigabyte had no interest in biting Finn, despite the open mouth and tickling tongue. He intended to knock Finn off his feet, wrap himself around the boy, choke the life out of him, and swallow him whole.

The snake's tail flew through Finn's legs, making no contact. Gigabyte, having expected to hit the boy, rolled off-balance. The snake recovered quickly and took aim at Finn once more as Finn's arms began to tingle and his physical sensations returned. He'd managed to hold the all-clear for a few precious seconds, but having a snake's tail whip through his projection proved more than Finn could bear. Every piece of him was sparking and prickling—he was substance again, half hologram, half human, the same as the others. The human aspect of his DHI would prove crushable—if Gigabyte got hold of him, Finn was going down.

The snake folded in half, reminding Finn of a jackknifing semitruck. Finn jumped over the body like a hurdler but caught his trailing foot and tumbled to the ground. The snake reversed course, jerking into a mirror image of itself—more of a *V* than a *C*, with Finn at the center; from Finn's right swung the huge head; from his left the pointed tail. The serpent was closing around Finn, who retained enough presence of mind to skid to a stop before those snapping jaws got hold of him. He'd seen a video in science class of a reticulated python catching and crushing a wharf rat; the snake had struck with lightning speed and snagged its prey in its mouth; it then ate the wiggling rat as it quickly coiled tightly into a death knot that hid all but the rat's desperately quivering tail, which soon went still.

The look in Gigabyte's eye as his head swept around told Finn that just such a strike was coming.

Finn turned—*trapped*—with the snake quickly closing around him. He shut his eyes and regained his focus. His arms lost their tingling.

A girl screamed.

* * *

To Finn's six friends, Gigabyte's head strike appeared to happen with the speed of a fighter jet. The massive head seemed to be feather light as it flew like a spear at Finn's body.

Amanda screamed.

The head pierced Finn's projection and drove right through the boy, once again making no contact. Once again, confusing the predator.

The snake lifted his head up into the sky, already twisting and turning its flashing tongue in search of the scent that connected to the piercing scream he had just heard.

Philby tugged hard on Amanda's arm and got her running. The planting was thick; it would not be easy going for such a large snake. He could take nothing like a straight line to reach them, but was forced instead to stitch his way through the dense undergrowth. Perhaps this explained the serpent's attraction to Finn, who was out in the open and looked like easy prey. If anything, the very size of the snake was an impediment. He was powerful and strong, yes, but his weight and mass slowed him and prevented him from traveling well in dense terrain.

Gigabyte launched himself in the direction of Amanda's scream, cutting a rut into the soft lawn, throwing mud and grass to either side.

* * *

Finn, who lost his brief state of all-clear the moment he heard Amanda scream, was struck in the back by the snake's departing tail and knocked six feet up in the air before sprawling onto the ground. Like a pendulum, the snake's tail swept back toward him, this time aimed for his head. Finn reached out to block the blow, but for reasons unknown to him, ended up clutching to the tail and holding on for dear life. This softened the blow and prevented another, but left Finn rushing along the grass at nearly thirty miles an hour, swished from side to side, and wondering how long he could hold on.

Gigabyte sensed the parasite holding on to him. The snake didn't give free rides. He turned his head just far enough to get a glimpse of the glowing boy clinging to his tail—but at the exact wrong moment.

The snake's head collided with a light blue steel-rail fence. It bent and popped through the railing's two center pipes which, as the snake turned, put him into a headlock, with his jaws stuck like a key in a lock.

Finn let go and took off running. The snake turned farther to catch sight of him, but in doing so further turned the key in the lock, preventing his own escape. He struggled briefly, writhing with the effort.

Finn ran, and ran hard.

Gigabyte, not able to pull free, went still. The snake dislocated his lower jaw, thrust his upper jaw forward and, as the mechanism came apart, pulled his head from the fence. He looked to the right, licking the air—the scent there was fading; to the left there was only a blur of light running away—no scent at all.

Finn heard a ferocious hiss charge the air from somewhere behind him. Farther and farther behind him, as it turned out.

He would soon try to describe that sound to others.

"Like it was . . . cursing," he would say.

Upon reaching the rendezvous, Finn demanded that Philby return the borrowed pants and shirt, something even Willa believed beyond the call of duty, given the somewhat desperate nature of their current situation. But Philby did not object and took off, returning a minute later in only his underwear, having left the clothes outside the door of the store. Again he was subjected to a volley of cackles and derisive snorting.

"Don't look now," he said, out of breath, "but we've got visitors."

Finn peered around the edge of the building and out toward the fountain.

"Did they see you?" he asked, over his shoulder.

"No, I don't think so."

"Who?" Charlene asked.

Philby answered, "It's the Vikings and the caveman and his boy."

"They're looking for us," Finn said in a whisper as he joined the others. "Must be." He glanced around for a place to hide the fob, somewhere they could find it when they next crossed over. The gardens and grounds were out—Cast Members worked on the landscaping every day of the week. The stainless-steel water fountain had no hiding places; Finn couldn't just leave the fob out in the open.

"We'd better think of somewhere fast," Charlene said, who had nominated herself as scout and was keeping one eye on the fountain. "They're getting closer."

"How can this be so difficult?" Finn asked.

But it was. Unlike the teepees in the Magic Kingdom, there was no obvious out-of-the-way spot in which to conceal the fob.

"It's going to have to be the bushes," Maybeck said. "Someplace any of us can get to. We're just going to have to trust that no one finds it."

"Hurry!" Charlene hissed.

Finn showed everyone where he was tucking the fob: nestled in beside the bricks that lined a raised garden of shrubs and flowers.

Maybeck produced a pen from his pocket and passed it to Finn. If any one of the kids held the fob as they crossed back over, the fob would travel with them. If Finn pushed the button with a pen, the pen would come along, but the fob would remain behind.

"Ready?" Finn asked.

Charlene abandoned her post and the Kingdom Keepers huddled together around Finn, alongside the raised garden bed.

He stabbed the button with the pen.

26

FOR THE NEXT DAY and a half the texts flew back and forth between the Kingdom Keepers. Finn used lunchtime to keep Amanda apprised of developments: no one had seen or heard from Wanda; Philby had buried himself in research, finding out everything he could about disappearing inks, and believing they should try to return to Wonders to try out his theories; Charlene was consumed with trying out for a dancing part in a school pageant.

"What about Maybeck?" Amanda asked Finn as they sat together in the lunchroom.

"He texted Philby to tell him to bring him the paper box this afternoon, after school. Said he figured something out."

"That sounds promising," Amanda said.

"What about Jess?" Finn asked.

"She's fine," Amanda answered dismissively, without a moment's thought.

"I'm just asking," he said.

"Who said you weren't?"

"As in: has she had any more . . . uh-oh."

Lousy Luowski was headed in their direction with a tray bearing only a dish of jiggling lime green Jell-O. Finn thought he had a pretty good idea what Luowski had in mind for the Jell-O.

"Hello, Greg," Amanda said in a disarmingly warm voice.

Her tone stopped Luowski in his tracks. The dish of Jell-O bumped against the lip of his tray and stopped.

"We've got some unfinished business," Luowski said. Mike Horton nodded at his side, like a translator.

"Greg," Amanda said softly, drawing him in. "Have you heard about the wind here at school?"

"That's a trick question," Mike Horton whispered too loudly into Luowski's ear. "Wind is invisible, in the first place."

"That's a trick question," Luowski said.

"Think hard, Mike," she said. "Science class about a month ago when Denny Fenner shoved Lois Long into the corner."

"And all the beakers went flying off. . . ." Horton stopped himself.

"And broke all over the floor," Amanda said.

Horton nodded, his skin going pale.

"What's going on?" Luowski asked, taking another determined step toward Finn.

"It wasn't pretty," Horton answered.

Luowski now had the dish of Jell-O in hand, but an arm's length from the top of Finn's head.

"What I've heard," Amanda said, fixed on Luowski unflinchingly, "is that the wind is actually like some kind of ghost that inhabits the school and helps defend the innocent."

At that moment, Luowski's hair lifted off his oily face, blowing straight back. His shirtsleeves fluttered and rippled. Horton's hair was caught by the wind as well, but not nearly in the same way. Luowski had to lean forward steeply just in order to remain standing.

"What . . . the . . . heck . . . is . . . happening?" The terror in his eyes conveyed Luowski's predicament. If he stood up straight he was going to be blown over backward, but the gale-force wind seemed confined to him, with only a tiny fraction spilling past behind him.

The green Jell-O cubes were no longer square, but stretched into trapezoids. Several of them skidded across the dish. One escaped, splatting onto Luowski's shirt.

"Stop it!" Luowski said to Finn, who just shrugged. "Stop it, you witch!" he said to Amanda.

"Me?" she gasped, backing her chair up as if afraid of it. "I don't think ghosts hear so good, Greg. I've heard you have to scream to get their attention. You have to scream an apology."

Whatever force held Luowski suddenly doubled.

He was leaning impossibly far forward, like a ski jumper, the soles of his running shoes fixed to the cafeteria's tile floor.

Some of the other students turned. Only a few seconds had passed since the wind had begun to blow.

Amanda had never stopped staring at Luowski, whose red face was now gripped in such terror that he looked like a big baby.

"I don't think they can hear you," Amanda said.

"I'm sorry! I'm *so-o-o-o-o* sorry!" Luowski crowed.

At that instant, the Jell-O flew off the dish and into Luowski's face and for a moment he wore a slimy green mask with only his eyelids popping through. Then the wind stopped all at once, as if a door had been shut, and the forward-leaning Luowski fell flat on his face, to the delight of most of the cafeteria.

There were cheers and applause.

Finn looked across the table to see Amanda's face filled with the light of mirth, her eyes sparkling, her smile a mile wide. She chortled and covered her laughing mouth with her hand, and for the first time looked away from Luowski and over at Finn, whose startled expression clearly caught her attention. He shook his head faintly side to side. She wiped the smile off her face, suddenly self-conscious.

"I think the school ghost has your number, Greg,"

she said, as she grabbed her tray and stood up. "I'd be careful of making threats if I were you."

The green-faced Luowski rolled over and looked up at Finn, about to say something when he thought better of it. Instead he turned his growl onto Horton, who had laughed himself to tears.

"Where are we meeting after school?" Amanda asked Finn calmly as they were returning the silverware and dishes off their trays.

"That was you," Finn mumbled. "You can direct it like that?" He'd seen Amanda use her power once before. There was no denying she was different.

"There are all sorts of things I can do that you don't know about, Finn."

"You can't just . . . do that in school."

"Of course I can," she said. "Who's going to believe *anyone* can do something like that? There will be a dozen explanations for what happened to Greg. None will involve me. Just wait and see."

They left the cafeteria, on their way back to their lockers.

"Do other Fairlies act so—"

"Bravely?" she said, interrupting.

"I was thinking more like . . . stupidly," he said.

"Ha, ha!"

"I'm serious. That was stupid."

"Greg Luowski was going to smear green Jell-O into your hair. The least you could do is thank me."

"You're right: thank you. But you should follow the same rules as the rest of us. You're a DHI now. You can't draw suspicion."

"I'm a DHI who's about to be sent back to Maryland to a halfway house full of Fairlies. I'm desperate, Finn."

"And how is misbehaving going to help your situation?"

"How's it going to hurt it?" she asked. "If I can do a little good before I leave, isn't that better than doing nothing at all?"

He knew he should have an answer for that. Even something trite would have been welcome. But a part of him understood that she was right: when it came to doing good, it was better to do something risky rather than nothing at all. He felt the same way about attempting to find Wayne.

"Where and when?" she asked, just before they split up off the stairs.

"Jelly's place right after school."

"Gotcha," she said, ascending the stairs effortlessly, as if a stiff wind blew at her back.

* * *

Maybeck lived above Crazy Glaze, his aunt Jelly's pottery shop. The shop's front room was crowded with shelves of pale, unfired clay vessels that customers painted and adorned with glazes and other treatments, while its back room contained more raw stock, a desk in the corner, and a small kiln. The two big kilns were out back, as were three motorized pottery wheels, and two manual ones; the whole back area was covered in a gray wash that spoke of years of use. Adjacent to the desk in the back room was a drafting table, and next to it a sewing machine and a light table, each pertaining to a particular hobby of Maybeck's multitalented guardian.

The heavyset woman, whose real name was Bess, had not been given her nickname as a result of her girth—substantial though it was—but on account of her own mispronunciation of the name Shelly as a child. Jelly had a choir girl's smile, kind eyes, and four chins. Her voice was low and husky, and when she looked at you it felt as if she could see things others could not—like a fortune-teller or priest.

With all the Kingdom Keepers assembled in the tight space, Jelly opened the kiln and carefully extricated a baking sheet containing a dozen chocolate chip cookies, which explained the incredible smell of the place. She moved some bricks and pulled out a second sheet of the oatmeal variety. Maybeck headed upstairs and returned with a box of cold milk and the after-school ceremony began. Once lips were properly licked free of remaining crumbs and the last drops of milk had slid down sugary throats, Jelly left them, shutting the door to the outer room to deal with her customers.

"So," Maybeck said, "I was doing an art project for school, this thing of layering colors, when something occurred to me, so I texted Philby. I suppose you know that or you wouldn't be here. The point being, I could be way wrong about all this, and I didn't mean to call a massive meeting or anything."

"No one forced us to be here," Willa said. "We wouldn't have come if we hadn't wanted to."

"Yeah, right. The thing is," Maybeck continued, "we all know how tricky *our friend* is. He's always doing stuff that has multiple meanings, multiple *layers*. That's what got me, I think: layers. Working with the colors. 'Cause the thing is, you layer yellow over red and you get orange, orange over yellow and you get yellow-orange. It's all about what's in front and what's behind."

"You kinda lost me there," Charlene said.

"It's the shapes on the box. They're like symbols or something. Curves. Lines."

"Code?" Philby said.

"Yeah, I think. In a way at least." Maybeck extended

his open palm and Philby produced the small paper box and handed it to him. Maybeck switched on the light box, which consisted of a sheet of white glass in front of a powerful, uniform white light, like the devices radiologists use to view X-rays.

"My theory," he said, continuing, "is that Wayne expected us to figure out what others would not: that what alone looked like symbols combined to something more."

"You mean, kind of like us?" Charlene said. "We make more sense as a group."

"We're capable of more," Philby added.

"Exponential," Jess added.

Finn realized this was something new—the DHIs talking about themselves as a group. It had always been there, lingering just below the surface—the idea that Wayne had intended them to act as a group, not as individuals, but this was the first he could remember anyone actually acknowledging it.

"The whole is greater than the sum of its parts," Finn said.

"Yeah, like that, I suppose," Maybeck said, "but all I'm interested in is layers." He held up the box. "See, on this side is a parenthesis—the left side. Turn the box around, and there's another parenthesis, also the left, like a stretched *C*."

"Matching," said Willa.

"You think they're both meant to be capital *C*s?" Philby asked Maybeck.

Maybeck didn't answer. He spun the paper cube to show a different face. "And this weird shape." He turned the box to show the opposite side. "And this one."

"I've looked through a dozen languages and a few hundred fonts: Cyrillic, Greek, Roman, of course," said Philby. "Those symbols aren't part of any modern alphabet. A few of those marks are pretty close to some accents used in modern languages, but I don't see where that gets us."

"Because it's Wayne," Maybeck said. "If I'm right, it's not about the individual symbols, but the way they combine."

He moved the paper box closer to the light table, the left parentheses facing the kids. For a moment the box caught the light and glowed like a lightbulb; it appeared to grow between Maybeck's fingers. Then, as he delivered it atop the light box's glass plate, the mark on the opposing face came into crisp focus. The kids pressed together in a tight huddle.

Charlene gasped.

"OMG!" said Willa.

"I thought so," said the ever modest Maybeck. "The left parenthesis joins the right parenthesis and together—"

"They form an *O*!" said Philby. "Our alphabet after all!"

Maybeck picked up the box, turned it, and replaced it. The letter was a backward *N*, but reversing the box formed the letter correctly. There was another, fainter, *V*, but it looked like something drawn and then erased. He rotated the box a third time. Each pair of images on the opposing sides of the cube's six faces combined to form a letter.

"Turn it around!" Willa said. "It's either a lowercase *b*, or a lower-, or uppercase, *P*."

"Then it's a *P*," Maybeck said, "because the *O* and *N* are both uppercase."

"Agreed," Philby said, already grabbing a shaping tool and drawing the letters into some soft clay on the table beside him: P N O.

"Initals?" said Amanda. "A what-do-you-call-it?"

"Abbreviation?" said Jess.

"No," said Amanda. "A . . ."

"*Piano*?" asked Charlene.

"Try again," said Maybeck. "A different order."

Philby wrote: N P O, then N O P.

Each of the kids was throwing out an idea of what the various letters stood for.

Philby moved the tool through the wet clay . . . O . . .

Before he'd reached the second letter Jess said quietly, "Open."

The shouting stopped. The kiln hummed, or maybe it was the light box or the overhead lights.

"Open," she said again. "O P N."

"Open," Maybeck repeated. "Of course."

"That is *so* Wayne," Willa said.

Maybeck carefully found the edge, sealed with a thin strip of tape. It took him a minute to locate a razor blade, but no one was going to suggest they hurry into this and tear the box in the process. At last, he ran the blade through the tape and the flap was loose. Two more incisions through the gaps, and all sides were free. Maybeck carefully unfolded the box.

"I've done this in math a hundred times," said Philby. "It forms a—"

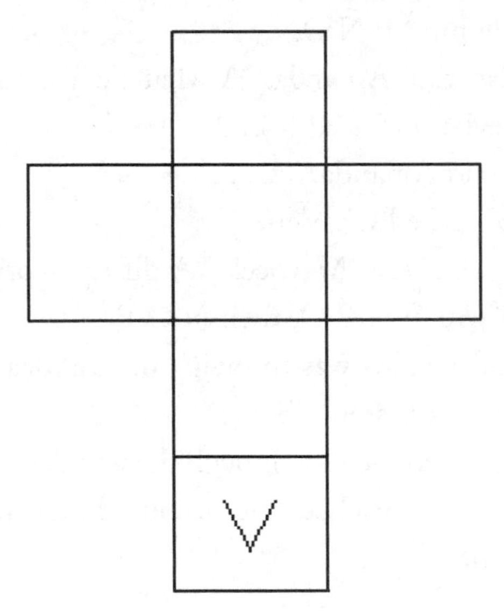

"It's a cross," said Amanda. Maybeck turned the box around in his palm to make it a proper cross. The *V* now pointed down, toward his wrist.

"That's not a *V*," said Finn. "It's a point."

Philby said, "It's a tip of a—"

"Sword," said Maybeck.

"Only boys would see that as a sword," said Charlene cynically. "It is so obviously a cross."

"It's a sword," Philby said, agreeing with Maybeck. "This is Wayne, don't forget."

"It's a cross. And in Epcot, that means France."

"And it was outside of France," Amanda said to Jess, "that you felt . . . you know . . . felt something the first time you crossed over."

Jess nodded timidly.

Willa said, "And France also means Notre Dame. The Hunchback—that's Disney."

"It's a sword," Maybeck repeated.

"And in Epcot," Philby said, mimicking her, "that's . . ." He squinted his eyes. "Norway. The Maelstrom ride—"

"I love that ride!" said Finn, immediately wishing he hadn't.

"—has a sword in it," Philby said, finishing his thought.

"*Impressions de France*," Willa said, "is a film in

Epcot's France. It shows the cathedral, as does an exhibit while you're waiting to get into the film. He's left us another clue or the answer there. Maybe he's being held in France."

"Maybe he's being held in Norway," Philby fired back.

"Maybe we split up and figure this out," said Finn.

"Divide and conquer," said Amanda. "Girls to France, boys to Norway."

"Tonight," said Maybeck.

"Nine o'clock," said Philby. "I can cross over and program the projectors. . . . I have to cross over to program them; there's no way past the firewalls from out here. I can't promise the system won't go down at midnight. I tried to reprogram that, but things got weird, and I'm not sure I did any good."

"That will give us about three hours," said Charlene. "Isn't that enough?"

Philby answered for the boys. "It depends on what we find."

27

BY NINE-FORTY THEY HAD ALL crossed over into Epcot. They arrived into the same location as before—near the public restrooms on the way to Test Track. This time Philby wore dark clothes, while Charlene arrived in the same cotton nightgown she wore so often, a victim of her single mother's lying down on Charlene's bed with her and both of them subsequently falling asleep.

Finn's DHI appeared, on his side with his legs tucked up against his chest, his hands flat under his head, in the same position in which he slept in his bed at home. He sat up and headed for the concrete block planter before even saying hello to anyone.

His hands dug around in the planter.

"Okay! Who's got it?" he said, trying to keep his voice calm.

The others looked at him blankly.

Jess said, "Got what?"

"The Return," Philby answered, understanding immediately. "The fob."

"Our way home," said Maybeck. "Without the fob, we're stuck here."

"The Syndrome," Charlene choked out.

"Seriously," Finn said. "This is no time for games. Who's got it?" He searched their faces in the dim light and knew immediately that it was not a practical joke.

"You've got to be kidding me," he said, desperately.

"Listen," Philby said. "It may not be stolen. It could have easily been found by a gardener who thought it had fallen out of someone's pocket when they were sitting on the wall."

"Lost and found," Charlene said.

"Exactly," said Philby.

"Oh, perfect," said Willa. "How are we supposed to find lost and found?"

"By looking for it," Finn answered. "We can't freak out. Stuff happens."

"Yeah, but it happens to us *all the time*," Willa said.

"That's part of it, I think," Finn said. "Part of being whatever it is we are."

"Kingdom Keepers," said Amanda. "Don't you guys get it? You think it's coincidence that we've all met? That Jess and I just happened to meet you? I don't think so. Wayne put you together for a reason. Each of you has a purpose, and together we have some bigger reason for being here."

"We get it," said Maybeck. "We just don't talk about it a lot."

"It's kind of freaky," said Charlene.

"Finn is right," Amanda said. "You—we—can get through this. We *have* to get through this. I have the ability to move things around. Finn can walk through doors. He and I will look for the fob. Once we get it back I'll go to France and Finn will go to Norway—how ridiculous does that sound?—and catch up with you."

"Sounds like a plan," Maybeck said. He rarely agreed with a plan, so Finn took this as a major endorsement. "Philby and I will head to Norway and look for the sword."

"Jess, Willa, and Charlie," Finn said, using Charlene's nickname, "will make for Paris and the possible connection between the box and a cross. You'll also make sure no one attacks Jess from her left."

"I think that threat is over," Jess said.

"No matter what," Finn injected, fiddling with his mobile phone, "we meet here before midnight. No matter where any of us are at eleven-forty-five, we head back here to return."

"We apparently can use our phones," Philby declared. "In case you're interested," he said to Finn, reading the screen, "lost and found is in a gift shop to the right of the entrance." He held up his phone. "I Googled it."

"I'm interested," said Finn. He reached out and grabbed Amanda's arm above the elbow. "You okay with this?"

"I'm following you," she said.

* * *

Willa voiced what Charlene and Jess were both thinking. "They didn't try to stick a boy with us."

"I was sure they would," Charlene said.

"It's the sword," Jess said. "Boys and swords. I'll bet if you asked Finn, he'd have rather gone after the sword than the lost and found."

"Stay down," Willa said. "No matter what, we can't be caught or get in trouble. The boys would fry us if that happened!"

The most dangerous moment lay ahead: crossing the fountain plaza. Their DHIs shimmered in the dark, like the face of a wristwatch losing its glow; they didn't throw light—they wouldn't be easily seen from any kind of distance, but within ten to twenty yards they were visible.

"We'll go one at a time," Willa instructed. "Charlene, you're the fastest, so you'll go first. If you're chased, don't lead whoever's following to France, so you'd better have a plan now for where you'll go."

"There are trees behind The Land," Charlene

said. “And on the other side of The Living Seas is a small forest. I can lose anybody in there.”

“We’ll meet at the Eiffel Tower in twenty minutes if we get separated,” Willa announced.

“Later,” Charlene said.

Crouching low, she raced out across the open expanse and into the trees across the way. She waved at them and then stepped deeper into the vegetation, disappearing.

Jess went next. She, too, was a fast runner and reached the trees apparently without causing any alarm. Her DHI sparkled in the shadows.

Willa waited, a tingle tickling her at the base of her neck. Something wasn’t right. She waited, looking both directions. It was a hum. Not an engine—not exactly—but a bike maybe, that sticky sound of rubber on concrete. To her left she saw them: a pair of Segway scooters, those two-wheeled motorized scooters that maintain perfect balance and are ridden standing up. Police used them in airports and malls. But it wasn’t policemen riding the two Segways; the riders were . . . crash-test dummies.

She squinted and blinked, believing she’d seen wrong. Despite everything she’d learned about the parks after dark she still couldn’t always accept what she saw.

The dummies were talking to each other, riding the

Segways side-by-side, their voices too faint to be heard at a distance, but voices nonetheless; there was no mistaking that sound.

The Segways followed the path curving around the World Showcase Lagoon and, a moment later, were gone.

Willa sprinted across the plaza and into the trees, making a mental note to ask Philby about the Segways. If crash-test dummies could get hold of a pair of the things, why couldn't the Kingdom Keepers manage to as well?

"Did you see that?" she asked the other two as she reached them, deep into the trees.

"What?" Charlene asked.

"No," said Jess.

"Ah . . . well . . . you probably wouldn't believe it anyway. Let's just say there are patrols out, and I'm not talking Disney Security."

"Overtakers?" whispered Charlene.

"That would be yes," Willa said. "On Segways, and moving fast."

"That's random," Willa said.

"Is it safe?" Jess said, clearly frightened.

"It's never safe for us," Willa informed her. "The thing to remember is we're nothing but projected light. I mean, that is, that's what we are when we're pure DHI, which is basically never."

"Unless you're Finn," Charlene said. "And Maybeck

once. And I've been practicing."

"If we could make ourselves pure projection—what Finn calls 'all-clear'—then there would be nothing to catch—like waving your finger through a flame, or one of those laser pointers." Willa sounded like Philby but with a high voice. "But the minute you let fear into it, which is basically all the time, then you're catchable."

"So let's get this over with," Jess declared.

They worked their way through the planting around and behind Canada and past some bathrooms to a spot where Willa motioned for them to stop and squat down behind a merchandise kiosk. The Eiffel Tower, shimmering with lights, rose to their right. The night air made it look so impossibly close.

"This is the worst," Willa whispered. "The only way over to France is across that bridge. Unless you feel like swimming?"

"No thanks," gushed Jess.

"We'll be totally exposed," Charlene said. "Totally out in the open."

"That's right."

"It turns at the island," Willa said. The bridge was supported by what amounted to a large rock at the middle. "We might be able to hide there, but I doubt it. The trouble is, you can see that bridge from just about anywhere in the World Showcase. Even from across the lagoon." She pointed to the two Segways moving past Japan: small, swift, silent shapes.

"Their backs are to us," Charlene said. "We could go for it."

"There are more," said Jess in a chilling voice. She rubbed her forehead as if fighting a headache.

"You feeling okay?" Charlene asked, with evident concern.

"Pictures in my head," Jess whispered. "It hasn't been like this before. Same thing last time. It must be this place."

"Or," Willa said, "maybe becoming a DHI did something to you. Maybe we should have thought about that."

"I think it has to do with getting older," Jess said. "Every week it's different now. Stronger."

"We don't want to lose you to some surprise attack."

"Don't worry about me," Jess said. "How do we get over the bridge?"

Charlene answered. "We don't."

The two looked at her intently.

"We go *under* it," she said.

* * *

At Spaceship Earth Finn and Amanda crossed to the west side of the plaza and then into a jungle planting, heading toward the entrance and the gift shop. They were both jumpy, alert for Overtakers.

"It's so weird when it's empty like this," Amanda said softly.

"Yes, it is. Same with the other parks. I thought I'd get used to it, but I don't. It freaks me out."

"Totally."

"There are Overtakers here. We saw them. Let's not forget Gigabyte."

"Oh, thanks. I really needed that image." Amanda crossed her arms and looked afraid.

"If we have to run, head for the parking lots. The projectors only work in the park itself. We'll turn invisible out there. Once we do, once we lose them, make your way back around and into these trees. On hands and knees if we have to. We'll meet in the middle, so circle toward the center. Circle again if you don't see me."

"The really creepy part," she said, "is that you say that all so calmly. Like I should expect to be chased. Like wandering around on my hands and knees in some Disney jungle, glowing and sparking like some kind of defective light, is normal."

"You kind of get used to it," he said.

"Which makes it all the weirder, believe me."

They'd traveled twenty yards or more. Finn held his

fingers to his lips and signaled her that they were looking at the back side of the gift shop.

He moved close to her and spoke incredibly softly. "I'm going to try to get through that back wall. If anyone shows up, or if I come running out of there, I may need you to do that wind thing of yours: to stop someone chasing me."

"No problem."

"You can do it just like that?"

"Same as with Greg," she said.

"And is there anything else you can do? Any other powers you're keeping from me that might be helpful?"

"I guess we'll find out," she said.

"What kind of answer is that?"

"The only one you're going to get."

* * *

Philby and Maybeck had sneaked along the west side of Epcot, past Test Track and Mexico to a place where they had a clean view of Norway's central building with its many sharply pointed roofs and barnlike wood construction.

"Inside," Philby said, "there's a Norwegian village—"

"And Maelstrom," Maybeck reminded him.

"Exactly."

"So what are we waiting for?" Maybeck asked.

"The Segways."

"What Segways?"

"The trouble with you is you don't pay attention. Two Segways passed in front of Germany about five minutes ago, heading counterclockwise."

"Toward us."

"Correct," Philby said.

"Those scooter things."

"Correct."

"So we hang."

"Until they pass. Yes. Then we'll stay close to the edge there, make our way into Norway and head straight for Maelstrom. That is, unless you have a better idea?"

"No need to be like that."

"Like what?"

"Like the way you're being."

"There's every need," Philby said. "You challenge everything I say, Maybeck."

"You're a nerd. That's what I'm supposed to do."

"Says who? Like there's a handbook or something?"

"Listen: you're the nerd and I'm the dude. What can I say?"

"I thought you're the one who doesn't like stereotyping."

"That's true."

"So?"

"So I could cut you some slack some of the time."

"Like now, for instance."

"Okay, I get it. What you don't understand, is how annoying it is to hang with a know-it-all."

"Then don't hang with me."

"I don't mean it that way: you're okay. It's just . . . annoying that you know so much."

"Pardon me for living."

"You wouldn't understand because you don't have to be around it."

"I happen to like to know stuff."

"I'm not knocking that."

"Of course you are."

"You make the rest of us look dumb . . . feel dumb."

"No way."

"I'm telling you," Maybeck said.

"I don't mean to do that," Philby said. "I get excited about knowing stuff. Maybe I take it too far."

"Maybe?" Maybeck snapped sarcastically.

"Message received," Philby said. "But you're no prince, either."

"Don't tell the ladies that."

"Ssh!" Philby spotted a pair of slender shadows on the path and at the same time heard a whining hum of

an electric motor. *The Segways!* He stretched out an arm, driving Maybeck into shadow with him. Both boys wore black—all that showed of their DHIs was a thin glow along their shoulders and legs. It looked like nothing more than the light that wavers from a lighted swimming pool at night; you would have to stare long and hard to make any sense of what you were seeing.

Maybeck gasped aloud as the Segways passed and he saw not people but crash-test dummies riding the scooters.

Philby went rigid and stayed absolutely still as the nearest Segway came to a gradual stop. The Segway spun in their direction and the dummy was looking right at them. He spoke in an eerily electronic, monotone, computer-generated voice like from a bad science fiction movie.

"Rover Two reporting audible anomaly, detected four degrees south by south-southwest from current position."

The second rover slowed, turned and returned to join the other. "Source of anomaly?" He had the *exact* same voice.

"Unknown. Presumed human."

"No visual. Do you copy?"

"Copy."

"Errant signal. Will file at conclusion of patrol."

"Copy."

The two rovers spun in unison and motored off past Mexico, growing ever smaller.

"That was . . . bizarre," Maybeck said.

"Overtakers."

"Ah . . . Duh! For as smart as you are, sometimes you can say the dumbest things."

"Test Track dummies."

"But they can *speak*," Maybeck said.

"I kind of noticed that. I suppose the term *dummies* is not quite fair. They're probably some kind of hybrid Animatronic, to be more exact. Robots built from leftover equipment like the kind of stuff I saw in the maintenance shed that time with Finn."

"You think Maleficent is building herself an army?" Maybeck said.

"Maybe Wayne found out about it. Maybe that's what got him in trouble. Except that I was with him when he disappeared, and I didn't see anything to do with any robots."

"But if there're Overtakers patrolling Epcot . . ." Maybeck said.

"There has to be a reason," Philby completed. "Yes, that's right."

"The sword," Maybeck said.

"Let's go."

* * *

With her incredible speed Charlene led the way, running from their hiding place in the shrubs to the junction of the bridge and the main path. Once there, she slipped over the low wall and skidded down on her bottom, grabbing onto one of the protruding rocks in the wall and keeping herself from plunging into the canal.

Next came Jess, so that Willa would be last. Jess bent over and ran hard, mimicking everything Charlene had done. She crawled over the wall and found Charlene's outstretched hand awaiting her.

"Way to go!" Charlene said in a hoarse whisper. They waited. One minute. Two.

"What's taking her so long?" Charlene said. She started back up the face of the bridge, but Jess stopped her.

"If she isn't here," Jess said, "there's a reason."

A moment later Willa vaulted the wall, and caught up to the two girls.

"The dummies stopped over by Norway. I couldn't see what was going on, but because Philby and Maybeck are over there. . . ."

"You think they're okay?" Charlene asked.

"The dummies stayed there for a minute and then moved on. I assume they're all right."

"Okay, then," Charlene said. "Have both of you

done uneven parallel bars?"

"No," said Jess. "But I played on the bar on the playground when I was little."

"Could you hold yourself up?"

"Yes."

"That's all you need to do. Willa?"

"I'll do okay," Willa said.

"Hand over hand," Charlene advised. "Keep your feet pressed against the bar so you're hanging with your back to the water. We can't be dangling our legs or they might see us."

"Who goes first?" Jess asked. When neither girl answered, she said, "I will."

She clambered over the rocks, surprising the other two with her agility and flexibility, and found her way to the cluster of metal pipes and plastic tubes connected to the underside of the bridge. She reached up, hooked her fingers around the biggest pipe, and pulled herself up, hanging from it like an opossum from a tree limb. She inched her way backward, wrenching her neck around so she could see.

"It's not so bad," she whispered to the others. After a minute or two she reached the rock island that supported the turn in the bridge. She let herself down, found the same pipe continuing on the next section, and reached the far side.

"You're next," Charlene told Willa as she waved to Jess and gave her a thumbs-up.

Willa said, "I'm not the most coordinated person, you know?"

"You'll do fine. Don't look down. Just keep moving. You might want to go feet first."

"Okay."

Willa inched around on the rocks tentatively and grabbed hold of the pipe. She tested it by hanging from it, then gripped it again and swung her legs up so that her legs faced the island, and looked once over her shoulder at Charlene, her expression desperate and filled with concern. Charlene offered her a bright expression and hoped for the best.

Willa worked herself out over the dark water, moving slowly, but with increasing confidence.

"Psst!" It was Jess from the opposite shore. She was pointing wildly up the canal away from the lake.

Charlene held her palm out like a traffic cop to stop Willa. Willa obeyed.

A small motorboat pulling a single barge was headed toward the lake. The barge had some gear on it—anchors or something. It was probably part of the support crew for the IllumiNations fireworks show. No matter: there was no way Willa could make it over to the island in time without being seen. If she remained perfectly still, the boat driver might not see her as he passed beneath her.

Charlene hand-signaled Willa to stay put. Willa nodded her agreement, but Charlene knew it couldn't be easy, since she was holding all her weight by only a few fingers and using her leg strength to clamp her feet to the pipe. Charlene gestured with her chin for Willa to flatten herself so she wouldn't hang down so far. Willa nodded, lengthened her hold, and pulled herself up closer to the pipe.

Willa struggled to hold on, arching her back, straightening her legs. And then it happened: she fell. Her feet slipped off the pipe, swinging down. The momentum proved too much for her tired hands. She lost her grip, letting go of the pipe, falling feet first, and dropped. Charlene expected a splash, but amazingly, Willa landed on the barge and despite her claim of not being athletic, she hit with the grace of a gymnast—her toes, ankles, knees absorbing the shock so that she arrived on the deck of the barge with only the most minimal sound, a small thud, which might have been nothing more than a wave lapping against the side of the vessel, and might have been lessened too by her being in her DHI state. The pilot didn't turn around or react in any way.

A terrified Willa met eyes with Charlene, already

scurrying across the deck of the barge and looking for a hiding place. Charlene had the presence of mind to point toward France and Willa nodded. They would meet up there if at all possible.

Willa and the barge motored out into the lake, the darkness soon masking them. The sound of the boat motor faded. Charlene scampered across the pipe like a monkey and reached Jess.

"What do we do?" Jess said.

"What we came to do," Charlene answered. "We don't have a choice."

"How do you people *do* this?" Jess said, her voice straining to confine her emotions.

"You'll get used to it," Charlene said. "After a while, you actually kind of crave it."

* * *

Finn walked calmly and steadily across the short distance to the back wall of the gift shop. He forgot about Amanda, he forgot about Wayne; he pictured the light of the train in the tunnel, wheatgrass blowing in the wind, a sailboat on the water, all things tranquil and gentle.

His hands and feet tingled, the sensation spreading up and down to meet somewhere in the center of his chest, near his heart, from where he felt a wonderfully peaceful swell of satisfaction and pleasure.

He walked straight through the cinder block wall, through a desk and a chair, arriving in an office space at the back of the gift shop. The shelves were neatly stocked with boxes and plastic bags crammed with items to replace all those sold out front. There was a computer terminal on the desk, a stapler, a phone. A Disney picture calendar hung on the wall alongside several cartoons that had been cut from the newspaper and a newspaper column titled "No Glass Slippers for This Little Princess." Post-its hung from everywhere like ornaments from a Christmas tree. Along the wall by the door was a steel cabinet taller than Finn divided in half by a big door on the left and two smaller doors on the right, the lowest of which bore the title: LOST AND FOUND.

Finn proudly approached the locker and tried the lever: locked. He jiggled it several times to no avail. Next, he tried the desk's center drawer, hoping for the key to unlock the lost and found: locked. In fact, every desk drawer was locked. He searched for a nail or hook where the keys might have been hung or hidden: nothing.

He knew he could reach through the metal locker door, but to do so he would have to be in all-clear, while to touch and pick up the fob he would have to be out of his all-clear state. He couldn't even imagine the pain of losing his all-clear state while his arm was divided by a piece of steel. Besides which, the fob had not crossed over with him—it would remain fully material whether in his hand or not. Only items the DHIs held in their hands or carried in a pocket when they went to sleep achieved the DHI state; the locker door would need to be opened so Finn could remove the fob.

But to make sure he had the right place, he kneeled on the floor, settled himself, and stuck his head through the door and into the locker. His DHI's glow shone enough light for him to see several cell phones and cameras, a sweatshirt—and the small black fob. The Return. He backed out of the locker before his own frustration removed his all-clear state and the metal bit into his neck.

So close, he thought, wondering if there wasn't something to be done. How could he just leave it there? He tried another search of the place, including sticking his face through the top of the desk—like looking into a pool from the edge—and he spotted a set of keys he was certain would open the locker.

But there was nothing to be done about it. Just as there was no way into the locker, there was no way in to the desk. The only way to retrieve the fob was to do so while the locker was unlocked and open. During business hours, when Epcot was operating.

He calmed himself, walked through the wall and back outside and caught up with Amanda.

"We're in trouble," he told her. "We can't cross back over until the park opens."

"But that's hours away," she said. "And doesn't that mean—?" She stopped herself because Finn was already nodding.

"The Syndrome," he said. "Every one of us will be stuck in the Syndrome."

28

PHILBY WHISPERED TO MAYBECK. "I don't like this. Reminds me of Small World."

"I hear you," returned Maybeck in an equally soft voice.

They were inside the doors of Maelstrom, walking quietly through the empty waiting-line area, approaching the attraction's loading dock. The main lights had been turned off. There was no music. As they arrived at the loading area, where guests would board the boats, the enormous painted mural facing them was barely lit, so that only the most brightly colored paint jumped out at them: a red-and-white striped sail, the top half of the sun, a village of white buildings.

"How do you spell *creepy*?" Maybeck asked.

A boat awaited them, the water gurgling around it.

"Why do I not want to get into that boat?" Philby said.

"It wouldn't have anything to do with the Norwegian and his son who just happened into Wonders, would it?"

"And the axe he was carrying?" Philby said.

"I didn't see that."

"I didn't mention it to any of the others, because I don't think they saw it either, but oh, yes: the redhead was carrying a very large axe."

"You're so comforting."

"I try."

"Well, try a little less, would you?" Maybeck said.

"Get in the boat," Philby advised. "I'll turn on the ride," he said, pointing to a control console, "and jump in as it's moving."

"And if you happen not to make it and I end up in there alone?"

"The sword," Philby said.

"You'd better not chicken out and leave me to do this alone."

"Don't sweat it. I'll make it to the boat in time."

Maybeck climbed into the second row. Philby hit the START button on the console and ran to the edge and, with plenty of time to spare, climbed in alongside Maybeck.

"Okay, we've got problems," Philby said, practically before he had sat down. He pointed to a curving bow of a boat that stuck out of the mural; it was wooden and three-dimensional.

"Yeah? So?" Maybeck said.

"That's where the dude and his son are supposed to be."

The front of the display boat was empty.

"Meaning?"

"They could be anywhere."

"An axe," Maybeck stated.

"True story."

"In here somewhere?"

"Could be."

"Why can't we be normal kids?" Maybeck asked.

"I think we have Wayne to thank for that. Wayne and our parents who wanted the college funds."

"College funds don't do you any good if you aren't alive to go to college."

"True story."

The boat began to climb. Into the dark. Into the sound of rushing water and the pounding of their own hearts in their ears.

* * *

"But what if she's in trouble?" Jess demanded.

"Then she'll get out of it, or she'll call or text," Charlene answered. The two were hunkered down where the bridge abutted the path, only a matter of thirty yards from the entrance to France. Street lamps cast a soft light.

Charlene led her to their right, along a retaining wall where a bicycle and canoe were fixed to the wall to simulate the towpath along the river Seine. Reaching the end of this retaining wall, they climbed over and into some well-manicured shrubs, and higher up, to just behind a bench, overlooking the plaza in front of France.

"But . . ."

"Our job is to get in there and find out if there's a connection to Wayne. Willa is smart. She'll think of something. If she needs us, we'll hear from her. I'll go first. You wait until I signal you. Okay?"

Jess clung to the rock wall, looking timid and afraid.

"Jess, we're good at this. You have to trust me, the same way we all trust your dreams. We wouldn't be here if it weren't for you. All this, everything we're doing is because of you, because Wayne picked you somehow, and don't ask me to explain it, because I can't. None of this makes any sense out there in what everyone calls the 'real world,' but this world is just as real, believe me. And it's the world we're in right now, so you've got to trust me."

"It's just so . . . different," Jess said, looking at her own hand glowing.

"I know what that's like. I remember what it was like the first few times. I thought it was some kind of dream. If it wasn't for the others, I'd still think it's a dream. But it isn't. We're here and we've got stuff to do, and I need you to trust me. Willa's going to be okay, and if she isn't we'll help her. It's just the way it is."

Jess nodded, still mesmerized by her illuminated hand. "I'll bet you're a good cheerleader."

"Sit tight and wait for my signal."

Charlene sprang into action. Up and over and past the bench, looking this way and that, stitching her way through the tall, mature trees along the embankment. She faced the Tuileries Gardens as she crossed and found a hiding place tucked into a storefront.

She waved and Jess followed, repeating her steps nearly exactly, amazed how it suddenly felt as if they'd crossed the Atlantic and stepped into a foreign country. The Parisian buildings were realistic and lovely, with tall windows and curving copper roofs. There were shops and cafés with little tables outside, incredible fountains, bright awnings, gas lamps, and street signs. The flowers and landscaping were all neatly manicured and perfect, the air heavy with perfume.

"It's . . . amazing."

"Yes," Charlene said. "But hold the applause. We need to find the Notre Dame exhibit."

"The *Impressions* movie."

"Yes."

"The main pavilion would be the next street over, wouldn't it?" Jess asked.

"Must be."

The girls kept to the front of the buildings and worked their way around to the entrance to a second, more elaborate courtyard. This, too, had gardens and gas lamps, shops and fountains. The plaza ended at a formidable structure behind which rose the needle of the top of the Eiffel Tower.

Just then, Jess heard the scuff of footsteps and pulled Charlene down with her, behind a large trash can and some potted plants.

A pair of court jesters appeared, clownlike in their colorful costumes and facepaint. They danced and leaped up on benches beneath a row of trees, with comical movements.

But Charlene recognized them for what they were. "Overtakers," she whispered into Jess's ear. She motioned for Jess to stay still. The two jesters were unpredictable, turning this way one moment and that way the next. Suddenly one of them, with powdered sugar all over his lips, approached the trash can behind which they were hiding. He crunched up a piece of paper and threw it away. If Charlene had reached out, she could have touched him.

"Pardon!" he called out to the other in French.

"Oui!" answered the other.

"T'entends un ronronnement?"

Charlene looked at Jess with a puzzled face. Jess leaned in so close that her lips touched Charlene's ear. "'Do you hear a hum?'" she translated.

"Non!"

"Viens ici."

"'Come here,'" Jess whispered.

The other jester bounded over, still playful and childlike in his movement.

Charlene held her breath and tried to calm herself, knowing the closer she got to all-clear, the less of a hum her DHI would emit.

The second jester, unable to leave his character, held his hand to his ear in a silly way, overemphasizing the effort.

"Aha! Je l'entends!"

"'I hear it!'"

"Qu'est-ce que t'en penses?"

"'What do you think it is?'"

"Je pense qu'il y a quelque chose qui ronronne!"

"'I think there's something humming!'"

"Mais qu'est-ce qu'il y a qui pourrait ronronner ici? Je ne l'ai jamais entendu avant. Et toi?"

"'But what could be humming here? I've never heard it before. Have you?'"

"Moi non plus. C'est un des fluos, peut-être? Comment pourrais-je savoir?"

"'Me neither. Maybe it's one of the fluorescent lights? How should I know?'"

Charlene nodded, appreciating the translation. Then she shook her head and made her fingers walk, indicating they had to move.

The jesters, only a few yards away, were going to find them. She felt certain of it. At the same time, she felt her hands and feet tingle, and the same odd sensation pass all the way through her until warming the center of her chest, just below her ribs.

All-clear, she realized, having heard Finn describe it so many times. She motioned for Jess to stay down, as close to the trash can as possible.

Then she stood up, looked right at the two jesters and said, "Looking for me?" There was no sense reciting DHI lines as she might have had they been Security guards or Cast Members; these two were Overtakers, patrolling for only one reason: to find and capture Kingdom Keepers.

As she moved toward them, the jesters lunged for her—*and ran right through her*. They fell to the path and turned their faces back toward her, clearly jolted by the experience.

Charlene, glowing more brightly with the thrill of having achieved all-clear, ran off, leading the two away from Jess's hiding place, where she was crouched behind the trash can. She vaulted over a bench, just as she ran hurdles for the track team, and heard one of the jesters crash into the bench behind her. She leaped up onto the edge of the fountain and across the water, landing a foot on the retaining wall, springing off it, and ducking under a tree.

She heard a splash—the second jester had gone down in the fountain.

Charlene cut left and vaulted over a second wall through a narrow gap between young trees. She was in a courtyard, blocked to her left by the same line of trees. She ran right and then sharply left as she reached a street between two French buildings. She never looked back, having learned from her coaches that to do so cost precious time in a footrace. The jesters were no match for her agility and speed. If she had looked back she would have seen the two a good twenty yards behind, and slowing as she continued to develop more speed.

She faced more gardens and trees—knew she could lose them for good here and circle back around, with any luck, in time to meet up with Jess.

But just as important, she needed to keep the jesters busy, to give Jess time to enter the pavilion and look for any clues. She fought the urge to be rid of these two. For the moment, she needed them to follow her. She slowed just long enough for them to see her enter the landscaping, just long enough for them to think they had a chance in following her.

Back in the courtyard, Jess stood and watched the footrace under way. She ran toward the pavilion, remembering the importance of getting inside. She entered and stopped abruptly, overcome by the magnificence of the exhibition hall. Ahead of her was the empty waiting line for the film *Impressions de France*. There was a model of Notre Dame in Paris, and a huge gargoyle crouched on a pedestal. She felt paralyzed, wondering what she was supposed to do. She wasn't about to go in and sit down and watch a movie. What clue had Wayne intended for them?

She closed her eyes, wondering if she could make herself see one of her visions. She heard a cracking sound and chunks of something, like rock, striking the floor.

She opened her eyes to see the gargoyle breaking apart from his recoiled pose. Small cracks appeared in his neck, widening as his head moved and swiveled toward her. Pieces of concrete and particles of dust fell away from him. His eyelids cracked and began to open.

She felt light-headed. She stepped back and knocked over a stanchion.

The gargoyle's ugly monkey eyes ringed with spikes locked onto hers, hypnotizing her. The small wings on his back began to flutter, sending more dust into the air. He wrenched his unseen legs up and out of the pedestal to stand four feet high, crouching and craning toward her as he blinked his dusty eyes in an effort to clear them.

"Over here!" came a girl's voice.

Jess, spooked with the surprise, let out a short cry, and glanced over to see Willa, drenched head to toe.

The gargoyle pivoted toward Willa.

"Over here, monkey-man!" Willa said.

"Or here!" Jess said.

The gargoyle jerked his head in Jess's direction, unable to decide which way to go. More dust flew, and Jess could see more cracks appearing in his body.

The beast's wings beat more furiously, and he lifted into the air, flying toward Willa. She dove to the floor and slid. The gargoyle landed heavily, shaking the entire building, but missed her. Willa came to her feet, grabbing onto the waiting-line rope.

"Help me!" she said.

Jess grabbed the other end of the rope. The girls dragged the stanchions with them as they charged the gargoyle. It struggled to turn around, moving slowly, like someone trying to get out of a chair.

The waiting-line rope caught the beast on his side and wrapped his wings tight against his body as the girls continued around him and met on the other side. They tangled the rope clumsily as the gargoyle fought off being captured. But his wings were caught and ineffective.

The more he struggled, the more cracks appeared in his body. Dust was everywhere, like a thick cloud. The girls ran for the exit.

"He's coming apart!" Jess said.

"Out of the way!" shouted Charlene.

The girls turned in the doorway to see the gargoyle in silhouette. They reacted instinctively. Charlene charged like a sprinter, left the ground, flying at the strange creature, feet first. She hit hard, driving the beast over onto his back. He smacked the floor and, as he did, broke into a hundred pieces.

The cloud of dust settled. Charlene scrambled to her feet.

"Everyone okay?" she asked.

"Where did you come from?" Jess asked.

"What was *that*?" Willa said.

"Gymnastics," Charlene answered. "A vault without the follow-through." She smiled widely. "I always wondered if I'd get a chance to use any of it."

Willa said, "We'd better get out of here."

"And fast," Charlene said, agreeing. "I left the jesters halfway to Morocco. At some point they'll figure out I circled back."

"We just leave?" Jess asked.

"Not enough excitement for one night?" Charlene teased.

"We find the others," Willa said. "The Overtakers know we're here now. There isn't much time."

"We've got to warn them," Charlene added.

"If we can," Willa said.

* * *

"What's going on?" Amanda asked. She and Finn had been on their way around the east side of Epcot—past the Universe of Energy pavilion, Mission: Space, and the abandoned Wonders of Life—when Finn had grabbed her by the wrist and jerked her down behind a gift cart.

"Look low to the ground."

She gasped.

"Our friend the python."

"Where's it going?"

"Away from Wonders toward the east side of the park."

"Jess!"

"Yes . . . France is over there."

"But then—"

"They're in trouble." Finn took out his phone and texted Charlene.

snake comin ur way

They stayed hidden, awaiting Charlene's reply.

ovrtkrs evrywehr need help tell me when da snake croses da bridge...

"We need to follow him."

"I was afraid you were going to say something like that."

"At a distance. It'll be all right."

"Why don't I believe you?"

"I can leave you off at the arrival point, if you want."

"Alone? Hello? I don't *think* so!"

"Okay. Stay low."

Finn and Amanda followed the snake for the next several minutes, staying well behind him. Finn kept licking his finger and holding it up when they paused.

"Wind direction," he explained. "He's going to smell us before he hears or sees us. But with the wind coming off the lake as it is, we're fine."

They reached the central fountain, and tucked behind its low wall.

"He's just so disgusting," she said of Gigabyte.

"He's a twenty-foot snake. What'd you expect?"

He hurried out across the plaza and Amanda

followed. They turned right toward Canada, from where Finn had a good view of the bridge to France.

Gigabyte slithered along, moving with astonishing speed.

snakes crosin da bridge...
tell me wen hes ovr

"Finn . . . to the left . . ." Amanda said.

Finn looked across the water, where he saw the pair of Segways at Showcase Plaza coming toward them.

uhoh more ovrtakrs...dont move

He hoped he'd sent the text in time.

But suddenly Charlene appeared from *under* the bridge. Then Jess. Then Willa.

"I don't believe it!" Amanda said. "Where'd they come from?"

"They aren't going to make it!"

At that moment, the two dummies on the Segways changed course, spotting the girls.

"They're going to get caught!" Finn said, standing up. He looked around trying to think what to do.

Amanda stepped out alongside of him. She closed her eyes, raised her hand, palm up.

The Segways briefly lifted off the asphalt as if they hit a speed bump, but then continued to scoot along normally.

"Not the same," Amanda mumbled. Finn could feel her concentrating. Being a DHI had lessened her powers. She was trembling as she squinted her eyes and lifted her outstretched hand for a second try. This time the Segways rose and floated, went off-balance and fell to the asphalt. The two dummies went flying and broke into pieces as they landed. One lost a leg and an arm. The other, both arms.

The one that still had its legs stood back up, turned its head back around a hundred and eighty degrees to face the front again and went off in search of its missing arms.

The girls took off at a sprint, joining Finn and Amanda, who were already running away. Finn glanced back to see the two dummies piecing themselves back together. It would be a few minutes before they were able to ride the Segways again.

"Was that you?" Jess asked Amanda.

"Sorry. It was a little bit strong," Amanda said.

"It did the trick," Finn said.

Charlene was well out in front of the others, since she was a much faster runner.

"Where to?" she called out.

"Norway!" Finn shouted, suddenly concerned that he hadn't heard from either Maybeck or Philby.

* * *

"Those who seek the spirit of Norway face peril and adventure," a Norwegian man's voice cautioned from inside a dark tunnel.

"I don't like the sound of that," Maybeck said.

"Me, neither," Philby agreed. "Especially since it was Wayne who sent us here."

The boat worked up a long incline, then leveled off, facing an Audio-Animatronic figure of a woman standing at the door of a cabin. She said something, but Philby missed it. Two men were working by a burning log.

"There!" Maybeck said.

Leaning against a rock were two axes with a sword in the middle.

Philby hadn't been expecting it so soon.

Maybeck stood.

"No!" Philby cautioned. "The alarms!" He'd studied Maelstrom. It had dozens of autostop features to keep guests from the danger of leaving the boats.

But Maybeck jumped anyway. It was a brilliant jump, nearly straight up. He came down four feet into the display. By jumping so far, he avoided tripping the light beam that would have caused an autostop—if the autostop was even in effect after hours, which Philby wasn't sure of.

Maybeck grabbed for the sword and pulled, but it didn't come free. Philby and the boat continued moving, now pulling even with the two men by the log. Maybeck would soon be left behind.

"It's wired to the rock!" Maybeck struggled to free it, pulling the sword and then untwisting the wire.

Philby heard the ring of metal, like the sound of a sword coming out of its sheath. Maybeck, sword in hand, came running around the two male figures, vaulted over a pile of logs, and landed on a large boulder. He timed it perfectly, sliding down the rock and back into the boat, onto the same bench where Philby sat.

"Ta-da!" he declared, making the sound of a brass fanfare.

They passed more rocks, and some guy with a cape holding a horn. The horn sounded.

"That isn't supposed to happen," Maybeck said. "That's not part of the ride."

Philby looked worried.

They approached another gateway into the next scene.

"That was way too easy," Philby mumbled, half expecting the next Audio-Animatronic mannequin to spin around and challenge them.

"Agreed," Maybeck said. He passed the sword to Philby, who took a quick look at it, then passed it back.

"We'll deal with that once we're out of here," he said.

As the bow of the boat passed the gateway a creepy voice called out.

"What's this?" came the voice from a white-bearded old man in white clothes. He didn't look like any robot; he looked *real.* "How dare you come here! Stop! This is Troll Country. Begone! I cast a spell . . ."

At mention of "a spell" Maybeck snapped his head around to check with Philby.

"I heard it," said Philby.

The scene's events were happening quickly now—too quickly.

An incredibly ugly troll appeared at the old man's side.

"Yes, yes. You'll disappear. Disappear! Bye-bye!"

"It's *them,*" Philby said, for it seemed to him the script had to have been written by the Overtakers themselves. Spells. Disappearance. Everything the Overtakers wanted for the Kingdom Keepers.

"'Bye-bye,'" Maybeck quoted the man. "That can't be good."

The boat suddenly spun around to face backward.

They fell away fast, falling down a surging waterfall.

"I hate going backward!" Philby announced.

"Makes two of us," Maybeck said.

"GURR-OWLLL!" roared an animal from behind and above their left shoulders. Maybeck instinctively ducked. "I am not seeing this!" Philby declared as a *live* polar bear slashed his huge paw through the air—right where Maybeck's head would have been.

The bear came back the other way just as Maybeck found the wherewithal to lift the sword. He sliced the bear's left arm nearly in half. Smoke rose as sparks zapped from it. A bunch of wires dangled from the stump.

"But I could have sworn it was real. . . ." Philby said, realizing the bear was no longer alive, but just an Audio-Animatronic.

Another roar, ten times as loud as the first. Philby dove into the bottom of the boat. Maybeck leaned away.

A second polar bear, standing eight feet tall on its rear legs, bent over and shoved its teeth right into Maybeck's face and snapped, trying to get a bite of him. Maybeck screamed and dropped the sword. It rattled around in the bottom of the boat, and Philby grabbed hold of it.

The bear's mouth bit into the side of the boat and

stopped. The bear's left paw grabbed the boat as its right clawed for Maybeck, and caught his shoulder.

Maybeck screamed horribly and reached for the wound. Philby reacted instinctively, doing the one thing he'd always been told not to do: he stood up in a moving boat. In part, he was trying to save Maybeck. In part, he was trying to *be* Maybeck.

He jabbed the sword at the bear. The beast saw it coming and reared back, taking a swipe at Philby. Only then did Philby realize that the bear's rear legs were fixed to the display—it couldn't come after them. But the bear hit the sword. Philby clutched his left hand around the grip to hold onto it and was spun like a turnstile.

He flew out of the boat.

But instead of thunking down onto the opposite display, Philby landed softly—too softly.

He lifted his head to see Maybeck's eyes go impossibly wide. Maybeck grabbed Philby's feet and pulled.

"Get out of there!" he said.

Philby tried, but he couldn't move. Something was holding him. He rocked his head, not really wanting to see. . . .

Gnomes!

There had to be a dozen of them. Tiny things, no taller than a ruler—*alive!*—with old-man faces and warts, and long, disgusting noses and weird ears. They supported Philby—they had caught him. But now they held onto him, claiming him as a prisoner, while Maybeck fought to keep in the boat.

Gulliver's Travels, Philby thought.

The boat continued moving, leaving Philby behind.

Philby was wrenched at an inhuman angle, his shoulders held by the intrepid gnomes, his feet by Maybeck.

He swatted at the gnomes. One of them stabbed his hand with a miniature gnome knife—it was like getting poked by a knitting needle. Thankfully the Imagineers hadn't armed the gnomes with sharpened weapons. Philby banged the sword over to his right, where it connected with a clank. He knew he must have hit a gnome when he felt his right shoulder jolt free. Philby next slapped the blade over his left shoulder, and now he was clear. But Maybeck had not let go; he'd moved to the back of the boat as it had moved forward and now had nowhere left to go.

All at once, Philby was being dragged half in, half out of the boat, with six angry gnomes racing on their miniature feet in a flurry to catch up to him.

The polar bear grew smaller and smaller, framed by the tunnel as the boat continued moving.

Maybeck finally hauled Philby into the boat just before they entered through the next scene's gate—

where Philby would have been knocked free and left behind.

There were trees. It was a rocky cave. The narrator said something that Philby couldn't make out. He was trembling from head to toe.

"Thanks," he said.

"You saved us, not me!" said Maybeck, in a rare display of humility.

Just as Philby thought he'd regained his balance, the boat dropped away, out from under them. It raced down an incline and into yet another scene. It was night. They were on the ocean under the northern lights, with an oil rig to their left.

"Cold!" Philby said, warning Maybeck, who understood what a drop in temperature meant.

Maleficent.

Darkness.

"We're almost through," Maybeck said.

Thankfully, a sea village appeared, not the green witch. Not this time.

Standing onshore were Willa, Charlene, Finn, Jess, and Amanda. A ship's horn sounded.

"You guys get all the fun!" Willa complained.

"Yeah, fun!" Maybeck said, pulling his bloody hand away from his wounded shoulder.

Finn reached out and helped the two to shore.

29

THEY HID BEHIND MEXICO'S Mayan temple, where they thought it unlikely they'd be found. Willa proved herself worthy of her Girl Scout merit badge by cleaning up Maybeck's wound. It looked nastier than it was—the line of deep scratches had stopped bleeding.

"First, I have some bad news," Finn said. He told the others about his experience at Lost and Found, how he thought he'd touched the fob inside the locker, but that they'd have to wait until morning before trying for it again.

A depressing silence settled over the group.

"My mother is going to freak when she can't wake me up," Philby said.

"Mine too," said Willa.

"Jelly can never get me out of bed," Maybeck said, "but she'll remember the last time. This won't be good."

"I wish there was something I could tell you," Finn said.

"If we're trapped here," said Charlene, "shouldn't we make the most of it?"

The others looked at her with total surprise. Charlene was usually the whiner of the group.

"Excuse me?" Willa said.

"I mean . . . if there's nothing we can do about it, if we have to be here anyway . . . and it seems to me we do . . . then shouldn't we try to find Wayne or something? What about the sword? Isn't that why we came here in the first place?"

"Somebody pinch me," Maybeck said.

"Charlene?" Willa said. "Is that really you?"

"Get off my case," Charlene protested. "Listen, we're all in big trouble, okay? Our parents, our aunt," she said—"and our guardian," she added, addressing Jess and Amanda—"they're all going to lose it when we can't be woken up. And if we do get back there—tomorrow morning—we're going to be in big trouble because they're going to know it has something to do with us crossing over. Who knows what happens after that? Right? I mean they could contact Disney or something, and maybe the program gets shut down again. Maybe we lose our places as Disney Hosts. I don't know. I'm just saying if we're going to do something, it probably should be tonight, as in right now, because my mom is going to put handcuffs on me or something. I'm going to be grounded for eternity."

"It's all wrong," Philby said, tracing his fingers along the blade of the sword, which was lying atop his crossed legs.

"Well, maybe you have a better idea," said a disgusted Charlene.

"Sorry, not you, Charlene," Philby said. "The sword." He motioned down at it. "The sword is all wrong."

"How can a sword be wrong?" Amanda asked.

"Wayne gave us the box," Philby said, "and the box became the sword . . . or the cross. But if it's a sword, I think this is the wrong sword. If it's a cross, maybe the clue is: France."

"The only thing we got in France," said Charlene, "was a lot of hassle."

"But if there are Overtakers guarding France, couldn't that mean something?" Jess asked.

"Of course it could," Finn agreed. "We won't give up on that."

"But I'm telling you it's the wrong sword," Philby said.

"There he goes again," Maybeck said.

"And that's got to be significant."

"Wrong how?" asked Amanda.

"The Maelstrom is Norway, so the sword should be Norwegian, right?"

No one challenged him.

"But it's not. It's an Irish sword."

"And you know this, how? Speaks with an Irish

accent, does it?" Maybeck said.

The others chuckled.

"Norwegian swords have circles of metal, like a doughnut, above the grip, not crosses. And you see this round shape, like a coin, at the center of the cross? It happens that that's an Irish design. It's an old Irish sword—very old. And what makes it particularly strange is that there's a fly in the coin on one side, and a shamrock on the other." He passed it around.

"Engraved," Jess said, handing it to Maybeck.

"No, not engraved," Maybeck said. He picked at the coin with his fingernail and caught an edge. "It's drawn on Scotch tape, clear tape that's been stuck on."

"Wayne," Finn said.

"Irish. Fly," said Philby. He held out his hand to Charlene. "It's a clue."

"Fly Irish?" Willa said. "Isn't there an Irish airline?"

"Maybe the airline sponsors one of the World Showcases," Finn said.

"We're getting ahead of ourselves," Philby cautioned, working Charlene's phone. "Wouldn't he have drawn a plane if he wanted us to go searching Irish airlines? But it's a fly. A housefly. Why?"

"SWAT?" Maybeck said. "Like a police SWAT team?"

"You are such a . . . *boy*," Willa said.

"Better than the alternative," Maybeck said.

Philby looked up from the phone. "Wiki lists a bunch of things for *The Fly*."

"This is *so* Wayne," Willa said. "I hate to say it, but this just seems so exactly what Wayne would do. You know? I mean, when does he ever just leave a message like: Maleficent is under Pirates? He's always so—"

"Careful," Finn said. "He makes sure no one could figure it out but us. It's too much for one person to process. But the five of us—"

"Seven now," said Charlene.

Philby read from the phone. "Okay . . . There were a bunch of movie versions—"

"I love that movie!" said Maybeck, interrupting.

"Hush!" said Willa. "Let him speak."

"A short story. There's a magazine . . . a U2 song—"

"That's it!" said Charlene. "U2's an *Irish* band."

"And you would know this because?" Willa questioned her.

"My parents listen to them all the time. Definitely Irish. And they've been around for like forever."

"Okay, people," Finn said. "Are you telling me that Wayne, who is approximately nine thousand years old, would have any idea who U2 are?"

"I'm just saying: it's a song," Charlene said. "And the words are wicked. It's all about stars falling, and secrets, and human consciousness. It's heavy stuff.

Eclipses and friends and . . . it could easily be some kind of message."

"I can Google the lyrics," Philby said. "But there's more here. There's a Dave Matthews song—"

"Sweet," said Charlene. "I know that song too!"

"—and a poem by a guy named Blake," Philby continued.

"William Blake," said Amanda. "He's British. Northern Ireland's part of Great Britain. All of Ireland was part of Great Britain before Irish independence—so we can't rule out Blake."

"And a *Simpsons* episode."

"I love the Simpsons," Maybeck said. "There're a couple where Bart is the Fly."

"Blake," Amanda said, "A dead poet. Dead for a long time. Dead as in can't be changed. That's Blake."

"An old dead poet?" Finn said. "That's got to be near the top of our list if Wayne's behind this."

"The Dave Matthews song is about *being saved*," Charlene repeated. "How much more do you need than that? Wayne needs to be saved."

"Wayne wouldn't have a clue who Dave Matthews is," Finn insisted.

"You can't know that."

"I do know that," Finn said. "And there's no way he'd know about U2 either."

"That's ridiculous!" Charlene protested. "*Everyone* knows U2."

Philby angled the phone in the limited light.

"Here's the poem."

"Read it," Finn said.

Philby looked around. No one objected.

"Okay. . . .

'Little Fly,
Thy summer's play
My thoughtless hand
Has brush'd away.

'Am not I
A fly like thee?
Or art not thou
A man like me?

'For I dance,
And drink, and sing,
Till some blind hand
Shall brush my wing.

'If thought is life
And strength and breath,
And the want
Of thought is death;

'Then am I
A happy fly.
If I live,
Or if I die.'"

For a moment, no one said a thing.

"Whoa," Maybeck grunted out. "Heavy."

"Note to self," Charlene said, "the U2 song is about stars falling and secrets being kept. I mean: come on, people!"

"And this is about life and death," Finn said.

"And dancing and drinking and singing," Amanda added, "all of which happen in Epcot and the other parks."

Willa said, "It's the part about how thinking is the strength of life, that gets me. And about how not thinking is death, and how as long as that's true, he's happy. That is so Wayne. And I think he's telling us something deeper—"

"Oh, please, give it a rest," said Maybeck.

She ignored him. "That it's not about him. It's not about whether he lives or dies but that he wants us to figure this out—to think."

"Flying," Philby said.

He won everyone's attention.

"Don't you see?" he continued. "Willa's right: it's

about thinking. It doesn't matter if it's the poem or a U2 song. It's a fly. It could be something in The Land, or A Bug's Life over in Animal Kingdom. But *think* about it. Fly. Right here in Epcot: Soarin' is about flying. And . . ." He pulled out and unfolded a sheet of paper from his back pocket, and read it. "Soarin' just happens to be on the maintenance list for areas with unexpected temperature drops."

"You carry that thing with you?" Maybeck said. "What are you, a Boy Scout?"

"Finn and I took a big risk collecting this data. I intend to make use of it."

"Mission: Space!" Finn added. "It involves flight."

Philby checked the sheet. "Also on here."

Jess touched her forehead and closed her eyes. Amanda noticed the reaction, though the others were too excited to spot it.

"And on Test Track you go fast enough to fly," Willa said.

Philby nodded. "Ditto," he said.

"There's that Star Wars ride where you're in a space pod," Maybeck said. "Over in Hollywood Studios."

"I don't have that data," Philby said.

Maybeck scoffed.

Amanda leaned into Jess. "What's wrong?"

"Not sure." With her eyes closed she reached out in

front of her, like a blind person groping in the dark. Then her eyes popped open. "That was strange. . . ." she whispered.

While the other kids continued talking—arguing, was more like it—Amanda probed Jess's sudden confusion with an inquisitive look. Jess shook her head. "I saw something—a pattern. Three rectangles. Just for an instant."

Finn had the attention of the others. "We keep the sword with us. It has to have something to do with either finding him or finding the Overtakers," he said. "It's got to be a clue."

"Of course it's a clue, Whitman," Maybeck said. "The question is, what are we supposed to do about it?"

"We have the entire night to check it out," Charlene said. "We can sit here for six hours, or we can actually do something."

"For instance?" Maybeck said.

Philby spoke up. "Check out any ride, any exhibit, any pavilion, that has to do with flying and that shows up on the maintenance list."

"Spaceship Earth," Willa said.

"That goes onto the list," said Philby, confirming its existence on his list. "And Finn, yes, we should keep the sword with us. But it should be *you*: that's what Wayne would want. He could have gotten the fly message to us without all the sword stuff, so the sword must be important."

"There are seven of us," Finn said. "Three teams of two and one lookout. The lookout has to get to some place with a view of the—"

"Fireworks," Philby said.

"No," Finn said, "the whole park."

"The control center for the fireworks is at the very top of this temple—the Mayan Temple."

No one was going to question Mr. Encyclopedia.

Finn arched his head back to look nearly straight up at the top of the Mayan temple.

"How do we get up there?" he asked.

"There's a door on the east side," Philby said. "It leads to a staircase that goes all the way up. This time of night, no one will be in there. As long as we don't touch anything. . . . Finn, you could all-clear through the door and let someone inside."

"That would be me," said Amanda, also looking up. "I was the lookout last time, right?" She didn't wait for anyone to answer. "Okay, I'll do it. But I'll need to borrow someone's phone in order to reach you."

30

As Finn's mother drifted off to sleep at a few minutes past eleven her body twitched in a serious convulsion that rocked the bed. She sat bolt upright, throwing the covers off the bed. Her husband reached down, pulled the covers back up, and went back to snoring.

The code! Her mind had played tricks on her by replaying as a dream the afternoon spent sorting out the code with Finn and his friends, Willa and Philby.

"Wayne's missing," she recalled Finn telling her—accidentally telling her, if she were any judge of her son.

How could she have been so stupid? The code had nothing whatsoever to do with any competition, and everything to do with Wayne going missing. It had all made so much sense in her quick dream: she relived the expressions on the faces of the kids as they worked together to solve the code, the exchanged glances. How could she have been so obtuse to miss it all at the time?

She threw her legs over the edge of the bed, tugged at her nightgown to straighten it, and hurried out of her bedroom and down the hall. Late or not, she had every intention of confronting Finn. The family policy was, *no lying*. They were not about to change that policy just because Finn was now a teenager—if anything, it was more important than ever.

She opened the door to his room, moved to the bed, and hesitated a moment as she saw her son's peaceful face cast in the glow of his various electronics. In that instant, the thought crossed her mind to turn around and leave this for the morning. How could she disturb his peace over some dream she'd had? Why was she so suspicious of her own son? Where had her trust gone?

She turned and took two steps back toward the door. But then she spun around sharply, her eyes scanning the floor. She'd been working on Finn for five years—*More like ten!* she thought—to put his clothes away when he took them off. She'd even bought him his own laundry hamper. Yet every morning, there were his clothes from the day before, strewn about the room as if a tornado had hit.

So where were they?

No boots. No pants. No shirt.

The anger she'd felt in the bedroom resurfaced. This seesaw of emotion was exhausting her. While her adrenaline was still charged, she marched to the bed and gently pulled back the covers.

Fully dressed. No pajamas.

Could this possibly mean . . . ?

She shook his shoulder.

"Finn? Sweetheart?"

She shook him harder. In the past two years he'd taken to sleeping so soundly she could sometimes have a bear of a time waking him.

"Finn, dear?"

Not a twitch. Not a complaint. He didn't roll over; he didn't squint or moan or tell her to go away. He didn't *move*.

It was as if . . .

"Oh, Lord . . ." she said aloud. She stepped back away from the bed, her bottom lip trembling, and crossed her arms, tears forming in her eyes. She returned to his bedside and shook him again.

"Finn? Finn! *Finn!* This is not funny!"

She shook him so hard that his lifeless, limp, sleeping body just rocked back and forth like . . . like. . . .

She couldn't bring herself to admit what it was like.

"Wake up! Wake up!"

Tears spilled from her blotchy face as droplets on his pillow.

"You did *not* do this. Tell me *you did not do this!* Where are you? Come back! Please, God, come back!"

Then she fell to her knees and wailed.

31

IT TOOK PHILBY THREE TRIES to find the right door, but finally he got himself, Amanda, and Finn into the back of the Mayan Temple and up its long staircase. They reached a glassed-in booth at the top. It was high enough and well disguised enough so that it couldn't be seen by park guests from within Epcot. Finn used all-clear to enter the control room and unlock the door.

Inside it looked like a miniature version of something NASA would build. There was a wraparound console with two computers, several dials and switches, and two phones.

"IllumiNations," Philby said, studying some of the switches up close. "This is where they run the music and the lasers for the show. Maybe even the fireworks—I can't tell, but if I had to guess—"

"So you're saying don't touch anything," Finn said.

"Amanda," Philby said in his Professor Philby voice, "the idea is that by being here maybe you can see the Overtakers move around. Tell us what's going on. You touch any of these buttons, or mess with the computers, and you'll announce to the whole park that something is way wrong. You'll also tell them exactly where you are, and they'll come after you. So whatever you do—"

"I've got it," she said.

"You're sure?"

"I'm sure."

Together, the three tested different locations, discovering that there was a projection shadow beneath the main console: if you tucked yourself under the console on hands and knees, you disappeared. Knowing that invisibility could prove critically important to her survival, Amanda took a seat in the center chair behind a console. The boys left her there, Charlene's cell phone in hand, Amanda's DHI glowing just enough to allow her to see the console panel clearly.

In its center there was a single word on a plaque: DANGER.

* * *

"They could have tried to make it girl–boy," Willa said. "You know, like every girl had to have a boy with her to keep her safe? Personally, I'm glad we were teamed up the way we are."

"I've never done anything like this. Not exactly like this," Jess said.

"It's a lot to get used to, I know. Being crossed over is not exactly what you'd call normal, is it?"

"Definitely not."

"The important thing," Willa said, "is for you and me to stick together. Safety in numbers and all that."

"And if we're . . . I don't know . . . attacked?"

"Overtakers? We try to avoid them. If we can't then we run, and if we have to, we split up and meet at the rendezvous when it's safe. And when you can, you want to practice going *all clear*. Finn got it really early. Maybeck managed it once. Philby, too. If you can pull that off you can do things like walk through walls, and if someone tries to grab you, they can't. Not that I'd know. But with your . . . powers . . . or whatever you call what it is you do—"

"Dreams."

"Yeah . . . your *dreams* . . . maybe you can figure it out quicker than the rest of us. Finn says it's all about relaxation, about not thinking about anything."

"Not so easy for me," Jess said. "I tend to think about the present *and* the future. I'm not so sure I can just turn that off."

"Good point," Willa said. "For now we just stick close and try to figure out if there's anything different about Soarin'. Any clue Wayne might be wanting us to get. The first time we did this, we had to solve the

Stonecutter's Quill and the clues were pretty obvious. Last time—"

"I was the one giving the clues."

"Exactly."

"So do we know what kind of clue Wayne might leave us?"

"Something weird. Wayne is definitely weird. And it won't be obvious. He never makes it easy."

"That doesn't exactly narrow things."

"No, it doesn't."

"So it could be anything," Jess said.

"Hopefully we'll know it when—if—we see it. But we should try to remember everything we see and hear. Maybe it won't make sense until later."

"I love Soarin'," Jess said.

"Me, too. But if the Overtakers are in control of it, maybe not so much."

"Like Small World."

"Exactly. You never know what to expect."

"I'm kinda scared," Jess said. They'd been sneaking along the edge of the path and were now only fifty yards from the entrance to Soarin'.

"Finn says that's a good thing," Willa said. "But I think he only says that. I don't think he actually means it. I think what he actually means is you can't help but being scared so you've just got to learn to live with it."

"So you're scared too?"

"Definitely. As cool as it is to go on these rides when the parks are closed, more often than not something bad happens. I can't help but be . . . apprehensive, I guess you'd say."

"You say *apprehensive*. I say *scared*."

"That'll work," Willa said, smiling faintly, her DHI sparking in the dark.

Creepy was more like it. She and Jess entered the Soarin' pavilion and went up the waiting-line ramp between huge aerial photographs that gave Willa the chilling sensation she was being watched. As they pushed through the door and into the vast chamber that fronted a curved, white projection screen sixty feet high an automated voice spoke into the cavernous theater: *"If you have loose fitting shoes, such as slip-ons or sandals, please remove them once you take your seat and leave them on the floor in front of you. If you have any carry-ons that are too large or fragile to fit inside the under-seat compartments, please leave them on the floor in front of you as well and our flight attendants will be happy to store them for you. Thank you and have a nice flight."*

"The ride is about to start!" whispered Willa.

"We're one minute to go," said a woman from near the front of the building.

Jess pulled on Willa, wanting to leave immediately.

Willa shook her head, held her finger to her lips, and pointed to the back bench of seats. As far as she was concerned if there was someone in here doing something, then maybe that was what Wayne wanted them to discover. It seemed incredibly late at night to be running tests, although she had no idea when regular maintenance was done on the rides, and she supposed nighttime was the only free time the engineers had. If she and Jess could get into third-row seats, once the mechanism lifted, they would be well back into the dark room. If they held their legs up, and kept them from dangling, they would be basically impossible to spot.

She pulled Jess with her. They took middle seats—more hidden than the end seats—and pulled their legs up into their chests, wrapping their arms around their shins.

"We're go in thirty!" called out the woman.

"Rachel, let's watch the sync on the aroma trigger." It was a man's voice from off to their left.

Willa caught a glimpse of stairs rising from the left of the hall, something she'd never seen before.

At once the room grew even darker. Loud music started. Willa felt a flutter in her chest. She *loved* this ride—her favorite in all of Disney World—but something told her this wouldn't be any ordinary flight. If they were testing the equipment, did that mean there was a problem?

Jess reached over and laid her hand on Willa's right arm and squeezed. Willa, in the glow from the screen, indicated that Jess should grip her legs with her arms: they had to keep from being seen at all costs.

As the mechanism began to lift and rotate, Willa caught a man's silhouette passing in front of the screen heading in the direction of Rachel, whom she now could see was standing at a console at the screen's lower right corner.

The man caught up to Rachel and the two shouted at each other over the roar of the music.

Willa looked up: New York City, not California as she had expected. She and Jess were flying over the skyscrapers and diving down into the avenues. They banked steeply left, then sharply right, and the air smelled of bagels as they reached a bridge. A seagull squawked and Willa had to clamp her hand over her mouth to keep her squeal from being heard.

They were changing the location of the flight. Rachel and the man were troubleshooting the timing and the effects. Suddenly the air smelled of hot dogs and mustard. Far in the distance Willa could see a long beach crowded with families in swimsuits. The water was frothing white from thousands more out swimming.

The girls pitched down, diving toward the beach.

"No! No! No!" shouted the man.

The music stopped, the screen went dark. Then a few emergency or work lights came on. Willa and Jess were well hidden, but they were hanging facing down, in the dive position. If Rachel or the man happened to look up, Willa knew she and Jess would be spotted. Making things more difficult, it felt as if she was going to fall out of the seat.

"We need the smell of hot dogs on the Coney Island flyover," the man said. He called on a walkie-talkie. "Mr. Devlin? We need to move aroma effect number two twenty-one-point-five seconds forward. Something's wrong with the time code."

A nasal voice replied. "Roger that, John. I see that here, too. I'll sync aroma effect two with the flyover and we'll go again."

"Will wait for your say-so."

Willa glanced over at Jess to see how she was doing. Her eyes went wide.

Jess might have been doing fine, but her hair had cascaded over her head and a barrette on the side was slowly creeping down her hair, drawn by gravity.

If Willa called out to Jess, she might be heard. If she reached over and touched her Jess might jerk, and if she did the barrette was going to fall. It slipped another inch, and judging by her expression, this time Jess felt it, and knew she didn't dare move.

Willa stretched to try to reach the barrette, but came up several inches short. Letting go of her leg to do so, she allowed it briefly to hang down. She strained against the safety belt, trying to buy herself the precious few inches needed. As she did Jess moved, however slightly, and the barrette slid down the remainder of her hair and went airborne like a small black moth—with rhinestones.

Willa swiped the air and missed the barrette. Instinctively, her leg kicked out to stop it. It was a soccer move, like trapping and balancing a ball on top of your foot. The barrette now lay atop Willa's Converse sneaker, perched there. If she moved her leg in the slightest, it was going to slip off.

More walkie-talkie chatter. Willa was too consumed with the balancing act to pay attention. But when the words rang out, "Good to go in thirty seconds," she knew she had trouble. She bent and lifted her knee, trying to bring the barrette high enough that either she or Jess could grab it. But in the process, it slipped from her shoe and her reflex was to kick straight out. It was a perfect kick, connecting with the barrette. She sent it flying toward the screen. It careened off a piece of the steel superstructure and into the set of seats suspended a row in front of them.

It disappeared. Though loose, it had not fallen to the floor.

The theater went dark and the flight started again. This time the ride might have been even more exciting since she knew at least some of what to expect, but Willa's full concentration was on the row of seats ahead of them and the unseen hair clip.

As they dove down toward Coney Island, the smell of hot dogs filled the air.

"Yes!" she heard the man shout. "That's better."

They buzzed a windsurfer and water sprayed in their faces. There was no music now, just the light sound of wind.

Clack! An abrupt, brittle sound.

"Full stop!" the man shouted.

The music and film stopped and the cars descended. As Willa approached the poured-concrete floor she spotted Jess's barrette on the floor, up near the front of the three rows of seats.

She tried her seat belt.

Locked!

Tried it again.

Locked!

The row of seats hit bottom and came to a full stop.

The seat belt released.

She tapped Jess on the forearm and Jess released her seat belt as well.

They had to get away from that hair clip. They couldn't make for the entrance as they'd step right into view of the man and Rachel. Willa took Jess by the hand, crouched, and made a mad dash for the far wall and the staircase she'd spotted. Reaching the end of the line of machinery, she paused, holding Jess back. It had to be timed exactly right.

The man walked past the first row, no doubt searching for the source of the unfamiliar sound. His eyes would be trained on the floor.

Three, two. . .

She raced across the open space, Jess right behind her, and reached the staircase. She pulled them flat against the wall, wishing now, more than ever, that she'd perfected the art of all-clear.

"It's a hair thing-a-ma-bobby," the man called out. "Someone lost it and it chooses now to fall off. Can you believe that dumb luck? Stopped the whole test for a freaking hair clip. Okay! Let's run it again."

Willa pointed up the stairs to a red-and-white exit sign. She turned an imaginary crank by the side of her head, signaling Jess they would make their move when the film ran again.

"Thirty seconds!" Rachel called out.

Jess nodded back at Willa, looking terrified, and sick to death with guilt.

"You okay?" Willa asked.

Jess squinted and put her hand to head. "No," she said in a forced whisper. "I keep *seeing* something."

"As in—?"

"Yes. Like my dreams. Like that. And the thing is: I've seen it before in other dreams. Recently. Like in the past couple of days. Rectangles. Buttons, maybe. A TV, I think. And I've seen it *twice* tonight: the same pattern. It's always the same pattern."

"Buttons? Like the kind you sew on?"

"The kind you push."

"Mission: Space."

"What?"

"Buttons. Monitors. That's Mission: Space." Willa glanced up at the exit sign. "I think you're on the wrong ride. . . ." she said.

* * *

At nearly the same moment Jess and Willa had entered Soarin', Finn and Philby had been poised outside the Test Track pavilion.

"What do you think?" Finn asked quietly. Tucked behind a FastPass kiosk to the right of the entrance, the boys were keeping an eye out for trouble.

"I'm thinking about those crash-test dummies."

"Yeah, me too."

"And how this is where they live."

"I'm with you."

"And that we're basically asking for it."

"I hear you."

"But we're going in there, aren't we?"

"We are," Finn said.

"I suppose if we can all-clear, we're okay."

"It's hard to do when everything's coming at you at once."

"It's hard to do, period. You're the all-clear expert. I'm a newbie."

"I don't know that I could do it with a pair of crash-test dummies coming at me."

"But it's *because* of the crash-test dummies that we have to go in there," Philby said. "Or am I missing something?"

"That, and the flying thing." Finn looked down at the sword in his hand. "I feel totally stupid carrying this around with me."

"Live with it. I think Wayne wants us to have it."

"Besides which, it's heavy. Have you ever lugged a sword around? It's like carrying a tuba."

"You play tuba?"

"I did for two weeks in fifth grade. Then I got wise and switched to trumpet."

"I'm clarinet," Philby said. It sounded like a confession. "And I sing in our church's youth choir, but if you tell anyone I'll have to kill you."

"If the crash-test dummies don't do it for you."

"Don't kid around like that."

"Like what?" Finn asked. "You think I'm kidding? If those things get hold of us. . . . It's not like they have brains or something. . . . They're obviously being controlled by someone or something else, and we both know who that is."

"Programmed is more like it," Professor Philby said, correcting him. "My guess is that at some point the Imagineers toyed with the idea of Audio-Animatronic crash-test dummies. There were probably a couple of those things lying around in a room somewhere, and the Overtakers got hold of them and 'enlisted' them by updating their software. That's the thing about this place: the Imagineers are like human wizards. They think up all this stuff, half of which none of us ever sees. But someone knows it exists. Right? And in the wrong hands. . . . Well, the thing is, there's probably a lot more stuff like the dummies, stuff we've never even *thought of before* that can be used against us."

"Are you trying to give me a pep talk?" Finn asked. "Because it isn't working."

"I'm just saying, we—*all* of us—should keep our eyes open. And we shouldn't trust anything we see. And we should be looking for stuff we don't see. We know Maleficent can transfigure herself into various animals. Who knows what Chernabog can do? Who knows what the two of them can do together? All I'm saying is: if crash-test dummies are out patrolling on Segways, and trolls are coming alive in Maelstrom, and jesters are attacking the girls in France, then this place is lit up by Overtakers. You know what I mean? They are like: volume on ten. They are working it. And we need to be ready for them because we're who they're after. In their world, we're the bad guys. And we know what happens to the bad guys."

"You are really depressing me here."

"Reality check. That's all."

"Can we go inside now? You've got me totally paranoid."

"If something happens, you go all-clear and get gone," Philby said. "Don't worry about me. If one of us gets out of this, it's way better than if we're both caught. Right? I know you'll come back for me. So no heroics. Just get out and figure something out and come back. I'm good with that."

"Not going to happen."

"No heroics," Philby repeated.

"I've got your back," Finn said, holding his ground. "Now let's take a ride."

* * *

Mission: Space was basically a bunch of pods on a giant turntable. Maybeck held an arm out to keep Charlene from going any farther into the room. She was a little too cheerleader for him, a little too gung ho. It worried him that she might be more athletic than he was, might show him up in some way. He didn't want her making him look bad.

"I hate this ride," he said. "I went on it once and I felt sick the rest of the day."

"I thought we ended up together on this because we could both take it."

"Who said I couldn't take it?"

"I thought you just did."

"Did not. I said it made me feel funky, not that I couldn't take it. But you're the one does all the flips and gymnastic stuff, not me."

"That's the point. I love this ride," she said. "It goes so fast it peels your face back."

"Yeah. Terrific," he said.

"If you want to be lookout, I can do this alone," she

said. "It's not like anyone has to know."

"Are you calling me chicken, girl?"

"That would be no," she said. "It was only an offer."

"Well, keep it—" Maybeck cut himself off, reaching for his pocket where his phone was vibrating. He checked the caller ID and answered. "Not the best timing," he whispered into the phone. He plugged his open ear with a finger. "Say again? . . . You're serious? . . ." He gave Charlene a weird look. "Can she describe it? . . . No . . . not now. Three minutes. Call me back in three minutes." He ended the call and returned the phone to his pants pocket.

"Madame Houdini has been having visions about this ride."

"FYI," Charlene said. "Houdini was an escape artist, not a clairvoyant."

"Yeah? Well Ms. Claire Voyant's been zooming on Mission: Space, according to the Willow Tree. Something to do with buttons and TV screens."

"And?"

"And she's going to describe it to us once we're inside one of those pods."

"So we should get going," Charlene said.

"Yeah. We should get going."

"So why are we standing here with your arm blocking me?" she asked.

He lowered his arm. "Because it looks too easy," Maybeck said, still speaking very softly. "How can it be this easy? It's almost like they're inviting us to get into one of those pods."

"That may be right. But there's only one way to find out."

"I told you that I hate this ride. Yeah?"

"You might have mentioned it," she said. "But you're tougher than the other guys, right?"

"You're going to head-trip me?"

"I'm building your confidence."

"My phone's going to ring. We gotta get in there."

"I'll go first," she said.

"The heck you will." He crossed the curved crack in the floor—it had appeared when the ride began allowing the floor-size turntable to spin—and approached the nearest pod. To the left of the closed door was a pale blue panel containing four green buttons. The bottom left button was marked DOOR OPEN, written vertically. The two on top were marked DOOR CLOSED and SEAT RESTRAINT. The bottom button wasn't labeled.

"Give me your phone," she whispered.

"What?"

"Don't you get it? One of us has to be out here to push the door-closed and seat-restraint buttons for the other person."

Maybeck studied the panel for a second time. "You think?"

"I know. That's the only way it's going to start."

"Maybe it doesn't need to start. Maybe we just go in the pod and look around?"

"And there are how many pods? And a whole 'nother room of pods next door. You think we picked the right one?"

"How should I know?"

"Give me your phone," she repeated. "I trust Jess. This has something to do with Jess and her dreams. I accept that, even if you can't."

"I didn't say anything."

"You called her Houdini."

He looked guilty as charged.

She held her hand out.

Maybeck passed her his phone.

* * *

On-screen, the hang glider flight dove over Yankee Stadium on its way back toward Manhattan. A crowd of fifty thousand cheered for a Derek Jeter home run as the smell of popcorn filled the air.

Jess and Willa used the cacophony as cover, fleeing up the staircase toward the exit sign. Willa made the mistake of looking back at the screen and lost her balance as the route dipped left and low over the East River. Jess reached out and caught her just as Willa was about to fall down the stairs.

"Don't look," Jess whispered.

Both girls averted their eyes, looking up the stairs instead of down—toward the back of the theater, instead of the screen.

Jess caught sight of something Willa did not. As they approached the exit door, Jess nudged her and pointed.

"'Projection Room,'" she said, quoting the title on the door.

"Yeah?"

"I think we need to check it out," Jess said.

"Because?"

"It's an IMAX projector," Jess said.

"So?"

"They're supercooled. As in very low-temperature. And majorly climate controlled."

"You're channeling Philby all of a sudden?"

"I wrote a report for science class. I happen to love IMAX theaters. And anything three-D. I know all about that booth, and believe me, it would be Maleficent heaven, or a perfect place to hide Wayne. Think about it: no one goes in there—it's all automated. It's kept cool. It's climate controlled. And it's tucked up at the back of this theater, way out of the way."

"I suppose it could have been the reason Soarin' showed up on the maintenance list," Willa said.

"So we're going in there," Jess said, making it a statement.

"I think we are," Willa agreed. "But you need to call Maybeck first and tell him what you saw. It's been three minutes."

Holding on to the rail, Jess looked back at the screen. The hang glider was flying down Broadway toward Times Square at night. It was a magnificent sight.

"Right about now," she said, "I wish I had Finn's sword."

"We'll make the call from inside the booth. It'll be quieter," Willa said, ever practical.

"But shouldn't we tell someone what we're doing, where we're going? What if they don't hear from us again, and can't find us?"

Willa took back the phone and started typing in a text.

Jess couldn't tell for certain, given the flickering light from the film, but she thought Willa's face had gone suddenly pale.

32

TEST TRACK'S WAITING LINE turned back on itself, weaving through a General Motors assembly line of car parts, partly constructed vehicles, and testing areas where car doors were moved remotely to test the durability of their hinges. Empty, it was a confusing tangle of steel railings, a labyrinth of tools and heavy machinery.

Finn and Philby moved through the line slowly, on high alert, both feeling uneasy. No matter how many times they had entered attractions or taken rides after a park's closing, the events always had a haunted quality about them, as if removing the people removed the life of the place as well, leaving only ghosts behind.

They had encountered Overtakers or succumbed to traps so many times that they now expected them. The characters took over the parks after closing, and the Overtakers did their best to take over the characters. The DHI kids could not enter into this conflict without a strong sense of personal risk.

Finn and Philby kept their heads up, their eyes

moving and their ears alert. An attack could come from anywhere at any time.

"Do you smell it?" Philby asked. A metallic, dusty aroma filled the area, like the air during a lightning storm.

"Could be just the machinery. There's a lot of stuff in here."

"Or it could be her," Philby said.

When Maleficent entered a room that same electronic smell preceded her. She could throw fireballs—St. Elmo's fire—off the tips of her fingers, could draw laserlike electronic fences in the air to contain and capture the Kingdom Keepers. She was clearly capable of generating her own electricity, like an electric eel. This smell in the air set both Finn and Philby back on their heels.

Contained within the rails of the waiting line, they turned to see an Audio-Animatronic mechanic, an old man, maybe 40 or 50, with fat hands and red cheeks sitting by a flashing computer monitor. They both stopped short at the same moment, reminded of the crash-test dummies. They stood perfectly still. The dummy did not move. They advanced cautiously, inches at a time, their eyes never leaving the dummy for long.

A moment later, they looked back at the mechanic as they passed a half dozen traffic signs. The line moved over against the wall here. They were getting closer to the loading zone and the start of the ride. They passed through the empty turnstiles and on through the darkened room where usually a nerdy guy who looked like a young Dan Patrick from ESPN talked you through what you'd experience on the ride.

"It isn't what we'd normally go through that worries me," Finn said. "It's what we don't expect to happen."

"With you there," Philby agreed.

They entered the loading area and moved to the far end where a car awaited.

"Ready?" Philby asked.

"Are you sure this is even possible?" Finn asked.

"I don't mean to sound too much like Maybeck, but this is *me* we're talking about. I know every attraction, every ride, inside and out. That's my job, right? And I take it seriously."

Philby's plan was for him to go up into the control booth and start the ride while Finn took a seat in the lead car.

"There has to be at least one seat belt fastened for a car to move," Philby explained. "Since the second car won't have any seat belts fastened, it won't start up. The others can't go either, but even if they could, the computer will hold them back. It'll mean ours is the only car out there, and I trust that a lot more than some car coming up from behind us and hitting us, or forcing us to go faster or something."

"But that also means I'll be strapped in," Finn said, "and you won't."

"That's correct. If I hurry, I can jump into the car in time. The seat belt may not work at that point—I don't know."

These were three words one never heard from Philby's mouth. Finn savored hearing them and almost made a point of it, but decided to keep his celebration to himself.

"If we see something . . ." Philby continued, "if for any reason it's needed . . . if I'm not strapped in I can get out of the car and meet you back at the start of the ride."

"We shouldn't separate. That's one of the rules."

"Rules are made to be broken, Finn. You know that. This is one of those times."

"Couldn't we just skip the cars and walk the test track?"

"The cars trigger the scene events. If Wayne left us a clue, if he wants us to see something, it'll be somewhere along the ride. We want—no, it's more than that—we *need* the scene events and the effects engaged."

"I still don't love the idea of me being strapped in and you not being."

"I'll hold on tight, believe me, *Mother*. But it's the only way to start the ride. It's this, or we bail right now."

"Okay." Finn didn't feel right about doing it this way—they'd instituted the buddy rule after losing Maybeck, and so far the rule had kept them safe. But Philby had convinced him there was no other way; and Philby knew this stuff.

The loading area was gloomy with most of the lights turned off. Thankfully, there were no crash-test dummies in sight. Finn climbed down into the lead car and fastened his seat belt. He laid the sword on the bench next to him. The click of the belt issued a sense of finality that he found disturbing. He drew in a deep breath and turned to find Philby looking down through the control booth's window.

Finn gave him a thumbs-up. Philby returned the gesture. There was a loud popping sound. The car hummed and vibrated slightly. It rolled forward.

Finn looked back over his shoulder to see Philby hurrying down a ladder and dodging obstacles and vaulting line railings in an effort to reach the moving car. Lights blinked on overhead with the car's movement: the ride was coming online; Philby had done it.

Philby was now only a few yards from the end of the loading dock and running fast. He had a good chance of reaching the car in time.

Finn spotted someone in the shadows—the same mechanic they'd been afraid of in the waiting line, the mechanic they'd seen at the same time that they'd smelled the electricity in the air.

He carried a heavy wrench in his right hand.

"Look out!" Finn shouted.

Philby skidded to a stop, and ducked just in time as the wrench ripped through the air where Philby's head would have been.

"Catch!" Finn shouted. He tossed the sword—pommel first—to Philby, who caught the grip perfectly.

As the car paused at DISPATCH, for what was announced as a seat belt check—not that there was anyone checking his—he looked back.

The mechanic took another swipe at Philby with the wrench.

Philby caught the wrench with the sword blade and a clanking of metal rang out.

Finn twisted in the seat to watch. His test car faced the HILL CLIMB. He saw two more contacts between the wrench and the blade, sparks shooting off at the second. Philby went down on one knee with the second blow, and the last thing Finn saw as the car climbed out of sight of the loading area was the mechanic lowering the wrench toward Philby's head with a vicious deliberateness.

* * *

Charlene got the call seconds after Maybeck hit the seat-restraint button.

Jess spoke softly into the phone and so it was difficult for Charlene to hear. "I see a screen," she said, "like a TV screen. There are two squares beneath it to either side and switches to the side. Three labels. Willa thinks the labels mean it's your ride, Mission: Space."

"Yes! She's right. I'm looking at a bunch of screens right now, and there're a gazillion square buttons and switches all over the place."

"'Valves' . . . 'Hypersleep' . . . 'First Stage,'" Jess said. "Those are the labels. I don't know what they mean, or even if they mean something, but Willa thinks it's important."

Charlene repeated the three labels, her eyes searching the console. The Hypersleep button was directly below the Engineer screen. Next, she spotted the 1st Stage Sep button below the Commander's screen.

"That's all I've got," Jess said.

Charlene thanked her and was about to ask her to describe the location of the Valves button, when the doors hissed. Maybeck hit the button. The door was about to close.

"I need you in here!" she shouted to Maybeck, realizing that with her seat belt locked around her waist, she couldn't reach the 1st Stage button, only the Hypersleep. *"Now!"*

For once, Maybeck listened to someone else. He dove through the opening as the door slid shut, landing across her knees, extended the full length of the capsule. He caught a foot, and just wrenched it free—his running shoe coming off—as the door sealed shut.

Charlene had reached out to pull on his leg to free his stuck foot. It was in that confusion that her eye lit upon a set of switches stacked vertically: Electrics, Hydraulics, Valves.

Valves! she realized. They were in such an out-of-the way location, she might have missed them entirely had she not reached for Maybeck's leg.

But now, as the interior lights went dark, rendering the capsule pitch-black, and a screen flickered, showing a blue sky filled with soft white clouds, she worked to imprint the exact location of those switches: to her right, and a little lower than her elbow.

"How long is this ride?" she asked Maybeck, who had pulled himself to sitting, feet on the floor, facing the far left screen.

"I don't know. Five minutes? Feels a lot longer than that, but that's what I'm guessing. Did I happen to mention that I hate this ride?"

The screen showed they were lining up with a launch platform. The pod began to shake and the roar of rocket engines drowned out all thought.

"We . . . have . . . to . . . focus!" she said, her teeth rattling. "We have five minutes to figure out these buttons."

"What buttons?"

"You take the Commander screen."

"Got it."

"Lower left button is marked—"

"First Stage Sep," he said.

"That's it. I've got the Hypersleep button and, I hope, the Valves switch. My guess is that we need to work these buttons in the right order and something will happen."

"That doesn't sound so great," Maybeck said. "What if we don't want it to happen?"

The capsule lifted and, as it did, the force driving Charlene back into her seat became intense. She sensed the capsule's spinning and began to feel dizzy.

"Note to self," Maybeck said, "I could easily hurl, or pass out, or whatever. So if we're going to do something, I would suggest sooner than later."

The liftoff was causing the capsule to feel like it might break apart.

"What . . . happens . . . first?" she managed to ask.

"Stage separation," he answered. "I know that much."

"And that's you. Okay. . . ."

"And like right away!" he spit out.

At that instant, the narrator's voice instructed the Commander, "Initiate first stage separation. . . .*Now!*" The 1st Stage Sep button lit up.

"Push the button," Charlene hollered too loudly, "and hold it! *Do not let go!*"

"Got it!" Maybeck said, depressing the button. "Hyperspace is next."

The Mission Control woman told them they were looking good. Maybeck had a few choice words for her, but kept them to himself. The man's voice told the pilot to fire the second-stage rockets.

"Don't do anything," she said.

"But what if—"

"It's not part of Wayne's instructions."

"But we're not even sure—"

"*Do not* touch any buttons. Not until I say so."

"Who put you in charge?"

"You did, remember? You wanted me in the capsule. Well, here I am."

They might have been able to see each other given the glow of the monitors, but Charlene couldn't sit forward. She was pasted back in her seat. The capsule slingshot around the moon and the Mission Control man told the engineer to activate Hyperspace.

"Okay. . . ." Charlene said, reaching out and pressing and holding the Hypersleep button.

"He said Hyper*space*, not Hyper*sleep*."

"Yeah? Well, we're making this up as we go," she said. She could see Maybeck's outstretched arm—thankfully, he was still holding the 1st Stage Sep button.

While holding the Hypersleep button, she stretched to find the Valves switch. She felt in the dark—top switch, middle switch, lower switch. She walked her fingers up and counted them again.

She talked to herself: "Top: Electrics. Middle: Valves. Lower: Hydraulics."

"What's going on? We're about to . . . crash on Mars."

"I'm going to throw the switch," she called out. "Hold on."

"Hold on? I'm flat as a pancake over here, Charlene, and I'm about to lose my cookies. And that makes pancakes and cookies, and that's not pretty."

Charlene touched the switch, hesitating only a heartbeat. Then she pushed it down.

Suddenly, the pressure against her chest tripled.

"It's speeding up!" Maybeck cried out.

"I . . . know," she managed to choke out. But she could barely breathe.

* * *

Willa turned the handle of the projection-booth door, pausing before pulling it open. She double-checked with Jess, who nodded. Willa cracked the door open just far enough to peer inside.

The overhead fluorescent tube lights flickered and came on automatically—motion sensors had sensed the door opening. A bar of light escaped the crack in the door and Willa did the only thing that made any sense to do: she jerked the door open, pulled Jess inside with her, and eased the door shut as quickly and quietly as possible.

The first thing that impressed her about the space was how neat and clean it was. The equipment was big and clunky—white metal boxes, and a tall glass one just ahead, all carefully labeled and covered in warning stickers. The projector itself was enormous, situated in the middle of the narrow room. Wide film fed from the glass case into the projector and then looped around and returned to the case.

"The IMAX film," Jess said, "is a continuous loop. This box," she said, indicating the glass tower, "keeps the film organized—see all the rollers?" The glass box held the film between rollers top to bottom so that a hundred yards or more of film could be stored in a four-foot-by-three-foot box, just four feet high.

"Maybe I get the four-one-one another time, if it's okay with you?" Willa said, her face sweaty, her eyes nervous.

"Sure, no problem." But Jess studied all the equipment with fascination, having read about it and studied it, but never having seen it in person.

Willa moved quickly through the projection room to a far door and carefully opened it as well. "He's not here," she said. "It's a storage room."

Jess took her time at the projector.

"It's like one of those computer clean rooms," Willa said. "And check it out: the temperature and humidity are monitored. So I'm guessing this is the place that reported the temperature drop back to maintenance."

Jess finally broke away from her study of the gear. "And that means . . . Maleficent?"

"If Maleficent entered this room the temperature would sure drop considerably, so yes, I assume at some point she was here."

"For what reason?"

"That's what we need to figure out. Does it have to do with their testing the new New York film? Something to do with Wayne? Was he kept here for a while? I don't know the answers."

"We're assuming Wayne is here somewhere in Epcot," Jess said. "Because of my dream—the jacket he's wearing and our discovery of the boardroom mural. Okay?"

"Okay."

"So what if the Overtakers found out that Wayne had discovered their plans? I mean, when they took me, it was to keep me from seeing into the future and knowing what they were up to. So what if Wayne presented the same problem: he knew what they were up to?"

"Okay, I'm with you."

"And Wayne had been all over the park putting this together. Right? I mean that's what he would do, isn't it? Make sure he was right? And let's say that the Overtakers had some way of knowing where Wayne had gone. A GPS chip in his phone, or maybe a memo he'd written, or questions he'd asked to the wrong person. That's not so important. What is important is that the Overtakers had some way of knowing where he'd been, what he'd been up to."

"Which could have happened in any number of ways."

"Exactly right."

"So," Willa said, "Maleficent or the Overtakers retrace Wayne's steps, and in doing so trip all the temperature sensors because the temperature drops wherever she goes."

"She's smart enough to hide somewhere that won't happen. We're not going to find her in one of the places on the maintenance list. I don't believe that's going to happen."

"But we're here because Wayne was once here," Willa said. "I think this makes a lot of sense."

"Me, too. So that means we need to figure out why Wayne came here. Why Soarin'? Why the projection booth? He must have been onto the Overtakers' plan. They followed him here, just as we have."

"So they probably took whatever it was that he was after—if he didn't take it himself," Willa said.

"Possibly."

"Probably, is more like it."

"But you're forgetting something: he went missing during all the trouble in the Animal Kingdom when you guys were trying to find me. There's a time thing here. The maintenance logs are more recent than that, so the Overtakers came here *after* they already had Wayne. So they were or *are* looking for something that Wayne didn't have on him when they got him. You can bet they searched the Firehouse—and they obviously didn't find it there either."

"So it's still here," Willa said.

"I think so. I think there are clues of some sort all over the park. Wayne left them in the attractions that have to do with flying. He's trying to save the park. You *know* that's his main concern. That's just Wayne. The

Blake poem was trying to tell us that he's willing to die to save the parks, if necessary. So whatever he was worried about is here."

"Unless they found it," Willa clarified.

"True," Jess said. "But if they found it, then why did they keep looking? The maintenance log has Maleficent—or at least temperature drops—happening all over the place."

"So they never did find it!" Willa said.

"Or, there's more than one thing to find. More than one clue, one piece of evidence. Wayne spread it around, knowing that would increase our chances of figuring it out."

"There's something here somewhere," Willa said, spinning around.

"I think so," said Jess.

"So we conduct a search. A methodical search, just the way Wayne would expect Philby to organize it."

"We start at the door and work our way forward," Jess said.

"One question," Willa said. "Could it be in the film? If he spliced a single frame into the film, would it ever be spotted?"

"At twenty-four frames per second," Jess said, quoting her research, "I doubt it. It might flicker, but you wouldn't see it. Good point. What a hiding place! That's brilliant, Willa!"

"Thank you."

"But we're not going to catch it. Not while the film is moving. Your eye can't pick it up with the film moving so fast."

The film was moving as the test downstairs continued.

"So?"

"Wayne would know the film is stored in the glass box. It's too hard for us to see it all in there. If he left a clue spliced into the film it would have to be right at the start, right where we'd see it when the film was stopped and waiting to load and, I hate to say it, but it would be the California film, not the New York one they're testing." She pointed to an enormous aluminum wheel—a case—sitting on the floor. "That's the California film. It's basically a crime to open that box. The film is incredibly sensitive to dust and dirt in the air. You handle with special white—"

She was interrupted by Willa's pointing to a pair of the very gloves she was describing.

"Okay," Jess said. "I'll check the film while you search the room. But you have to be thorough."

"We both have to be thorough."

"And fast," Jess said. "If they have a problem with their test, they may head up here."

They got to work. Five minutes passed. Ten. Jess

had the case open and was carefully reviewing each frame of the film's leader by holding the film up to the overhead light.

Willa was working her way through the room, inch by inch, making note of every piece of equipment and anything that might be unusual about it.

"Got something!" Jess said, her white-gloved hands carefully holding the film over her head. Willa joined her.

"See the splice line?" Jess said. "I mean, there are several in the leader, so it's not anything huge by itself, but see this second splice? It's a single frame that has been cut into the film. And that is unusual. This is the only one I've seen."

"But it's black."

"It's dark, yes. It blends in that way with the rest of the leader. But it's not actually black, just very, very, dark. We need more light."

"Such as?"

"I'm not sure. The projector's light is incredibly bright. If we could slide the whole can over there, and I could get close enough to where the light is leaking out, maybe . . ."

"So let's do it," Willa said.

The film can was incredibly heavy. Even working together, the two couldn't budge it.

"We'll have to unwind the film far enough to get the leader over there," Jess said. "And it can't touch the floor or it's ruined. Use your socks as gloves."

"What?"

"Take off your socks and use them as gloves. You're going to have to hold the film."

A minute later Jess was uncoiling the film from the can and Willa was supporting it, keeping it from touching the floor. Jess managed to get the splice up to the edge of the projector, from which a brilliant white light seeped out and illuminated the dark rectangle of spliced film.

What she saw astounded her.

"It's a seat belt sign," she said.

"A *what*?"

"You heard me. Like you'd see on an airplane or something."

Jess had turned to look back at Willa. In doing so, she'd lost track of her hands. They wandered into the projector's beam, interrupting it. She noticed this immediately, but it was too late: she'd broken the image being projected to the screen.

"Uh-oh," she said. Glancing out through the projection windowpane she could just make out the two tiny figures well below, at the control console. The bigger of the two—the man—was pointing up toward the booth.

"The *lights*!" she said to Willa. "The room lights can be seen from below. They know we're here!"

Willa kept her calm, immediately coiling the film back into the can. Jess fed her the extra length.

"I saw something. . . . I have to check something," Willa said.

"Saw what?"

"In this book over there. It's a journal. It's marked A-three, whatever that means. But I think it's some kind of maintenance log. There was something about seat belts. . . ."

"No way," Jess said.

"Way."

The projector stopped.

"This is not good," said Willa.

They'd fed enough film into the can that Jess could take over and finish it up. Willa pulled her hands from her socks, dropping one in the process. She hurried over past the projector. The journal was an oversized notebook with a hardcover. She flipped through the pages as Jess finished putting the film away and closing the canister.

"He's got to be on his way up here," Jess said. "I know he saw the light on."

"I knew it!" Willa said. "The last entry lists a seat belt inspection. Some of the seat belts were locking but not opening. And get this! The dates of all the other maintenance work . . . it ends like two *years* ago. They must have automated the work or something. But this seat belt thing . . . it's dated three weeks ago."

"Right when Wayne went missing."

"Bingo," Willa said.

"It has to mean something."

Willa moved to the projection window.

"Oh, no . . ." she gasped. "He's on his way up here."

"Well, we can't go out the door."

"And it's not like we can hide in here."

"There!" Jess said. She pointed beyond Willa to a door.

They hurried and opened the door. It led into the upper-level superstructure of the ride—a catwalk that led out into the dark and the steel girders that supported Soarin's huge swings below.

"We're supposed to go out there?" Willa groaned.

"Just don't look down!" Jess said.

They stepped out into the dark and pulled the door closed. Jess made the mistake of not following her own advice: she glanced down. One misstep, and they would fall sixty feet through steel pipes to a concrete floor.

"Keep moving," she said, her voice dry with fright.

* * *

As the test car crested the hill, the Dan Patrick voice announced the start of rough road tests and the car turned and dropped back down a ramp, shaking and vibrating its way to the bottom. Finn remembered this as the place his sister would try to talk and her voice would rattle, amusing the family.

Thought of his sister and his family made him wonder what would happen when he couldn't be awakened, when his mother discovered him stuck in the Syndrome. An unpleasant thought, he pushed it aside.

He heard Philby scream, a skin-crawling sound that echoed through the ride and he called back, shouting his name. *"Philby?"*

The stupid seat belt wouldn't let him out of the car no matter how hard he wrestled with it. The more he fought it, the tighter it gripped him; he suddenly saw what an easy target he would make if anyone came after him. He'd given Philby his own means of self-defense; but Finn was a sitting duck. A *strapped-in* sitting duck, at that.

The brake test came next—the car racing headlong toward a barrier. Finn held a dozen thoughts in his head at this point, one of which was the notion that if the mannequin had attacked them, then the Overtakers had been expecting them; and if the Overtakers had been expecting them, then would they have sabotaged the test car? And if they had sabotaged the test car, wouldn't the brakes be the first thing to go?

The test car flew toward the end of the line. Finn knew where to expect the sensation of being slowed by the brakes, and it didn't come. Instead, the car maintained speed as it swung left, following the track. The left wheels lifted off the concrete, then thumped back down. The car swung right as the narrators both said something but the car was moving too fast for Finn to hear it. Finn reached out and grabbed for the dash as the car entered a second brake test at a speed he'd never felt before. Propelled down a straightaway at an unbelievable speed, it seemed certain to crash. Again Finn fought the seat belt. Again, he did nothing but tighten it a notch across his waist.

"Braking!" the woman's voice shouted.

But the car didn't brake. It swung left again and, as before, nearly jumped the track—throwing Finn to his right, the left wheels lifting, the car balanced only on its two right wheels, then slamming down as it turned right.

It rolled to a stop inside the heat chamber, the narrator saying something about "extreme test conditions." Banks of infrared lights came on and the room quickly warmed. Finn knew the ride, knew the car was supposed to continue right on through to the next chamber. He could see it ahead: the cold room.

But the car stopped. The hundreds of heat lamps remained on and Finn felt the temperature quickly rising, dangerously rising. For a moment the heat had actually felt good, but now it did not. He guessed it was well over a hundred degrees inside the car and gaining rapidly.

105. . . .

110. . . .

He was beginning to bake. Sweat ran into his eyes, stinging. He struggled against the restraints. His face was burning. The metal of the car was too hot to touch. He pulled his hands in. He thought he smelled his hair burning.

Plastic began to melt. The disintegration moved toward him from both sides, trying to meet in the middle. If that kind of heat reached him. . . .

Smoke rose from the vehicle. A label adhered to the side caught fire, flames licking up to his right.

Finn was crazy now, jumping and bucking and fighting the seat belt restraint, trying to slip up and out. The thing was impossibly tight. If he hadn't tried so hard to break out earlier he might have made it; but it had cinched so tight that he felt choked around the waist, and he wasn't coming out of it. If he could calm down he might all-clear his way out, but he was anything but calm.

"Welcome. . . ."

He looked up through his blurred vision—it felt as if his eyelashes had burned off—and into the blue-and-white cold room only twenty feet in front of him.

She was taller than he remembered, her green face longer, her chin more pointed, the purple lining of her robe more . . . purple. Smoke swirled around the car. The melting plastic inched toward him, a thermometer warning him of how little time he had. He was going to combust.

"You never know when to quit, do you, Finn?"

He had never liked that she knew his name. Did not like to hear her say it now. He understood the heat now—it had less to do with the lights, and much more to do with this witch. Her association with electricity—was she part electricity herself?—explained the intense temperature. And what better place to trap him than in a room adjoined by a walk-in freezer big enough for a car?

"Where is he?" Finn called out.

"You never let well enough alone, young man." She raised her hand and pointed at him and what looked like the trail left by a laser welder crept up the car's hood, melting a line into the metal.

Finn could smell burning rubber. The tires were going.

"You are dabbling where you shouldn't be dabbling," she said.

"You and Chernabog should have kept moving, should have moved on. But you can't, can you? You can't leave the parks. You're stuck here, where you were created. You want so badly to scare us—to scare everyone—but you're pitiful really. A sad, silly witch who can't do anything but make trouble. How sick is that?"

She moved her green finger and the red laser line melting through the sheet metal of the hood changed direction as well.

"Silly? You still think so? It's fun to watch you burn. To watch you pay for all the trouble you've brought me. You and your self-righteous friends. You will come and go, the five of you, your friend Wayne. You'll see. But I will live here forever. I am immortal, am I not? Fifty years old and I haven't aged a day. You try that."

"Oh, I don't know," Finn said. "You look a hundred to me."

She didn't like that. She twisted her horrible face into a ball of meanness, of spite and hatred.

"It wouldn't do to just kill you. You must be made to suffer first."

Where had he been? What had he been thinking? He felt like Dorothy in Oz: he'd been wearing the slippers all along. Slippers that this green witch did not know he possessed.

He closed his eyes and pictured a train tunnel.

"Don't you dare pass out on me, boy! I want to hear you scream. I want to see you suffer. Open your eyes."

He pictured a deep, bottomless void of black—a cool dark pit so perfect that no sound escaped.

He felt his hands tingle.

She might have been saying something, but he didn't hear.

He felt his legs twitch and jump with static, like his nerves misfiring just before sleep.

The train's light came toward him, growing brighter and more intense. He leaned forward and came out of the chest strap—there was no heat, no cold. He felt nothing but the intense tingling in his limbs and a fullness in his heart. He sat forward. The waist strap passed through him. He pulled up and out of it.

The melting plastic crept from either side and joined, melting the seat he'd been sitting in, just as the witch's laser went straight up his legs and chest, passing right through him.

In complete disbelief she looked first to her finger

and then to the boy, as if there had to be something mechanically wrong, as if she needed to put another battery in her finger, or sharpen her dark purple fingernail.

Finn stood in the smoking car, shimmering.

"Things are really heating up," he said to her, moving to jump out of the car.

"Finn! Catch!" It was Philby! He was running up the track toward Finn, his left forearm raised against the intense heat. He threw the sword. It flew through the air, end over end, and Finn reached to catch it, to snatch it out of the air the way they did in movies. But he was *all clear* and the sword passed right through his hand and landed. He would have to come out of all-clear to pick up the sword—and that would also make him vulnerable. His arms tingled. He picked up the sword.

He slashed and sliced as he jumped free of the vehicle and marched steadily toward Maleficent, who was already retreating deeper into the cold chamber.

As she backed up, the heat on Finn's back quickly lessened.

Finn heard a spray behind him: Philby had grabbed a fire extinguisher.

Maleficent was backed up to the end of the cold room now. Finn didn't feel the cold, only the swinging steel in his hand.

The infrared lights went off as Philby doused the last of the flames.

"We will defeat you," Finn said, still advancing steadily. "The longer you drag this out, the less likely it is that your character will survive. You understand that, don't you? The stories can be rewritten. Some of us die, it's true. But others are simply written out of the story. Edited out of the film. Removed. Permanently. Erased." He witnessed her reaction—a horror he'd not seen on her confident face before. "It's what you fear the most, isn't it? What you Overtakers are running from? Erasure? Insignificance? The fear that your ride, your attraction will be removed from the park the way others have been? One day you're here. One day you're gone."

"What do you know?" she said.

He didn't quite believe his eyes as he watched her melt into the gray concrete floor, watched her reform into a snake equal in size to Gigabyte, but bearing a definite green hue. His hands and feet tingled, and he realized that fear had gotten the better of him.

He didn't like snakes.

She came after him with a flick of her mighty tail, slithering toward him with blinding speed. She opened her awful mouth, revealing a pair of fangs that had to be two feet long.

He raised the sword and prepared to strike.

Maleficent flicked her tongue in the direction of the half-melted test car, and the car made a popping noise and came to life, its headlights snapping on brightly. It rolled toward Finn, gaining speed.

From the front—Maleficent in snake form. From behind—the car. And Finn in the middle, raking the heavy sword left to right, right to left, keeping the eager snake at bay. Maleficent lunged, fangs extended, but Finn sliced for her head and she retreated.

"Look out!" Philby said. "Jump when I say!"

Finn dared not look back. Maleficent struck again. Finn caught her on the side of the head with the blade. She bled—green blood—crying out as she jerked her head back.

"Now!" Philby said.

Finn jumped straight up.

The car cut under him. He tumbled backward, rolled along the hood, and was dumped into the seat area, where Philby grabbed hold of him.

"Duck!" Philby roared.

Finn tucked into a ball just as Maleficent's bleeding snake head cut through the air overhead, its fangs dripping a venom that looked like pus.

The car took off, gaining speed. The narrator said something about robots and picking up the pace.

The car moved faster and faster. And faster still.

"I don't like this," Philby said, struggling to sit down in a seat. He helped Finn turn around and planted him in the seat next to him.

The test car was moving much too fast. Faster than it was engineered for. Through one turn. Around another to the left. Another to the right. The tires screeched through the next turn to the left and louder still to the right. More turns, the car rocking up onto its partially melted tires. A truck came at them head-on and nearly hit them—a projection that Finn had forgotten about. The car should have slowed then, but it did not. It was moving far too quickly for them to jump.

It whipped through a few scenes that should have been taken at a leisurely pace and headed for the barrier test at far too high a speed. The barrier was timed to lift out of the way of the oncoming car at the last second—one of the ride's many thrills—but the timing was set up for a much slower speed. The car arrived before the barrier lifted. It rammed the barrier head-on, punched a hole through it, and broke out into the night air outside—onto the oval track and the fastest, most dangerous part of the ride.

33

CHARLENE STRUGGLED TO maintain consciousness as Mission: Space flew out of control. The center screen, which was supposed to simulate a view out the space capsule, showed them landing on Mars, balancing on a precipice above a thousand foot fall, and then. . . .

Falling over the edge.

The sensation inside the capsule was of both falling and weightlessness, a nauseating combination that left Maybeck making unpleasant noises next to her.

Oh, please don't, Charlene found herself thinking. If he puked inside the pod it was going to reek, and she would likely follow.

They crashed at the bottom in a roar of metal and rock and she wondered if she hadn't been half-DHI at that moment what effect it would have had on her body. She assumed she would have passed out. But she remained awake and hyperalert, charged with adrenaline.

The screen had gone dark upon impact. It now sputtered static and came back to life.

A man's face filled the screen: an old man.

Wayne.

"If you're seeing this, you have survived an arduous journey and Jessica has managed to see what I'd hoped she'd see, and that means I am speaking to one or more of the Kingdom Keepers, and only to the Kingdom Keepers. It also means that something has happened to me, either of a temporary or permanent nature, and that necessitates diligence on your part, and likely requires a great deal of you in the hours to come. It's probably dark in the capsule, so let me take care of that."

The lights came on. The effect was eerie—as if he were right there with them.

"That should do it," he said. "If you want to take notes, you'll find paper and a pen beneath the center seat."

Charlene found them and prepared to write.

"I don't believe this," Maybeck said. "I thought I'd seen everything."

"Hush!" she said.

"The Overtakers are planning something of a scale we've not seen before," Wayne continued. His eyes tracked to his right. He was afraid of being discovered. "It will come on the heels of a deception of the worst kind. Beware your friends and know your enemies. I trust you have found the carousel and that Philby knew what to do or you wouldn't be here."

He was being vague, perhaps in the fear that despite his efforts the Overtakers might discover his message. Charlene scribbled down as much as she could of what he was saying.

"Remember: we stand under it to get out of the rain but it lives above our brain." He glanced furtively to his right again.

"I haven't got long." He smiled, wincing. "None of us do. The solution is in Norway. Finn must know that. Trust it. By all means, he must *use* it. Now and later. He—you all—will need more help. What I'm talking about: it *is* mightier than the sword. . . . At some point you will meet my daughter, I presume, if you haven't already. I didn't name her by chance, you know? Do you know? If you don't now, you will before long."

The image fizzled and went black. But just before he disappeared into a curtain of static, Wayne's gaze shifted to his right and froze as terror filled his kind face and Charlene felt a horrible hollow in the pit of her stomach.

"That's all?" Maybeck said.

"I wrote it down," Charlene told him.

"Why is he always so . . . Wayne?"

"Because he is," Charlene said. "He knows what they're capable of. He's careful because of that."

"Yeah, but I mean, I seriously doubt any Overtaker could have survived what we just went through. He planned it brilliantly: being DHIs we don't have the same mass, so there isn't the same gravitational pull as on a normal person. A Cast Member or character would have tossed their cookies and passed out. He could put us through something no one else could make it through. So why not spill the beans once we get through all that?"

"Because that video is on a computer server somewhere. Maybe only a DHI could see it here, but what if it was discovered and viewed another way?"

Maybeck nodded. "I hadn't thought of that." A rare moment of humility. The spinning must have gotten to him, she thought.

"We need to tell the others," she said. She tried the phone. With the pod's door closed she had no reception.

"Which begs the question," Maybeck said. "Now that we're both in here, who is going to open the door?"

The screen spit static.

The door to the pod opened.

* * *

The catwalk led nowhere. Willa and Jess had walked only a few feet when the metal mesh bridge arrived at a dead end. Behind them loomed the closed door to the projection booth.

"There!" Jess said, pointing.

Through the small window that allowed the projector's beam to reach the screen they could see a man's head moving around.

Willa said, "Wayne wanted us to find that maintenance diary. We're done here." She glanced down. It was such a long way to the floor. "How are you with climbing?"

"As in?"

"There's a ladder right here. It probably goes down to another catwalk. Maybe we can find our way down."

"Probably? The best we can do is probably?"

"It's better than being caught."

Jess said, "Okay, I'll go first."

Jess forced herself not to look down. She placed her feet on each rung, careful to make sure she made contact. The rungs were no more than a thin piece of steel, and slippery with a glossy gray paint.

"He's coming!" Willa hissed down to Jess. "The door!"

Jess looked up through the mesh of the catwalk and saw the doorknob turning. She hurried down, moving dangerously fast. If she fell. . . .

Willa climbed down quickly, and found that her ankles were suddenly in Jess's face. Jess leaned back to avoid Willa's shoes and nearly lost her grip. At last the toes of Jess's shoes touched the catwalk below. Willa, moving too quickly, lost control. She slipped and fell the remaining few feet, crashing down onto the catwalk.

"Who's there?" the man called out.

Looking down Willa saw at least four levels of catwalk, each connected to the next by ladders. The catwalks provided access to various levels of machinery, for repair and maintenance, creating a three-dimensional bridge system, a maze of narrow walkways that branched out or terminated in dead ends. Level 3, where the girls now stood, accessed the upper reaches of Soarin's swings, the bench seating that lifted forty feet off the floor to provide the sensation of hang gliding.

Behind them, the New York flight was replaying, causing the light in the room to shift and change color, now a brilliant blue, now nearly pitch-black. The effect created a strobelike flicker so that one moment Jess couldn't see Willa, and then a second later she got a clear look. It was a confusing and difficult environment to move around in without losing your balance or going over the rail.

Jess heard the clanking of the man above them running to the end of the Level 4 catwalk, and knew that once there, if he looked down he would see them.

Jess stumbled and lunged to the right.

Her arm disappeared.

She stopped and thrust her left arm forward: it vanished.

Now she hurried forward and tapped Willa on the back, not wanting to speak. Jess showed her how both hands disappeared when she put them beneath the two-foot-thick pipe that was the top hinge of the Soarin' swings. Thick black rubber hydraulic tubing hung beneath the hinge arm, held there by wire strapping.

Jess motioned up.

They glanced back as they heard a rustling of fabric: the man was coming down the ladder!

Jess jumped up on the railing, grabbed hold of the hydraulic tube, and hung there, her back to the floor, her toes gripping the tube.

She went invisible. Beneath the pipe was a DHI shadow.

Willa jumped up and joined her, farther down the pipe, just as the man banged down onto the catwalk they had been standing on.

Jess slowed her breathing, since she was able to hear it herself and knew it might give her away.

The man walked toward them, peering into the dark. He switched on a flashlight and waved it from side to side.

Jess didn't know how any of this worked, and perhaps Philby could have explained it, but to her surprise, as the flashlight struck her she wasn't illuminated. But she realized a fraction of a second later that she cast a shadow anyway. It was actually Willa's shadow she saw, cast onto the swing to their right. As long as they both remained absolutely still, the shadows didn't look like much. It seemed doubtful he'd even notice.

Then the scene in the film changed and the machinery reacted to lower the benches far below.

The pipe holding them moved, dipping lower toward the screen. Jess fought to hold on to the black tubing, but it was no use. Gravity claimed the aspect of her that was not fully DHI and she began to slide, as did Willa in front of her.

The man must have heard them, even over the music of the ride, for he looked right at Jess—right into her eyes—though he didn't know it.

Down, down, down, she and Willa slid, away from the man who remained up at Level 3. And there, to Jess's right, she spotted the Level 2 catwalk.

She felt her fingers letting go of the rubber hose. She had no choice. She swung left and then right, building momentum. With each effort, as she cleared the projection shadow created by the pipe above her, part of her DHI showed.

"Hey!" cried the man.

She was too focused on her dismount to look up, but she understood that he'd spotted her DHI as it appeared.

"You!" he called out.

She let go and sailed over the railing, throwing herself forward and landing briefly on her feet before falling to her knees.

She heard a clanking ahead of her—Willa, she hoped—but had no time to figure any of this out. There was a red-and-white exit sign thirty feet behind her.

"Go for it!" she heard Willa hiss.

The man was screaming now for help.

"Spies!" he cried out, believing them to be Disney fans no doubt—fans interested in Soarin' changing from California to New York.

If only he knew. . . .

Jess ran for the exit sign. She felt the vibration of the catwalk beneath her feet and knew that Willa was on it as well.

The man's feet appeared ahead of her—he was coming down another ladder.

She ran harder and faster.

"Right behind you!" she heard Willa call out.

A wave of relief surged through her: Willa was okay. Willa was with her.

She banged into the exit door's panic bar and threw the door open. An alarm sounded.

The man cried out for them to stop.

She charged down the fire escape as fast as her feet would carry her, the warm night air splashing onto her face never more welcome.

* * *

As the test car gained speed, Finn turned to Philby and said, "No brakes."

"I remember," Philby shouted above the clatter. The outside track formed a circle around the Test Track pavilion where cars could accelerate to speeds in excess of sixty-five miles per hour. Philby and Finn were quickly approaching ninety miles per hour.

"The system is not designed for this speed!" Philby said, his red hair flying, both hands gripping the melted dashboard. "It's going to jump the track!"

It occurred to Finn that Philby knew such things, though this was one time he wished he didn't.

"As in?"

"We're going to wreck!"

The acceleration pinned them back in their seats. Finn knew by the intense pressure how far from all-clear he was, and how he wasn't going to get back: he was scared. There was no changing that now. No easy fix.

The boys fought against the g-force, heaving forward.

"Give me your shoes," Philby said.

Finn looked at him with bewilderment. It seemed an odd time to be locked in fashion envy.

"Your shoes!" Philby shouted. *"Now!"*

Finn tore them off his feet and Philby hurriedly untied the laces. He kicked off his own and worked the laces loose on those as well.

"Tie 'em together!" he shouted. "Keep the laces as long as possible."

Finn did as he was told. The car was moving dangerously faster now, beginning to jump off the track. The boys felt an eerie sensation combining both gravitational pull and weightlessness that suggested the car was about to go airborne. The intense centrifugal force caused both boys to lean over toward the track's outside rail. No matter how they fought against it, they could not sit up. If it went much faster they would be lying flat on the scat, a position from which it would be impossible to do anything. Without seat belts, each little bump lifted them and drove them against each other on the far right of the car where Finn sat squished.

Philby, furiously checking his knots, happened to look back.

"Bad news!" he said.

Finn battled the forces and managed to turn his head around to see an empty car gaining on them. If the excess speed didn't throw their car off the track, then a collision would take care of them. It was the perfect Overtaker move: the wreck would be blamed on two "vandals" who had broken into the park, switched on the ride, and then been hit and killed by an empty car. No one to blame but the boys themselves. He could almost hear Maleficent laughing. None of them had ever talked about it, but they all believed that should their DHIs ever be killed outright, their sleeping selves would be locked in the Syndrome forever. They would never awaken.

"We've got major problems!" Finn hollered to be heard over the roar of the ride.

"You think?" Philby roared back at him.

Philby had his string of shoes ready. Strung together, the four running shoes looked like an awkward kite tail or string of dead fish. They looked like something invented just to pass the time, with one lace tied to the next in a daisy chain.

Finn felt like challenging Philby, like holding his feet to the fire and asking why now, of all times, the guy was stringing shoes together. But he knew better. Philby was a man of purpose. Everything he did seemed calculated, a means to an end; if anything, the guy didn't loosen up enough. So if Philby wanted to tie a bunch of shoes together while going in excess of ninety miles per hour, riding in a car about to jump the track and kill Finn along with him, then so be it: tie away.

"Here's . . . the . . . deal," Philby said, each word an effort to produce because of the surprising amount of pressure imposed upon his chest by the g-force. "When I say *now* we're going to jump. We're going off your side, over the rail, and then hold on tight. We're too high up—and probably over concrete—to let ourselves fall. So we're going to hang from the outside of the retaining wall. The safety wall. Okay? But listen, we have to get over the wall. It's going to be messy."

"Messy? You think I can time a jump going a hundred miles per hour?" Finn gasped.

"We won't be going a hundred," Philby said. "Hang on tight. . . ."

Finn made the mistake of looking back: the empty test car was bearing down on them. It was either going to collide and throw them from the car, or bump their car off the track. What was Philby thinking?

Philby flung the string of shoes over the windshield toward the vehicle's right front panel.

"What the—?" Finn said.

"The emergency stop," Philby said. "That's why we've got to hold on tight."

Finn understood then: leave it to Philby to figure this out. He hunkered down and braced himself, knees thrust forward into the melted dash. He recalled all the times his parents had chided him about wearing seat belts, but that wasn't an option now, the seat belts were no longer functioning thanks to the excessive heat.

Philby launched his kite tail a second time. The lead shoe slapped the side of the car, just missing the large red plastic emergency stop button.

"Close!" he shouted. He had meant Philby's attempt, but he noticed that the word applied to the trailing car as well: they were about to be rear-ended.

Philby wound up the chain of shoes and launched it again. Finn's running shoe slapped the side of the car, but missed the button again.

Wham! The empty car smashed into the back bumper. The boys whipped forward and Finn nearly left the moving car. He pulled himself back inside.

Philby tried a different technique. He swung hard and got the string of shoes going over his head in a circle, like a cowboy's lasso, like a helicopter blade. The car bumped them from behind again, and then backed off as if it had a mind of its own.

Finn saw what was happening: the trailing car's rear tires smoked as it took aim to knock them from the track.

Philby propped himself up with just his left hand

holding the dash, dropping his right and lowering the circle of shoes with the deftness of a golf pro. Finn's running shoe smashed into the red button and the car's brakes screeched. Finn reached out and grabbed Philby by the belt as Philby lifted off his feet, both hands over his head, ready to fly to his death. Finn held on with all his strength. The test car screamed, shuddered, and slowed.

Behind them, the empty car, its tires smoking, barreled toward them, a collision imminent.

"Now!" Philby shouted.

Finn jumped from the moving car. His chest hit the sheet-metal retaining wall, and he turned, his fingers seeking purchase. He caught hold, stopped himself, and then let go, dropping another three feet. He snagged hold of the lip of the ride at track level, his feet dangling twenty feet above the plaza below.

He caught sight of Philby, in roughly the same position, about twenty feet in front of him.

It sounded like an explosion. The trailing car crashed into their stopped vehicle, sending car parts overhead in a shower of metal and plastic. Some pieces went forty feet up or higher, falling onto the plaza below in great thunderous crashes. An electric motor sailed fifty yards out into a parking lot behind the pavilion. Smoke curled above them, while Finn pictured himself somewhere in the midst of all that destruction, knowing what it would have meant for him, understanding what had just happened. Philby had saved his life.

They moved hand over hand along the perimeter of the track until they were over an awning.

"On three," Philby said. And they let go, falling in unison. They bounced off and slid down the awning and landed on their feet with only a few scratches to show for their adventure. Finn's face was sunburned from the infrared lights and his hair was singed above both ears into tangled curls.

They found the sword point-end down in a flower bed, which reminded Finn of *The Sword in the Stone*. He retrieved it and found he could slip it between his belt and pants and that it would hold.

"Don't know where our shoes ended up," Philby said. "Sorry about that."

Finn faced his friend, thinking about all that had happened in the past few minutes.

"Sorry?" he said. Their shoes were the furthest thing from Finn's mind. Then he smiled at Philby. "Yeah, you'd better be sorry."

He threw an arm over Philby's shoulder, and Philby did the same. The two headed off to the rendezvous in stocking feet, the point of the sword clanking against the concrete plaza with each determined step.

34

AFTER SOME TEXTING, the group met at the rendezvous. It was a few minutes past 3 AM, but no one looked tired. Maybeck was missing a shoe; Willa, a sock. Finn and Philby were shoeless.

Finn pointed out that they couldn't just stand around talking—they were far too visible, far too vulnerable. Surprisingly, it wasn't Philby or Willa who came up with the idea of secreting themselves into a corporate lounge, but Charlene.

"Remember that charity event we did at *The Seas with Nemo and Friends*? The one with the hospital kids? How 'bout there?"

"Brilliant!" said Philby. "It used to be the United Technologies lounge. The company left the park in 1998 and—"

"Spare us the history lesson," Maybeck quipped. "Let's just get out of here."

The Living Seas pavilion was across the plaza and toward the entry gate, a location Finn liked because they needed a place to hide until the Lost and Found opened—and it would be close by to the lounge.

They divided into two groups in case they were spotted or attacked. Maybeck's group went first. Finn followed with Willa, Amanda, and Philby a few minutes later.

The lounge's dark wood paneling, retro furniture, wall decorations, and acrylic piano were a throwback to 1980s decor. A large metal sculpture of a fish stared out from one wall. But the prize of the room was the one entire wall consisting of a window into Nemo's five-million-gallon aquarium, offering dazzling views and endless visual thrills as fish and sea animals swam past.

Finn asked Amanda to speak first. He couldn't take his eyes off her as she recounted what she'd witnessed from the control room atop the Mayan Temple.

"I never had to warn any of you," she said, "but what I saw surprised me. Twice the drawbridge over the lake raised and lowered—"

"That would be the bridge opposite where we crossed," Charlene interrupted, speaking to Willa.

Amanda continued. "And anyway, the globe left the lake the first time, but the second time I couldn't see what it was about. Nothing much happened. It just went up, and a few minutes later, back down. Also, the robot guys on the Segways—the dummies—are constantly patrolling. Around and around the lake. It seemed to me the Overtakers basically have full control of the place."

Willa told them about her and Jess's trials at Soarin' and her discovery of the maintenance journal and the single frame of film with the image of a seat belt on it.

Charlene told about Wayne's video, holding everyone in rapt attention. She read from her notes his exact words, looking up between each comment: "'a deception of the worst kind . . . beware your friends and know your enemies. . . . Remember: we stand under it to get out of the rain but it lives above our brain . . . the solution is in Norway. Trust it . . . Later, you all will need more . . .' He talked about Wanda and said he didn't name her by chance, that 'it is mightier than the sword.'"

The group was silent for a long time after that as they mulled over what it all meant.

Then, before getting into what Charlene had said, Philby joined Finn in talking about their confrontation with Maleficent, Finn's new sunburn, and the wreck of the car on Test Track.

"You can bet the Overtakers will have it all cleaned up by morning," Philby said. "They're clever that way."

"I can confirm that after the wreck," Amanda said, gazing at Finn, her face a knot of both concern and relief, "all sorts of characters headed in that direction. I heard and saw them."

"Which is good for us," Finn said. "That should keep them busy the rest of the night."

"As if we're going anywhere," Willa said. "I'm so glad we found a place to hang out."

She found herself the brunt of everyone's staring.

"What?" she asked.

"Wayne left us a half dozen clues," Philby said.

"He expects action," Finn said.

"You have got to be kidding me! You two nearly got killed. Maybeck and Charlene had to be let out of that pod by Amanda or they'd still be locked in there. And Jess and I were nearly captured. You want to go back out there? Be my guest. I'm happy right here."

"What's any of it mean?" Jess asked. "What was Wayne trying to tell us?"

"'A deception of the worst kind,'" Charlene read from her list.

"Betrayal," Philby said, "is the worst deception."

"Betray—" Willa spit out, unable to completely say the word. "No way!"

"A traitor?" Charlene choked out.

"One of us is going to betray the others?" Maybeck asked.

"That's not possible," Willa said. "Is it?"

"Anything's possible," Finn said.

Maybeck grew sober, suddenly more serious than any of the others had seen him before. "Are you going to tell me that after all we've been through . . . ?" But he, too, could not complete his thought.

He didn't need to: everyone understood him.

"Okay. Well, I, for one, do not believe it," Willa said.

"Neither do I," Charlene said.

"No matter what," Finn added, "it's bad for us to doubt each other, to question our friendship—"

"Or loyalty," Philby said.

"But apparently," Maybeck said, "that's what Wayne had in mind."

"I can't see him doing that," Charlene said. "Why would he turn us against each other?"

"To save the rest of us," Maybeck said. "To keep us alert."

The group sat in a deadly silence for a long time. Looks were exchanged, some of them suspicious.

"I think we should move on," Willa proposed. "What's next?"

Philby said, quoting Wayne, "'We stand under it to get out of the rain, and it lives above our brain.' That's a hat." He won nods from all. "And 'The solution is in Norway.' That's the sword."

"That has to be right," Charlene agreed.

"But what *about* a hat and a sword?" asked Jess. "Do they mean something?"

"They must," said Willa. "That's the way Wayne is. It all means something."

"And a pen is mightier than the sword," Philby said. "Everyone knows that expression. But maybe not the Overtakers, which is why he left part of it out. It's got to be Walt's pen, right?"

"No doubt. But we have to figure the rest of this stuff out," Maybeck complained. "I mean, I'm glad to know what he was trying to tell us—but what was he trying to tell us?"

Everyone turned to Philby. He collected himself and said, "As to the first part: he wants us on guard for a traitor. None of us likes the thought of that, but I think what's done is done. We're not going to look at each other the same way for a while, and we're just going to have to live with that."

Most everyone nodded.

"Wayne shot that video himself. That means he chose what order to tell us stuff in. So after the possible betrayal comes the hat. Right? We need to focus on the hat. Maybe the rest of the stuff will make more sense when we figure out the hat."

"There are so many hats they sell," Charlene said. "Princess hats, baseball caps—"

"Pirate hats."

"Witches' hats?" said Amanda.

"I suppose we should go look at them all," Philby said. "In one of the stores, I mean. I'm not sure we can do this on our own."

"Do not tell me you want to leave here!" Willa said. When everyone looked at her, she sat upright. "Hey . . . now wait a minute . . . enough with those looks. We've got to get something straight: just because you may disagree doesn't mean you're the traitor! You should see how you're all looking at me! What if I'm the one voice of reason in all this? Huh? What if I'm right and Philby's the one leading us out for the Overtakers to catch us?"

They all looked at Philby, whose expression didn't change one bit. "Nice try," he said to Willa.

"I'm not trying anything!" she protested.

"Except to make me out to be a bad guy."

"I'm just asking, are we safer in here or out there? And I think the answer's pretty obvious."

"Willa has a point," Maybeck said, his attention fixed on her. She smiled at him for backing her up and Maybeck looked away. "A couple things are pretty obvious. First of all: we need to stay paired up at all times. If there is a traitor, we can't allow him or her the chance to signal anyone. Secondly: there are too many of us.

We're too big a group to go sneaking around. I'm thinking we send a search party for the hats. I nominate Finn, Philby, and Charlene."

"I hate to point this out," Charlene said, "but whoever the traitor is, he or she would love nothing more than to see the three of us captured. Philby is our brains, Finn our leader—"

"And you're our jock," Willa said. "Yeah. I see what you mean."

Everyone turned his or her attention—and suspicions—onto Maybeck. Finn knew that of all of them Maybeck had been a captive of the Overtakers the longest. He could have been compromised and no one would know it.

"Can I say something?" Amanda said. "Do you people see what's happening? Jess and I, we're new to this. But one of the things that's so impressive about you, about this group, is how you work together. How one person picks up where the other person leaves off. I mean . . . it's actually pretty awesome. And now, all of a sudden, in like five minutes, no one is trusting anyone and every decision is taking about twice as long as you usually take. Just an observation," she said, sitting back.

"How do you undo something like this?" Charlene asked. "It's not like I *want* to see any of you as the traitor, but how am I supposed to not? Wayne wrecked it."

"But he wrecked it for a reason," Philby said.

"He knew how this would mess us up," Finn said.

"Wayne operates on serious bandwidth," Philby said. "He wouldn't have thrown this out there if it wasn't important."

"We'll pick from a hat," Finn said. "Three names. They'll go to the store."

"No irony there," Willa said. "A *hat*?"

"We don't even have a hat!" Maybeck said.

"It's an *expression*," Finn said.

The gloomy mood was broken.

Charlene wrote out their names on small pieces of paper and folded them up. Jess drew three from the pile.

"Philby, Finn, and Charlene," she announced, unfolding and reading them.

"Fate," said Philby.

"I rest my case," said Maybeck. "I *am* the man."

35

FINN HADN'T SAID ANYTHING, but he'd known he had to be part of the scout team; they would need him to fully cross over to all-clear and enter the gift shop in order to open it for the others. After a few minutes of sneaking over to the Mission: Space Gift Shop, being careful not to be seen, Finn unlocked the doors from the inside and admitted Philby and Charlene.

"I don't feel good about this," Finn said. "Seems Security—the real park Security—would know if someone was cruising the gift shop."

"If park Security's doing anything, they're dealing with whatever the Overtakers failed to clean up after the Test Track wreck."

"We still should make it quick," said Charlene. "We don't even know if this is really the clue Wayne meant for us."

"Hats," Philby said. "It has to be hats."

It was dark and gloomy in the shop despite the abundance of cheerful gifts, lending the vast space a sense of foreboding. They split up. Charlene knew where the princess hats were; in fact, she knew much more about the layout of the gift shop than the boys did. She directed Philby to the back and Finn to the left.

Finn found a collection of khaki-colored ball caps for sale. The caps bore a variety of logos and emblems, which made him wonder if those details had anything to do with whatever Wayne wanted them to see. Philby discovered a space helmet and some character hats. Finn joined him in the back, feeling overwhelmed. How were they supposed to make any sense of this? There were a dozen or more different hats, any one of which might be important.

"If we only knew *why* the hat is important," he said.

"Over here," hissed Charlene.

By the time he and Philby joined her Finn felt they'd already spent too much time in the shop. He also found himself wondering who the traitor might be, and when he *or she* might turn on the rest of them. He tried to push the idea from his mind, but it wouldn't yield.

"We've got to get out of here," he pressed.

"So what jumps out at you?" Charlene asked the boys, indicating a shelf of Mickey and Minnie accessories.

"Let's not make this into twenty questions," Finn said.

"I want to make sure this makes sense," she said. "I

don't want to just tell you, I want you to see it."

"You're worried we'll accuse you of being the traitor if it doesn't work out," Philby said, picking up on her tone of voice. "Aren't you?"

"I didn't say that."

"You didn't have to," he said.

"Mickey ears?" Finn said. "A Minnie hat?"

"OMG!" Philby said, stepping toward the display. He reached out and took Mickey's sorcerer hat in hand. He looked at Charlene. "This is what you wanted us to see," he said. She nodded timidly.

Finn took a good look at the pointed sorcerer's cap. It was decorated with a crescent moon and several large stars. "You stand under it to get out of the rain."

"We are *so* dense!" Philby said. "Where do stars never grow old? These stars are always there."

"But the Channel!" Charlene said. "The Channel got us here."

"Maybe by accident. Or maybe there was something else showing that day besides *Dumbo*. We can check on that."

"I'll bet it was *Fantasia*. I'll bet we missed it. Mickey wears that same cap in the movie," said Charlene.

"But the point is," Finn said, "that the sorcerer's hat fits the riddle in keeping off the rain, and about it being on your brain, but it isn't this hat, it's the one in

Hollywood Studios. *That* is the hat that keeps you out of the rain."

"Fantasmic!" Philby said. "It all adds up. You see? Mickey's hat. Hollywood Studios. The sword. Mickey defeats the dragon in the show with the—"

"Sword," Finn said.

"And the dragon is Maleficent," Charlene said. "It's either Chernabog or Maleficent that turns into the dragon. Right?"

"It's Maleficent," Professor Philby said. "First Mickey encounters the Wicked Queen from Snow White, then she summons all the baddies—Ursula, Cruella, Scar. Jafar becomes a genie and Mickey accidentally calls out Hercules and Chernabog. It's Chernabog who summons the dead, and who brings Maleficent. And it's Maleficent who transfigures into the dragon."

"Where does the sword come in?" Finn asked.

"It doesn't. Mickey defeats the dragon with a wall of water. In the movie, *Fantasia*, it's thc ringing of a bell that drives Chernabog back to his mountain."

"No sword?"

"Maybe this is a new version," Charlene said. "With a new hero." She was looking intently at Finn.

"This is what Wayne wanted us to find," Philby said. "I'm sure of it. The stars. All the clues. And

Fantasmic! is the perfect place for Maleficent and Chernabog to hide. That show is all about them, and it's virtually deserted twenty-three hours a day."

"You and I saw her right here," Finn reminded.

"We did," Philby agreed. "But the parks are close to each other. She can transfigure herself into a bird. I'm not saying she's in two places at once. I'm just saying Wayne wants us over at Fantasmic!"

"Not before we find him."

"We may not have a choice on that," Philby said. "What if we don't find him here?"

"We will," said Finn.

"If only we could go back in time, we could have rescued him from Wonders."

Charlene's comment stopped Finn cold. For a moment he faced her as if in a trance. Then he took her by the shoulders and all three of them thought Finn was about to kiss her. Charlene looked terrified; Philby looked surprised; Finn looked out of it.

"We blew it!" Finn said.

"You don't have to sound so excited about it," Philby said. Then he added, "Blew what, exactly?"

"'Go back in time.' Charlene just said: 'Go back in time.'" He still held her shoulders; she still looked panicked.

"Yeah? So what?" Philby said.

Charlene was speechless. She turned her cheek toward Finn so that at least if he tried to kiss her it wouldn't be on the lips. But she didn't push him away, and she would later secretly wonder why not.

"Think about Jess's dreams," Finn said. "Her visions. What's the one thing we know about them? About when they take place?"

"The fut—" Philby said, catching himself. "No way!"

"What's going on?" Charlene asked, still braced for the possibility of a kiss.

Philby answered for Finn. "When we went to Wonders, the writing wasn't on the wall behind the chair. It wasn't exactly like Jess's dream. No Wayne. No words on the wall."

"I was there. I know all this."

"We were all there. But we were *too soon*," Finn said. "Wayne hadn't been brought there yet. We got there *ahead* of Jess's vision. It wasn't that she'd gotten it wrong—"

"We were just early," Philby said, completing his thought.

"So at some point he's still going to end up in that chair?" Charlene said.

"At some point they start moving him around to keep him hidden," Philby said.

"Like, for instance," Finn said, "after the Kingdom

Keepers cause a car crash at Test Track."

"Or discover the maintenance log at Soarin'," Philby said.

"Or end up on Mission: Space," Charlene added.

The excitement sparked between them. Finn finally released Charlene's shoulders, apologizing, and she quietly sighed in relief.

"He's there now," Finn said. "I can feel it. He's leaving a message on the wall for Jess that she got days ago. We can still save him."

"If you're right, he'll be under heavy guard," Philby said, not contradicting Finn.

"Since when has that stopped us?"

36

WONDERS OF LIFE loomed out of a gray ground fog sucked from the earth as the night stretched its cold arm toward morning. Four AM had come and gone beneath an overcast sky that seemed to darken by the minute. It was as if Maleficent herself were in the sky, directing the darkness to continue, blotting out any attempts of a dawning sun to hint at its impending arrival.

From within the jungle landscaping, not far from their original position, seven pairs of eyes studied the abandoned pavilion, seven hearts beat wildly from a combination of fatigue, fear, and anticipation. Where was the snake? The cavemen? Where were the Norwegian and his son?

The plan, hastily thought up by Maybeck, but agreed upon by all, was a simple one of tactical diversion: Maybeck and Finn, both capable of all-clear—though Maybeck less so than Finn—would enter the pavilion first and position themselves with a view of the boardroom. Charlene would arrive to provide a distraction, making herself the object of pursuit. Her athletic ability was supposed to best any effort by the

Overtakers to capture her. While she kept the Overtakers busy, Maybeck and Finn would rescue Wayne.

Jess, Willa, and Amanda were to take up positions outside the pavilion, keeping it under constant surveillance, while Philby would infiltrate the pavilion's utility area—which they believed to be in the basement—hoping to be able to monitor, if not control, the structure's electricity and security.

It took them ten minutes to finally spot Gigabyte. The humongous snake came from their left, up the path toward the pavilion, its tongue lashing the air for unexpected scents. It circled the pavilion and headed back down the path and through the line of potted trees that blocked the view of the pavilion from the park.

Philby checked his watch. "Twelve minutes," he said. "We need to be in and out in ten, or the snake is going to present a major problem."

"Is everyone clear on what to do if we find Wayne?" said Finn.

"It's up to Charlene," Jess said, "to create a diversion."

"Eleven minutes," Philby warned, "and counting."

"Let's go," Finn said to Maybeck.

The two approached a side window together, avoiding the front door.

“I can do this,” Maybeck said. He closed his eyes, let out a deep breath and stepped forward, knocking into the window as he tried to step through. He fell back, but Finn caught him.

“A little quieter wouldn’t hurt,” Finn said, standing him up again. “Picture a train—”

“I said I can do this!” Maybeck said. He tried again, but the window blocked him for a second time.

Finn could imagine Philby counting down the minutes. He checked his watch: ten minutes left.

“One last try,” he told Maybeck. “Then I go it alone.”

Maybeck closed his eyes, released a cleansing breath, and said, “Okay. A train light at the end of a tunnel. Now what?” Maybeck did not enjoy having to ask anyone for help with anything.

“Let the train come toward you. It takes over all the darkness, it blots out all sound, even the sound of my voice.”

Maybeck stepped through the glass. Finn closed his eyes and followed. They were inside.

* * *

Charlene entered through the front door, left open by Finn, exactly three minutes after Finn and Maybeck had been seen stepping through the pavilion’s side window.

Had Finn set a trap for her? Was he the one Wayne had warned them about?

She hurried up the main stairs, keeping low and holding on to the banister, knowing that Finn and Maybeck would, at this same moment, be ascending the stairs.

She didn't look back, but heard Philby enter shortly behind her, wondering if he'd have time to be effective but putting nothing past him.

In the back of her mind lingered Wayne's warning: *"Beware your friends and know your enemies."* If ever there were an opportunity for betrayal, this hastily put together plan was it. All it would take is one of them failing to fulfill his or her responsibility and any number of them might be captured. It was an obvious place to set a trap. She pushed away all her negative thoughts and kept her mind on what had to be done. She was supposed to do the distracting, not be the distracted. She was the decoy, the diversion. It was time for action.

To be effective, her decoy could not be spotted as such: it had to look as if she intended to rescue Wayne. If she just went in yelling and screaming, the Overtakers might sense that her intrusion was merely a ruse and she would put Maybeck and Finn at risk.

So she came into the lounge area quietly, raised up on tiptoe. She kept to the wall and then quietly slipped between it and the circus tent, moving slowly enough not to ripple the tent canvas.

The door to the boardroom was partially open. To her right was another doorway that led into the room where Finn and Maybeck would be hiding. If she was chased, her plan was to lead her pursuers right beneath Maybeck and Finn, who, by agreement, would be up the ladder and hidden in the circus tower in the center of the room.

With the door open, she could just make out the Norwegian in profile. He had a mane of red hair, a strong jaw, and a weight lifter's biceps.

She moved closer, inch by inch, the clock ticking in her head. The young boy lay fast asleep with his head in the man's lap.

Was that all? she wondered. *Just the two of them?*

She didn't trust it. Wayne's warning about a traitor in their midst made her question everything, everyone. She hated this change in herself. She stood stone still and took in her surroundings, alert for someone hiding in waiting. Seeing no one, she darted across the carpet and planted herself behind the open boardroom door, and placed her eye to the crack.

Wayne! He was sitting in the chair, his wrists bound, his eyes wide with expectation. Could he possibly know she was there?

It all seemed so possible now—everything they'd worked toward. She didn't want to blow it. Wayne, a few feet away. One man between her and Wayne's freedom.

It didn't make any sense. It *had* to be a trap. Finn was always the first to point out that where the Overtakers were concerned, when it looked too good to be true, it probably was. There were more Overtakers nearby. Had to be. Maybe already watching her. Just as she feared that Wayne's rescue now looked suspiciously too easy, the Overtakers, she thought, must be holding back, wondering why it looked so easy to grab her. Nothing was as it seemed.

The clock kept moving in her head. Philby would cut the lights with five minutes left—exactly thirty seconds away.

She used her gymnastic skills and her exceptional sense of balance to stretch her legs between the lower door hinge on her left, and a piece of molding to her right. Her foot found the middle hinge, and she went up the wall like Spider-Man. Now with her left foot on the top hinge, she paused, hooked her fingers over the door and swung it open slightly.

"Hvem er der?" the man said. "Who dere?" he tried in heavily accented English.

Charlene struggled to hold herself high above the

far side of the door. Finally she heard the man move the boy off his lap and the whisper of his clothing as he came out of the boardroom. She dove over the door, reached back, and caught her hand, flipping herself over and landing squarely on her feet.

As the Norwegian left the boardroom, Charlene entered it. She pulled the door shut behind her and locked it.

Wayne, in the corner to her left, was tied to a chair. His mouth was gagged, his eyes fixed straight ahead. He didn't look over at her and she wondered if they had him drugged. This time it was obvious that the wall behind him had been scrubbed clean—she could imagine the cryptogram having been written there. It was now erased.

The boy was waking up in front of her.

Four heads poked up from the far side of the table.

Trolls!

They'd been sleeping in the boardroom chairs, but they were too short for Charlene to have seen. They came awake groggily, but with looks of fierce determination. She'd heard trolls called cute, but there was nothing cute about these. Two jumped up onto the table. Two others leaped down to the floor and ran beneath the table toward her.

The sleepy boy rubbed his eyes and looked at her as

if she were a ghost. It was too late for her to try to all-clear. She ran to Wayne and was reaching for the knot on his right wrist when a troll grabbed her legs from behind, pulling her away from the chair. She kicked back and the little man went flying into one of his friends.

Wayne continued to stare off into space.

"Hang in there," she said, no longer able to think about untying him. A third troll latched onto her lower leg. He opened his mouth and bit her.

Charlene cried out and kicked him. The little man rolled like a soccer ball and crashed into the far wall below one of the Mary Poppins Carousel horses.

The door banged as it was struck hard from the other side.

She had to time this just right. The trolls were going to make a mess of that. The three had recovered and now joined hands with the fourth to form a semicircle of small, ugly dwarves taking small steps toward her.

She didn't have to worry about Wayne—Finn and Maybeck could take care of him. Her job was to get back through the door and lead the Overtakers away from here. Timing her exit was critical.

Another tremendous crash. One more of those and the doorjamb would give.

She judged the height of the trolls—three and a half feet. If they raised their arms, maybe as high as five feet.

Her track hurdles were set at "low": thirty inches. The trolls were too tall for her to hurdle over.

She stepped to the wall and ran at them at an angle, envisioning herself in the high jump. She lifted her chest, arching her back, and kicked her feet high. She flew over them upside down.

As she smacked down onto the floor—wishing there had been some kind of mat for her to land upon—the surprised trolls turned around. The Norwegian boy stood up in his chair. At the same moment, the door blew open in a spray of splinters.

Charlene spun the boy in the swivel chair and pushed him; he fell into the trolls and they collapsed as a group.

The Norwegian barreled through the broken door and was carried forward by his momentum straight into the boardroom table.

Charlene timed it perfectly, sprinting behind him and out the door. She had no doubt that everyone in that room would now be chasing her, but she never looked back to confirm it. She took off at full speed, through the door to her left, and out to the glassed-in sunroom, making for the same window she'd used only hours before.

The lights went out.

At the same time, a loud electronic *clunk* signaled that the elevator was in use and coming up.

Three feet from the window Charlene saw the brace. It was an adjustable and lockable tube of metal that now prevented the same window from opening. Every window had a similar brace in place. She was locked inside.

The elevator clunked again. The doors were coming open. Behind her came the Norwegian and his posse of trolls, but she wasn't sure they could see her in the dark. They stopped and looked around.

If she made for the elevator and it turned out Overtakers were inside, she would be caught. If she waited even a second or two longer the Norwegian was going to see her crouched down beside the wall.

Something winked at her from high up on the wall: a piece of glass reflecting the small amount of ambient outdoor light that came through the glass ceiling and walls.

A security camera.

Philby.

He'd seen the locked windows. He'd sent the elevator for her. It was a gamble. If she guessed wrong . . .

Behind the Norwegian, Maybeck and Finn would have by now descended from the room's tower and gone after Wayne. She had to keep the Norwegian and his pals busy for a few seconds longer.

The elevator doors . . .

She ran and dove like she was sliding into third base in a tied game—and slid right into the elevator.

The empty elevator.

Was about to reach for the panel when the CLOSE DOORS button lit up, as did the 1.

Philby.

The doors eased shut just a fraction of a second ahead of the Norwegian trying to stop her.

The problem was, the elevator was far slower than the Norwegian. He raced down the curved staircase to meet the elevator on the first floor.

He stood there—all six-foot-four of him—as the elevator doors slid open.

It was empty.

* * *

Finn and Maybeck sneaked down the circus-pole ladder and then hurried to the door, where they paused, with the boardroom to their right. Maybeck's phone vibrated in his pocket.

"Do I answer that?" he hissed at Finn.

"Not now," Finn answered.

The area in front of them was dark and eerily

empty. The circus tent to their left posed the greatest threat—anything could hide in there—though its canvas walls remained motionless, suggesting that the tent was empty.

Finn stepped tentatively toward the boardroom, Maybeck right behind him.

Maybeck's phone buzzed in his pocket for a second time.

Finn peered around the splintered doorjamb. The seat in the corner was empty. He ran to the chair, angry and frustrated. A pattern had been scratched into the wood of the arm. It looked something like a sword or a cross, but on closer examination there was a second crosspiece beneath the top bar.

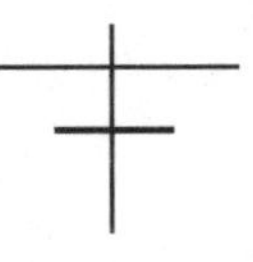

"It's a combination of an *F* for Fantasmic! and a cross for the sword," Finn said. He now knew the purpose of the sword and where he would use it.

But in his chest was an empty hole where his heart should have been.

Wayne was gone.

* * *

As the Norwegian stepped into the empty elevator, Charlene was hovering directly over him, each limb extended between the walls to hold her there. She looked like a four-legged starfish.

Just as he raised his head to look up, she let go and dropped, catching his shoulders from the back and using the momentum of her fall to pull him over backward. They went together, crushing the trolls and knocking them down like bowling pins. She released him just before hitting the floor so that she could land on her feet. The Norwegian hit the floor hard. The elevator alarm went off as the doors tried to shut but couldn't. Philby must have overridden the safety feature, because suddenly the doors slid shut, catching and pinning the Norwegian's legs. He tried to free himself, kicking out, but the doors held him. At the same time the elevator began to climb, lifting the Norwegian and hanging him upside down. The elevator stopped four feet off the floor, so that his shoulders were touching the carpet, and the elevator held his legs.

Charlene spotted a security camera in the corner and she threw a thumbs-up toward it. As the trolls attempted to recover, she took off out the front door but quickly skidded to a stop.

Two Foo lions—that should have been stone lions

from China, but seemed not to be made of stone at all, but from flesh and blood that only *looked* like stone—blocked the path in front of her. The lion on the left cocked its head toward her—it held a lion cub with its left front paw. The lion to the right growled.

Charlene fought to catch her breath, terror rippling through her.

"Good kitties," she said.

* * *

Maybeck held his phone to his ear. "It's a trap," he told Finn. "There are lions at the front door."

"Lions?"

"Gigabyte's at the back." He spoke into the phone—"Wayne?"—and then listened. "They haven't seen him leave." He paused. "We were set up, man. This is a trap."

"Is not!" Finn said, trying to make sense of it all. "Stop thinking like that!" But the truth was: he was thinking about the possible traitor as much as anyone. He and Maybeck had spent, at most, thirty to forty seconds coming down the ladder. Somehow the Overtakers had managed to move Wayne, an old guy who didn't move that fast, in that short time.

"They should get back to Nemo ASAP," Finn said. "No use in all of us getting caught."

"No way anyone's catching me," Maybeck said,

though his voice lacked his usual confidence.

Only then did an unwanted thought surface in Finn's mind. The kind of thought that on one hand made little sense, but on the other hand could not be easily dismissed. Suddenly Finn feared that the Overtakers knew that the Kingdom Keepers were unable to activate the Return—that the fob was missing. What if the Overtakers had somehow determined the Keepers' vulnerable status and were now set to exploit it? As long as that fob remained in the Lost and Found there was no way out for the Keepers. They were easy prey, in danger of attack and capture. Maleficent must have been licking her chops. Whether by accident or design, the Keepers had made themselves easy targets.

Maybeck took out his phone to relay the order to return to the Nemo lounge as Finn looked on, but he speed-dialed without thinking, and had no idea who he had called. Whomever he was speaking to, Amanda, Willa, or Jess—Finn guessed it was Willa—obviously tried to argue, but Maybeck shut her up. "Just do it!" he shouted into the phone before disconnecting the call. "Sometimes I hate girls," he said to Finn. "All the talking. . . ."

I would bet they don't exactly love us either, Finn was about to say, but he kept the thought to himself.

"Easy!" Maybeck pulled Finn against the wall. Through the lounge windows that looked out onto the pavilion's dark lower level, lit only by the dim glow of exit signs, the boys could see two jesters and a crash-test dummy. They appeared to be searching the various scenes and attractions.

The crash-test dummy turned and raised its head toward the lounge. It lifted its robotic arm and pointed.

"Wayne must still be in the building."

"Forget about him, would you?" Maybeck said. "Right now, we've got to get out of here. And we've got to make sure Charlene and Philby make it too."

He pushed the phone's direct-connect button. "Philby?"

"Here."

"We've got—"

"Trouble. I know. I'm watching everyone. I heard Willa just now. Charlene's at the front door, pinned there by the lions. Willa's right: the snake's at the back exit. That dummy—there are two of them, actually—looks like he's headed for the stairs. I cut the lights. I don't know what else I can do."

"Direct us?" Finn asked, leaning toward Maybeck's phone. "Can you get us out of here?"

"There are a lot of cameras, to be sure. But it's not like I can see everywhere."

"How many exits are there?" Finn asked.

"Twelve," came Philby's answer immediately.

"And they only have two blocked?" Maybeck

said. “So what’s the big deal?”

“The pavilion is closed. Remember?” Philby said. “The other exits are locked—not electronically, but with actual keys. Front and back are the only ways out. The sunroom windows are locked as well. That stopped Charlene.”

“Roach motel,” Maybeck said.

Finn knew he was right: the Overtakers had let them in, but were now blocking their way out. The situation had every appearance of having been a trap from the start.

“Did you see where they took Wayne?” Finn asked Philby. Maybeck grimaced; he didn’t want Finn hung up on rescuing the old man.

“Never saw him,” Philby reported. “Not in any of the cameras.”

“Then he’s probably still on this floor somewhere,” Finn said to Maybeck. “We can find him and get him.”

“Leave it alone, Whitman. He was bait. That’s all. We need to get out of here.” To the phone he said, “Any ideas, genius?”

“Yeah, but you won’t like it,” Philby replied.

“How do you know?” Maybeck barked into the phone. “Let’s hear it.”

“Because it involves heights.”

Maybeck’s shoulders slumped. To Finn he said, “How did I know he was going to say that?”

Philby told them his plan.

37

CHARLENE HAD MONITORED the direct-connect call between Maybeck and Philby. She cut in.

"Philby, I could use a little help here," she said. "The door is locked behind me."

The stone lions were advancing one heavy step at a time, making the path shake.

With each step, Charlene had backed up until her spine was pressed against the pavilion's front-door glass. The four trolls had collected on the other side of the door but obviously had no intention of becoming involved with the lions, even if, theoretically, they were on the same team.

"Philby?" she repeated.

Charlene considered running for it. Being made of stone, the lions were moving sluggishly. But maybe their slow movement was nothing more than them stalking her. She had three cats and loved to watch them stalk their toys, or a lizard in the backyard, or a seagull. She loved the controlled complexity of the hunt, the cats' unwavering focus and fierce concentration. She saw that same look now in the gray stone eyes of the lions. She was willing to bet that they could move very fast if need be, and had no desire to test her theory.

"Okay," Philby said after an exasperatingly long pause. "I've got it. My theory is—"

"Lose the theory," she said.

The lions were less than fifteen feet away and moving steadily toward her.

"Now would be a good time to actually *do something*," she added. "As in . . . right now. This very second."

Right on cue, the lawn sprinklers erupted, spewing cold water. There were spray nozzles edging the entry path, as well as circular sprinklers out in the lawn. Thankfully, none of them was perfectly set, meaning that all the planters, the grass, and the entry path were suddenly wet and getting wetter.

The lions moved away from the edges of the path and bumped into each other, frantic to avoid the spray. Cats hate water!

Charlene vaulted over the green metal fence and took off running, keeping herself in the thick of the spray. She heard a collision as one of the lions attempted to charge her but struck the fencing, denting it. It whined as it was hit by the water.

She ran in a zigzag pattern in case one of the cats had dared to pursue her, but glanced back and saw with relief that they had not. Together they had moved to the one place the water didn't reach—the front doors—conveniently trapping the ugly trolls on the other side.

Soaking wet, Charlene vaulted the metal fence twenty yards further on, pulled out her phone, and thanked Philby, telling him she'd meet him at the rendezvous.

"And oh, BTW," she said, "I'd avoid the front door if I were you."

* * *

Finn pulled the grille off the air conditioning duct. "I hate small spaces," he said.

"Get over it."

"I've seen this in movies, but I always thought it was fake."

"If you're not going in there, I am," said Maybeck. He squeezed himself through the small rectangular vent opening, aiming to the right. "It's tight," he said, his voice now muted, "but I can see the other vent up ahead."

Finn crawled in behind him, wishing his edgy nerves would have allowed him to fully cross over and not need to seek a human way out of the pavilion. It would have been so much easier to just walk through the second story wall and find a place to jump down.

But the truth was, Maybeck needed him; even if Finn had been able to all-clear, he couldn't leave Maybeck alone. Finn struggled to pull himself through the horizontal airshaft. The ducting ringed the pavilion's interior with vents on both sides, providing air conditioning to both the pavilion's showcase area and the public and private rooms on the second floor that surrounded it.

"I'm going to suffocate," Finn complained.

"Shut up," Maybeck called back to him harshly. "I can see those clowns," he added, meaning the jesters.

"There's a ladder," Maybeck said a moment later, his eyes on the vent. "Some kind of work going on. Philby's right: it might work."

It had to work, Finn felt like pointing out. Once they popped out of the ventilation system through one of the vents, the jesters and crash-test dummies—and anyone else down there in the showcase—would see them. At that moment the chase would become a footrace. Only their unexpected route might save Maybeck and Finn, and only then if they could really move fast once they left the safety of the duct.

"We have to wait," Finn said.

"I'm aware of that."

"So be patient."

"You be patient, if you want to. I don't exactly feel so patient."

"He'll make it."

"Yeah. Okay. But if he doesn't, maybe we've wasted our chance of getting out of here. And what if that's the plan?"

"What are you talking about?"

"Isn't it a little too convenient that we and Charlene were attacked and Philby wasn't? He turned off the lights. Why didn't they go looking to turn them back on?"

"How do we know that they didn't?"

"I'm just saying."

"You're accusing him."

"Am not."

"You are too. Listen, Maybeck," Finn whispered while lying on his stomach. "We can't do this to each other. We just can't. Okay?"

Maybeck was silent.

"He's going to show up. We don't have to expect the worst in each other."

"Excuse me. I left my violin at home," Maybeck said.

Another three minutes passed. Even to Finn it felt more like an hour.

"How long do we just wait here?" Maybeck asked. "At some point they're going to come looking for us, and that vent grille we removed is out there sitting on the floor, and it's not like you'll be turning around and pulling it back into place. I say we go for it. If Philby makes it, he makes it."

"Call him."

"Are you kidding me? I can't get my phone out of my pocket. You can't either! That's ridiculous." He waited about two seconds. "We've got to go without him."

"We can't!"

"There's no choice. I'll tell you what: it has been too long. I'm going. If you want to stay, then stay."

"It's going to take two of us," Finn said. "He said it was going to take two people. If we don't wait for him, there's no one to help him."

"Like I said: you can wait. But I'm out of here."

Maybeck popped the grille free of the vent and pulled it back inside. "So far, so good," he whispered back at Finn. "I don't think anyone saw that."

Finn desperately wanted to wait for Philby, but the small confines of the ventilation shaft were making him nauseated. He'd broken out in a sweat. His hands were shaking. He had to get out, Philby or no Philby.

"Go!" Finn said.

Maybeck squeezed out of the open grille, and onto the maintenance scaffolding Philby had spotted behind Cranium Command. Finn couldn't move fast enough: he crawled ahead, pulled himself through the vent, and was helped to his feet by Maybeck.

"Check it out," Maybeck said softly.

The pavilion, lit only by ambient light coming through the sand-dollar skylights in the roof, was enormous, forty or fifty yards across, its floor filled with colorful marquees announcing attractions, kiosks, red and blue street lamps, and lush green garden beds. At its center was a large carousel. Finn and Maybeck were level with the carousel's roof, and this was their destination.

Finn didn't immediately spot the jesters or crash-test dummies, wondering if Philby had somehow distracted them.

Where is he? Finn wondered, glancing toward the open vent and wishing Philby would arrive in time.

"I'm going for it," Maybeck said. He bent to pick up one end of a narrow aluminum plank from the scaffolding. Finn pitched in, grabbing the opposite end. Together they fed the long, slender piece of metal out toward the tall stepladder, attempting to build a bridge between them and the carousel. On the third try, they managed to land the end of the plank across a step in the ladder. Maybeck tested it and it held his weight. It aimed slightly uphill.

"We'll need another from there," he said, removing a second plank from the scaffolding. Together they placed this plank atop the first. Maybeck drew a deep breath and walked across, his arms out at his sides for balance. Finn stood on the planks at the near end to steady them and caught himself holding his breath. Maybeck was anything but steady. He wobbled and dipped and leaned, and several times appeared to be going over the side but managed somehow to reach the stepladder. He grabbed hold of it like a drowning man to a raft, and looked back at Finn as if to say, Whoa.

Maybeck fed the second plank out toward the carousel's canopy, extending the bridge. He crossed to the carousel and waved Finn foward.

Finn had excellent balance. He crossed easily, being careful to take it slowly, and reached the stepladder without incident.

"Three o'clock!" Maybeck called out.

Finn looked down to see the two jesters running toward him. His eye measured the distance to the carousel as his brain calculated the time required to reach it. Maybeck held the end of the plank.

"Come on!" Maybeck shouted.

Finn stepped out onto the wobbly plank. Two steps toward the carousel the first jester hit the stepladder, trying to tip it over. But the two planks complicated his efforts. The ladder rocked, but did not fall.

Finn, however, did.

He slipped and banged down onto the plank, now halfway between the ladder and carousel.

The second jester arrived and immediately jumped onto the stepladder and climbed with an unnerving confidence: he, too, rocked the ladder side to side, trying to dump Finn.

Maybeck reached out a hand toward Finn, whose knee slid off the plank, dumping him to the right. He stretched out a hand for Maybeck, but their fingers only danced around, unable to touch.

The climbing jester lunged heavily to the left. The stepladder tipped and Finn felt it reach the point of no return: it was going over. He scrambled forward, grabbed Maybeck's hand, and felt the plank and the whole contraption go down. Maybeck swung Finn strongly like a pendulum. Finn hooked the carousel canopy—metal, not fabric as it appeared—with his knee and, with Maybeck's help, rolled up and onto it.

The ladder and bridge collapsed with a crash. The boys watched as the jester jumped away from it at the last second, landing effortlessly on his feet.

And there was Philby on the scaffolding. He'd come through the air vent but was now stranded by the fall of the bridge.

Finn saw him, looking for some way to get him over to the carousel.

"Go!" Philby shouted.

"No way!" Finn said.

The silent jesters hopped and ran around frantically. Then one disappeared beneath Finn, who realized with dread that the thing was climbing toward them.

"Go!" Philby repeated.

"We go together," Maybeck said. "Or it won't work."

Finn looked up. Overhead was a large mobile of metal arms and colorful shapes. Above the mobile was a projection room—a booth with lights and projector lenses aimed out of it. Philby's plan had been to evacuate the pavilion through the small projection room. But now Philby was stuck on the other side—a world away.

"The arms of the mobile are balanced," Maybeck said. "We have to do this together or we can't do it at all."

* * *

Finn saw he was right. If he tried grabbing onto the end of any one of the sculpture's arms, the arm would simply tilt down to meet him. But if both boys took hold of opposite arms they could balance the structure, keeping it level. With three of them—including Philby—they could include one boy to hold on at the fulcrum in the center of the arc. But if Philby were left to follow, even if he reached the carousel, he wouldn't be able to climb the mobile alone.

"I'm not going without him," Finn said.

"Are you *kidding* me?" Maybeck said. "He's a freaking genius! He'll think of something."

"We go together," Finn said.

"In case you missed it, the joker and his buddy are pretty much planning a different ending."

Finn strained to figure this out. Philby wasn't the only one capable of thinking. And there it was, right in front of his eyes.

"The wire!" Finn shouted, across the void.

Connecting the top of the carousel to both sides of the pavilion was a wire that had been strung to hang lights. It looked thick and strong enough to bear a person's weight.

"You'll have to tightrope!" Finn called to Philby.

"But I can't tightrope!"

"You're a DHI," Finn called back. "You weigh less than half what you normally do. Maybe less than that. You can do this. Push for all-clear. The lighter you are, the easier it'll be."

Two crash-test dummies marched into the space. The jester Finn could see picked up the tall stepladder and dragged it toward the carousel. This was not good.

"You've got to do this. You've got to hurry," Finn shouted.

"Grab that flag for balance," Maybeck said, suddenly into the idea.

Philby reached the end of the scaffold, removed a flag from the wall, and climbed up to the wire. He tore the flag off the short pole and held the pole in both hands at waist level. He put one foot onto the wire and shot Finn a look of pure terror.

"No sweat," Finn said.

"Easy for you to say."

"Close your eyes. Be as calm as you can be."

Philby shut his eyes and took a step out onto the wire. He fluttered back and forth, then found his balance and took another step, and another.

"Wish I had a camera," Maybeck said.

The stepladder was pushed up against the edge of the carousel awning.

"Hold me," Maybeck said, going down on his knees.

Finn grabbed Maybeck's ankles as Maybeck lay down and stretched to reach the edge of the canopy and the top of the ladder just beyond.

"Lower!" he called back to Finn.

Finn leaned forward, clutching Maybeck's ankles. If he let go, Maybeck would fall to the floor.

Maybeck's outstretched hand reached the top of the ladder just as the jester's hand appeared. Maybeck made a fist and smashed down onto the jester's fingers, then took hold of the ladder's top step and shoved.

The ladder went over, taking the jester with it.

Finn pulled hard and Maybeck scrambled back up the metal canopy.

They both turned to look at Philby, who was now three-quarters of the way across the wire. Three more steps and Finn called out. "Open your eyes!"

Philby's eyes popped open and he jumped off the wire and onto the canopy. "Piece of cake," he said.

With Philby in the middle, Maybeck on one end, and Finn on the other, on a count of three, the boys took hold of the lowest arm of the mobile. Finn moved slightly toward the center and the arm leveled out. Maybeck kicked out, and the mobile began spinning.

The next lowest arm swung above them. Finn reached and steadied it. "On three!" he said.

They climbed the mobile as if it were a jungle gym, from one arm to the next, and reached the top. Finn and Maybeck climbed through opposite openings in the projection booth and then joined to pull Philby through yet another. As Philby had discovered, there was a roof-access emergency exit, much like the one they had found in Space Mountain, so long ago now that it felt like a dream.

Out on the roof, in the night air, there was no time for celebration.

Looking down, they saw nothing: the lions and Gigabyte had apparently chased the others across the plaza, or had gone off looking for them. The boys descended the fire escape ladder to the ground and took off through the jungle toward the Living Seas.

"When my eyes were shut," Philby said, as they ran side by side. "When I was on that wire—"

"Yeah?" Maybeck said.

"I figured it out. Wayne's message."

"You're telling me. . . ." Maybeck said breathlessly, "that while you were *tightroping* you were working things out?"

"It's not like I've had a lot of free time," Philby complained.

"Figured *what* out?" Finn said, struggling to keep up with the other two.

"What connects Mission: Space, Test Track, and Soarin'. What connects what each of us found: you and I, Maleficent; the girls, that maintenance journal; you and Charlene," he said to Maybeck, "Wayne's video."

"And?" Finn said, huffing.

"Seat belts."

"Huh?" Maybeck grunted.

"The Overtakers are targeting rides with seat belts. Maintenance problems on Soarin'. Finn would have been killed by being stuck in that Test Track car if he hadn't been able to go all-clear."

"Seat belts," Maybeck said, with obvious cynicism.

"I think their plan is to hold hundreds of guests hostage by locking them into seat belts that won't come undone. Trapping them on rides. Making the rides do dangerous things they aren't supposed to—just like what happened to all of us. Maybe they plan to make demands. Maybe they just plan to hurt everyone. But if we don't stop them at Fantasmic!—if we don't change things—bad stuff is going to happen. The seat belts are going to fail—that's the message. That's what Wayne found out."

Finn, aching over the loss of Wayne, suddenly found his legs. He didn't just catch up with his friends, he ran past them. It wasn't only Philby's discovery that put a fire under him, or the near miss at saving Wayne, but something much bigger.

The sky was beginning to soften in the east.

Morning was fast approaching.

38

THE MEETING AT THE rendezvous had gone quickly. Everyone was overtired, irritable, and anxious. Finn had found himself sitting on a couch in the Nemo lounge next to Amanda and, as the discussion had dragged on, she'd reached down and found his hand and given it a squeeze. It was a small gesture of confidence, but to Finn he imagined this was what drinking a double-shot espresso latte must be like. His fatigue vaporized; his heart raced out of control.

With his racing heart came racing thoughts. Amanda had opened some creative gate in his brain and a dozen ideas came spilling out, most of them finding their way to his tongue. For a moment he babbled at the others, having little idea what he was actually saying. Then a memory popped into his head and he realized that this was where his mind had been leading him for the past several minutes.

"Five AM," he blurted out, interrupting Philby who was, for the third time, attempting to explain why he believed the Overtakers planned to take park guests as hostages. But Finn had won the attention of everyone in the room, and went quickly about explaining himself.

"When I got stuck at the Studios I kind of hitched a ride with some Imagineers—at least I think they were Imagineers. One of the guys was the pyrotechnics crew chief, a guy named Pete. He was talking to the driver and mentioned that all this week they were doing run-throughs of Fantasmic! at five AM. He was bummed because he had to get up so early to be there."

"That would make sense," said Philby, ever the philosopher. "It would have to be dark to conduct a tech rehearsal of Fantasmic! with all the projectors and fireworks and lighting. They wouldn't need all the Cast Members, but maybe there'd be some. And they certainly couldn't have anyone in the audience in case something went wrong with whatever they're testing."

"It's our chance," Finn said. "No audience. Maleficent and Chernabog using it to hide. They act out the parts and the rest of the day no one bothers them."

"We attack them there," Maybeck said.

"On their turf," Philby said. "I don't love that."

"It's where it's supposed to happen," Finn said, resigned to the idea. "Wayne told us as much. The sorcerer's hat. The symbol I found scratched into the chair. He wants us to challenge them at Fantasmic!"

"He wants us to defeat them," Philby said, correcting him. "*You* to defeat them."

"Us," Finn said. "Even if I'm the one carrying the sword, it's going to take all of us."

"And how exactly are any of us supposed to get there?" Maybeck asked.

"He's right," Philby said. "The monorail and buses don't start running until two hours before opening. That's seven in the morning."

"Yeah," Finn said, "but Pete has to be there. And so does his buddy, the driver." He checked his watch: 4:24 AM. "We can still make it."

* * *

Locating a pickup truck with a bobblehead Mickey Mouse on the dash in such short order required them to split up. They kept their direct-connect phones at the ready as they snuck backstage. The "backstage" side of Epcot, as at the other parks, looked entirely different from the side the public saw: flat-roofed, steel-framed buildings housed the rides and attractions, the food storage, the costume and prop storage, the maintenance and administration facilities. There were large parking areas and a network of roads connecting it all. The kids fanned out to search for the pickup truck.

Word soon came over the phone intercoms that Willa had found the pickup near some cream-colored containers behind China. Finn and Amanda caught up to her quickly, followed a few minutes later by Philby, who brought a tarp with him that he'd borrowed from another vehicle. Charlene arrived out of breath, saying she'd seen Maybeck and Jess heading in the opposite direction, toward America.

"I think Maybeck might have gotten turned around," Charlene said. "I don't think he knew where he was going."

It didn't surprise Finn. It was not only dark but the back of the park was totally unfamiliar. All the buildings looked the same, and there were very few signs.

Finn was about to check on Maybeck when a man appeared from a trailer who Finn recognized as the driver. The man moved toward them and the pickup truck.

"Turn your radios off," Finn whispered, fearing they might be overheard if Maybeck suddenly called.

"What do we do?" Willa asked.

"We're too late," Finn whispered. "We needed to be in the back of that—"

The man patted his coat and turned around, returning to the trailer.

"This is our shot," Philby said.

The moment the man entered the trailer, the kids took off running. They climbed up into the truck bed and pulled the tarp over them. It was dark enough out, and early enough, that Finn hoped the guy wouldn't notice the tarp. Less than a minute later, he felt the truck rock as the driver climbed in and started the engine. Again Amanda found his hand and held on.

There was still the chance that Maybeck and Jess would find their way to the Studios. Finn considered calling Wanda and asking her for help, and the more he considered this, the more he thought it a good idea. Wayne had mentioned his daughter on the video Charlene and Maybeck had seen. Maybe she would know something about Fantasmic! or be able to help them in some way.

Finn couldn't see much in the darkness under the tarp. He texted the others, warning them that once out of Epcot they would be in DHI shadow and would remain so until near or inside Disney Hollywood Studios.

As the pickup arrived at the Hollywood Studios Security checkpoint Finn's warning proved critical: the guard pulled back the tarp to have a look. The Kingdom Keepers held their breath and remained perfectly still.

"Funny," a guard said, presumably to another guard, "the way it was bunched up like that I could have sworn there was something underneath."

"You think too much," a lower voice said. "I've told you that before: don't think so much."

"We're supposed to think, you jerk," the first guard said. "How are we supposed to keep this place safe if we're not thinking?"

"You're trying to trick me. Just by asking me that, you're making me think. I know your type."

The guard left the tarp in a heap at the back of the truck, exposing Finn and the others. Finn understood the risk that presented: at any time they could come within range of the DHI projectors; when they did they would reappear, and if the driver happened to look back . . .

The truck rumbled and rolled slowly out of the gate.

"Jump," Finn said.

"What?"

"No time to argue. Jump!" He stood and leaped over the side. As he was in midair, his DHI sparkled, first in black and white and then in full color. He landed feet first on the pavement, but was thrown off balance by his forward momentum and went down hard. Like salmon leaping from a mountain stream, the other DHIs jumped: first Amanda, who had not questioned Finn for a second. Then Charlene and Willa and finally Philby.

The brake lights on the pickup truck lit up bright red—the driver had felt something and was stopping.

"The ditch!" Finn called out, as he rolled off the asphalt into the grass and down into a dry ditch meant to carry off rainwater. The others quickly did the same. He didn't dare lift his head to see if the driver was coming over toward them. All he could do was stay perfectly still and hope.

And hope.

Through the chirping of cicadas and the hum of electric power, Finn thought he heard the sound of the tarp being moved around. The driver knew he hadn't put the tarp in the truck in the first place. Maybe he hadn't felt them jump from the truck; maybe it had just finally registered that Studio Security had looked under a tarp in the back of his truck. If he'd seen them and now pursued them over to the ditch they would have no choice but to run. It would create big problems for them—park Security would be alerted, and with the testing at Fantasmic! being the only event that was probably taking place at this early hour, their ability to infiltrate the attraction would likely be compromised.

They had no choice but to lie there and await their fate.

At last they heard the door shut and the truck rumble off. Finn directed the group behind an outbuilding. Amanda had gotten Wanda's phone number from the visit she had paid to Mrs. Nash's house, but she didn't have it in her phone's contact list. It turned out not to matter, because Philby had Wanda's number memorized, though no one knew how he'd gotten it in the first place. That was the thing about Philby: you learned not to ask.

Finn apologized for waking Wanda up and then attempted to explain their situation. She stopped him several times, whenever he mentioned her father—first in the Mission: Space video, then in person at Wonders. She agreed to pick up Maybeck and Jess, saying she could meet them at Epcot. She offered to get Maybeck a Studio Cast Member Security uniform if possible, and said she'd have Jess come dressed as one of the cast of Fantasmic!

With everyone now accounted for, Finn felt better. He led the four others deeper into the backstage area of the Studios. The Fantasmic! technical rehearsal was scheduled to start in less than five minutes. As they walked, Philby caught up to Finn and Amanda.

"Why do you suppose they'd be conducting technical rehearsals on a show that's been playing for so many years?" Philby asked. "Have you thought about that?"

"I just assumed. . . ." Finn said. But he didn't finish his thought. "You're saying it has something to do with the Overtakers?"

"What else? Something is disrupting the show.

Tech rehearsals are all about the effects—the timing, the lighting, the music, entrance cues. It could have been what got Wayne going. Right? He hears a rumor about Fantasmic! having problems. The problems came on recently and aren't going away. The first few attempts to fix them don't work, so they schedule a whole week of tech rehearsals to strip the show down and build it back up, scene by scene, minute by minute."

It made sense to Finn. "Okay. But he went missing way before now, way before these rehearsals."

"But the first time Jess gets one of her telepathic visions was this week. Right now. Because he knew something no one else did: if we were going to stop them with the least risk to the audience, we had to do it now, when the rehearsals are going on. The genius of Maleficent and Chernabog hiding at Fantasmic!—if that's even what they're doing—is that the only time anyone's around that place, there are like five thousand guests hanging out. Who's going to put them at risk?"

"The genius of them hiding there," Finn corrected him, "is that they *belong* there. All they have to do is stash an Auto-Animatronic figure or a Cast Member or two and then take their place. Who's to know? Who looks that closely at Maleficent? It's probably dark backstage. From out front she's pretty far away and not very big. Green skin. Weird chin. Who's going to pull her aside and ask for a Disney ID anyway?"

"So what you're saying, Philby," said Amanda, "is that they aren't tech rehearsals at all. They're more like exorcisms. The Disney people are actually searching for Overtakers in hopes of finding them and locking them up, or whatever they do with them?"

"If they know what they're up against," Philby said, "then that's exactly what they're doing. But—"

"If they don't know what they're up against . . ." Finn said.

"—then everybody involved in those rehearsals is in danger," Amanda said. "Including us."

"Most definitely including us," Philby said.

Finn said, "The Imagineers will want to lock them up and *study* them. If anyone's going to take them on, if anyone's going to try to stop them permanently it's going to be . . . us."

The word died on the tip of his tongue. Amanda could have corrected him; Philby could have corrected him. Finn reached down and touched the grip of the sword.

Why had Wayne put him in charge, anyway? Why couldn't it be Maybeck with the sword, or Philby with his encyclopedic knowledge of famous Disney sword battles? Why him? The answer came to him indirectly, as it so often did. He had been the first one to cross over; the first one to meet Wayne; he was still the only one who could all-clear nearly at will. He was the one because Wayne had chosen him. There it was, as simple as he could break it down. Asking why Wayne had chosen him would only send him running in circles right back to the fact that Wayne *had* chosen him. He needed to stop questioning it and start doing something about it. His hand gripped the sword so tightly that, just for a moment, his fingers appeared bloodless, his knuckles white, the sword's grip welded to his hand. At one with it.

"I can do this," he heard slip past his own lips. As faint as a whisper, not something anyone heard—or so he hoped. But Amanda shot him a fearful and sympathetic look that said otherwise. At the very least she had heard; at the very least one other person knew his deepest fear.

Willa and Charlene caught up to them.

"Assignments?" Philby asked. That was another thing: when they'd first come together as a group, everyone was constantly jockeying for control, trying to come up with a better idea, a better plan. Now only Maybeck voiced that kind of discontent, and even so, less and less. Philby wasn't telling, he was asking; and no one but Finn would be expected to answer.

"Give us the layout," Finn said. Maybe that was why Wayne had chosen him: because he understood the value of each Kingdom Keeper, knew when to seek advice.

"A control room. Seating for several thousand. Two acres of water with a channel down the middle and a natural-gas pipe running just under the surface. A flotilla of a dozen barges. A multitiered performance stage complete with various trapdoors, zip lines, stunt pillows, all over five stories high, including another three stories below stage level with multiple staircases, dressing rooms and enough pyrotechnics on hand to be monitored by the federal government."

"Sounds . . . dangerous," Amanda said.

"Sounds big," said Willa.

Philby, hearing their comments, snapped his head toward Amanda, then shot Finn an intense look.

Finn said, "Are you thinking what I'm thinking?"

"I can't believe we missed it."

"Missed *what*, you guys?" Amanda said.

"You nailed it," Philby said. "Fantasmic! has everything, including isolation, to make it—"

"A base of operations for the Overtakers," Finn said.

"If they ever got their hands on all the ordnance—"

"That's fireworks," Willa explained to Amanda, in case she hadn't heard the term, but Amanda nodded as if she already knew that.

"—together with the boats," Philby continued, "and the way Fantasmic! is laid out, it would give them a base of operations. A fort. A defensible position from which to launch strikes on the various parks."

"Willa," Finn said, "you'll hang back. We need one person keeping watch on the whole place while the rest of us focus on specific tasks."

"I can do that," Willa said.

"You're our go-to person. Anyone needs help," he told the others, "Willa's it. She's our wild card."

"I've been called worse," she said.

"I don't know if I should say this or not," Amanda said. "But couldn't the Overtakers hang out in place like this for a long time before anyone ever figured it out? I mean it's so far removed from everything else."

"I think that's the point," Finn said. "That's the point exactly."

"But what if that's what Wayne discovered?" she asked. "What if they already control Fantasmic!—then aren't we walking into a trap?"

Philby glanced at Finn, who looked back at Philby. Their DHIs shimmered, revealing they were on an edge of the projection range. Their DHIs spit static and glowed off-color.

Finn said, "No, we'd be *running* into a trap." With that, he and Philby picked up the pace and the girls followed. Five glowing figures stealing through the dark up a path toward flashes of light reflecting off the low-lying clouds as booming explosions combined with a narrator's excited voice rippling through the air.

The show had begun.

39

"YOU'RE GOING TO HAVE to duck down on the floor," Wanda said.

"On the floor?" Maybeck complained, "But it's a subcompact!"

"Besides, we're invisible!" Jess said, finding the state disconcerting and upsetting. Invisibility wasn't the thrill she'd imagined. It left her feeling half dead, as if she didn't exist and never would again.

"Keep low," Wanda said. "There's no choice. You're going to reappear at some point, and though I doubt they'll search the car, they might glance in through the windows or something and it would be bad luck if that's when you showed back up. I put a blanket back there, and some clothes. Just make it look messy."

"Messy," Maybeck said, "I can do."

He told Jess he'd take the bottom so he wouldn't crush her and instructed her to pull the blanket completely over them. She nodded, feeling nervous about lying on top of Maybeck, nervous about the Security guards at Hollywood Studios, nervous about her invisibility and the thought she might suddenly reappear at the wrong moment. In short, nervous about everything.

"Hurry. We're coming up to the booth."

The two scrambled to get down onto the car's floor. Maybeck lay down face-first and Jess piled onto his back and tugged and kicked at the blanket until she was completely covered. Hopefully the blanket would keep them in the projection shadow and allow them to retain their invisibility.

"And for heaven's sake stay absolutely still," Wanda said.

The car arrived at the backstage checkpoint. She rolled down her window and showed her ID.

"You're not on the list," the guard informed her bluntly a minute or so later.

One of the longest minutes in Jess's life. She and Maybeck were as close as ham and cheese; she wanted out of there.

"Listen, friend, there's a tech rehearsal at Fantasmic! That should be on your list somewhere. If you check with Alex Wright you'll find that not only am I expected, but I'm late. Or try Rich. Any one of them will tell you not only to let me in, but that you should chew me out for being late."

The guard snickered. "Stand by," he said.

Wanda put her window up.

Jess saw a flicker of light beneath the blanket. She

realized it was her right elbow—sticking out slightly from the blanket—their DHIs were active. She drew her arm beneath the blanket, hoping she'd fully covered their feet.

She whispered into Maybeck's ear. "We're in range." He nodded and the back of his head hit her chin.

The hum of Wanda's window coming down sent a jolt of panic through Jess. She fought against the anxiety, knowing she could ill afford it. She tried picturing the ocean. All of a sudden she felt her hands and feet tingling, then her arms and legs. She was pressed up against the backseat—and watched her left hand disappear *through* the seat itself. She understood immediately what was happening to her.

She found Maybeck's ear under all that hair and whispered something to him.

"You trying to get me fired?" the guard said. "I woke up Mr. Wright and he was none too happy about it."

"But he backed up everything I said," Wanda stated boldly.

"Well, yes, ma'am, he did. All that's left is for me to search the car. Won't be but a second." The guard cupped his hands and peered through the rear side window. He tried the door.

"Would you unlock the door please, ma'am?"

"Whatever for?" Wanda said, sounding threatened.

"I just need to take a look."

"You've had your look. I told you: I'm late."

"Then the sooner you unlock the doors, the sooner you'll be on your way."

Wanda heaved a long sigh and threw the master switch. All the doors popped. The guard opened the rear door.

"Listen, officer," Wanda said, turning to see into the backseat, "there's no need to—"

"Just doing my job, ma'am." He took hold of a corner of the blanket.

"Listen. I can explain everything if you'll just—"

The guard pulled the blanket away. The backseat was empty.

"Explain what, ma'am? What was that?"

"Ah . . . the messiness. I'm not usually . . . this messy."

"No crime in that. If you'd just pop the trunk, I'll have you on your way."

As she popped the trunk, Wanda reached between the seats to pull the blanket back into place over the kids. She whispered softly, "Thank goodness you stayed invis—" But she caught herself as the blanket fell flat to the floor. The kids weren't there.

Then, as the guard pulled open the trunk, a bulge appeared and the blanket rose up from the floor on its own, first about a foot high, then rippling and rising another foot. Wanda lifted the edge and saw Jess lying on Maybeck's back. Jess grabbed the blanket from Wanda and pulled it back into place, hiding them.

Wanda, who knew nothing of all-clear—had no idea how the two might have moved into the trunk and then returned to the floor of the backseat—stuttered and tried to say something coherent, but was brought up short by the guard tapping on her window. She had no recollection of his shutting the trunk.

"You're set to go, ma'am. And I wouldn't worry about, you know . . . ?"

She offered him a puzzled look.

"The messiness," he said.

"Ah! That!" she said. "You have a good day."

"And you, ma'am."

She pulled the car through the raised barrier and released another pent-up sigh.

"What the . . . ? What was *that*?"

"Tell us when it's safe to come up," Maybeck said, his voice sounding strained.

"I think I'm squishing him," Jess said.

Wanda parked in front of the costume department and led them inside. "You can probably pass as a Security guard," she told Maybeck, who stood up taller, appreciating the comment. "That would get you inside as Finn told you he wanted. And you . . ." she said to Jess.

"I will be of the most help as close to the stage as possible. There's at least a chance I'll see something before it happens and be able to warn someone."

"A stagehand," Wanda said excitedly. "I can get you the headset and everything. It won't be hooked up to anything, but no one will know that. You'll look official, which is all that matters."

"We can hook it up to one of our phones," Maybeck said. "Philby can do that stuff."

"As a stagehand, you'd have full access backstage," Wanda said.

"We need to find the dressing room Maleficent uses."

Maybeck said, "Amanda's going to do that. Finn said so."

"She's going after the missing Cast Member," Jess said.

"You are *not* going to take on the real one by yourself," Maybeck said, trying to make his statement sound irrefutable.

Jess studied him thoughtfully. "Of course not. But the closer I can get to her—physically closer to the real one—the more likely I might be able to see her thoughts. Have a vision. Think about that, Donnie:

what if I could find out what she was thinking? Planning? What if I could see *her* future? We'd be one step ahead of her from now on. How could she possibly win if we knew what she was going to do before she ever did it?"

Wanda looked deeply troubled. "You're beginning to scare me," she said.

"If it's okay with you, we need you to get to Philby to figure out a phone for Jess," Maybeck said. "And it would be great if you could manage to get me a Security radio—a real one."

"What?"

"I need to be able to know what's going on with them. Can you do that?"

"I can try, I guess."

Jess looked at her with sympathetic eyes. "That's all any of us can do."

40

MRS. WHITMAN KNEW all the expressions: *Be careful what you wish for. You can't undo what's already done.* Had calmer heads prevailed, she might have considered the ramifications of her initial panic, might have thought through the effect her contacting the other parents would have, might have sat down with her husband and talked this through. But as it was, she'd considered nothing, reacting instead to a mother's concern for the well-being of her son and believing she was acting in his best interests.

"An ambulance is taking our son to the hospital," said Gladis Philby over the phone.

"But. . . ."

"Listen," Philby's mother said. "I know we think we know what's going on. I've heard the theories from the Imagineers, and I hope to God they're right. Of course I do. But the fact is, college fund program or not, my son's in a coma, and I can't take any chances. If they disqualify him, take him out of the program, well, honestly, maybe that's for the best as long as I get my son back. I can't stand this anymore, to tell you the truth. I'm done with it."

"But if the Imagineers are right," Mrs. Whitman said, "then the doctors might just make matters worse. That's why we're keeping our Finn at home. You heard what Bess Morton, Donnie's aunt, said about Donnie? She has been through this—she's the only one who has been through this—and the fact of the matter is, Terrance just woke up at some point and climbed out of bed fit as a fiddle."

"If you want to count on that . . . on the word of a . . . of an . . . *artist*," she said with a good deal of disdain, "that is of course your prerogative. We have elected to put our faith in the doctors."

"I want to do what's right," Mrs. Whitman said. "I was just hoping we, the parents, might approach this in a similar—"

"We are doing what we feel we need to do. If you are trying to pressure me into—"

"Not at all!" Mrs. Whitman said. "I'm not trying to pressure you into anything."

"What if they should never come back?" Mrs. Philby said, her words choked. "I don't accept all this nonsense our children have told us about dreaming and traveling . . . If you ask me, it's . . . well, I can't even say it. It's horrible is what it is. The evil of our society. Where our children, our dear, precious children, could ever get hold of such things—"

"It is *not* what you think!" Mrs. Whitman gasped.

"The doctors will run tests. We shall see what we see."

"Our children—their holograms—are trapped inside the parks somewhere."

"And you actually *believe* that nonsense," Mrs. Philby replied, "which means this conversation is over."

"If we work together," Mrs. Whitman said, "maybe we can figure out where they've gone. Maybe we can find them and bring them back."

"Listen to you!"

"The Overtakers have kidnapped Wayne. I . . . Finn . . . your son was here at my house. We . . . There was a cryptogram, a kind of mathematical—"

"I know what a cryptogram is!" Mrs. Philby said. "Will you listen to yourself, Mrs. Whitman? Will you listen to what you are saying?"

"I know it sounds—"

"Ridiculous? Absurd? Impossible? Yes, it does! And you? You're delusional if you believe such . . . such garbage." Mrs. Philby was breathing heavily into the phone. "What do you mean, he was at your house?"

"After school. He and our Finn and another of the—Willa . . . Listen, I know how far-fetched all of it sounds. We've been asked to endure so much. But my point is: if there is some truth to what they say about what happened to Donnie Maybeck that time, about where they go at night, about Wayne and this . . . this war they seem to be fighting—"

"Would you just listen to yourself?"

"But if there is," Mrs. Whitman persisted. "If there should be—"

"But there isn't. How could there be?"

Mrs. Whitman felt a tremendous headache coming on. She gripped her head with her free hand and tried to be objective about what she was saying. She knew that if she were the one on the receiving end of her own argument she'd think the other person a nutcase.

"I don't know," she muttered.

"When the doctors render their opinion," Mrs. Philby said, "I will contact you and the other parents."

"Kind of you."

"It's the least I can do. Should I call this number?"

Mrs. Whitman gave her her mobile number instead.

"Are you . . . going out?" Mrs. Philby asked, as if Mrs. Whitman would be committing the ultimate bad-parent crime by leaving her comatose son in his present state.

"My husband will be here with Finn," Mrs. Whitman said. "I . . . that is . . . Donnie's aunt and I—"

"The *artist*?"

"The same. Yes. Donnie let slip something about Epcot." She hesitated, knowing the scorn she faced for bringing up the subject. "We can't just sit by and do nothing, you see?"

"But . . . you can't possibly believe any of what they tell us!"

"Actually . . . Well . . . That is . . . Yes. I'm afraid I do."

41

PHILBY KNEW HE HAD IT in him. He stood behind the control room that overlooked the expansive but empty amphitheater facing the Fantasmic! stage and walked through the wall, thinking this must be how Harry Potter felt when entering Platform 9 3/4 for the Hogwarts Express. Philby had always considered that to be purely fictional, impossible—and yet here he was, doing it. He stepped through and found himself alongside gunmetal gray shelves holding a dozen flashing computer slaves. He was standing to the left of, and looking over the shoulder of, a man wearing a Disney ball cap and a dark blue sweatshirt. The man's full attention was on the show onstage, and it was a good thing too, for his angle of view allowed Philby to spot his own reflection in the control room's slanted windows; if the man looked slightly to his own left he would have seen the boy spying on him. Philby stepped behind an open locker door, screening himself, so that he could peer through the crack between the door and the cabinet. He studied the man's every move—where he looked, how he controlled the array of knobs and buttons on the board and various boxes in front of him as well as off to his side. Philby quickly identified the lighting and sound boards. Everything was computerized: the show's effects were brought together on a single computer screen that tracked by hundredths of seconds and started and stopped each particular function, from the opening and closing of a trapdoor to a light changing color. Everything was synchronized with the music. The show played out on a large flat-screen display that showed dozens of different rows of categories: five for music; six for live sound; fifteen for lights; six for pyrotechnics; plus a dozen other stage events.

The man wore a headset through which he communicated with the rest of the crew, keeping one eye on the display, the other on the stage below.

"Okay," Philby heard the director from the house say over an intercom, "we're through the opening without a glitch, let's keep it running." The technician clicked a button on the console in front of him, keeping his eyes on the screen.

Philby quickly saw that the variously colored segments of each row on the master display related directly to events happening onstage below. The tech director stopped the show to adjust one of the lighting cues, and the technician, following his instructions, tapped a few keys on his console, extending one blue bulge on the lighting display. When they ran the cue again, a corresponding blue light on stage remained lit a fraction of a second longer than before. Satisfied, the man let the show continue.

To the right of the console were several other computer screens, and while this might have overwhelmed any of the other Kingdom Keepers, Philby found himself right at home. The top screen was a list of pyrotechnic effects and, as Philby studied it, he realized that the other screens pertained to the other categories on the larger flat panel. The screens on the right expanded and explained the events on the main screen. The discovery intrigued Philby: if he could get into that chair, he would have full control over every light, sound, trapdoor, and explosion that happened on stage.

Including those that were never supposed to happen.

* * *

Charlene, Amanda, and Finn were tucked into a thicket that looked out onto the backstage entrance to the Fantasmic! stage. From here the structure looked like an oil-rig platform, a series of open concrete platforms rising higher and higher, enclosed in steel-pipe railings painted a sky blue. For safety's sake, there was only a single entrance to the backstage area. And though that entrance was presently unguarded, something warned

Finn not to try it. *Don't go there,* a voice said in his head, and he took this to be not only his own unconscious thought, but somehow—and he didn't pretend to know how it might be possible—a message from Wayne. He felt something guiding him, like the kind of power a song could have over him, or the way he felt sometimes late at night when nothing in the world made any sense, and then he'd picture his mother or father and for no explainable reason he would feel okay again. Like that. Weird, strange emotions that carried through and penetrated his core, so deep that he knew to obey them.

"We need another way in," he said, bracing himself for the challenges he felt certain to come. But on this night he was to be surprised.

"Okay," Charlene said. She'd never taken her eyes off the stage's superstructure. She seemed to be breaking it down level by level, bolt by bolt. "I have a theory. Just a theory. I need like thirty seconds to check it out."

"Involving?"

"If I'm right," she said, "I can get you in there."

"Go for it," he said.

"It's a little risky," she added. "So if anything happens . . . well, don't forget about me. I'm not saying that. But do what needs to be done first and figure me out *after*. You got it?"

Was this the same girl who had once tried to make

everything all about her? Could one person change like that? So quickly? So completely? Charlene herself attributed the change to her participation in the adventure at Animal Kingdom. And where Maybeck might have questioned her, or accused her of being the traitor they all expected, Finn decided to do otherwise.

"Should I talk you out of it?" he asked.

"No. I hope not. Stay tuned. BRB."

As she took off, running out into the open, Finn reached for her arm to stop her, but missed. As far as he could tell she had not yet taken her eyes off the superstructure. Whatever her idea was, it seemed to consume all her attention. Even now, as she sprinted across the paved area, as Finn feared she was going to go against what he'd said and use the backstage entrance anyway, as he rose and felt his jaw drop to allow him to yell out to stop her, she never flinched, never looked away from the superstructure above and ahead of her.

As he was about to call out, Amanda took his arm and pulled him back down. He shook her off and broke her grip, furious that she'd stopped him. What did she know? If something happened to Charlene, it wasn't Amanda who'd get blamed. No, the blame would fall squarely on him. Being the leader also meant being the loser if there was loss.

Charlene jumped and spun around and was suddenly running *backward* nearly as fast as she had been going forward. She'd broken her staring contest with the stage, and was now looking back at the trees, at her friends. Her eyes were defiant, as if she possessed a secret none of the rest of them knew. Finn felt as if she were looking him straight in the eye. For a moment an icy panic stole through him: she was the traitor about to betray them.

And then she disappeared.

Vanished.

Gone.

Amanda took Finn's arm again, but her face was filled with exhilaration, not the terror and dread he felt.

"DHI shadow," she said softly.

The terraced audience seating of Fantasmic!'s outdoor amphitheater sloped down a hundred feet or more toward the artificial lake in front of the stage. The back of the stage rose to the same height as the highest level of the audience area. Charlene had figured out that if she ran down to the lowest level—the stage-door entrance—she would be in a projection shadow.

"See?" Charlene said, causing Finn to jump. She was standing a few feet behind them. "I cut around and came back through the landscaping. The projection line is just about dead even with the door. It runs about a quarter of the way around that far side. I found the other edge. But there's a nice solid shadow, thirty or forty feet or more."

"That was some kind of risk to take," Finn said.

"Would you have said that if Philby had been the one to discover it?" She waited for his answer, but he wasn't going to encourage her. "I think you need to open your mind, Finn Whitman. It took some calculation, I admit it, but it wasn't a total guess. There's never been any voiceover work, never any green-screen work, never even any discussion of our taking part in Fantasmic! Why?"

"Because our DHIs don't reach over here," he answered.

"Or there's enough interference to make it a hassle. And they're not about to install one of those projectors for a single attraction. Not when they cost as much as they do."

Finn had had all this same information at his disposal. Why had she figured it out while he had not?

"I can get you in there," she said. "I can climb up there, find some rope—there's got to be a ton of rope backstage, or strapping, or something, and get you both up there. Amanda's new at this, so maybe she can't touch stuff when she's invisible, but you and I can haul her up. Once we're in, we're in. No one's going to question our being there. I've counted twenty-five people so far."

Finn realized that had been part of what Charlene had been doing earlier: counting Cast Members.

"There will be costumes somewhere. Stuff like that. We can make this work. We can get you onto the stage before Maleficent's scene."

Finn reminded her, "When you go to sleep, things in your pockets or a wristwatch or necklace cross over with you. Things held in your hands do not—maybe because as you fell asleep you let go. What if when I go down there into projection shadow, the sword doesn't come with me?"

"Good point. So you'll have to tie it to the rope. We'll haul it up after you two have made it. That way it won't give you away." She pointed. "We'll go this way, through the woods. Once we disappear, that's it. We're doing this blind. I'll do my best, but I won't know where you are, I won't be able to see you, and you won't be able to see me, so here's the code: one tug on the rope means go. Three means stop."

"What about two tugs?" Amanda asked.

Finn answered, "Two means nothing. We won't use two tugs, just to make sure there's no confusion."

"You guys have done this before," Amanda said in a voice of resignation.

"Just a little bit," said Charlene, motioning for them both to follow.

42

THE PLAN WAS A SIMPLE ONE: to get Finn into position prior to Maleficent's appearance in the show. Assuming the Overtaker Maleficent had taken the place of the Cast Member playing her—in order to "hide out in the open"—and that Chernabog had done the same thing as well, Maleficent's appearance in Fantasmic! would be the moment for Finn to attack her with the sword.

Charlene had an equally difficult assignment: she was to try to figure out a way to trap Chernabog, hopefully preventing his becoming a dragon, as he did at the end of the show. The way it played out, the dragon was eventually subdued by water, which worked nicely for theater; but if the Overtakers realized they were under attack, they weren't about to let some water stop them. The dragon would battle back with everything he had, including fire breathing. Finn didn't want to get up close and personal with that.

The bigger issue facing Finn, Amanda, and Charlene at the moment was how big a grip the Overtakers had on the show. Was it just Chernabog and

Maleficent, or were others involved? And if so: characters in the show, or stagehands, or both?

"Remember," Finn said to Amanda, as they stared at an empty wall where they believed an invisible Charlene was climbing, "once we're in shadow, you won't be visible, and maybe we shouldn't speak either. Don't want someone hearing a ghost."

"You're taking Mickey's place, right?"

"Yes."

"But what if they've already gotten to him?"

"If they've kidnapped and replaced the Cast Member who plays Mickey, then we've probably lost already. Mickey's got to be on our side. Maybe they're ultimately after him. You've seen how the major Cast Members—all the Cast Member princesses, Minnie and Mickey, Goofy, Pluto—always travel around the park with a 'handler?'" he said. "Guests are made to believe the handler is there to guide the character, manage them, speak for them when necessary. Wayne says they're actually bodyguards. Even the smallest handler is trained in martial arts. They've been around ever since the Overtakers appeared. The Imagineers protect them at all costs. If the parks were ever to lose the Mickey and Minnie who show up after the park closes. . . ."

"Mickey's a big part of the show."

"He *is* the show. His character has obvious powers—powers greater than Maleficent's, and he has the show itself on his side—it's written and staged so that he wins. For all we know, Maleficent *wanted* these additional tech rehearsals—she arranged for them to take place—so she could study and practice how to defeat Mickey, to defeat him in battle. Then, at some point, the plan is to lure the *real* Mickey, not the Cast Member Mickey, from the Magic Kingdom over here to the show. That wouldn't be terribly difficult. He steps onto the stage and she defeats him, and the balance of power is shifted forever. We can't pretend to know the way she thinks. She's cunning in that way: it's never as simple as it looks."

"Sometimes it is," she said. "Sometimes things are really obvious and really simple."

"You think?" he said. *Was that the traitor speaking?* he wondered. "You call scaling a wall while being invisible simple? Do you know how much a person relies on looking down and seeing his or *her* foot take a toehold, or see her fingers grab a rock? It's like climbing blind. It's incredibly hard. That's why Charlene went first," he said. "She's half-monkey."

Amanda looked hurt. Finn wasn't sure what he'd said to cause that.

"I wouldn't let her hear you say that," Amanda

said. "She likes you, you know?"

"What's that supposed to mean?"

"She just does."

"And you know this because?"

"Girls know this stuff, Finn, and we talk about it. And we text about it. And we IM about it. It's what girls do. You guys do sports and Xbox. We figure out who likes who."

"Ah. . . ."

"She's beautiful. You have to admit that. Pretty enough to be on TV or in the movies. And she's a jock. What's not to like?"

"I guess."

"You ought to give it a shot."

Finn felt the center of his chest turn to stone. Why was Amanda trying to do this?

"Maybe I will," he said.

"Maybe you should."

Why was she bringing this up now? Why was she pushing him?

"But I thought. . . ." he said.

"What?"

"About us. Never mind. It's nothing."

"You thought what? That we're something or we're nothing?"

"I guess so. I don't know. I guess that's right.

Nothing I guess." He felt his world implode and didn't understand any of it. He thought that he and Amanda—after all the hand touching—had something going. He thought they were more than just friends. His heart wouldn't stand still when he was around her; he got all jumpy and found himself hearing her voice among all the others. He wanted to catch her looking at him. Wanted to see that she was listening when he spoke.

And now this.

"There," Amanda said.

A blue nylon strap had dropped down from the second backstage level above them. Finn followed it with his eyes and saw it tied to one of the steel stanchions supporting the railing.

"I'm supposed to go first," he said, "and Charlene and I will pull you up."

"Whatever."

He reached out and took her hand in his, but she shook him off and let go. He reached a second time and grabbed hold; the warmth of her arm surprised him. He tried to make eye contact with her, but her eyes were dark and hard and cold. She wouldn't look at him.

They stepped into the DHI projection shadow and, as they did, he let go of her hand.

He walked. Looking down, he saw some leaves

scoot to the side and decided that it had to be her feet shuffling through them. She was right there with him.

He wanted to speak, but didn't.

He found the nylon strap and tied the sword to its end and then climbed the strap like a rope at a ropes course. He wrapped the dangling strap around his leg and shinnied up, taking several minutes and a lot of energy to reach the second level. If Charlene was there, he couldn't tell. He neither heard nor saw her.

But the blue strap moved, and Finn turned and put his hands to it. He felt Charlene tug once: she was telling Amanda it was safe for her to tie herself to the strap.

Finn held to the strap, waiting for something to happen; Amanda would give them a single tug when she was tied on and ready to be lifted.

Finn counted to thirty. To sixty. He felt Charlene tug the strap for a second time. He knew immediately that the only weight on the end of that strap was the sword. He could see it stand up and dance a few inches off the ground.

The frustration of his invisibility and silence built up so much that he just wanted to scream.

He heard the scuffle of feet and went rigid. Glancing over his shoulder Finn saw a stagehand and another guy—who appeared to be a rigger, judging by the tools he was carrying. The men were coming right at Finn and Charlene. The Keepers were holding the strap, a loop of which lay over the railing and was gathered on the platform. Finn knew that the way the strap hung there had to appear unnatural, because it wasn't really *hanging* there: they were holding it.

Finn held his breath.

The stagehand and the rigger walked right past.

Finn moved slowly and tracked them until they, too, disappeared down a staircase.

Amanda wasn't tied to the strap. If she was down there, she wasn't playing along.

A deception of the worst kind. Beware your friends and know your enemies.

Charlene began hauling up the sword. She took her time to prevent it from clanking against the concrete and drawing attention.

Finn recalled Amanda breaking away from him. He felt a shiver. He thought back to a conversation they'd had while waiting for Charlene to climb.

You're going to try to find the Cast Member, he'd reminded her.

"The one playing Maleficent," she'd said. "I know my job."

"You're mad at me."

"I think I could be of more help than as a messenger."

"Your . . . powers. I know. But it's too dangerous."

"And that's ridiculous."

"If we can get the Cast Member playing Maleficent to talk to the show's stage manager—"

"While the real Maleficent is out there on stage," Amanda had said, "then maybe the stage manager sees the problem—sees he has two Maleficents, and then maybe he believes what's actually going on is going on. We went over it all, Finn. I get it."

"I'm worried about you, that's all." He had blurted it out. It sounded awkward now that he recalled it.

"I can *help* you if you'll only let me. Don't forget Expedition Everest."

Amanda had saved Finn's life inside Everest. He had thanked her, and they'd never discussed it since. Now she apparently wanted the chance to play the same role, but the risk to her was too great. Finn had the sword. It seemed likely that only the sword could defeat Maleficent and Chernabog. A gust of wind wasn't going to change things.

Amanda had said, *Don't worry about me so much.*

It wasn't that simple, and he wished he could have told her why.

Finn was distracted from his reverie by the arrival of the end of the strap, delivering the sword at last. Finn untied the knot and tucked the sword away in a corner to hide it. He couldn't go walking around the stage area with a sword stuck through his belt. He'd have to come back for it.

Amanda was down there somewhere. Gone. Only the warmth of her remained, searing the tips of his fingers where he'd held onto her.

Finn looked high up into the void of the gray-blue dawn sky, a knot in his chest, confusion in his thoughts, remorse in his heart. He felt utterly alone.

* * *

Philby spotted a possible answer to his needs. The engineer kept glancing at the clock and then at a key chain thick with keys.

The show's control booth was too important—since it gave access to the control for all the pyrotechnical devices—to be left unlocked. No, it had to be under lock and key, and only a few people would possess such keys, would be given that kind of access. This man and how many others? Certainly not your average Security guard. It would have to be someone much higher up—the head of Security for sure, and a few other key technical personnel.

There! He glanced at the clock again. Philby's curiosity was satisfied as a voice over a speaker announced: "Break in five minutes. Prepare the stage please."

All Philby had to do was get the guy outside the

booth without his keys. Philby saw a solution to his two problems: the first, getting the keys away from the man, or removing the booth's key from the key chain, would have to be handled quickly; the second, stopping the show, would happen in just under five minutes, with the break.

Philby slipped out the Nextel, made sure it was in silent mode, and wrote a text, targeting the phone's "KKS" group.

philitup: need fantasmic shut down 4 5 min....

He hit SEND. The text would be sent to the four other Kingdom Keepers.

Philby kept his eye on the key chain. He was going to have to sneak across on hands and knees and come up from behind and grab them—he didn't see any other way to do it. He would wait for a particularly busy part of the show. The mist projectors would be coming up soon; the stage would go dark as characters hurried out into place. That seemed a perfect time to go for it.

A message arrived.

MYBEST: need ur cell

philitup: no way...locked in da booth

MYBEST: Jess is a stagehand...needs 2 b able 2 rech us all...

FINN: she can hav mine...ill leav it bhind da 2nd levl firehose...

MYBEST: k

WILLATREE: phil...i can mess up da boats is that good???

philitup: fantasmic...lol get it?

WILLATREE: no...phil...realy...r u kiddin?? stay 2 da teki stuff...stand by

Beyond the window of the booth, the stage went dark. Philby watched the flat-panel display and saw the approach of a confusion of colorful bubbles crowding nearly every line of the music and effects readouts. Whatever scene was next, it was big and busy.

This was to be his chancc.

He crouched down, keeping his eye pressed to the crack beside the locker door. His body tensed with the first onstage explosion, which was quickly followed by another.

Philby crawled around the door and directly behind the engineer's seat and eased his hand toward the keys.

But the engineer's head swung in his direction, and Philby yanked back his hand. He was but the thickness of a chair away from the man. Had he been human instead of DHI the man might have felt the heat from his body, or smelled him, or sensed him some other way. Instead, Philby held his breath as the man's chair pivoted to within an inch of contact. Then it swung back to the left, and the man's head with it.

Philby reached up, clutched the keys slowly and tightly to keep them from making noise, and slipped them off the console. He crept back to behind the locker door and carefully studied them. The engineer had too many keys to keep track of—he had marked them all with color tabs and had written on each tab. Philby worked through them, making sure not to allow them to jangle.

F CNTL

He kept a finger separating this key from the others and continued through the rest.

MSTR

Philby marked this key's place as well. None of the ten or twelve others were marked with anything that he found interesting. Only these two. Maybe if things worked out perfectly he might get them back onto the ring unnoticed.

Feeling jittery to be working so close to the

engineer, and knowing that Willa could pull off her boats maneuver at any moment, he worked furiously to remove the keys from the ring. It was a ring that required the desired key to be worked two full turns around a circle. Philby had to pull a piece of the ring away, as if he were trying to pry open a stubborn spring. He got the first key off, trying to memorize what order the keys were in; then the second. He pocketed both, putting one in each front pocket to keep them from clanking together.

There was no waiting. He didn't have any choice but to crawl back out behind the chair and return the key chain. He did so with as little feeling of dread and anxiety as he could muster—he wanted to be prepared to attempt to go *all clear* if it came to that: if the engineer came after him, he would walk through the wall if possible.

"What the—?" the engineer said loudly into the small room.

For a moment Philby convinced himself he'd been seen. But then he realized the man was reacting to something outside the window, not inside the booth.

Philby darted back behind the locker door.

"Come on!" the man complained. "We're like one minute to break." He spoke into his headset, having a nasty conversation about the incompetence of the people managing the boats.

Willa had come through.

The technician looked at the clock as the minute hand moved to exactly five minutes before the hour. The technician tugged off the headset and grabbed his keys. He headed to the door, then hesitated a second as he glanced back toward the console.

Philby wondered if the technician had seen him, or his glow, or somehow felt his presence. The man stepped outside and pulled the door shut with authority.

It would be at least a five-minute break—the union technicians on the Kingdom Keepers DHI soundstage had taken regular five-minute breaks. Philby allowed himself an undisturbed five minutes. He slipped into the chair and hunkered down low.

He'd been watching the flat-panel display for quite a while, observing what effect each line controlled. Now his fingers found the mouse and he went about clicking and extending events the same way he worked a video editor or music composition software—changing both the order and length of specific events. By doing so he was changing the show, and, he hoped, stacking the deck and buying Finn a dealer's odds.

With any luck, even with the engineer back in the chair, Maleficent wouldn't know what hit her.

* * *

Finn left his phone—an invisible phone, but one he could feel—tucked in behind the firehose, feeling suddenly lost without it. Perhaps it was his invisibility doing this to him. But he suspected something else.

He would take visual cues—if they were given—from Charlene if possible, and would also keep an eye out for Jess playing a stagehand. Maleficent's entrance wasn't too far off. He had to get in position.

Amanda would be down on the dressing-room level; he had no idea where Willa was, but from her text he suspected she was responsible for the break in the technical rehearsal that had just occurred. Philby was inside the control booth, leaving Maybeck's identity and whereabouts unknown to Finn, though again from the text he knew that Maybeck was in the area.

In situations like this time played tricks on him. Clocks sped up. Reaction time slowed down. Soon it would all reach a fevered pitch, a boiling point, with him in the center of the cauldron.

"You okay?" Charlene asked. They'd found their way out of the DHI projection shadow, visible now, and had tucked themselves into the entrance of a darkened—and Finn hoped, unused—hallway. The stage was a labyrinth of these hallways and staircases, all of them interconnected in a way it would take days to memorize. Some led to the wings of the stage itself while others returned Cast Members to subterranean dressing rooms, and still others to the platforms beneath trapdoors or up high into what from the audience appeared to be a towering mountain. Some of these areas were lit and some were not, suggesting which ones were being used during the technical rehearsal.

"Been better," Finn said.

"She's okay," Charlene said, answering a question that Finn hadn't asked. "There's a reason for her not getting onto the rope, and it isn't the reason you think."

And it isn't the reason you think. Charlene was the reason Amanda hadn't gotten onto the rope. Finn felt certain of it.

"She probably saw those two coming toward us and took off. Who knows what that looked like from down there."

Charlene put her hand on his shoulder and rubbed the tightness away. He wanted to ask her to stop, but didn't. He wanted to ask her about what Amanda had said, but didn't know how.

She was about to put herself at as much risk as he was. They were attempting to tackle forces with powers far greater than their own. There was little to no chance they could prevail on their own.

"This is only going to work if we time it right," she

said, as if reading his thoughts. How could she do that? How could she know him so well?

"Just what I was thinking."

"So I'd wish you luck, but that would mean I thought you need it, and I don't. I don't think any of this is about luck or chance or fate. You know? Destiny maybe. I think somehow we are supposed to be here right now. The five of us. The *seven* of us. Not because Wayne wants it, or we want it. But just because."

"Because," he echoed.

"Yeah. Think about where each of us was before we tried out to be the Disney Hosts. Does that even feel like you? Like the same person? Not me. I can tell you that. It's all so totally different. I was like this yahoo cheerleader, right? I don't know that girl. Not now."

"I know what you mean."

"Right?"

"Yes. It's all different."

"We are where we're supposed to be."

"You sound like my mother," he said. "She's always laying that stuff on me."

"I'm freaking," she said. "And when I freak I talk too much. All I meant to say is that if anything happens—"

"Do *not* say it."

"But—"

"No! Do not go there." He felt his hands shaking.

Over the speakers, he heard the mirror speaking to the Evil Queen.

"*. . . in Mickey's imagination, beauty and love will always survive.*"

"Beauty and love! Did you hear that?" Charlene asked.

"I . . . yeah." Beauty and love. They seemed to define Charlene.

It was time to return for the sword. Maleficent would be on the stage soon.

"That's our cue," Charlene said.

"Right."

"Okay then," she added.

"Okay."

43

GLADIS PHILBY, wearing a Hawaiian housedress over her nightgown, stood sobbing in the hallway outside her son's bedroom as paramedics with the ambulance service moved her comatose son from his bed to the wheeled stretcher that would move him to the vehicle.

As they lifted him, not a muscle responded. He looked . . . She couldn't bring herself to think it. But that was the way he looked, and there was no holding back the tears.

Her husband came out of the room. "Okay, they've got him ready to move. They've started an IV. They've got monitors on him. They'll be in touch with doctors from the back of the ambulance and may give him something on the way. I signed a release allowing them to treat him. If it's . . . you know. . . ."

"Drugs?"

"Then the IV should help. In any case, they'll do blood tests at the hospital and figure this out soon enough. One of us can go in the ambulance with him, but I told them I wanted to stay with you. We should change—quickly—and try to follow them to the hospital."

She nodded. She couldn't get any words out.

"I know it doesn't help much, but they say his vitals—it isn't a deep coma. They say it's more like . . . he's just sleeping soundly."

Now she found the strength to speak. "Do not tell me that you believe for one second all this nonsense about—"

"I didn't say that, Gladis. All I said is, he seems okay. We need to change and get in the car. The best way to help him now is to be with him."

She nodded again, but Mrs. Whitman's words flew through her thought like a wounded bird: *We can't just sit by and do nothing, you see?*

"Frank," she said to her husband, "they'll be testing him for an hour or more, don't you think?"

"Yes, two or three, I suppose. It's never fast. Why?"

"And you say he's sleeping comfortably."

"What is it, dearest?"

"I want to be with him, it isn't that. I'm his mother. But more than anything I want him free of this."

"Gladis?"

"I think . . . I'm not saying I believe any of this, you understand. But I think for the time being we can put ourselves to better use than sitting around a hospital waiting room."

"Whatever are you talking about?"

"There's a phone call I have to make."

"At this hour?"

She drew in a large breath, swelling the housedress and filling her face with color for the first time since she had discovered her unresponsive son.

"We're going to Disney World."

44

JESS HAD NO IDEA what she was doing. Dressed in a black T-shirt, a black fleece, and black jeans—all courtesy of the Studios' costume shop—and wearing a black baseball cap and a headset, she was currently wandering the maze of hallways and staircases at the back of the Fantasmic! stage. The black clothing helped reduce the glow from her DHI. Every so often she paused and closed her eyes and tried to summon whatever it was that allowed her dreams to turn to visions. If you'd asked her a week or two earlier if she could bring on this state she would have answered an emphatic no. But since the visions of Wayne had begun, since she'd picked up something *while awake* in the middle of walking around Epcot, she'd convinced herself otherwise. Why should such "powers" be limited to sleep? Besides, she had a secret weapon working for her: technically she *was* currently asleep; her body was lying in bed at Mrs. Nash's, snoring softly, no doubt. Being a DHI didn't count as being awake; it didn't even feel like being awake. So why, if her sleeping self could imagine and dream, couldn't she tap into that as a DHI and experience it here, now, wandering the hallways of Fantasmic!—why?

Jess understood the potential risk of her efforts. You didn't summon the dark thoughts of someone—something—like Maleficent without uncertainty. Who knew the depth of her darkness, the gravitational pull of her menace? What if once Jess got inside Maleficent's mind there was no way out—what if it was a mental maze that took you prisoner and never relinquished you? What if Maleficent had been waiting for just such an opportunity? What if she were powerful enough to manipulate her own thought so skillfully that she could send an image to Jess that was a lie? What if she could use such a lie as a tool to mislead the Kingdom Keepers? Wouldn't she, Jess, then qualify as the traitor?

Layer upon layer her doubts began to accumulate. Jess felt like she had worms in her stomach and wondered if she possessed enough strength for this task. Maleficent had feared her, had captured and imprisoned her—twice!—had made her a target for some time now. Maleficent saw Jess as the obstacle to the Overtakers' success, whether because of Jess's ability to see the future, or because of some other quality Jess had yet to recognize in herself. But actively seeking a way into an evil fairy's thoughts suddenly struck Jess as crazy. What had she been thinking? Worse: how had the others allowed her to do this?

But it wasn't the others. It was only Maybeck and Wanda, and Jess still didn't know how much she trusted Wanda anyway. What if Wanda was Wayne's traitor? It helped that Wayne had mentioned her in his video message—it helped a lot. It helped that Wanda had gotten up in the middle of the night and taken huge risks to smuggle her and Maybeck into the Studios. But there was something still bothering Jess about the woman. The performance at Mrs. Nash's house had been impressive, and yet it had also felt somewhat authentic, as if Wanda had bigger plans for her and Amanda than working with the Kingdom Keepers. Perhaps she intended to place them both in a boarding school far away from here. Jess didn't like other women making plans for her: Maleficent had played mother for months.

Never again, Jess swore to herself.

She felt it then: an eerie cold, and a strange feeling, as if an animal had crawled inside her and were looking for a way out. Images flashed in front of her eyes: colors in the sky; a jet airplane; a man wearing a beret; Mickey Mouse, but with Japanese anime-style eyes.

OMG! Finn. Was he conducting an orchestra? Directing traffic? And Maybeck and . . . *Wayne*, hunched over in some kind of box, struggling to breathe.

She threw her head to the side because there was

the horrid face of Chernabog bearing down on her as the chill increased to a deep freeze. She squeezed her eyes tightly shut and then forced them open and, *Thank goodness*, she was standing in the subterranean hallway beneath Fantasmic!

I'm close, she thought. *She's nearby.* Where was Amanda?

Jess worked the phone Finn had left for her.

She wrote a text to all of the others:

I can feel her. lower level 1. she's here.

But not for long. The door swung open. Jess lowered her head, putting the brim of the cap between her face and the person who came out of that room. She could see only the feet.

It wasn't a person at all. It was a black robe with purple trim. And as the robe parted slightly it revealed . . . green ankles and shins.

"You!" the familiar voice called out. A voice like breaking ice. "I'm late for my cue. Are you the one taking me? Where is Annie? Are you going to answer me? Hello? Listen, sweetie, if Annie's late, if she's not going to do her job, I'll need you to throw the switch on the lift. Rehearsals! Why are they so understaffed? Do you think you can handle that? *Hmm?*"

"Yes, ma'am," Jess said, lowering her voice to disguise it. "The switch."

"Well, hurry it up! We haven't got all day."

The cold was intense. Jess realized it was seeping out from beneath the door—Maleficent had the temperature in the dressing room turned down to icehouse freezing. She had no idea where the Cast Member playing Maleficent had gone; but this *thing* was no Cast Member.

Jess followed thc flowing black robe deeper down the hall, followed into the depths of the structure, through two more hallways and down a narrow stairway like something on a ship. The show's soundtrack grew louder than could be explained by the small speakers along the wall, backstage monitors that allowed all the Cast Members to hear the music and action onstage, so that they could keep track of their cues.

Jess followed the icy creature as if she had no choice, wondering when the *thing* would figure out who it was coming up behind, and knowing she couldn't allow that truth to be revealed. Finn would be up there waiting.

Finn and the sword: the Kingdom Keepers' best and perhaps only chance to defeat *it*.

* * *

Charlene found exactly what she wanted: a long length

of pirate chain, complete with an old lock and key. There were three lengths of the chain coiled backstage alongside a stock of bows and arrows and some rope. The chain was impossibly heavy and cumbersome, but she draped it around her shoulders like a Hawaiian lei and looked straight up the emergency ladder that led down to the back of the stage from the very top of the mountain.

There was no time to waste: someone could arrive at any moment and stop her. She struggled to keep herself upright with the newly added weight, took hold of the ladder railings, and began to climb.

Five feet into the climb she heard voices approaching. She managed two more rungs and then froze, her face pressed against the cold metal. The two men Finn had heard now stood directly below her, with her feet no more than a few inches from the top of the head of the tallest one.

"Do you think they'll find it this time?" one of them said. It was impossible to tell who was doing the talking.

"No. For one thing he's supposed to appear only on film. For another, it doesn't happen all the time. It's like a typical glitch, you ask me. Can't make it happen when you want to fix it, can't stop it from happening when you don't."

"I'm done with these early morning tech-rehearsal calls."

"You and me both."

"Think they'll cancel the show if they can't get it right?"

"*Dah!* Who are we talking about? Of course they'll cancel. And then you and I will be laid off until they resolve it."

"You think?"

"No. I know."

"But what are we supposed to do about it?"

"Don't ask me."

"But I am asking you."

"But you shouldn't be."

Back and forth they went, sniping at one another. Charlene dared not move for fear the chain might rattle or clank against the fire ladder and give her away.

Unless or until they moved, she was trapped here.

And if she didn't get up to the top soon, then Finn would be in serious trouble.

* * *

Wearing a Security guard costume, Maybeck watched from stage left as the Evil Queen turned into the Hag from Snow White as a bubbling cauldron appeared in front of her. She summoned "the forces of evil" to turn the dream into "a nightmare Fantasmic!"

This was Finn's cue, the only time the title of the show was mentioned from the stage. It was also significant that this seemed the mission of the Overtakers as well—to turn the dream into a nightmare—to stop Jess's dreams. It all made so much sense all of a sudden. Everything Wayne had asked them to do at Magic Kingdom and Animal Kingdom focused laserlike into the storyline of Fantasmic! The good becoming bad; the bad wanting to ruin the dreams. It was as if Fantasmic! were the outline for an Overtakers' charter of evil.

One thing seemed certain: whatever happened here in the next few minutes was to be cataclysmic, irreversible, and it would affect the Kingdom Keepers for a long time to come. Without any real evidence, Finn knew this to be true.

Because someone's going down, he thought. *And it had better not be us.*

* * *

Philby had changed the timeline, blocking Mickey's trapdoor lift and Maleficent's flashy exit. Maybeck or Amanda or Willa—or all three—would still have to stop the Cast Member playing the Brave Little Tailor Mickey from getting in the way, but Philby had no control over that.

What he could control. . . .

Philby's arm stung. It felt as if someone had pricked him on the inside of his elbow.

His head swam; he felt lightheaded and slightly sick to his stomach. His arm burned and his vision blurred and he looked down to see a computer mouse in his hand and he couldn't remember why he was holding it.

There was still something incredibly important to do.

A dragon?

What did he know about dragons?

He blinked rapidly, reaching for his arm and trying to remove whatever was making it sting so badly there—it felt like he'd been climbing a tree and had caught a splinter in his arm—but his fingers came up empty.

Fire. It was something to do with fire. Stopping the fire? Starting a fire?

There was a pounding on the door to his right.

Where was he?

A show was happening onstage beyond the window. The colors were beautiful—the lights amazing.

A man's face appeared in the glass. Some older dude wearing a ball cap. He looked frustrated as he tried to cup his eyes to the window, but he clearly couldn't see in. Something told Philby the glass was treated with a mirror surface on the outside, but he wasn't sure how he knew this. He wasn't sure how he knew anything. Why was his brain suddenly void of all the random thoughts that always filled it? He spent his every waking hour awash in numbers and facts. He drowned in them, morning to night. Yet now, ever since that stinging in his arm had started, things seemed much more peaceful. Dreamy.

He felt tired. He didn't like the feeling at all.

The woven office chair he occupied was unusually comfortable. As comfy as a couch.

What could a little nap hurt?

The door jiggled again. Someone wanted in.

Philby stood to open the door, but caught himself when his hand was only inches away from the door knob.

I'm not supposed to open that.

He didn't know why, exactly. Just that he wasn't supposed to.

He looked back and saw the flat panel. The computer mouse.

Something to do with fire. And dragons. Or was it only one dragon?

His parents had lectured him about drugs and about drinking alcohol. He had no interest in either. Drugs and drinking messed up your mind and Philby valued his mind far too much to go experimenting with its chemistry. He understood chemistry at an advanced level. He understood a lot of things that not many other kids his age understood and he took great pride in that fact.

Yet he felt drugged. Or drunk. He didn't know the difference, so he wasn't sure which. That is to say, he didn't feel himself. Something strange had overtaken him from the moment he'd felt that sting on the inside of his elbow.

His foggy mind sought an explanation, for that was the way his mind worked: question/answer. Logic lived inside him like a prized gem in a vault.

For every action there's an equal and opposite reaction.

He was definitely on the reaction end of things. But no matter how hard he tried, he couldn't think why he couldn't think. He couldn't place what action might have made him this way.

The thought of that got him laughing. Softly at first. To himself. But then the silliness of the moment spread through him like a wildfire and—

Fire.

There it was again: something about fire and that flat-panel computer screen and that mouse.

But even that seemed funny.

His laughter began anew and he found himself owning the cozy office chair, bouncing to the rhythm of the music—*good music*—and wondering what it was about that flat-panel screen that was so incredibly important.

* * *

Jess kept her head down and moved to the rectangular box with the red and green buttons inside. Big buttons that reminded her of the controls outside the Mission: Space pods. Above the box was a smaller green light—dark for the moment.

Something told her this all had to do with Philby, as Maleficent stepped onto a square platform and tightened her robes so that they didn't hang over the edges of the platform. She clipped a safety strap around her waist, keeping her right hand on it. Jess could envision her arriving up on stage, releasing that strap, and stepping out of a blinding spotlight to take the place of the Hag—a woman who had come *down* on the same platform only moments earlier.

Jess had watched how the Hag's handler had handled things: when the little warning light turned green, the handler pushed the large green button. A moment later the stage had opened overhead and the Hag had appeared, descending on the platform. Now Maleficent had taken the Hag's place and Jess assumed the device worked just the same to take someone back up onstage:

the computer would cue the handler. If all the proper safety precautions had been observed, then the handler pushed the green button, allowing the computer to start the lift when the show's timing called for Maleficent's entrance. If anything was awry, the handler could hit the red button marked ALL STOP and prevent the lift from rising through the trap door and anyone getting hurt.

Like Finn, she thought, knowing that tonight the script had been rewritten.

The smaller light flashed green. Jess's finger shook uncontrollably as it hovered at the large green switch. Maybe there was some other way. Maybe Finn was taking too great a risk.

"Go on push it, you fool!" said Maleficent. "It's my entrance!"

Jess's finger straightened, all the indecision gone from her, and with it the shaking. Her finger inched closer to the button and, at the last possible second, she turned her head toward the green *thing* standing on the lift, and she raised her head just enough to allow the cap's brim to reveal her face.

In that moment, she and Maleficent met eyes and she took great delight as the evil fairy's whites widened in the sea of green skin, as consternation overcame the witch—for this *thing* before her never showed fear.

"You?" she gasped dryly.

Jess smiled widely. "Me," she said, gloating. "Enjoy the show."

Jess pushed the button and in a flash of light and smoke Maleficent was gone.

45

AS THE FIRE-BURST surrounding Maleficent's entrance receded, leaving a coil of gray smoke twisting high above the stage, Finn saw a Security guard holding back Mickey, the Brave Little Tailor, preventing the Cast Member from going onstage. Finn had no time to glance overhead and try to spot Charlene and prevent the dragon from rearing its ugly head—all forty-five feet of it; no time to ensure he wouldn't be burned to a crisp by Chernabog, who he assumed had taken the dragon's place the same way Maleficent had taken the place of the Cast Member playing her. What odd fun this substitution must have been for them—acting out themselves in front of audiences and tech rehearsals, subtly changing the show in ways the Imagineers couldn't troubleshoot. Preparing for something much bigger, much more sinister. Taking the audience of ten thousand hostage? Threatening to burn them if they left their seats? Such an act would give the Overtakers the kind of clout they sought, would provide them a negotiating position.

Maleficent turned to taunt Mickey, as was her role.

Finn noted that she had a green bandage on her neck—where he had cut her with the sword.

Finn stepped out onto the stage, the sword held down at his side. He'd wondered how hard it might be to determine if he had the right Maleficent and not the Cast Member playing her, but his question was answered immediately. Not only was her skin green and bandaged, her eyes were bloodshot, and the look in them pure hatred. But there was also that twisted smile—a smile he'd witnessed in the back corridors of the Animal Kingdom's veterinary clinic.

"Silly, silly boy," she said, her voice amplified by the microphone she wore.

Presuming that Charlene was in place and that Philby had temporarily turned off the fire effect in the dragon, Finn took another step closer.

"We know about Epcot," he said. "The seat belts."

Her face reacted like a child opening a Christmas present only to discover coal inside the box.

The plan was in place. Finn was to antagonize her to the point she'd leave her mark on stage, stepping away from the cauldron. He would keep her focused and mad, so that she would direct Chernabog, or whatever force inhabited the stage dragon, to lash out at Finn with his fire breathing. But Finn would lead her mistakenly to enter into the path of the fire—the release of which would be controlled by Philby, not the dragon—and just as the beast unleashed its fury, Philby would drop Finn through Mickey the Brave Little Tailor's trapdoor to safety, while Maleficent would be caught and consumed—and eliminated—by her own evil plan.

If all else failed, he had the sword with which to defend himself, though he had known all along he would never actually strike her with it. The idea of that repulsed him, no matter how many times he'd seen it in a movie, or made it happen in a video game. No matter that Wayne had obviously believed it would come to that.

Finn crossed the stage, keeping the steaming cauldron between himself and Maleficent. Philby had done an excellent job—none of this was in the script. The cauldron should have been gone by now. Maleficent should have already summoned the dragon. As agreed, Finn took these changes to mean that Philby was in control and would trip the trapdoor when needed. Knowing that Philby had his back gave Finn added confidence.

"You silly, silly boy," she retched at him. "Do you actually believe a few *children* have any sort of chance against our powers?" She waved a hand and the cauldron tipped over, spilling a steaming green, viscous goo that would have caught Finn's feet had he not jumped quickly out of the way.

The Fantasmic! cauldron was always empty; the steam that poured from it was merely an effect. *She did that!* Finn thought.

The fairy reeled back her arm, and a fireball appeared in her hand. She launched it at Finn, who raised the sword and deflected it. The ball flew into the wings and exploded. He heard fire extinguishers whooshing as stagehands tried to extinguish the flames.

A pair of stagehands approached her. "Loretta!" the first one called at the witch. "What's going on?"

She threw a second fireball at them. They ducked and that fireball also flew offstage.

"We have a rehearsal going on here!" she hollered crisply. "The show's been through a rewrite, didn't you know?"

One of the stagehands held up an outstretched palm—he didn't want any more of her. The pair gingerly backed off the stage.

"The new show includes the defeat of the Kingdom Keepers." She motioned toward Finn and, as she did, a fence of bright laserlike beams surrounded him.

Finn heard, "The Kingdom Keepers! Of course! I knew I'd seen that kid somewhere!" and other such remarks trickle through the wings.

Finn couldn't allow Maleficent to hold him—it would all be over quickly if she contained him. He drew in a calming breath. The sword fell from his hand as he achieved all-clear, and he stepped through the beams without harm.

She snarled, her eyes rolling back in her head.

Finn glanced back at the sword—it was trapped inside the lasers, out of his reach. He wondered how much of this Philby was aware of. Things weren't exactly going according to plan.

"Tricky, tricky," Maleficent said. "That's a new one."

Finn had to move her, had to shift her to her left, his right—and he had to do so quickly. *Any second*—

Maleficent raised her arm.

BOOM! A blinding flash of white light preceded a dazzling wash of fog and smoke that rose high into the sky revealing . . . *Chernabog*. It was her spell, her show now—no longer Fantasmic!, all Maleficent's doing. Finn had to change that somehow—to take it away from her.

The creature was only visible for a matter of a second or two. Had anyone else even seen him? But his image lingered in Finn's thought: a horrific giant of a beast. In his place appeared a four-story dragon. It looked like the dragon puppet that Finn had seen before in the show—only it was *real*.

Charlene was supposed to keep the dragon up there on the platform. The one thing they could ill afford was for the dragon to leap down onto the main stage and come after Finn. He couldn't fight both Maleficent and the dragon at the same time.

Maleficent grinned and threw another fireball at him. Finn stood still. It passed right through him and landed in the water.

"Old green fairies are no longer needed here," he said, continuing to move to his right. "Did I mention—*ugly*, old green fairies?"

She boiled, but began moving in concert with him now. "Little *children* should know their place. And you know what they say about children playing with fire?"

She raised her arm to signal the dragon.

It all seemed wrong. Finn had not yet reached the mark on stage indicating the trapdoor he was to fall through. The dragon craned its huge head toward him, its red eyes—eyeballs the size of cars—blinking at him, while a clear goo ran down from them. It opened its jaws. It moved its feet.

Charlene was not in place! Worse, Philby had not opened the trapdoor.

Finn rushed Maleficent and took hold of her arm and prevented her from lowering it, stopped her from signaling the dragon to release his flame.

Her arm was ice-cold. His hand stuck to her green skin, like a tongue sticking to a dry piece of ice.

Finn now saw something extraordinary in Maleficent's eyes: uncertainty. Confusion. She had ridden that platform to the stage expecting to perform the same scene she'd been performing for some time now. Finn's arrival and Philby's manipulation of the stage effects had thrown the show off-script; she clearly wasn't sure what to do next. She had tried hurling her fireballs to no effect; her laser cage had failed to contain him.

Or was it fear he saw in her eyes? Fear that he might do to her now what he'd done once before: choked her to near-unconsciousness, rendering her powers useless. Did he possess that ability still?

But no. The arm he held began sprouting feathers, the skin turning prickly and leathery. Her face elongated and changed from green to brown. Her pointy nose stretched and hardened into a beak. A flap of skin stretched from under her jaw and turned a brilliant red.

Finn heard the cursing of men horrified by what they saw. He heard loud footfalls as the stagehands fled for the emergency exits.

She was transfiguring into a hideous vulture. Finn drove into her and knocked her backward, sending her sprawling over the fallen cauldron. Her right wing hit the spilled green goo and the feathers started dissolving. But a talon came up between them and found his chest and pushed him back, throwing Finn across the stage.

The vulture rose to its feet, its wings extended. It was a foul-looking thing, with a bald head, a hooked beak, and sagging eyes. Finn backed up, looking for the open trapdoor in the floor.

He glanced up higher without really meaning to: the dragon was practically falling off its perch, its neck extended, its mouth coming open.

Finn was going to get flamed.

"*Philby!*" he shouted.

He needed that trapdoor to open *right now*.

* * *

Philby's head felt as if someone had hooked up an air hose to his ear and pumped his head full to exploding. The stinging in his elbow continued. He couldn't make sense of what was happening to him. The only other time he'd felt like this he'd been . . . *at the hospital.* He'd come down with a terrible fever and his mother had taken him to the emergency room and they'd put a . . . *needle in his arm* . . . and it had felt . . . *exactly like this*.

The Jell-O brain was a new sensation entirely, but

even with his thoughts clouded, Philby could imagine his parents finding him in the Syndrome and overreacting. His mother had overreacting down to an art form.

Doctors! They were messing with him and his DHI was experiencing what his normal self was experiencing the same way his normal self suffered what happened to his DHI.

He breathed deeper and faster. They were medicating him. He had to fight it and get past it.

Fire.

He had to do something related to fire. For the first time in several minutes Philby looked out through the control booth's main window.

There was a huge, butt-ugly bird on stage flapping its wings at—*Finn!*

Perched above Finn was a—*dragon.*

Now things began to make a little more sense. Dragon, fire, Finn. This had something to do with him and the mouse in his right hand.

Had Finn called out his name? Had he heard that faintly through the speaker marked STAGE SOUND LIVE?

A sudden pounding on the control booth door made him jump in the chair. He heard a man's voice. "Is someone in there? Open up!"

Philby kept silent but wondered how long it would be until that man got inside.

That jolt of panic briefly cleared his thought. Philby felt much more like himself all of a sudden.

He spotted a small video camera in the upper left corner of the window. It was focused down toward the show. He followed its wires with his eyes, back behind the console to his left, past several wireless receivers and steel boxes. He reached behind to make sure he had traced the correct wires. They led to a silver Panasonic digital video recorder; its lights were on, including an illuminated red RECORD button. Plugged into the front of the machine was a silver thumb drive bearing Mickey ears, also with a red light flashing. To the left was a box containing a pile of similar thumb drives. It only made sense they would record the shows and use the recordings to troubleshoot or improve things.

The flashing red lights triggered something inside him.

Finn: trapdoor. Dragon: no fire.

He checked the flat-panel display. Yes! There were several lines labeled TRAP, and a separate monitor to his left displayed a stage floor plan with TRAP-1, TRAP-2, TRAP-3, all the way through TRAP-7.

Philby wiggled the mouse, drawing the cursor across the screen, and went to work.

* * *

Charlene had to move because the guys beneath her were never going to. At this point, what did it matter if they saw her? The dragon was alive up there. He was *huge*, and she had to stop him.

As she climbed, the chain around her shoulders rattled again the steel ladder.

"Hey! You!" came an angry voice from below.

"You can't go up there! *Get down here!*"

She thought she heard *Security* mentioned. No matter what, she wouldn't have much time.

As she arrived to the top of the ladder, Charlene's head swooned. The mountain peak rose at least forty feet above the stage and much higher than that off the ground to the back of the structure—it looked like eighty or a hundred feet. She felt dizzy and a little sick to her stomach. It took her an extra second or two to realize that the greenish-brown tree trunk in front of her was the dragon's right leg. The size of it shocked her. She'd known her task was to lock down the dragon, but she'd never expected *this*. At that moment, the beast was hunched so far forward, his neck craned down toward the stage, that he seemed poised to jump. Her job was to prevent this from happening and her first reaction was that she'd failed. She'd let Finn and the team down.

But the dragon didn't jump. He just stayed there leering toward Finn as if. . . .

He's going to spit fire! she thought.

Charlene's conscious thought was replaced by instinct and action. It wasn't so different from a soccer game or gymnastics: you stopped thinking and let your body take over. She ducked her head and caught one end of the chain as it fell off, springing up and over the disgusting, scaly skin of the dragon's right foot, grabbing hold of a spine of leathery skin—if you could call it skin—across the bridge of his four-toed foot, all the while dragging the chain with her. She couldn't allow the beast to slip his foot out, so as she landed back on the upper platform she climbed the foot again to put a full turn around the dragon's ankle, but by now he'd felt her, by now his attention had been distracted from the stage, and one gooey eyeball slid to the side of its socket and caught the gnat-size girl doing something down there on his foot and . . . *kicked her off.*

Charlene flew from the dragon's foot like a bug being brushed off a child's arm. But she held on to the chain, so that instead of being flung to her death, she ended up being swung out and around and coming back down to the floor with a thud, but with the chain now looped around the dragon's ankle exactly as she'd wanted it. Bruised and aching, she forced herself up on her hands and knees and crawled toward the free end of the chain, where it was hanging over the rung of the nearby safety ladder.

The dragon briefly lost his balance in his attempt to lose the bug. He stepped back to recover, driving his heel down.

Charlene saw it coming and rolled, letting go of the chain. The heel came down with a stomp. Right on top of the chain.

Charlene stood and pulled with everything she had, but the chain would not budge.

The dragon—irritated and bothered—reared back his head, ready to throw a tongue of flame at his target.

She caught something out of the corner of her eye: a small pile of props, including some bows and arrows and four or five spears. They looked like they'd been there forever. But she took hold of one of the spears, tested its strength, and thought back to the one time her track coach had let her try to throw the javelin. She looked up at the dragon, remembering her Language Arts block on Greek mythology.

Achilles.

His mother, Thetis, had dipped him in the river Styx to make him immortal. But since she had held him by one heel to dunk him, this one part of his body had remained dry, and was the only part of him vulnerable to any weapon.

Achilles' heel.

She ran to the side of the beast's ankle, searching for the indentation at the back of the ankle—the soft, fleshy part between ankle and tendon.

She reared back the spear, then in an instant coiled down, using every muscle in her abdomen and back to whip her body forward, her arm hesitating and waiting for the sling effect that would draw first her shoulder, then her elbow, wrist, and hand ahead, up, and over her head, so that the spear seemed now to be part of her body.

She let go.

* * *

Finn froze, locked in fear as the vulture moved toward him, pushing him farther back and away from any of the glow-tape *X*s that marked the various trapdoors on the stage floor. If he couldn't get himself atop one of those *X*s, he was going to fry. Get barbecued. Roasted. Killed.

The dragon had been about to flame-throw when he'd suddenly looked away and stumbled.

Charlene, Finn thought. *At last!*

But nothing was going to stop Maleficent. The vulture threw her neck forward, trying to peck Finn's head off his shoulders. He looked over at the sword inside the glowing cage of laser light.

If only. . . .

"You and me," Finn said, looking directly into the hideous, drooling eyes. The vulture advanced another step, her pink tongue appearing as its beak opened.

"It's over."

He heard the voice but didn't quite believe it. A trick of his mind, perhaps. *Wishful thinking.* For there was no questioning whose voice it was: Wayne's.

He looked to his right. High above him on an outcropping of rock stood the old geezer with his khaki pants, his white hair, and his Epcot windbreaker. *Exactly as Jess had envisioned him.*

"We've lost. It's over. Surrender is the only option."

"No!" Finn shouted. "They'll trap us in the Syndrome. We'll be there forever."

"Listen to him!" the vulture croaked out in a grating voice much like Maleficent's. "He's trying to help you!"

"No!" Finn said, taking another dangerous step even farther from the series of trapdoors.

"It's over," Wayne said, turning and looking down at him. "Save yourself. . . ."

"Finn!"

Finn reeled in the opposite direction toward the voice. Her voice.

Amanda appeared at the edge of the stage. Amanda, who had deserted him. Was she behind this?

Had he allowed himself to be fooled all along? Was she going to try to tell him to listen to Wayne and give up?

"Don't you dare surrender!" she called out. She lifted her hands palms out and prepared to levitate, as he'd seen her do to Greg Luowski.

The wide-eyed vulture pivoted in Amanda's direction. Amanda had nearly killed Maleficent at their last meeting; the vulture raised her wings as if defying Amanda to levitate her off the stage. Finn understood her choice of transfiguration then—a bird had nothing to fear from being lifted.

But as Amanda made a waving motion with her hands, it wasn't the vulture that felt the pulse of energy.

It was the sword. It slid beneath the laser fence, casting sparks as it passed through to safety, and floated across the stage to arrive at Finn's feet, just as the vulture spun and lunged its beak for Finn's head.

He clenched his hands around the sword's grip and hoisted the blade, putting it between him and the vulture's head, piercing the feathers and the leathery neck so that the vulture shrieked and cried out as thick green blood flowed from her neck.

As the blade withdrew the vulture shrank and contracted, reforming into the green-faced fairy Finn feared more than anything on earth. Maleficent was bleeding green from her neck. She staggered, her bloodshot eyes rolling back white in their sockets. She tried to speak but gurgled and spat and stumbled.

"Kill him!" she hollered, grasping her wound with both bony hands.

The dragon roared, throwing himself forward. Just as the flame released from his gaping mouth, he too screamed painfully and lurched to the side, yanking his leg into the air and revealing some kind of stick stuck through his heel. He fell to that side, awkwardly off-balance. His neck bent and twisted, and the flame shot high, missing Finn entirely.

All seven trapdoors opened at once.

It was not Finn who fell through to safety. It was Maleficent.

She vanished.

Finn fell back to the stage, recoiling from the dragon's fire only to see Wayne engulfed by the coil of blue-and-orange flame. It hit him like a blast from a flamethrower—a narrow torrent of roaring fire like a stream of water shot from a hose.

And Wayne was gone.

The dragon teetered and, unable to set down his wounded foot, hopped once to hold himself upright, and then went over backward, off the mountaintop. A length of thick chain flailed like a whip behind him.

Finn heard a tremendous crash of bone and trees and jungle. And there was Charlene, rising from behind where the beast had stood, and practically throwing herself over the rail to track his fall.

Amanda ran across the stage, leaping over two open trapdoors, and slid to Finn's side.

"Are you all right?" she cried, throwing her arms around him.

Finn dropped the sword and hugged her back. "You saved my life," he said.

"You saved us all," she whispered back to him.

46

AFTER THEIR RENDEZVOUS at the Studios' Soundstage B, and a lot of excited discussion of what had just happened, a distraught Wanda listened as Finn vented his frustration over losing the fob and held up her father's cluttered key chain.

"Use these if you like," she said, wiping away her tears. "I'm sure that one of them opens the gift shop at Epcot. And probably another, the Lost and Found."

"I think he wanted to save us," Finn said. "He meant to help us. He was a good man—"

"A great man," added Philby.

"The best," said Willa.

Wanda nodded solemnly. "I know he wouldn't want me crying over him," she said. "But I'm going to miss him so much. If it's all right with you, I'll drop you all at Epcot, but then I need to go home. I need to be alone."

Charlene and Amanda embraced her, and then Willa joined them and the boys, and for a moment there was a knot in everyone's throat and a tear on everyone's cheek, with Wanda in the middle sobbing and moaning and Finn thinking his heart might break for good. He saw in his mind's eye flashes of Wayne sitting on a bench, climbing Escher's Keep, driving a golf cart through an empty Magic Kingdom, of his face flickering on Finn's computer screen. Of the sparkle in the old guy's eyes and the calm in his voice as he faced danger after danger. Memories that would not soon fade.

"He taught us—" Finn said into the group.

"He loved these parks," said Philby.

"We're all going to miss him," said Maybeck.

"—about ourselves as much as about the parks," Finn added. "I'm a different person because of him."

"We all are," said Jess.

Finn didn't know how long they stayed like that, locked in a group hug, reflecting on everything Wayne had done, but it was not a short amount of time. Maybeck told a story. Philby recalled his and Wayne's voyage as avatars into the heart of the Imagineering computer system. Jess allowed how Wayne had saved her from captivity. Eventually they broke it up. They packed themselves into Wanda's car, sitting on laps and jammed into every free inch of space, and she drove them back to Epcot.

Wanda apologized as if she owed them something more, and then drove off down an empty access road as the sun rose above the green treetops. They sneaked back onto the property just as the first Cast Members were arriving to open the attractions. Finn got inside the gift shop courtesy of Wayne's keys, and opened the Lost and Found with another.

There, on the shelf, was the fob. And next to it, a yellowed and faded Disney sweatshirt that Finn recognized at once as belonging to Wayne. It was something Wanda would want as a keepsake. It had probably been left behind when Wayne had been held captive in Wonders. Finn carried it with him and took his time returning carefully to the Nemo lounge.

He walked in displaying the fob. "Ta-da!" he trumpeted. "We can return now."

"No we can't!" Philby faced a flat-screen monitor in the far corner of the lounge.

Maybeck groaned. "He's been replaying the show," he whispered to Finn. "He took this thumb drive from the control booth. Reliving it all. Truth is, he's not doing so good. He thinks maybe docs are messing with his real self. Like maybe they're medicating him. And I've got to say: he's acting like it."

"We can't go," Philby said.

Willa said to Finn, "Can I see that?"

Finn passed her the sweatshirt. She pulled in the other girls. "What does that smell like to you?" The girls all sniffed at it. Finn left them, crossing to Philby.

"We've got to return, Philby. I've got the fob."

"'Beware your friends and know your enemies,'" Philby said, quoting Wayne.

"We're all tired. It's been a long night," Finn said.

"Wayne was the traitor," Philby said.

He silenced the room. But it went beyond that. An unspoken anger filled the air with tension.

"He was warning us about *himself*, not one of us," Philby said. "Since when would Wayne ever—and I mean: *ever*—tell us to surrender?"

"I was outgunned," Finn said. "If Amanda hadn't—"

"I'm not talking about you. Or me. Or *any of us*. I'm talking about *Wayne*," Philby said. "Why would Wayne ever tell us to surrender? Answer: he wouldn't." Professor Philby had returned. "That was totally not him. No way. Not ever."

"We all *saw* him, dude," Maybeck said.

"And we saw Maleficent vanish through a trapdoor and the dragon fall from the top of the stage."

"I saw the dragon getting tied up," Charlene said. "He was hurt, but he wasn't dead. And Maleficent transformed back into that vulture thing and was being rushed to the veterinarian clinic at AK. That's what all the sirens were about."

"Should have let her die, if you ask me," Maybeck said.

"Forget about them for a minute," Philby said. "Being a DHI has taught us all that we can't always trust what we see. Right? I mean . . . look at us! Are we real?"

"You need some sleep, man," Maybeck said. "We all do. We've got to hit the button and return. As in: now."

"Shadows," Philby said.

"You're tripping, dude," Maybeck said.

Philby worked a keyboard that slid out from a cabinet beneath the flat screen. The thumb drive's red light blinked from the computer box behind the keyboard.

"Check it out," he said. He backed up the video footage of the battle on stage. "Willa!" he said. "There's a kitchen back there. Find me a match please."

"Dude!" Maybeck said. "You are way over-baked."

"We hear him out," Willa said. "When is Philby ever wrong?"

"When his real self is being medicated by doctors," Maybeck answered.

"Let him talk." Willa headed off toward the lounge kitchen in search of a match.

"What do you notice about the vulture?" Philby asked.

"Ugly?" Charlene said.

"Big?" Maybeck said.

"Scary," said Finn.

Philby pointed to the screen. "Shadows. All the stage lights make the thing cast about a dozen shadows going out from her feet like a star."

"Okay. . . ." said Amanda, stepping closer.

"And Finn?"

"Basically the same thing," said Jess. "Lots of shadows."

"And the dragon," volunteered Charlene. "Not as many, but that one shadow is really dark."

"He's closer to those top lights," Philby said. "Different pattern, but strong shadows nonetheless."

"And this interests us because?" said Maybeck sarcastically.

Willa arrived with a book of matches. "I found these," she said.

"Excellent!" said Philby. "Put your finger here, please."

Willa hesitated. "You're not going to burn me, are you?"

"A little trust please?" Philby said. "Stand your index finger on end."

Willa stood her finger alongside the keyboard.

Philby struck and lit a match and moved it closer to Willa's holographic finger. "Don't move," he said.

"Please don't burn me," she said.

"What do you see?" Philby asked Finn.

"A nervous finger."

"*Behind* the finger," Philby said.

"A shadow," Amanda answered.

"Gold star," said Philby, raising the burning match to his lips and blowing it out.

"I repeat," Maybeck said. "This interests us—"

"Because of this," Philby said.

He played the video forward. There was no sound. The dragon reared back, opened his mouth, and then fell as Charlene speared his heel. The column of fire erupted from his open mouth and Wayne was incinerated.

Every one of the kids looked away from the screen just before Wayne burned. "I cannot look at that!" Finn said. "Do not ask me to look at that."

"And maybe that was the point," Philby said. "That none of us would have the stomach to study it. But you've got to look at it."

All of them took deep breaths at nearly the same instant. Philby played it again.

"No way. . . . " muttered Willa.

"What?" said Maybeck. "I think I'm going to be sick."

"I can't do this," said Jess.

"One more time," said Philby. "Please. Just look. Not at Wayne, but behind him." He ran the segment one more time.

"I don't believe it," whispered Finn.

"How is that possible?" said Charlene.

Maybeck spoke. "It's *not* possible. It's some kind of trick of light. A bad angle by the camera."

"Lighting's fine," said Philby. "Angle is fine. But it *is* a trick of light. You're right about that."

"But there's no shadow," said Willa. "All that flame—all that light—"

"Finn," Philby said. "I want you to go *all clear*. And I want you to put your finger down here, right where Willa did."

Finn considered arguing, but he was too tired to do it. Instead, he closed his eyes and summoned the dark tunnel and the pinprick of light. He heard the sound of a match being struck and several of his friends gasping. He looked down.

His finger cast no shadow.

"It wasn't Wayne," Philby said. "It was a DHI of Wayne."

"'A deception of the worst kind,'" Jess said, quoting Wayne's Mission: Space video message.

"They tried to use a DHI of Wayne to trick you into surrendering," Philby said. "Wayne knew they modeled him for a DHI. He tried to warn us not to believe him. Not to believe the Wayne we saw."

"He's still alive!" Finn said, and a cheer went up among them.

47

"It's the same smell as the match," Willa said, placing her face into Wayne's sweatshirt again. "It's sulphur or something."

"Let me try," Philby said, sitting in front of the keyboard. He placed the sweatshirt in both hands and sank his face into it. He drank in a huge snort.

"Cordite," he said, pulling his face out. "Black powder. Fireworks."

"Fireworks," Finn echoed.

"IllumiNations," Willa said.

They all faced her.

"When I fell onto that barge from the bridge, it went all the way across the lake, under the drawbridge by China and around backstage to where they store that stuff until the next show, I guess. There are a bunch of the barges back there. Guards and all sorts of security. They were complaining about the Earth Globe. It was malfunctioning—'flashing'—they said."

"Wayne," Philby said.

"We don't know that!" Maybeck objected.

"Flashing? Are you kidding me?" Philby said.

"Flashing as in Morse code? Flashing as in SOS or 'somebody save me'? Flashing as in: somebody come try to fix this thing and find me hidden on the barge where my sweatshirt got all smelly from the fireworks?"

"Do you think?" Jess said.

"No," Philby said. "I know."

"He wanted his sweatshirt found," Finn said.

"As a clue," Willa added.

"Well, I'm tired," Maybeck said. "If we're going to do this, let's do it before we're all discovered in the Syndrome and put through what Philby's going through."

"But if Willa's right," Finn said, "then there are guards. That works for the Overtakers—no one's getting in there who doesn't belong. But it's not so good for us."

"One if by land, two if by sea," Philby said.

Maybeck groaned. "We've got to get him crossed back over before he hurts himself."

Philby said, "They're guarding the docks. The explosives. But Willa, you got out of there."

"I swam," she said.

"She swam," Philby said. "Two if by sea."

"She swam," Finn said.

* * *

The sun had just cleared the horizon as Finn, Amanda, and Charlene—the three best swimmers of the group—

lowered themselves into the chilly water north of China.

They stayed near the edge of the canal and swam slowly and silently through the dark water until facing a view of the dock area where all the barges were tied. Near the back of the group, on the right, loomed the Earth Globe.

The dock appeared empty. Finn assumed it was a trick. He motioned for them to stop swimming and the three grabbed hold of rocks on the wall of the canal and waited.

And waited.

Charlene began shaking from the cold water. Her lips were blue.

"Are you going to make it?" Finn whispered.

"I hope they hurry," she answered.

As if on cue, the dark shape of a guard appeared onto the dock. He'd come from the Earth Globe, something that Finn took as a good sign.

"Now?" Amanda asked.

"A little more," he answered.

"Who goes there?" shouted the guard.

His calling out prompted the door of a Quonset hut to open. Pete appeared—the pyrotechnics chief Finn had first seen when he was smuggling himself into Epcot. Pete appeared to speak to the guard, who then pointed off toward a grouping of several storage containers.

Pete motioned the guard forward and he headed slowly in the direction of the containers.

"Okay," Finn said. "Here we go."

The commotion behind the containers was Maybeck.

Willa appeared on a Segway from the guard's left. She came at him fast, and turned at the last moment, keeping out of reach. The guard shouted at her as well.

Finn, Amanda, and Charlene swam the sidestroke, the quietest of all the strokes, drawing closer to the flotilla of pyrotechnics barges. Maybeck and Willa took off, the guard chasing after them.

As the three reached the water side of the Earth Globe barge, the Quonset hut door opened and three more guards appeared. Pete directed one to pursue the kids. The two others separated and began a thorough search of the area.

Finn pulled himself up the side of the barge slowly, making as little noise as possible. He lay flat on his stomach. Amanda arrived next, and Charlene last.

At the base of the huge globe, which glowed in a color map of the world at night, was a metal box about the size of a desk standing on its side.

About the size of a person, Finn thought. There were

cables running into the box. It looked to be some kind of control room, encased and enclosed to keep whoever was in there safe while fireworks rained down all around it.

There was a carabiner holding a clasp shut on the front of the box—a door.

Finn crawled toward the box.

A van pulled up and off the pavement, skidding to a stop. It threw up a plume of dust.

Finn crept one knee closer to the box, but he still lay a good ten feet away.

He heard his mother's voice.

For a moment he didn't believe it. He had to be feeling the effects of the all-nighter. It couldn't actually be *his mother*. But she spoke again.

"I want to talk to whoever is in charge," she said.

That was his mother. No doubt about it.

Pete hurried over in that direction. Finn peered through the bottom of the globe. His father. His mother. And two other adults.

"We have been searching this park for over an hour," his mother complained. "And then, just now . . . we saw two—"

"Kids," Finn's father said.

"Yes," his mother said. "Running from this direction. If you have harmed these children in any way. . . !"

"Harmed?" Pete answered. "What children? We saw some vandals, some trespassers just now, and I sent a couple of guards after them. If those are your kids, they're in big trouble, lady."

"Do not 'lady' me, mister."

One of the remaining guards moved closer to the Earth Globe barge. He did so slowly so as not to arouse suspicion. But he was too close now. There was no way Finn was going to get the box open with that man standing there.

Finn felt a tug on his wet shirt. He looked over his shoulder. Charlene was pointing down to the far end of the barge where Finn finally spotted what she was trying to get him to see: an outboard engine strapped to the back. Unlike the other barges, the Earth Globe did not need to be towed into place.

Charlene pointed at herself, and then at the engine.

Finn understood the message. He nodded.

Charlene took off, slowly crawling on her belly down the far side of the barge, keeping herself flat and low, her wet, black clothing blending in perfectly with the barge's black paint.

Finn's eyes roamed, looking for . . . He spotted it: a single thick line tying the barge to the dock. But how was he ever going to get to it?

Amanda tugged on him next. He met eyes with her

and she held up both hands. Then she pointed to herself. Then the hands again, and she slowly pushed.

Finn nodded: *Brilliant!*

Only that one rope remained.

There are some things in this world that will never be fully explained. Even the existence of Fairlies did not explain them all: how a friend can think of a friend and the phone will suddenly ring with that same friend on the other end; how a twin will know the exact moment when his or her twin has unexpectedly died; how the same song will come into the heads of two people at the exact same instant; how a mother can see her child no matter how well the kid is hidden in a crowd.

Finn's mom spotted him. He saw the change in her face, and there was no doubt in his mind. Next, she spotted Charlene crawling toward the back. She went rigid. She was turning toward Finn's dad as Finn shook his head no, once and quite violently. She stopped.

His father said something to her. She shook her head, her eyes never leaving Finn. They filled with tears and she wiped them away and made excuses to Pete about how upset she was. She had no idea what to do. She stood there like a stone statue.

Finn knew it was now or never, but no matter how he planned to get to the line and release the barge, he knew the guard would stop him. He might avoid capture by going *all clear*, but that would also prevent him from taking hold of the rope. And if he tried to get the door open to the box, he'd never make it. The guard would pounce on him and he and the girls would be hauled off. They had no right to be on the barge or the Disney property. By the time anyone got a look in that box Wayne would have been moved and would be long gone.

Maintaining eye contact with his mom, Finn pointed at the line holding the barge to shore and watched as her eyes found it.

She looked back at her son, then once again to the line. Finn used his hands to mime untying and he pulled his arms apart to indicate separation.

If his mother turned him in now, all was lost. He was putting Wayne's fate in her hands. All their fates.

He waited. And waited.

"Oh, dear," his mother said. Her knees went out and she fell forward. She'd obviously caved under the pressure. Finn's plan had failed.

Pete caught her. Then Finn's dad took her under her arm and tried to stand her up. But she used being off-balance to propel herself toward the barge.

"If I can only sit down for a moment," she said. She practically dragged Finn's dad to the side of the Earth

Globe barge, and she sat down on the edge of the barge next to an old tire used as a bumper. Right next to the line that tied it to shore.

His mom. The performance of a lifetime.

Pete and the other parents were still talking when Philby showed up between the containers.

"Mom? Dad?"

Philby's parents—for they turned out to be the other two adults—cried out in surprise.

Everyone's attention focused on Philby as he stepped out. "I'm sorry. That's all I can say: I'm sorry."

Finn's mom slipped the line off the cleat that bound the barge to the dock. She stood up and stepped away from the barge.

Amanda locked her legs under a crossbeam that secured the globe, rose to her knees, drew back her hands, and pushed them forward.

The guard fell over. Mr. and Mrs. Whitman fell over. And the barge jumped away from the dock.

Charlene pulled the start cord and the engine kicked to life.

The guard scrambled to his feet, turned, and ran for the barge. He jumped, but splashed into the murky water, missing the barge.

Charlene motored them away from the dock.

Finn hurried forward, figured out the carabiner, and

removed it from the clasp. He swung open the door, fell to his knees, and felt tears running from his eyes.

Wayne, his feet pressed up into his chest, his white hair like a beacon of light, was crammed into the small box.

He was smiling.

"What took you so long?" he said.

48

DAYS BLENDED INTO WEEKS. Philby used his control of the software to keep them from crossing over in part because their parents were monitoring them closely and "heads would roll" if they went DHI again.

Philby's only conversation with Wayne had been brief, on the day of his rescue. Wayne had spoken in a whisper, not out of weakness, but in the interest of secrecy.

"There is more going on than meets the eye. It's much bigger than you think."

"The seat belts?"

"A small part of it, yes. Present your evidence to the Imagineers. They will believe you. They will do the necessary safety checks of the seat belts. It's not an issue if they have Maleficent. And I'm assuming—"

"She and Chernabog . . . I heard they were taken to the Animal Kingdom. To the vet clinic for her, and the elephant cages for him."

"That may buy you the time you need."

"Time to do what?"

"To finish it. They aren't done. There are more of

them—many more than we knew. And the only way to stop them. . . ."

But the paramedics approached. They grabbed Wayne's gurney and whisked him off into the ambulance. It was the last Finn had seen of him.

Finn had turned in his cell phone and computer as part of his punishment, accepting that it would be a month or more before his parents loosened up and gave him back some of his freedoms. But despite all the discipline, he and his mom would catch eyes every so often—at the dinner table, across the kitchen when Finn was doing his homework—and he would see her eyes smile back at him. It was more than his being safe. It was that she'd been part of the team—in solving the cryptogram, in untying the barge. She'd briefly experienced the thrill he lived with nearly every day. She'd touched it. She knew now. She would never look at him the same again.

School was school: b o r i n g . . . except at lunch, when a certain friend would slide onto the bench next to him off in the far corner, and sometimes he would feel her hand glance against his or would catch a look in her eye, or see her fighting back a smile.

"I don't know what happened outside the stage," he finally gathered the courage to say one day. "But whatever it was, it wasn't right. I like Charlene and everything, but I don't know why you said the things you said."

"Neither do I."

"And that's it?"

She shrugged. "I don't know how to explain this."

"It would help by trying to in the first place."

"I'm a Fairlie," she said.

"I think we've established that."

"We all have special . . . traits. Qualities."

"Powers," he said.

"We don't think of them that way. But okay. Whatever. We have them."

"I was talking about Charlene," he said.

"Shut up, Finn. Let me talk if I'm going to talk."

He felt himself blush. There weren't many people who could tell him to shut up without getting him steamed. But when Amanda said it, he wanted to laugh.

"My quality is . . . what I'm good at . . . what I'm able to do is to push. To levitate. To move objects away from me." He directed the intensity of her eyes onto his. "To move things away from me."

He swallowed. "And if they don't want to be moved?"

"I can move almost anything I want to. No matter how large. I mean, maybe not a building, but I moved a truck once."

"Just because you're good at something," he said, "doesn't mean it has to own you. There are people that let that happen, and there are people that don't. It's a choice, not a prison sentence."

"That makes it sound easier than it is."

"Let me put it this way: you can push me away all you want, but I'm like a human yo-yo. I'm going to come right back at you."

"It's what I do. I pushed my family away without meaning to—or I wouldn't be without them."

"You don't know that. You don't know what happened to them."

"I can imagine."

"Wayne taught us to imagine the good, Amanda. It is an option, you know? Seriously."

"The thing with Charlene."

"You were pushing me. I get that," he said.

"I'll never let anyone get close."

"You don't know that. You can't say that."

She sighed, deeply frustrated.

He placed his hand onto hers on the bench. Hers was icy cold. His, phenomenally warm from nerves.

"A human yo-yo," he repeated.

He won a smile from her.

"You're Kingdom Keepers now. You and Jess. You know that, right?"

She nodded.

"There are ways we do things," he said. "As a group. For each other. We always team up. No one ever goes alone."

She looked totally stressed out.

"No one ever goes alone," he repeated. "I'll tell you something: I don't like girls. But I like you. I don't care about girls, but I care about you, and Willa, and Jess, and yeah, Charlene, too. Nothing bad is ever going to happen to them. Never going to happen to you. That's just the way it is. You're a part of that now. You can't get out of it. We won't let you. No one ever goes alone."

"You going to eat that?" she asked, pointing to something that had pineapple in its name but was the texture of a kitchen sponge.

"No," he said. "Go for it."

She reached over and snagged it and ate it in two bites. "You haven't forgotten about Jeannie Pucket, right?"

"Who's Jeannie Pucket?" he asked.

"My roommate. Jess's and my roommate. You promised you'd meet her."

"Oh, great. . . ."

"I was thinking an ice cream cone at The Frozen Marble."

"You make it sound like a date."

"It kind of is."

"Help!"

"I could come along," she offered.

"It's sounding better," he said.

"Thanks," she said, still chewing.

"Well if it isn't Thin Wit-less!" growled a voice from behind them.

Luowski now had a string of zits from his nose all the way over to his ear. Mike Horton stood to the side and slightly behind him.

"And the evil witch," Luowski added. "Blown any houses off-course lately?"

"Take a hike, Luowski," Finn said.

"You and me, we've got unfinished business."

"Mike," Finn said, "I thought you were going to get him a better writer?"

Horton tried to keep the grin off his face.

Luowski said, "Your girly-friend isn't always going to be around, Whitman. Don't you think it's kind of spineless to need a girl to do your fighting for you anyway?"

"Sticks and stones, Luowski. You know I'm not going to fight you. You're a cretin. And if you don't know what that means, look it up. You'll be enlightened."

"I'm coming for you, Whitman."

"Mike," Amanda said, "do me a favor and get Greg out of here before there's trouble."

Horton led Luowski away. Luowski tried to look like he wanted to hang around, but Finn knew better. Amanda had him and half the school scared.

"You realize we're outcasts?" Finn said.

"Yes. I've been one my whole life. It's not so bad really. You get used to it."

"I'm working on it."

"I can help you," she said.

"I'd like that, I think. But remember: I don't like girls."

"Yes. So you said."

"Just so we're clear on that."

"Perfectly." She wiggled her hand under his. And he squeezed hers just a little bit tighter.

ACKNOWLEDGMENTS

Thanks to Nancy Litzinger Zastrow for running my office. To Amy Berkower, Dan Conaway, and, especially, Genevieve Gange-Hawes—all of Writers House, New York. Also to Matthew Snyder, of CAA.

At Disney Book Group I want to thank Wendy Lefkon, Jennifer Levine, Nellie Kurtzman, Frankie Lobono, Jessica Ward, and the whole publishing team for all the help on these projects.

The Kingdom Keepers books wouldn't exist without the on-site research, and this time around (Epcot and Disney's Hollywood Studios) the research wouldn't have happened without the dedication and time from all of the following: Alex Wright, Jason Grandt and Debra Wren, Pete Glim, Jeff Terry, Brian Ripley, Tom Devlin, Rachel at Soarin', and Lorraine and Philip at the Engineering Base.

Thanks to everyone for keeping the magic alive.

—Ridley Pearson
2010
St. Louis

Don't miss the next adventure:

1

"LET'S GET LOST," Finn said to the two girls.

DisneyQuest was a maze, a place where it was difficult to know where you were. An electronic funhouse filled with virtual rides, video games, and interactive attractions, the enormous building in Walt Disney World's Downtown Disney consisted of five floors subdivided into virtual worlds and activities, all interconnected in a way that seemed designed to disorient. Finn actually *was* currently lost—he couldn't quite figure out where he was or how to get out of there—but his suggestion to "get lost" stemmed from his spotting Greg "Lousy" Luowski at the other end of the gaming room, over near the Guitar Hero consoles. Luowski was the ninth-grade bully. Roughly the size of a kitchen appliance, the zit-faced, fingernail-chewing Luowski had it out for Finn, and Finn knew enough to stay clear of trouble. At least, *avoidable* trouble.

Over the past few years, trouble had defined him, had followed him as he and his four friends—now known as the Kingdom Keepers—had gained notoriety for their efforts to save Disney World from the Overtakers, a group of fanatical Disney villain characters within the Parks bent on taking over and "stealing the magic." Guys like Luowski didn't appreciate sharing the spotlight with anyone, and at the moment Finn was roughly a million times more popular than Luowski.

"How about the simulators in CyberSpace Mountain?" Charlene said. Charlene was to beautiful what Mount Everest was to high. A cheerleader and phenomenal athlete, she was the poster child for the Kingdom Keepers. Her Facebook page had more friends than Ashton Kutcher's—well, not really, but close enough. Boys liked her. Girls liked her. Teachers liked her. Parents liked her. It was enough to make you hate her. But no one could. She was too ridiculously Charlene to ever have an ill thought aimed at her.

Finn considered the suggestion and glanced over to Amanda to get her read. Amanda was a different kind of pretty: mysterious, her looks often changing from slightly Asian to Polynesian or Caribbean. Amanda was not officially one of the five Kingdom Keepers, but she and her "sister," Jess, had unique qualities and unusual abilities that made them important to the team.

Amanda and Jess had once been part of a group of foster kids called the Fairlies—as in "fairly human." Kids who could bend spoons just by staring at them, or hear clearly at absurd distances, hold their breath underwater for ten minutes at a time, light fires by concentrating, dream the future, see the past. Kids labeled freaks and weirdos; kids once studied by the military but dismissed to a special home in Baltimore when scientists failed to duplicate or explain what was termed their "controlled phenomena."

Currently, Amanda and Jess lived in an Orlando foster home for wayward girls run by the iron-handed Mrs. Nash. Despite sharing not only the same address, but also the same bunk room, they now attended different high schools; Jess had qualified for an AP program and went to Edgewater High along with two of the Kingdom Keepers, Willa and Philby.

Amanda had come to DisneyQuest this evening because the event was a school-sanctioned function, and Amanda had brought Jess as her one allowed guest. To Finn, it seemed like the entire ninth grade of Winter Park High was there.

Finn liked Amanda, which roughly translated to: he couldn't stop thinking about her, was often tongue-tied when trying to talk to her, and made a fool out of himself when trying to come off as cool. There was a friction that existed between Amanda and Charlene that he knew had something to do with him, but which he didn't like to think about. In general, he didn't like to think about girls all that much, but he couldn't seem to help himself.

"Okay," he said. "I guess." Finn didn't like roller

coasters—actually was terrified of them—but wasn't about to admit it.

The other three Keepers were also in DisneyQuest somewhere, as was Jess. Even though only Finn and Amanda attended Winter Park, it had been months since the whole group had done anything fun together. Their last outing, to Disney's Hollywood Studios' Fantasmic!, had led to an encounter with the Overtakers that nearly got Finn killed. The idea tonight had been to meet here and stick together, but they'd separated by ride and interest—Philby and Willa had gone to the ground floor to battle pirate ships, while Maybeck and Jess had gone to the bumper cars. Charlene had taken off to the bathroom a few minutes earlier, and Finn had considered ditching her in favor of being alone with Amanda; but it had only been a passing thought and one he didn't fully understand. He liked Charlene. A lot. But not in the same incomprehensible way he liked Amanda.

Luowski spotted Finn and made a face like a football player who'd taken a knee in the wrong place. Finn didn't want to get drawn into that.

"Come on, let's go," he said. The three located the stairs to the second floor, and Charlene led them to CyberSpace Mountain.

The ride was a virtual roller coaster that allowed visitors to pick preexisting twists and turns or to design their own. There were five levels of challenge, from easy to terrifying.

"I'll take mine lite," Finn said.

"Me, too," said Amanda. "I get sick on roller coasters."

"We should go together," Finn said, confessing, "because I'm basically a chicken."

"Oh, right," said Charlene. "You a chicken? I don't think so."

"Seriously! The Barnstormer is about as tough as I can take it."

Both girls laughed. Then they exchanged looks that had they been Taser shots would have dropped each other to the ground.

Bill Nye the Science Guy tutored Charlene as she scrolled through selections to create a wildly scary roller coaster for herself. Maybe she was trying to make a point to Amanda, maybe she just loved roller coasters; but it had enough loops and jumps to make an astronaut puke.

She used her entrance ticket to store it. Then she quickly worked with Bill Nye to make another, very basic, ride. She saved it onto Finn's ticket.

"I love it as scary as it gets," she said looking directly at Amanda. "It's awesome."

They headed for the short line of people waiting for the next simulator. Charlene was bumped into by someone, so hard that had she not possessed the grace of a dancer, she would have fallen to the floor.

Greg Luowski.

She dropped the two tickets in the process. In a surprisingly polite gesture, Luowski helped her up and collected the tickets and returned them to her. Finn caught this look in Luowski's eyes—the idiot liked Charlene; his bumping into her had been no accident.

"Lay off, Luowski," Finn said.

Amanda took Finn by the arm.

"Lay off what, Whitless? My bad for the knock-down. Can't I help her up?" He faced Charlene. "I really am sorry."

"No problem," she said. But Finn was still seething. "As in: We don't want any *problems*." She said this slowly, making sure Finn heard every word.

"I'll be around, Whitless. If you want me, you can find me."

"Try some deodorant, Luowski."

Charlene cupped her mouth, hiding her smile. Luowski didn't just smell like a jock, he smelled like an entire team that had been working out in the summer heat for five hours. He smelled like a guy who hadn't showered since sixth grade.

"Or maybe I'll find you," he growled at Finn.

"I'm not worried," Finn said. "I'll smell you coming."

The line moved. Finn and the girls were shown up

the stairs. The simulators were designed for a maximum of two people. Charlene lined up in front of door 1, Finn and Amanda, door 3.

"No holding hands, you two, if you get scared," Charlene called down to them.

Finn faked a grin; he was scared already.

A Cast Member wearing a name tag that said "Megan" accepted Finn's card from him and chose the only predesigned ride it contained. The door opened, and Finn and Amanda were escorted into the simulator chamber. Finn and Amanda climbed down into the padded seats of the red metal capsule. The seats faced a large flat-panel screen. Megan directed them to stow anything loose in their pockets. That was when Finn started to worry. She then pointed out the two red STOP emergency buttons, one for each rider.

Finn's stomach turned. He didn't like the idea of taking a ride that needed panic buttons. He pulled down the black padded chest brace into place, as directed. Amanda did the same. Megan double-checked everything.

"You're good to go," she said. She hit a button, and the simulator's lid closed slowly, locking in place. The only light came from the flat-panel display, where the ride's parallel tracks stretched out in front of them.

"This was a stupid idea," he mumbled.

"You're telling me," Amanda said.

"But did you see the course Charlene created for herself? No way I would go on that thing in a million years."

"She wanted to impress you."

"That's ridiculous."

"Trust me. She picked the scariest stuff possible. It would terrify the guy who *designed* it. But she's going to come out of there and tell us she loved it."

He wanted to disagree, but thought she was probably right.

The lights dimmed. The ride began.

"If I scream," Finn said, "it's just to make it feel all the more real."

She laughed. But not for long. Her amusement was cut short as the roller coaster car began to move forward on the tracks in front of them. A light flashed in their eyes. Sound effects roared from unseen speakers, and the car banked sharply left. Finn clutched the safety harness and shut his eyes.

"I hate this already," he said.

The capsule banked left again, did a complete flip in that direction, and then lifted into a double loop, dumping them upside down twice in a row. Amanda's hair fell like a curtain. Finn squinted open his eyes: the track dropped straight down, about a thousand feet. They plummeted down, as on the Tower of Terror.

Finn screamed a word that would have gotten him

grounded for a week if his mother had heard it. It just flew out of him.

"This . . . is. . . not . . . right!" Amanda cried.

They reached bottom, leaving Finn's stomach somewhere at his feet. He re-swallowed his dinner. The car shot up like a NASA rocket launch.

He screamed the same word again.

"She . . . tricked . . . us!" Amanda hollered. Then she screamed at a pitch so high it should have shattered the flat-panel display.

"Puke alert," Finn gagged out as they entered a triple loop.

"Please, no!" Amanda said. "Try shutting your eyes."

"Only makes it worse!" he choked out.

"Tell me this thing can't actually crash." She released another shriek at a volume that might have been heard in Miami.

"It can't actually crash," he said, though he wasn't so sure. What if the simulator was put through stuff it wasn't designed to handle? he wondered. What if its bearings froze or its motor overheated? The thing was, even Charlene's ride, as crazy as she'd made it, hadn't seemed this bad. Had she tricked them, to sabotage Amanda?

That was the first time he realized that maybe Charlene wasn't the only one involved. A ride this violent carried the fingerprints of the Overtakers.

Finn remembered Megan telling them about the panic buttons. He reached down to punch the red emergency STOP button. Just as he did, the car lurched left, and he leaned so sharply in that direction that his hand missed the button.

"Did you see that?" he hollered. "I think it *knew* I was trying to stop it!"

"You're losing more than your cookies," Amanda said. "So this thing can think?"

The car dropped again. Rose and fell. Leaned ninety degrees left and stayed there. Jerked totally upside down and did three more upside-down loops.

Amanda struggled to reach her stop button. But as she did, the track dropped away. She and Finn were thrown forward against their restraints. She punched down and hit the red plastic button.

"Got it!" she yelled.

The ride continued.

She hit it again.

They were flipped over seven times to their right, like rolling down a steep hill in an oil barrel.

"I swear I pushed it," she announced. "But nothing happened."

"Impressive," he managed to mutter to himself despite all the craziness, no longer thinking it was the work of the Overtakers, but *knowing* it. Wondering how they might have accomplished such a thing, and what, if anything, Charlene's role had been in it. She had designed the ride, after all. If it was the Overtakers, how had they organized any kind of attack, given that their two leaders, Maleficent and Chernabog, were currently locked up somewhere in a Disney holding facility? The Kingdom Keepers' mentor and designer, Wayne Kresky, had believed that "With the head cut off the snake, the body cannot survive." But someone had clearly taken over leadership of the Overtakers. The ride going out of control could not be considered coincidence. The Keepers were under attack.

Finn reached down, able to press his STOP button. Nothing.

"It's . . . *them* . . . isn't it?" Amanda was no dummy. She'd figured it out on her own.

"Yeah," he said. "It's them. By now Megan knows"—he gritted his teeth as the track lifted and fell so hard and so many times in a row that his neck hurt—"something is wrong. She's working to fix it."

"You're dreaming."

"Probably. But at this point, she's our only hope."

Outside the simulator bay, Megan was in fact hitting every switch and button possible. The system's mechanicals included a warning-light display used to alert Cast Members to potential simulator hardware failure: a single light that ran a solid green, amber, or red. It was currently *flashing* red—a warning level never seen before and one that attracted the concern and attention of three other Cast Members, including the ride manager.

"It's going to come off the gyros!" the manager shouted. "Like a wheel coming off a bike. The thing is going to basically explode if we don't stop it!" He, too, hit every known control trying to stop the ride. "What the heck?" he asked Megan, as if it were her fault.

"The power!" she said. "Call down and tell them to cut off the power."

"It's coming apart!" Finn said. On the screen, the parallel tracks rushed toward them at impossible speeds, reflecting the velocity of their virtual roller coaster car. Finn could barely look at it—another five loops coming up, then a series of left corkscrews and what appeared to be the edge of a cliff—another of the thousand-foot drops. It was no longer the pattern of the animated tracks that frightened him, but the sounds of grinding metal and the way the seats in the simulator were no longer level, but leaning heavily left. It was being made to do things it was not designed to do. Its parts were failing—the bushings, the bearings, servos, and gyros; it was like a car going down the side of a mountain with no steering and two of its wheels loose. It was going to crash.

"How could they know where we are?" Amanda cried out. "How is that possible?"

Finn didn't answer. He knew that when it came to the Overtakers, anything was possible.

"We have to stop it," he said, looking for options. He shoved his back against the seat and tried to slip out of the chest restraint. It was the same kind of restraint used on real roller coasters—a padded pipe that pulled down over your head. There was some slack in the way it fit. He got about halfway out before getting stuck.

"You're going to crush yourself!" she said.

The simulator spun sideways and rotated forward in full circles seven times. Finn felt his dinner coming up again. Each time he took his eyes off the screen he felt sick. He tried to focus on the screen the way his father had told him to focus on the horizon when seasick. The nausea passed. He was okay.

They fell hundreds of feet, facedown.

Finn squeezed back into his seat, unable to free himself.

"We . . . have. . . to . . . do . . . something!" he said.

"I'm up for suggestions," she answered. Oddly, Amanda sounded suddenly collected, and unaffected by the flips and twirls and drops. She could actually string a sentence together.

Then it struck him: Amanda had a unique power.

"Push . . . it . . . open," Finn shouted over the roar of the simulator's disintegrating parts. Amanda flashed him a look, her dark hair hanging fully upside down, her cheeks vibrating like Jell-O. Her eyes strained to find the hatch door that Megan had closed electronically. Neither of them knew exactly what was up or down any longer.

"It's too strong! I heard it lock," she said.

So had he, but what choice did they have? "You . . . have . . . to . . . try!"

If the seal broke, maybe it would initiate an automatic shutdown.

"Could be dangerous!" she said. For me, Amanda was thinking. How would they explain the damage to the simulator? Damage that would come from the inside? So far in her life her "gift"—as some called it—had only gotten her in trouble or made her the object of teasing. Subjugated at the age of eight to a foster home for freaks in Baltimore—the Fairlies—she'd been studied by scientists, doctors, and soldiers until she'd not had any choice but to run away with Jess. She had no urgent desire to make a scene with her gift and bring all that down on herself again.

They jerked violently left, right, front, back, and left again. Finn's head felt as if it was going to come off his neck. *Dangerous?* he wanted to say. *Really?*

Amanda couldn't risk Finn's getting hurt. She released her bloodless grip on the chest restraint, reaching toward the screen with outstretched arms. Finn watched her close her eyes, bend her elbows, and flatten her hands, palms facing out like a traffic cop's. She pushed up over her head—all at once, and with every ounce of strength she possessed.

The metal bulged like it had been hit with a battering ram. Red paint flakes rained down. Sparks flew.

"Again!" he hollered.

"Too strong!" she complained.

"You're all we've got." The vibrations climbed toward a climax. The push had made the simulator lean even farther to the left; the grinding of metal was now louder than the sound effects.

He smelled electrical smoke. They were going to suffocate.

"EVERYTHING YOU'VE GOT!" he shouted.